The Gates of Dawn

By Carl Sailor

THE GATES OF DAWN

Published by Carl Sailor Books
contact@CarlSailorBooks.com

ISBN:
Book: 978-1-7337630-0-4
Epub: 978-1-7337630-1-1

This is a work of fiction. All characters, organizations, and situations presented in this book are either products of the author's imagination, or are used fictitiously.

Story and characters ©2018 Carl Sailor
Cover artwork ©2018 Damjan Gjorgievski
Edited by Ariel Anderson, Mythcreants
All rights reserved.

Support the author online at:
www.patreon.com/carl_sailor
www.etsy.com/shop/CarlSailorBooks
www.facebook.com/PaulBowmansWar

Table of Contents

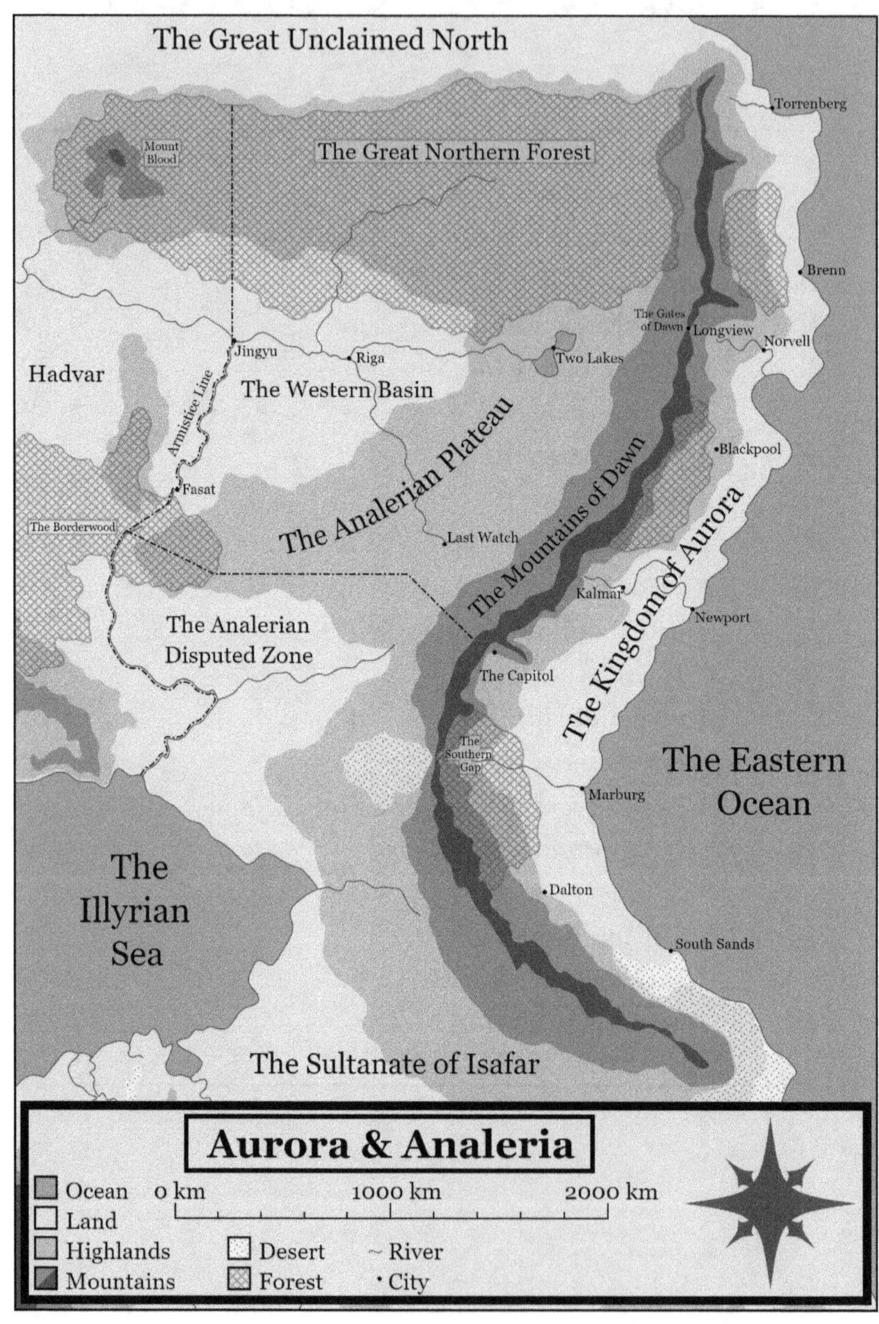

The Great Unclaimed North
The Great Northern Forest
Torrenberg
Mount Blood
Brenn
The Gates of Dawn
Longview
Two Lakes
Norvell
Jingyu
Riga
Hadvar
The Western Basin
Armistice Line
Blackpool
The Analerian Plateau
The Mountains of Dawn
Fasat
The Borderwood
Last Watch
Kalmar
The Kingdom of Aurora
Newport
The Analerian Disputed Zone
The Capitol
The Eastern Ocean
The Southern Gap
Marburg
The Illyrian Sea
Dalton
South Sands
The Sultanate of Isafar
Aurora & Analeria
Ocean
Land
Highlands
Mountains
Desert
Forest
River
City
0 km
1000 km
2000 km

Chapter I

At the Southern Gap

PAUL Bowman planted his shovel in the raw earth beneath him and leaned forward to catch his breath. The soldiers had been digging for several hours in the pre-dawn haze, and the trench was almost four feet deep. The men were exhausted, but now that there was more light, the work was starting to pick up speed.

The order to dig the trenches had come in the early morning hours. A party of scouts had returned with word that a force of a few thousand Isafari foot soldiers was camped on the other side of the pass. Baker Company of the Forty-Second Infantry was immediately roused and set to digging earthworks half a mile forward of the regimental camp.

Paul scratched at the four days growth of brown stubble on his chin. At six feet and two inches, he was a man of greater than average height, and his once less-than-average build had been strengthened considerably by six weeks of brutal conscript training. Idly, he ran his fingers over his short brown hair and straightened the black eye patch that covered the remains of his left eye. That eye patch was probably what had earned him the position of sergeant—that and the fact that at thirty-two years old, Paul was the oldest man by far in Baker Company, possibly the oldest in the entire Forty-Second Infantry.

As he rested, Paul looked about and took stock of the area. This place was called the Southern Gap, a thickly wooded pass through the Mountains of Dawn that marked the border between the Kingdom of Aurora and the Sultanate of Isafar. The soldiers were digging trenches among the trees just behind the crest of a ridge that spanned the width of the narrow pass.

Through the tall trees, Paul could see the vast dark shapes of the Mountains of Dawn, towering over the pass to the north and south. In the east, the pink dawn glow was beginning to slip through the high branches. And to the west, the dark remains of the previous night were shrinking away as the morning drew near.

Paul glanced to his right where three men were struggling to remove an exposed root before it collapsed the front of the trench. It was a simple task, but the three men couldn't decide how to go about doing it, and their collective indecision was threatening to bring down the front of the trench. Paul decided to leave them to their bickering, and wandered to his left where Lieutenant Stuart sat at a table which was far too fancy for the trench, tuning the company radio.

"You got that thing working yet?" Paul asked, and hastily added, "sir?" Some officers could be a bit prickly about that.

"I've found our frequency," Lieutenant Stuart said cheerfully, "Just waiting for the enemy now."

Paul frowned. Second Lieutenant Miles Anderson Stuart had just returned from the Coronation Ball in the Capitol, and he was in entirely too good a mood for the rest of the company. His custom-fitted green-and-gold officers uniform was steam pressed and spotless (contrasting sharply with the mud-caked olive-drab uniforms the rest of the men wore), and Paul had little doubt that the man had been eating very well over the past few days. Fiddling with the radio was probably the most demanding task the lieutenant had set himself to since leaving the officers caravan a mile behind the front.

"I hope either Able or Charlie Company shows up before the enemy does, sir," Paul said with a sigh. It was only common sense. In the past four days, the men of the Forty-Second Infantry had been packed into a train like livestock and marched over fifty miles through the woods. Baker Company in particular had been given barely three hours' rest before being roused and set to digging the earthworks. The regimental cook wagon had been serving cold beans in a stew for the whole trip, and at only one bowl to a man twice a day, nobody below the rank of second lieutenant had a full belly. More importantly, there were only six hundred men in Baker Company, nowhere near enough to man the entire length of the trench. If the attack came now before one of the other companies arrived, it would be a miracle if every fifth man escaped with his life.

"Come now, Bowman, old boy! Don't tell me you're not itching to see some real action," Lieutenant Stuart said, giving Paul a friendly clap on the back and not noticing the wince as Paul's rifle dug into his sore back muscles. "Where's your sense of adventure? Of pride in your country?"

"It got beaten out of me in boot camp, sir," Paul said, only half joking.

"Nonsense!" Stuart clearly wasn't listening, "It's the dawning of a new age; Hadvar is finally defeated, Aurora has crowned a new queen, and all bodes well for the future. Or at least it shall be once we give these southern barbarians a damn good thrashing!"

"I don't get what the big deal was about that whole 'Coronation Ball' thing anyway," Paul grumbled, "She's already been Queen for months, hasn't she? Why do they need to make such a big stink about it? Sir."

"*Making a big stink* is half the fun!" Stuart said gleefully, "What's the point of having a queen if we can't throw her a little celebration every now and again?"

"And what was that about Hadvar being defeated? I thought the broadsheets just said it was a cease-fire. Nobody mentioned any big defeat or anything," Paul said. He could be wrong of course; he couldn't read the broadsheets himself. But if there had been some large battle, Paul would definitely have heard about it from somewhere.

"Oh, I'll grant it wasn't nearly as climactic an end to the fighting as one would hope," Stuart admitted, "but it's still cause for celebration. The war is finally over and done with, after thirty long years."

"You don't really think this peace is going to last, do you?" Paul said grimly.

"Oh, we can't all be burdened with your cynicism, Bowman, old boy," Stuart said with a condescending smile, "The common folk need a sense of continuity. There's more than enough misery in the world these days, what with Analeria still in ruins, Hadvar expanding south beyond the Illyrian Sea, and now these upstarts from Isafar going on the march. The people need to be assured that, here in Aurora at least, law and order still reign."

Paul sighed and shook his head. "Let me know if we get any orders, sir," Paul said, as he wandered back to where he had planted his shovel to continue digging with the rest of the soldiers. Lieutenant Stuart was out of touch and a bit of an idiot, but he meant well. And it could always have been worse. All of the other company officers were still asleep in the officers caravan, a mile and a half back down the slope. The fact that Stuart had even bothered to join his men at the front at this hour spoke volumes for his character, if not his intelligence.

"So," a gruff voice said as Paul rejoined the digging, "whaddid Lieutenant Fancypants have to say?"

Paul looked up. David Fisher was a short, stocky man with a thick mustache, which he somehow managed to keep neatly trimmed even out here. He hailed from Newport, as his thick working-class accent clearly indicated. He was a drinker and a brawler who always had a strong opinion on hand, and his recent promotion to lance corporal had done nothing to temper his convictions. Paul knew full well that Fisher didn't think highly at all of Lieutenant Stuart, or any other nobleman for that matter.

"He's excited about the battle," Paul said, trying to be diplomatic.

"Well"—Fisher shook his head—"whaddya expect from a nerk like him?"

"I don't know," Private Ben Green said, "I'm looking forward to doing some actual fighting for a change."

"Yer kidding me," Fisher rounded on the taller man.

"I didn't sign up to dig trenches," Green said, a sharp movement of his elbow indicating the rifle slung over his back. "I signed up to fight. That's why I'm a soldier."

Private Green was a large man, more heavily built though not quite as tall as Paul. He was an unflappable optimist, and always had an encouraging word close at the ready. Paul could hardly believe that just six weeks ago, Green had been an unrepentant street thug who only joined the army to evade prison after nearly beating a man to death in a tavern brawl. His transformation from gutter scum to model soldier had been a thing of wonder.

"You ain't no soldier," Fisher said with a laugh, "Yer a *conscript.* We're all conscripts here." Fisher had spent a great deal of time over the past few weeks explaining the difference between soldiers and conscripts. Soldiers choose to fight, while conscripts were forced to it, or something of the like. It was the difference between taking action and being acted upon, so he said. Paul allowed Fisher his opinion, but Private Green was no conscript. Sure, he may have been pressured into the army at first, along with the rest of the Forty-Second Infantry, but he had grown to fit his role remarkably, and he was far beyond the need for coercion now. Fisher could run his mouth all he wanted, but Green was a soldier.

And what about me? Paul thought. *Am I a soldier or just a conscript?* He recalled the circumstances of his own recruitment and scowled. The story was a particularly bitter one, and he hadn't completely gotten over it just yet. *Probably best not to think about that,* Paul thought, *Getting sour about it won't do much good right now.*

"I'm not a conscript!" a third voice piped up. Everyone turned to see young Private Logan Carter, his shovel planted firmly in the ground. "I'm no conscript. I *volunteered!*" Carter was short, scrawny, and not much use in a fight, but unusually bright for a boy of his age. Officially he was sixteen, but anyone with any sense could see that he had lied about his age to get into the army.

"That is very true," Fisher said fondly, "You ain't no conscript, m'boy." He patted Carter on the shoulder. "Yer a *idiot!*" Everyone else laughed, and one by one, they all resumed digging. Paul started to wander back toward Lieutenant Stuart.

"Mister Bowman, sir?" Private Carter was suddenly beside Paul. "Are we going to fight soon?"

Paul could hear Carter's voice trembling as he spoke. The boy was putting on a brave face, but he was clearly nervous. "Pretty soon, yeah," Paul said, "but don't worry, kid. Reinforcements will get here before the enemy does. We just need to make sure these trenches get dug before the battle."

"Right," Carter nodded. He returned to digging for a few moments and then came back up. "Mister Bowman, what's it like being in a battle?"

"No clue," Paul shrugged, "Not looking forward to finding out neither."

"But..." Carter seemed perplexed, "Didn't you fight in the war against Hadvar?"

Paul stopped digging and stared at the kid. "Where'd you hear that?"

"From everyone," Carter said sheepishly, "They're saying you lost your eye at the Siege of Two Lakes. Is it true?"

Paul shook his head fondly at the boy. "I've spent the past fifteen years of my life *avoiding* the war against Hadvar. Hell, when the peace broke out three months ago, I thought I was finally in the clear! And you're telling me all those other guys are making me out to be some grizzled old veteran? I thought you were brighter than that, kid."

"But, you're a sergeant, right?" Carter said, "Don't you have to be an experienced veteran to..."

Paul laughed. "Listen, kid, that fool of a Lieutenant promoted me because I can shout and because I have this stupid eye patch. Beyond that, I'm just as green as everyone else in this damn regiment. I haven't seen a battle in my life."

"Then how *did* you lose your eye, Mister Bowman?"

"Quiet," Paul held up a hand to silence Carter as he strained his ears to listen. There was a distant sound, soft but growing. A low, steady rumble with a strange rotating quality to it. As the sound grew louder, other men stopped what they were doing and looked about in confusion. Some began to speak in hushed tones, and others clutched their rifles. "What's that sound?" Carter whispered, "What does it mean?"

"*That* is the sound of a fulgurite reactor," Paul said with a grin, "And it means that reinforcements have arrived."

"Is it one of the other companies?" Carter asked.

Paul pointed through the trees toward the vast northern bulk of the Mountains of Dawn. "See for yourself."

A massive dark shape emerged from behind the eastern side of the towering northern peaks. The vibrations flowed out of it in waves and washed over the earthworks. The soldiers below stared up in wonder, and then cheered as the airship floated gracefully through the sky to hover above the trenches. Paul turned to Carter, "Ever seen an airship before, kid?"

"N-no. Never," Carter stammered, "This is my first time."

Paul didn't remember the first time he saw an airship. He had practically grown up on commercial skyfreighters. During his thirty-two years, he had worked almost every job related to an airship imaginable, from hauling cargo to engine work to plumbing. He had even commanded a ship on his own for a few journeys before being conscripted into military service. Sure, the skyfreighter *Silesia* had been a rickety old first-generation relic, and he had only really been covering for another captain who was down with fever, but that didn't matter. For a few precious days, that ship had belonged to him.

But *this* ship... Paul had seen dozens of military airships, but never one like this! She had to be at least three hundred feet from stern to prow, sixty feet high, and a hundred feet wide at her thickest. Her hull narrowed almost to a point at her prow, which rested upon two long, thick columns that pointed forward, like the legs of a graceful mountain cat ready to pounce. The mouths of the columns glowed faintly blue; those would be the impact coils that held the ship aloft. Four more impact coils were positioned at the stern, two pointing downward for stability and two pointing directly astern for thrust. Paul had never before seen impact columns as large as those. And at such a high angle! They had to be at least sixty degrees from vertical in the bow and thirty astern. That high of an angle would eat up a lot of energy, but it would make her fast as lightning and stable enough to withstand a hurricane. This ship was a marvel of engineering!

Staring up at the mighty airship slowly coming to rest above the treetops, Paul made a promise to himself: Once his service in the army was up, he would travel north to the city of Longview, which sat in the cradle of the great mountain pass that the locals called the Gates of Dawn. That city was the closest thing he had ever had to an earthbound home. Once there, he would get an airship that was all his own. Yes, that was a fine ambition.

"I am the wind," Paul whispered to himself as he beheld the majestic sight.

"What was that?" Private Carter asked softly. Paul glanced at the boy, still staring spellbound at the massive airship. Paul couldn't fault the kid. He wouldn't expect the son of a tavernkeeper from the southern forests of Aurora to be very experienced in the ways of the larger world.

"Just something someone told me once," Paul patted Carter on the shoulder, "Let's get back to work, kid. The boys in the sky have got our back."

The acceleration bell sounded three times to indicate that the mighty airship *Celsius* was coming to a halt. "My lord," the young helmsman announced as the growl of the twin fulgurite reactors dropped to a soft hum, "we have reached the forward position at the Southern Gap."

"Thank you, Helm," Lord Wingate said, "XO, please note our arrival for the log."

"It is so noted, my lord," the executive officer Commander Theodore Barnes said as he scrawled his report in the ship's logbook.

His Excellency, Admiral the Lord Orpheus Chester Wingate stood from the captain's chair and strode to the observation window at the front of the bridge. Fifty metres below, the troops were hard at work constructing the earthworks. Lord Wingate frowned; he couldn't imagine a worse position to entrench. The trees would conceal the trenches from the enemy, but they would also give cover to an advancing foe, and that was never good in a defensive situation. That would lead to a drawn-out battle of attrition; and with the reported size of the Isafari force, such a battle would almost certainly end in a crushing rout.

"Will you take tea, my lord?" Lord Wingate hadn't noticed the small young woman come up beside him with the tea trolley. Her voice was uneasy, and she trembled slightly as she looked up at him, holding a teapot that was far too ornate for an airship like the *Celsius*. Her uniform marked her out as a member of the Women's Airborne Volunteer Echelon. Her young face was unfamiliar. Was this her first posting?

"I'm quite alright, girl. Thank you," he said, raising his hand to gently decline her offer.

As the WAVE girl wheeled her trolley away to make the rounds of the bridge, Lord Wingate returned his attentions to the earthworks below. Hopefully the trenches wouldn't be too significant in the upcoming battle. If all went as planned, the forward battery of the *Celsius* would be enough to repel the might of Isafar. And if that wasn't sufficient, the airships *Albion* and *Fearless* were only about an hour behind. Still, if the combined might of three Auroran airships proved insufficient to beat back the invaders, the brunt of their assault would fall upon the entrenched infantry. And even in the best possible scenario, there would be no stopping at least a few determined invaders from reaching the lines. Men would be lost today; there was no way around that.

Lord Wingate turned away from the window and wandered over to Commander Barnes. "Barnes," Lord Wingate said softly, "take a note for the log." Commander Barnes leaned in close to hear Lord Wingate's note. "Once this operation is over, remind me to find out which officer selected the location for the ground defences."

"So that you may commend him?" Barnes asked as he made his note.

"So that I can throttle him," Lord Wingate grumbled.

At that moment, the door slid open and the ships tactical officer, Commander William Travis Hanscom lurched onto the bridge, still fussing with the brass buttons on his uniform. He staggered up to Lord Wingate and tried as best he could to make a salute with his uniform jacket flopping open. "I reported as soon as I heard the bell," Hanscom wheezed as he resumed fiddling with his buttons, not waiting for Lord Wingate to return his salute. "Have we arrived at the Southern Gap?" His eyes were shot with blood, and Lord Wingate could smell the lingering reek of last night's whiskey on the man's breath.

"We have indeed," Lord Wingate indicated the forward window, "Would you care to observe the ground fortifications?"

"No need," Hanscom said, "I had a good look out a window while I was in my cabin."

"I see," Lord Wingate said, "What was your appraisal of their position?"

"It's a good enough location," Hanscom said, "It'll hold out if we can do our job right." He turned and shouted across the bridge, "Girl! Some tea!"

Lord Wingate frowned as the tea trolley girl scurried to serve Hanscom. Anyone could tell that Hanscom was bluffing about having observed the ground troops. It would have been bad enough if he was not also the ship's tactical officer; it was precisely his job to be aware of that sort of thing. But the worst part was that there would be no disciplining him. Hanscom was untouchable. His entire life had been handed to him on a silver platter, and it would remain so right up to the day he died. Such was the way of Old Nobility.

I'm also Old Nobility, Lord Wingate reminded himself ruefully. It galled him to accept that this revolting piece of human trash was of the same noble stock as himself. Sure, Lord Wingate had also been born to a life of privilege, but he had used his blessings and made accomplishments in his own right. He had even commanded his own airship when he was but three-and-twenty years old. Hanscom was eight-and-twenty, and he hadn't accomplished nearly so much. Still, in a few decades' time he would be made a lord, regardless of whether or not he deserved it. He would be an esteemed pillar of court life, an honoured patriarch of the Auroran aristocracy, married to some empty-headed young chit and sire to a new generation of Old Nobility. *And he'll still be a bloody drunken fool!*

Lord Wingate sighed. There was no use fretting over the shortcomings of his crew; there was a battle to be fought. "Helm," he called, "increase our altitude by one hundred metres. It's time we had a good look at the enemy camp."

"Aye, my lord," the helmsman responded, "increase altitude by one hundred metres." The acceleration bell sounded twice. *Brace for a short movement.*

As the *Celsius* pitched upward, Lord Wingate heard a loud crash, and the sound of shattering porcelain. He turned to see the WAVE girl with the tea trolley standing in front of a steaming puddle of tea. Right beside her, Hanscom stood clutching at his uniform where a light brown stain was soaking into the white silk undershirt beneath his uniform jacket. "I'm sorry," the WAVE girl said in a terrified squeak as she produced a handkerchief and tried to wipe the moisture out of his shirt, "I'm so sorry."

What is wrong with you, girl?!" Hanscom knocked the girl's hand away. Lord Wingate flinched at the volume of the shout.

"I'm sorry, sir," the girl said, slowly backing away. "I lost my grip when the—"

"I don't care if you're *sorry*, girl!" Hanscom continued to rant, "*Sorry* won't do me any good!"

"Please," the girl shrank back to her trolley, and knelt down to wipe up the spill. "I'm sorry. I'll do everything I can to—"

"Do you have any idea how much it costs to have this thing cleaned? Bloody hell, you girls are useless!"

"Hanscom!" Lord Wingate bellowed. Both Hanscom and the beleaguered girl looked up. Lord Wingate glared at Hanscom. "Leave her be."

"But Captain," Hanscom protested, "this girl—"

"I'm not a captain," Lord Wingate growled "I'm an admiral and a lord!" He didn't like pulling rank, but Hanscom rarely responded to anything less. "Go to the forward window and let me know when the enemy encampment comes into view."

"Aye, my lord," Hanscom turned and skulked away to the window, still fretting over his uniform.

Lord Wingate knelt down beside the WAVE girl. "Are you alright?"

"Y-yes, my lord," the girl stammered, "I'm sorry."

"What is your name, girl?"

"Halford, my lord." The girl stood up sharply, "Louise Halford, of the Women's Airborne Volunteer Echelon."

"Is this your first posting, Louise?"

"Yes, my lord," Louise blushed slightly.

"Don't worry about the spill, my dear," Lord Wingate said, putting a hand on her shoulder, "I think we've all had our fill of tea for now."

"My lord," Hanscom called roughly from the forward window, "The enemy camp is in sight."

"I'm on my way," Lord Wingate called back. "Alright, Louise, take your cart back to the galley. And tell the WAVE taskmaster to send someone else to wipe up the spill whenever they can be spared."

"Thank you, my lord," Louise smiled, curtsied, and wheeled the tea trolley off the bridge. Lord Wingate watched her leave. She would be alright. The WAVE had its detractors, and Lord Wingate had once been amongst them, but eight-and-twenty years in the Auroran Royal Airborne Fleet had tempered his opinions on the matter. *I also married one of them!* Lord Wingate thought with a smile.

Returning to the matter at hand, Lord Wingate walked to the forward window where Hanscom waited. "You coddle those girls overmuch, my lord," Hanscom grumbled as Lord Wingate stood beside him, "It will not do to have—"

"Let me make this perfectly clear, Hanscom," Lord Wingate said in a deadly whisper, "If you ever make a scene like that on my bridge again, I will transfer you to the *Dreadnought*."

Hanscom's expression changed instantly to one of horror. The *Dreadnought* had an ill name in the fleet. She had been the very first airship built by the ARAF, and though she had been impressive for her time, she was now an obsolete forty-year-old wreck of an airship that for some reason had never been decommissioned. Nowadays, she sat idle for months at a time, transferring from one port to another every so often, awaiting orders that would never come. But what really gave the *Dreadnought* her ill reputation was her crew. To the ARAF high command, she was the dumping ground of the fleet. Her crew was made up of troublemakers, pariahs, incompetents; people who were too politically sensitive to be discharged out of hand, but still couldn't be trusted with important duties. In short, the *Dreadnought* was where careers went to die. "Do I make myself clear, Hanscom?"

Hanscom hung his head. "Very clear, my lord."

"Good." Lord Wingate turned his attention back to the window. "Now then, what are we dealing with here?"

Beyond the crest of the ridge, the trees quickly gave way to open ground, which sloped sharply downward away from the mountains. At the bottom of the slope, a hundred metres or so back from the edge of the trees, lay the Isafari camp. It was still covered in shadow thanks to the mountains, but its shape and size were visible from above. It was a vast amorphous sprawl, at least two hundred metres across; and it consumed all the free space between the bottom of the slope and the white salt flats that stretched beyond the horizon.

"About... ten thousand strong, best I can figure," Hanscom said, "Three regiments worth?"

Isafar did not use regiments to organise its armies, but the analogy was appropriate enough. Three regiments, compared to only one on the Auroran side of the pass. There was no getting around numbers like that, not with the awful position that the troops in the pass had been placed in. If this army could not be dissuaded, or at least drastically reduced in size, then the battle was already lost.

The salt flats were a distinct advantage though. They prevented the Isafari from retreating due east. Those flats were called "The Anvil of the Sun," and for good reason. If the Isafari troops were desperate enough to retreat across the flats, they would be roasted alive by the sun within hours. If they wanted to retreat and *survive*, they would have to either head north into the Analerian Disputed Zone or south along a narrow corridor between the mountains and the flats. If they went north, they would be in cut off in unfamiliar territory, and if they went south, they would be in the shadow of the mountains for miles, and they could be pursued by ground forces without giving up the high ground. *Now, if only we can convince them to retreat...*

Lord Wingate squinted. There was something out in the salt flats, two hundred metres or so beyond the Isafari camp. A set of small dark shapes against the white expanse of the salt flats. Seven in total. Too large to be people. Lord Wingate walked to the side of the window where a spyglass hung on a peg.

"Shall we commence bombardment, my lord?" Hanscom asked.

Lord Wingate ignored him, brought the spyglass to his eyes and, adjusted the knobs and dials to bring the image into focus. What were those things?

Hanscom squinted, "What do you see, my lord?"

"Artillery," Lord Wingate announced as he recognised the shapes, "The enemy has deployed artillery in the salt flats."

"What?" Hanscom squawked, "That can't be right. What model are those guns?" He sounded genuinely troubled. And not without reason. There had been no mention of any artillery in the intelligence dispatches. Beyond that, Isafar was not an industrialised nation; they couldn't manufacture heavy artillery like that. How had they come by *seven* of them?

They're probably Hadvari, Lord Wingate thought, *sold off after the armistice to make good on war debts or something mundane like that.* Still it was worth further investigation. "Helm," Lord Wingate said, "slow ahead, and keep us close to the treeline. I want a closer look at those guns."

The acceleration bell chimed, and the *Celsius* dipped and glided over the treetops, slowly approaching the Isafari camp. Lord Wingate squinted through the spyglass, trying to glean as many details as he possibly could as the *Celsius* crept closer. Beside each gun sat a pile of crates. Ammunition no doubt. Small figures of people scurried to and fro amongst the guns. That was ominous. Had they already been given targets? Judging by the relative size of the people, their barrels were about three metres long.

Three? That was too large for Hadvari ordinance, the largest Hadvari boomers were only a metre and a half. And unlike regular Hadvari ordinance, none of thoee guns had blast shields. As the ship neared, Lord Wingate also noticed recoil compensators on their muzzles; Hadvar didn't make heavy guns with those. Only one country in the world could have possibly made them...

"Those are Auroran guns!"

"What? That's preposterous," Hanscom said, "How could they have gotten their hands on our weapons?"

"See for yourself." Lord Wingate passed the spyglass to Hanscom.

"Traitors!" Hanscom hissed as he peered through the spyglass, "Bloody turncoats!"

Lord Wingate shook his head. "Mercenaries, more likely. Probably one of the Analerian irregular companies. We armed quite a few of those bandits with heavy ordinance during the war against Hadvar." *I had a feeling that would come back to bite us in the arse.*

"If you say so," Hanscom grumbled, "but what are we going to do about it?"

"Sparks," Lord Wingate turned to address his communications officer, Ensign Jonathan Holloway, "Inform the ground forces that the enemy has deployed artillery. Advise them to pull back to a more —"

Before Lord Wingate could finish, a massive explosion rocked the airship. The shock sent both Lord Wingate and Hanscom sprawling on the deck.

"Helm!" Lord Wingate shouted as he picked himself up, "bring us about! All speed! Get us out of the line of fire." He steadied himself against the window as the mighty airship banked hard to starboard. "Hanscom, sound the general alarm! Sparks, damage report! All decks!"

"What about the warning to the ground troops?" Holloway shouted back.

"Belay that, Sparks," Lord Wingate shouted, "Damage report first."

"Aye, my lord."

Lord Wingate strained to keep his balance as the deck pitched violently. The roar of the fulgurite reactors returned in force, along with the screeching alarm that summoned all hands to battle stations. After about thirty seconds, the deck returned to a level position, and Lord Wingate dashed over to the comm officer's console. "Where did they get us?" he demanded.

"They hit the aft reactor," Holloway said, "It sounds bad. Want me to put them on the speaker?"

Lord Wingate nodded. "Do it."

The large speaker on the comm officer's console crackled to life. Holloway handed the mouthpiece to Lord Wingate, who took it firmly. "Aft reactor," he demanded, "what's your status?"

"They got us bad," a tinny voice huffed from the other side of the speaker through a haze of static, "We have a hull breach, coils three and five are leaking fast, and three of my engineers got hit by shrapnel. But I think we can— Wait, what?" The speaker cut out for a moment. Then the voice returned with a grave tone, "Bad news. There's a hairline fracture in the reactor body."

Ensign Holloway squeaked with horror. Lord Wingate could hardly blame him—a reactor-body fracture was all but a death sentence for an airship. Still, Lord Wingate wasn't about to give up just yet. "Can you fix it?"

"Not without shutting the reactor down," the voice said, "We can probably get half an hour out of her before then, but only if we keep her output low. Anything above 60 percent and we risk a full core breach in about five minutes."

"Keep output low, and do what you can to shore everything up," Lord Wingate said, and motioned for Holloway to close the channel.

"What are your orders, my lord?" Holloway asked unsteadily.

Lord Wingate ran over all their options in his mind. They couldn't come to ground anywhere on the eastern side of the pass; the thickness of the trees would prevent that, and the forest stretched for at least a hundred clicks in any direction. And if they came to ground on the western side, the *Celsius* would be captured by the Isafari within minutes, which was unacceptable. They couldn't stay in the air for more than half an hour, not with the larger of their two reactors out of commission, and backup was an hour away at least. That left only one option. *The final option.*

Lord Wingate took a deep breath. "Let me address the crew," he said solemnly. Holloway flicked a bunch of switches on his console and nodded.

"Attention all hands," He could hear his voice reverberating from beyond the bridge. The effect was unsettling. "This is Admiral the Lord Wingate. Whatever you are doing now, drop it or finish it in the next thirty seconds. Engine crew, disengage all safety mechanisms and standby to come to full power. Armoury crew, lock all blast doors in the open position. All other hands, proceed to your designated breach points and make ready to abandon ship. The Mordred Protocol is now in effect. You have five minutes."

"What was that sound?" Carter trembled as the sound of the explosion reached the trenches.

Paul quickly pulled out his rifle and ducked close against the front of the trench. "Cover!" he shouted over the rising growl of the airship's fulgurite reactor. The rest of the soldiers followed his example, pulling out their rifles and crouching low in their trenches. The earthworks were barely five feet deep now, but they would have to do.

"Are they coming?" Carter whispered as he clutched his rifle with white knuckles, "Is it the enemy?"

"Take it easy, kid," Paul gave Carter a reassuring pat on the shoulder, "Keep your head down for a bit. I'm gonna go see what's happening." Paul scrambled through the trench, keeping as low as he could without crawling through the dirt, toward Lieutenant Stuart, who was still fiddling with the radio as if nothing had happened.

"Sir?" Paul asked, "What's going on?"

"No word yet!" Stuart was grinning like a madman, his eyes full of wild anticipation for the coming battle, "But any moment now!"

"Sir," Paul said, crouching in the trench beside Stuart, "I recommend you take cover. We don't know what's coming."

"Ha! I'll tell you what's coming, Bowman, old boy!" Stuart laughed, "A disorganised mob of savages with rocks and spears, that's what! Our forces are superior in every way, and when those barbarians catch wind of it, they shan't—"

Shots rang out from the forest, and Stuart fell backwards off his chair. "Snipers!" Paul shouted, throwing himself against the earth at the front of the trench. The Isafari forces had arrived at last.

Paul glanced back at Stuart and was about to tell him to take cover, but stopped when he saw the lieutenant slumped in the dirt, blood running down his face from a single hole in his forehead. His eyes were blank, and his face was frozen in the same look of wild anticipation. Paul stared at the thing that had once been a man. He had seen dead bodies before, but never one with a familiar face. He didn't quite know what to make of it.

From the radio on the table, a sharp beeping noise began to chirp wildly from within a crackling tangle of static. *Orders at last,* Paul thought. He quickly snatched the radio earpiece and... *How does this thing work again?* He had never actually operated a radio before. There were a bunch of knobs and dials and a lever. What the hell were they supposed to do? *Carter could probably figure this thing out,* Paul thought, *That kid's smart; he can read.* Little did it matter, as a few seconds later, another volley of shots rang out and the radio exploded in a shower of sparks.

Paul pressed himself against the side of the trench and tried to comprehend the state of affairs. Lieutenant Stuart was dead, the radio was gone, the enemy was bearing down on them, and there were no signs of any reinforcements. The airship was still prowling the skies above them, but without the radio, there was no way to call down any support. There didn't seem to be a way out of this.

Paul crouched as low as he could and scrambled through the trench toward the huddled forms of Corporal Fisher, Private Green, Private Carter, and a few others he didn't know offhand. Fisher and Green leaned against the front of the trench, preparing their rifles. Carter was huddled in the fetal position, clutching his rifle for dear life.

"How's the lieutenant?" Fisher asked with a sour look. Paul shook his head. Fisher closed his eyes for a moment, then got to his feet. "Hell with this," he spat, "I'm getting outta here!"

"What do you think you're doing?" one of the other soldiers objected, "You can't just run!"

"You bet I can!" Fisher said, throwing off his rifle, "And if yer smart, you'll run too!"

"If you run, the provos will shoot you for a deserter," Green said. His eyes narrowed in a threatening glare.

"And if I stay, those savages are gonna shoot me anyway!" Fisher snapped back as he started to scramble out the back of the trench, "At least this way I got a chance!" Before anyone could say another word, another rifle cracked in the distance, and Fisher was dead. Nobody else tried to run.

After a few moments, one of the privates asked, "So what's our plan?"

On instinct, Paul glanced back toward Lieutenant Stuart, before remembering that he was still dead. Slowly, the realization dawned on Paul: *I'm the only one left in charge!* Baker Company was relying on him to get them out of this mess. If anyone was going to decide what to do, it would have to be him.

What was left to do? They couldn't just stay here and wait for reinforcements that might not even come. If they fell back, the Isafari snipers would pick them off with impunity. Moving out of the way of the snipers was just as bad; that would either lead to capture by the enemy or the entire company being shot for dereliction of duty. The only option that remained was going forward. Paul desperately racked his brain for another solution, but the more he resisted, the clearer the reality became.

Shit.

"We're going to attack," Paul announced.

"You can't be serious!" Green exclaimed.

"They'll slaughter us!" another soldier objected.

"We're going to attack," Paul said more firmly, "We can't stay here, and we can't retreat, so that means we're going to attack! Got it?"

"I'll follow you," Carter solemnly murmured as he came to a crouching position. Slowly, the other soldiers followed his lead. Paul fished into one of his coat pockets and pulled out a small tin whistle. He gave two short bursts and shouted, "Company! Fix bayonets!" Paul joined the rest of the company in fastening a long, sinister blade to the muzzle of his rifle. Paul could hear the distant sound of sergeants and lance corporals carrying his orders down the trench. Paul gave two more short toots on the whistle and shouted, "On the signal, company will advance!" Paul and the soldiers crouched close against the front of the trench, preparing to spring out with rifles at the ready. Paul clutched the tin whistle between his teeth and listened to his orders relaying down the line.

For a moment, everything was still. Paul glanced over at Carter. The boy was still as frightened as ever, but his face was set with determination. Paul gave him a reassuring nod, and Carter returned the gesture with a look that said he would follow Paul over the edge of the earth if that was what it took. Paul took a deep breath and let forth a long, steady blast on the whistle. He was still blowing as he sprang up out of the trench with the rest of his soldiers.

Almost immediately, a volley of gunshots erupted from deep within the forest, and Private Carter dropped to the ground screaming. This time, however, telltale muzzle flashes betrayed the snipers positions among the trees. Paul and his men charged forward at a dead run toward the enemy with a wordless cry of animal fury.

Indistinct shapes began to move deep within the woods. Paul couldn't make them out clearly in the low light with his one eye, but he knew well enough what they were: the Isafari snipers, pulling out of their cover before they were overrun. More shots rang out, but not from the Isafari. Some of the Auroran troops were firing at the fleeing enemy. Paul quickened his pace as much as he could.

One Isafari sniper tripped and fell. Green pounced on the man like a rabid dog, joyful murder blazing in his gray eyes as he drove his bayonet into the fallen man's flesh again and again. Paul kept running, not daring to look back at the carnage unfolding behind him. Green might be a model soldier on the outside, but he was still a brute at heart, and no amount of training would ever change that.

The trees vanished, and Paul emerged onto a hillside overlooking a vast campsite. The Isafari camp. A few dozen Isafari snipers barreled down the hill toward the camp. Paul jogged to a stop and took out his rifle to take a few shots at the retreating snipers. As he aimed, he noticed a battery of artillery in the salt flats a few hundred feet behind the camp. *Dammit!* They had boomers! Why hadn't their scouts reported those? Before Paul could react, something exploded overhead. Paul looked up.

It was the airship from before. She couldn't be more than a hundred feet above the treetops. Smoke and flame belched out of a gaping hole in her side. She gave off the most terrible sound, like the howl of a dying beast mixed with the shriek and groan of twisting metal. Paul could only watch as the once mighty airship plunged out of the red dawn sky directly toward the enemy boomers.

As the ship crashed, there was a brilliant blue flash, like a second sun erupting out of the salt flats. Paul raised a hand to cover his eyes, just as a terrific explosion of sound slammed into him, nearly knocking him over. Paul lowered his hand as the blinding light subsided, and he looked out upon the devastation.

The Isafari artillery battery was completely gone. All that remained of their position was a vast black scorch mark and a twisting plume of smoke. The salt flats beyond were littered with smoldering debris. The Isafari camp was largely intact, though quite a few fires burned brightly where none had been seen before. Most of the fleeing snipers had been knocked backwards off their feet by the force of the shockwave.

The Mordred Protocol! Paul gaped, *I thought it was just a rumor!*

"Look at that!" a voice cried out from behind Paul. He turned to look. Soldiers were beginning to emerge from the woods. Almost all of Baker Company was there. They stared in awe at the destruction, and some began to whisper among themselves. Finally someone shouted, "Look up there!" Paul looked up into the sky where the man pointed. Parachutes. Some of the airship crew had escaped.

And the wind was carrying them directly towards the Isafari camp.

Paul fumbled for his whistle and gave two short blasts. "Alright men," he shouted, "the enemy is in chaos! We're going to hit the enemy camp and protect the airship survivors. Follow me!"

And with that, he charged down the slope, and the rest of his men followed after him. As they closed the distance, Paul could see the fallen Isafari snipers picking themselves up off the ground. In the sky above, the survivors from the ship drifted toward the enemy camp. If this gambit failed...

I am the wind...

Chapter II
An Interview

LORD Wingate flinched as the force of the explosion struck him like a brick wall. Even at this range, the shockwave was almost a tangible thing. But what surprised Lord Wingate the most was the blinding flash of blue light as the reactors exploded. It was like nothing he had ever seen before. Instinctively, he checked the integrity of his parachute straps. Everything was holding. Good. Lord Wingate sighed in relief—not much to do now but let gravity take its course.

Once the blue blaze from the reactor explosion had subsided, Lord Wingate looked out across the devastation he had wrought. The *Celsius* had overshot the artillery position by about fifty metres or so. The battery had been completely obliterated by the blast, but apart from a few fires, the enemy camp was still largely intact. That was disappointing; Lord Wingate had hoped to take out a decent chunk of the Isafari foot along with their artillery. Still, as long as it took their heavy guns out of play and bought time for the Auroran troops to pull back and regroup, the gambit would have paid off.

Not too bad for a manouvre that had never actually been attempted before. *That's right,* Lord Wingate reminded himself, *This is one for the history books—the first ever successful execution of the Mordred Protocol in a combat situation.* If an airship sustained critical damage to its reactor and was unable to escape or make in-flight repairs, the Mordred Protocol declared that the ship was to disable its reactor safety measures, evacuate its crew, and crash itself into the nearest target of strategic value. It had been amongst the very first directives laid down after the catastrophic opening years of the war against Hadvar, but in all the years since then, this was the first time it had actually been implemented to any success.

Lord Wingate doubted that he would receive any official recognition for his actions. The ARAF was unlikely to reward a commander who lost his ship, especially a commander as high up as Lord Wingate. He would probably have to confine himself to desk duty for a while to control the political backlash from his actions, but as long as some strategic boon could be salvaged this day, he would be content.

Lord Wingate glanced down towards the ground, looming a hundred metres or so beneath him. The altitude didn't daunt him as it might a lesser man; this wasn't his first parachute jump, and more than two and a half decades in the ARAF had long since quashed his initial fear of heights. What did give Lord Wingate pause was the fact that the tops of the trees were behind him now and steadily getting farther away. He was drifting slowly but surely towards the east. Towards the Isafari camp.

Two other parachutes drifted close behind him, the helmsman, who had plotted the *Celsius's* suicide run, and Holloway, who had stayed behind to radio the order for the ground troops to fall back, and to notify *Albion* and *Fearless.* The rest of the crew had abandoned ship farther back near the earthworks; they would probably be safe. But as for Lord Wingate and his two companions, they would land right in the middle of the enemy camp. Lord Wingate's hand wandered down to rest idly upon the pistol holstered at his right side.

Lord Wingate heard a terrific shout from the ground below. He looked down and was horrified by what he saw: A disorganised mob of Auroran soldiers was spewing out of the forest and down the hill at a dead run towards the Isafari camp! What the hell were they doing?! They were supposed to fall back and regroup with the rest of the regiment, not charge blindly ahead! Lord Wingate glanced back at Holloway, floating close behind him. He *had* radioed them their orders, hadn't he?

As the horde of Auroran soldiers neared the Isafari camp, Lord Wingate's heart sank in his chest. He had sacrificed his own ship, the pride of the Auroran fleet, to buy them time to regroup, and they had squandered the opportunity. Lord Wingate glanced over at the Isafari camp. Dark figures were pouring out of the camp to oppose the oncoming wave of Auroran soldiers. This was going to be a damn massacre! Once the Isafari soldiers formed a defensive line, they would...

...Lord Wingate blinked in amazement. The Isafari soldiers weren't attacking; they were surrendering! Lord Wingate watched as the Isafari troops threw down their guns and sank to their knees with their hands over their heads, the universal signal for quarter. As they surrendered, more soldiers emerged from the camp and followed in their example. The oncoming Auroran soldiers broke off their charge. Some set about gathering the Isafari soldiers into groups while the rest moved into the Isafari camp, presumably to continue the surrender.

As Lord Wingate floated down to the ground on a lazy breeze, it all started to make more sense. The Isafari troops had narrowly missed being incinerated by the explosion of the *Celsius,* and a good portion of their camp had been set on fire by the blast. And to top it off, a horde of angry Auroran soldiers had come charging towards them. Still, if they were surrendering so easily, they must have had pretty low morale, even before the crash. These soldiers would likely have never even been a threat! Lord Wingate laughed; if he had known that before going into battle...

No battle plan survives first contact with the enemy.

Finally, Lord Wingate came to ground amongst the tents. Holloway and the young helmsman landed close after him. The camp was in chaos; hordes of dark-skinned men rushed hither and thither, shouting words that meant nothing to Lord Wingate's untrained ear. A significant number of women and children congregated amisdt the hustle and bustle. *Camp followers most likely,* Lord Wingate supposed.

"What are we going to do now?" the young helmsman asked as soon as he was clear of all the straps and buckles that fastened him to his parachute.

"We need to take charge of the situation on the ground," Lord Wingate said, drawing his sidearm as a precaution. "Do either of you speak Isafari?"

"I do," Holloway said unsteadily. "A little. I mean, I'm not quite fluent yet, but I think I can handle it."

"Good. Helmsman," Lord Wingate said, making a mental note to learn the boy's proper name, "run back to the rest of our troops, and relay a message. Let them know that the battle is won and the enemy has surrendered. Order them to join us here and assist with the clean-up operations with all haste. Do you understand?"

"Yes my lord," The young helmsman saluted hastily and scampered away.

"And you," Lord Wingate turned back to Holloway, "come with me. We need to find the commander of this force so we can formalise the surrender."

It was about that moment when Lord Wingate noticed that he and Holloway had begun to draw a small crowd. A dozen or so dark-skinned men were staring in slack-jawed amazement at them. They were bare chested and barefoot, and more than a few looked distinctly undernourished. Lord Wingate couldn't exactly fault these soldiers for their incredulity; he had, after all, just jumped out of an exploding airship and floated safely to the ground.

"This seems like a good place to begin our search," Lord Wingate said, "Ask these soldiers where their commander is."

"Right," Holloway nodded and stepped forward to address the crowd. His speech was halting, but hopefully it would be sufficient. The crowd only stared. Holloway addressed the crowd, more steadily this time, but still the crowd didn't react.

"I don't think they understand me," Holloway whispered.

"Try asking them something else," Lord Wingate suggested, "Ask them to identify themselves."

Holloway said something else in Isafari, but still there was no response. What was wrong with these savages?

Someone shouted something from outside the crowd. The great mass moved aside to accommodate the speaker; his skin was dark like the rest, but he was noticeably taller than the others. He also wore shoes and what looked like a tunic, in contrast to the other Isafari soldiers. *An officer,* Lord Wingate thought, *or whatever the Isafari equivalent is.* The new man marched right up to Holloway and began to speak. Holloway responded in Isafari as the crowd of soldiers dispersed.

"This man is a translator," Holloway announced after about half a minute of gibberish between the two of them, "He'll help us."

"A *translator?*" Lord Wingate raised an eyebrow, "Why would we need another one?"

"Because these people don't speak Isafari," Holloway explained, "They're Masada."

"*Masada?*" Lord Wingate had never heard the name before.

"Oh yeah," Holloway perked up, "He says they have all sorts of people here. Masada, Bangundu, Go'oh, Qâmâbullu, I think there's even a few—"

"Wait wait wait," Lord Wingate interrupted, "They're *not* from Isafar?"

"Well, yes they are," Holloway tried to explain, "They're just all from different tribes. You see, Isafar is composed of a number of—"

Lord Wingate stopped Holloway. "You can explain it to me later. Right now we need to find the leader of this force. Ask this man where we can find him."

Holloway turned back to the translator and asked the question. "He wants to know why we're looking for their commander," Holloway reported back.

"Tell him we are here to accept their surrender."

Holloway spoke again. The translator gaped at Holloway's request and glared as he responded. "He... uh, he says no," Holloway said, "Also... I think I may have just insulted him."

"Did you use the right words?" Lord Wingate whispered, his right hand wandering down to his sidearm, "Maybe you should try —"

"Hang on," Holloway held up a hand to silence Lord Wingate, "I think I can handle this..." Holloway made a gesture of deference and spoke what was very likely an apology. That seemed to placate the translator. "He says they cannot surrender to us..." Holloway translated, "because they have already surrendered to someone else."

That made sense; there had to have been an officer leading the charge that had first made the Isafari surrender. That officer would have most likely taken control of the situation himself. "We must find whomever they have surrendered to," Lord Wingate said, "Tell this man to bring us to him."

Holloway translated the request, and the translator led them through the camp to a large tent surrounded by a great milling throng of people. Most of these men were fair-skinned Auroran soldiers who moved aside and saluted as Lord Wingate approached and followed the Isafari translator into the tent.

Inside the tent, still more Auroran soldiers milled about. Each one was shouting about something, their sundry voices all combining into one tremendous note of discord. "Soldiers!" Lord Wingate bellowed. All at once, the crowd fell silent and looked up to see who had spoken. *Much better.*

"Which of you has command here?" Lord Wingate demanded. One by one, the soldiers moved to the side of the tent until only two men stood before Lord Wingate.

One of them was a dark-skinned Isafari, and most definitely someone of importance. He was just under six feet tall, and his head was shaven completely bald. The man was garbed in long robes of some intricately woven material, and thin hoops of gold hung from his... wait, was that a woman?!

Lord Wingate blinked. She was most certainly a woman upon closer observation, but she was like no woman Lord Wingate had ever seen before! She wasn't beautiful in the conventional sense, certainly not with her shaven head, but there was an unmistakable presence about her. She clearly commanded respect, but not in the same haughty way that a general or a great conqueror would; she just seemed to *expect* it of people. *A most striking woman,* Lord Wingate thought.

The figure beside her was an Auroran soldier, a few centimetres taller than she, but not nearly so striking. He had brown hair and an average build for a soldier. If not for the patch over his left eye, the man would be completely unremarkable. The man turned to face Lord Wingate and made a ragged salute. As he turned, Lord Wingate saw the three-chevron emblem of a sergeant on his sleeve. *Good enough for preliminary enquiries,* Lord Wingate supposed.

"Sergeant," Lord Wingate addressed the man in a loud, clear voice, "full report."

"Uh... w-what?" the man stared blankly at Lord Wingate.

"...What is your name, Sergeant?" Lord Wingate sighed. *Blasted grunts. Not an ounce of proper discipline between the lot of them.*

"Oh! Uh... Paul. Paul Bowman," Sergeant Bowman made another sloppy salute, "Sergeant, Baker company, the Forty-Second Infantry, sir."

A little better this time... Lord Wingate thought. "Where is your commanding officer?"

Bowman's expression changed, "Lieutenant Stuart was... killed a few minutes ago, sir, back at the—"

"I didn't ask for your *Leftenant*," Lord Wingate said, getting a little more frustrated, "I asked for your *commanding officer!*"

"Uh... sorry?" Bowman didn't appear to understand the distinction. *What fool of an officer had thought it a good idea to promote this idiot?!*

"Where is your *captain?*" Lord Wingate asked, his nerves beginning to wear thin.

"Uh..." Bowman scratched his head and glanced to the side, "Far as I know, he's still back in the officers caravan, sir."

"Then who is in command here?" Lord Wingate demanded.

"Um..." Bowman paused to think, "I, uh... I am, sir. I think."

Lord Wingate's jaw dropped, "You mean this entire army surrendered to *you?*"

"Pretty much, yeah," Bowman shrugged.

The bed was far from comfortable. It had one of those new mattresses with the metal springs instead of the canvas-and-straw ones Paul had grown accustomed to during training. He could feel one or two of the springs poking sharply at him through the cheap linen covering, trying to skewer him like a porcupine. Paul couldn't bring himself to care; this was the first real rest he'd had since before digging out the trenches, and he was tired as a corpse.

Paul glanced over to the door of his cell. Some overdressed guard stood outside, rigid as a post. That guard had been there when the provos had first tossed him in here; and by the looks of it, he hadn't moved an inch in all that time. *How long has it been?* Paul wondered. He knew from experience that time did funny things inside a cell.

The events from earlier in the day dashed across his mind with lightning speed. The memory of his charge on the Isafari camp and their subsequent surrender whizzed by like bullets. A little while after that, two more airships floated over the mountains and came to ground beside the Isafari camp. Paul had still been wiping the wonder from his eye when two random provos arrested him and put him in this cell aboard one of the two airships.

That had all happened in just over an hour, and yet the memories seemed to last only a few minutes. But here in the brig, there was only the vast, uncertain expanse of time. Minutes stretched out into hours and then shrank back into minutes again. Paul sighed and laid himself out on the uncomfortable mattress. He could rest until Lieutenant Stuart gave him something to do.

Lieutenant Stuart is dead. The thought hit Paul like a bullet. Stuart had been a friend, even if he was a bit loopy at times, and now he was gone. *Corporal Fisher too,* Paul remembered; him with his rhetoric about soldiers and conscripts. *And young Private Carter,* Paul thought as well. That one was worst of all; Carter died during the charge. Following him. *He's dead because of me,* Paul thought, *They're all dead because of me!*

Paul closed his eyes and saw them: Lieutenant Stuart lying in the dirt of the trench, blood running down a face forever frozen in a wild grin. The look of terror in Corporal Fisher's eyes when he decided to run. That reassuring glance from Private Carter just moments before the charge. *I should have saved them!* Paul thought, *Dammit, I should have done something. Anything.*

He sighed and rolled over, turning away from the bars and that damn statue of a guard. A *real* soldier would have found a way to save them all. *Not me though,* he thought, *Fisher was right. I'm just a conscript. It's all I've ever been. It's all I'll ever be.*

A loud banging noise from the door of his cell shook Paul out of his thoughts. The two provos from before were standing outside the cell. "Prisoner," one of them addressed Paul in a loud, arrogant voice, "get up." Paul pulled himself to his feet as the provo who spoke opened the cell door. "The prisoner will come with us." Grudgingly, Paul followed the pair out of the cell.

The provos marched Paul through the airship, one in front of him and one behind him. They led him up a tight, wrought-iron spiral staircase, down a long hallway lit by those fancy new wire-and-glass electric candles, then up another spiral stair, and down another similar corridor. Eventually, they stopped at the end of the hallway, before a fine lacquered wooden door that seemed entirely out of place on a warship such as this.

One of the provos knocked sharply on the door, and after a few seconds, the door opened, and a stocky man poked his head through. He was round faced with a ridiculous upturned golden mustache and beady blue eyes. He nodded at the provos and opened the door more fully to let everyone in.

Paul blinked. While the door had simply been out of place, the office beyond it looked like another world completely! The floor was covered with an ornately patterned carpet, and the walls were paneled with dark varnished wood. Several portraits hung on the walls depicting stern-faced military men in decorated uniforms. A ridiculous crystal chandelier hung from the ceiling. And was that a liquor cabinet in the corner? This room looked like it belonged in the palace of some well-off lord, not taking up space on a military airship.

A vast window dominated the back of the room and opened onto the mountains astern of the airship. In front of the window sat an expensive-looking desk, and behind that desk sat a large, imposing man in a perfectly tailored green-and-gold uniform that glittered with medals. His hair was light brown with wings of white at the temples and a neatly managed pair of sideburns that joined just beneath his nose. His face was like a stone carving, and though time had begun to crack it in places, it only added to the severity of his gaze.

Ah hell, Paul thought, *this guy again!*

"Sergeant Paul Bowman of the Forty-Second Infantry," The man said in a deep baritone, "we spoke earlier, but I don't believe we've yet been properly introduced. I am Admiral the Lord Orpheus Chester Wingate."

"Nice to... meet you?" Paul said awkwardly, "Sir?" The fleet was a separate chain of command from the Army, wasn't it? What was the protocol for a situation like this?

"Thank you, gentlemen," Lord Wingate nodded to the two provos who had escorted Paul into the room, "Would you please fetch our other guests?" The provos saluted, turned on their heels and marched out of the room. "Now then, Mister Bowman, I would like to ask you a few questions concerning your actions during this battle."

"Are you going to shoot me if I answer wrong?" Paul locked eyes with the man.

"I sincerely hope it won't come to that," Lord Wingate said, returning Paul's gaze without flinching.

"Not too damn reassuring," Paul grumbled.

"Watch your tone, soldier," snapped the blond, round-faced man who had opened the door, "You're addressing a lord."

"I'm not a soldier," Paul replied, "I'm a conscript."

"Easy now, Barnes," Lord Wingate said, raising a hand to silence the shorter, stockier man, "I'm not so pampered yet that I can't handle a little unpolished speech."

The man called Barnes straightened, glared at Paul, and said, "I understand, my lord."

Lord Wingate turned back to Paul and produced a quill and paper. "Now then, Mister Bowman, if you could begin by summarising, from your point of view, the events of this morning..."

"Alright," Paul said as Lord Wingate and Barnes both began to take down notes, "Well, they woke us up early and sent us up to the

—"

"Who is *they?*" Lord Wingate interrupted without looking up from his notes.

"The officers, of course," Paul said. *Who else would it have been?*

"I see." Lord Wingate still didn't look up, "Go on."

"Anyway," Paul continued, "the *officers* told us to go dig the trenches in the upper pass. So we got to the place they had marked off and—"

"Which of the officers accompanied you to the site of the earthworks?" Lord Wingate interrupted again.

"Only Lieutenant Stuart came with us," Paul said, "The others stayed behind."

Lord Wingate nodded slightly but otherwise gave no sign of anything. "Continue."

"We were digging the trenches for a few hours when that Airship showed up."

"Just to clarify," Lord Wingate interjected, "that would be the airship *Celsius?* Of the Auroran Royal Airborne Fleet?"

"Was that its name?" Paul said, "the one that got hit and did the Mordred Protocol?"

Both Lord Wingate and Barnes stopped taking notes and looked squarely at Paul. Their faces were numb with shock. "You *know* about The Mordred Protocol?!?" Lord Wingate asked, agape.

Paul shrugged, "Yeah."

"H-how?" Barnes stammered, "How could someone like *you* possibly know about—"

"I've spent most of my life working on commercial skyfreighters," Paul said with a smug grin, "Of course I know about it. *Everyone* knows about it." Until an hour or so ago, Paul had dismissed it as just another rumor, but there was no need to let on about that.

"Yes, well... getting back on topic," Lord Wingate said, regaining his composure and returning to his notes, "What happened after the *Celsius* arrived?"

"A few minutes later," Paul said, "we heard an explosion when the airship—I mean, when the *Celsius* was hit. Soon after that, we came under fire from Isafari snipers, so I decid—"

"And was Leftenant Stuart still present at the front?"

Paul frowned; what the hell was a *left*enant? "*Lieu*tenant Stuart," Paul assumed that was what Lord Wingate meant, "was killed by an

Isafari sniper."

"I see," Lord Wingate said, "Did you receive any orders at this point?"

"We did not," Paul said, "Our radio was disabled before we could receive orders."

"No officers *and* no radio?" Barnes laughed, "That sounds *awfully* convenient."

"Look, do you want me to tell you what happened or not?" Paul rounded on the stocky man.

"H-how dare you?!" Barnes spluttered, "You cannot speak to me like that! I'll have you know I—"

"Stop it! Both of you!" Lord Wingate snapped. "You're a commander, Barnes; start acting like one."

"Sorry, my lord," Barnes said, stiffening his posture even further.

Lord Wingate turned his gaze back to Paul, "And you," he said, "I expect to see a certain amount of decorum in a soldier."

"I'm not a soldier," Paul said again, "I'm a conscript."

Lord Wingate's eyes narrowed, "So you have said," He returned to his notes, "Commander Barnes does bring up a good point," he went on, "It does seem convenient that both your commanding officer and your radio should be disabled"—he looked up at Paul —"leaving *you* in command."

"Are you saying I killed Lieutenant Stuart and sabotaged the radio myself?" Paul glared.

"I'm saying it is possible," Lord Wingate matched Paul's glare.

"And I'm saying that's not what happened," Paul said firmly, "Isafari snipers shot Lieutenant Stuart, and then they shot out the radio."

"Why didn't you fix the radio?" Barnes asked.

"Are you serious?" Paul stared at the man.

"The sergeant has a point," Lord Wingate said, "It is unreasonable to expect *infantry* to make complex repairs during combat."

"Thank you," Paul said.

"Returning to the matter at hand," Lord Wingate said, "what happened after the radio was destroyed?"

"After the radio was destroyed," Paul said, "I ordered the troops to charge and—"

"Yes, this is what I wanted to ask you about," Lord Wingate gathered his notes, "Why did you order your company to *advance* of all things?"

"I looked at all our options and figured the only thing we could do was charge," Paul said.

"You should have fallen back," Barnes said.

"And get my whole company shot for desertion?" Paul retorted, "I don't think so!"

"Then you should have held out for reinforcements," Barnes fired back.

"And what if reinforcements didn't come?" Paul refused to back down.

"Then you should have—" Barnes was cut off by a sharp knock at the door. "I'll get that," he grumbled as he walked over to the door.

Barnes opened the door, and in strode the same pair of provos from before. They escorted three people into the room. One of the three Paul recognized immediately; a tall ebony-skinned woman with a shaven head. She was well-fed yet still slender, and she wore patterned robes that, for Isafar, must have been very fine indeed. She was the one who had surrendered to Paul after the charge. The second figure was a dark-skinned man, a few inches shorter than the woman and clad in distinctly less-fine garb than the woman. The third figure was a scrawny little blond kid in a green-and-gold uniform that marked him out as an Auroran officer, probably from one of the airships.

The woman strode to the center of the office, as through the provos weren't even there, and spoke in a confident, melodic voice. Paul didn't understand her language, and he suspected Lord Wingate and Barnes didn't either, but the woman addressed them as if they were subjects who owed her fealty. Paul was conversational in Hadvari, if a little out of practice, and knew a few useful phrases in Isafari, but he couldn't pick up on a single word the woman said. Paul also could have sworn that she clicked her tongue once or twice as she spoke. *Definitely not Isafari.*

The second man, clearly a translator, spoke in Isafari, though faster than Paul could pick out. Then as he finished, the young blond officer spoke: "She says her name is Batu of the Masada, and she wants to know why she has been brought here. I think she's nobility. Maybe even a queen!"

Lord Wingate stood up from his desk. He was taller than Paul and much more solidly built. "Thank you, Ensign Holloway. Please tell the Lady Batu that I have summoned her here in order to construct a report on the events of the day."

The boy, Holloway, turned back to the Isafari translator and began to relay Lord Wingate's order. His speech was halting; no doubt the poor kid was struggling over the right words. He couldn't be much older than sixteen, Paul reckoned; maybe a year or two older than Private Carter at most.

Private Carter is dead, Paul remembered bitterly.

Finally Batu's response made it back to Holloway: "She... erm, Lady Batu says she didn't ask you, sir."

Lord Wingate stared in shock, and Barnes looked as though he was about to burst. "What?" the two men said in unison.

Holloway quickly clarified, "She seems to believe that she was summoned here by..."

Holloway turned toward Paul, trailing off awkwardly as he did. Paul glanced at Batu; the woman's expression hadn't changed, but she was now watching him intently, as if awaiting his permission. Did she honestly think *he* was in charge?

Holloway cleared his throat, "Forgive me sir, but I don't believe I know your name."

"Paul," he extended his hand to the boy, "Paul Bowman, sergeant, Baker Company, Forty-Second Infantry."

Holloway took his hand and shook vigorously, "Holloway, Jonathan, ensign, communications specialist, the *Celsius,*" The kid blinked and corrected, "Erm, *formerly* of the *Celsius.*"

"Sorry about your ship, kid," Paul said, lowering his voice slightly, "Hell of a thing, losing a bird like that."

"Thank you, sir," Holloway nodded with a sad smile.

"Pay attention, Ensign," Lord Wingate said gently, "We still have business to take care of."

"Oh right!" Holloway jumped and turned back to face Lord Wingate, "Lady Batu believes that Sergeant Bowman is in command here. She is... rather insistent on the matter."

"Tell her," Paul spoke up and gestured at Lord Wingate, "that this man is my servant. Say that he..." *How did the phrase go again?* "that he *speaks with my voice.*"

"My lord, I really must protest—" Barnes began, before Lord Wingate cut him off with a sharp gesture. Lord Wingate locked eyes with Holloway and nodded subtly. Holloway quickly turned to the Isafari translator and began to speak. Barnes glared at Paul, who returned the look with a smug grin.

The trick seemed to work, and Batu began to tell her story. Paul didn't really pay attention to the details. Hell, he'd been there for most of the important parts. He did find it odd though that Lord Wingate spent quite a bit of time asking Batu about the artillery in the salt flats. What was the point of asking those questions? All those guns were gone, weren't they?

Just as Batu's story came to an end, there was a loud, impatient knock at the door. One of the provos went to open it, but it burst open, hitting the man in the face. A portly, balding man stormed through the door. Paul recognized him immediately: Captain Wilmont, his commanding officer, and he looked to be in a foul mood.

"My lord!" Captain Wilmont marched to the center of the room, shoving Batu and her translator roughly to the side, "I was told I might find you here." He struck a salute, "Captain Sir Alphonse Wilmont, commanding officer, Baker Company, the Forty-Second Infantry, reporting for debrief."

"Sir! Do you mind?" Barnes shouted, "We happen to be in the middle of—"

"Ah, Mister Bowman," Captain Wilmont snarled. Paul straightened his back; Wilmont was always one for formality. "I always *knew* you'd fall afoul of command before long!"

Wilmont turned toward Lord Wingate who had buried his head in his hands as soon as Wilmont entered, and said, "I spent so much time picking out the location for those defences, and what does this imbecile do? He goes and breaks position the very moment these scruffy savages show their faces!" He gestured at Batu and her translator with contempt, "Honestly, my lord, I've not the faintest idea what Leftenant Stuart sees in this oaf! I shall have to have words with Mister Stuart about this man's callous disregard for the chain of command!"

Paul raised an eyebrow at that last comment. Had Captain Wilmont not yet heard of Stuart's death? Paul was about to speak, but Lord Wingate spoke first: "Did I hear that right? Was it *you* who decided where to place the fortifications for the battle?"

"Why yes in fact, my lord, if I do say so myself!" Captain Wilmont said, puffing his chest out and beaming like an idiot.

"I was wondering who that was," Lord Wingate said with a smile. "I've been meaning to speak with you, as a matter of fact. I've some choice words for you," His smile broadened even more, "*Choice words* indeed."

"You honour me, my lord," Captain Wilmont blushed and

bowed slightly. Paul could barely keep from rolling his eyes. *Nobility sure love to pat themselves on the back.*

"Ensign Holloway," Lord Wingate said, "please thank Lady Batu and her... translator for their co-operation, and escort them back to their quarters." Holloway saluted and began to speak to the Isafari translator. Lord Wingate turned to Paul, "I believe we're done with you as well, Mister Bowman. You are dismissed."

"Thanks," Paul said as he turned to go.

"Not so fast, Mister Bowman," Barnes said. Paul stopped in his tracks, "My lord, this man has shown tremendous disregard for protocol, and given great insult to you personally. I recommend he be disciplined."

"I second that with a vengeance!" Captain Wilmont added, "These conscript-soldiers have no sense of what is proper! They want for the lash, my lord, every man jack of them!"

"I'm quite capable of meting out punishments on my own, Captain," Lord Wingate said firmly. He locked eyes with Paul, and a malicious grin crept across his face. "Besides, I believe I already something rather fitting in mind," He leaned back in his chair, "Guards, take this man to the white room and give him to Fairchild."

Paul slouched in the chair and shook his head. *Damn that Lord Wingate!* He had led Paul to believe that this 'Fairchild' person was some sort of disciplinary figure or a brutal interrogator. As it happened, the real Fairchild was something much, much worse...

She was a journalist.

Paul had only been around this Fairchild girl for a few minutes, but already he felt like clawing out his one remaining eye. Everything about her annoyed him, from her smile, to her too-eager blue eyes, to that strange wooden box she was fiddling with on the low table that sat between them. Even her outfit annoyed him—from that ridiculous pinstriped skirt she wore, to her tooled leather corset with brass gears sewn in patterns down the side, to the short jacket that barely reached down to her bosom, leaving a window of bare flesh exposed; it all seemed calculated to make him uncomfortable.

Paul glanced about the large room. *The white room* Lord Wingate had called it. It was an appropriate name; aside from the dark wood-paneled walls, everything in the room from the ornate carpet to the finely upholstered furniture was as white as mountain snow. It almost hurt to look. At the front of the room was a large domed wrought-iron window that looked out over the bow of the airship. This was clearly an observation deck of sorts. Paul shook his head; a room this large or fancy would never be found on one of the commercial skyfreighters he was accustomed to.

"So, Mister Bowman," Fairchild said in her much-too-lively voice, "or would you prefer *Sergeant?*" She had a way of emphasizing words that made everything seem overly dramatic. It made Paul cringe.

"Just Paul is fine, Miss Fairchild," he said.

"Oh, do call me Isabelle," she said, absently flicking back a wavy lock of red hair that peeked out from beneath an outrageous feathered hat, "All my friends call me Isabelle."

"Right," Paul groaned and slouched further in his chair.

"Now then, *Paul,*" Fairchild said as she finally stopped fiddling with that bloody wooden box, "Do please regale me with your daring exploits."

"Okay," Paul said as he straightened up in his chair, "well, we arrived at the Southern Gap late last night and we—"

A loud metallic rattling interrupted him. He blinked; Fairchild was doing... something to the box to make that sound. "What *is* that thing?" Paul asked, "Some kinda... radio or something?"

Fairchild giggled lightly. "Oh, is it not a marvelous contraption?" She turned the box around to show a mess of levers and buttons with a strip of paper peeking out of the top. "It's an *automatic typesetting machine!*" She emphasized every word as though each one was vitally important, "Made for me personally by *Newton and Sons* before I departed the Capitol." She gave a delighted squeal, "Oh, modern technology is simply marvelous! Do you not agree?" Paul just nodded along with her.

Fairchild turned the box-thing back to face her, "Now then, do please continue..."

"Right, well when we arrived, the officers set us digging out trenches in the pass," The ticking sound started up again. Paul ignored it as best he could. "It was early morning when the airship arrived. The *Celsius,* I think that was its name..."

"I heard the savages shot it down," Fairchild leaned forward, mercifully stopping that damn ticking sound for a moment, "Is that so? Oh, it must have been such a fright."

"Yeah," Paul admitted, "It was, a little bit. I mean, there was a lot of confusion and—"

Fairchild gasped dramatically, "Was that when the savages made their attack?"

"Well, it wasn't really much of an attack..." Paul began.

"Oh!" Fairchild giggled lightly, "Such confidence in the face of mortal danger!" The ticking resumed in earnest.

"No, no, no," Paul tried to correct her, "What I mean is that it wasn't a *large* attack. It was just a few dozen snipers."

"The savages had *sharpshooters* as well?" Fairchild said with mock fear, "Why, your comrades must have been quaking in their boots! Did you steady the line? I'll bet you steadied the line!"

"No, I didn't steady the line," Paul insisted, "I just gave the order to advance."

"Oh, I can just picture it now!" Fairchild sighed as her box continued making that damn noise.

"I really doubt it." Paul grumbled.

Fairchild babbled softly to herself as she worked, "Charging across the open field towards the foe, standard of the Queen blazing behind him in the dawn and not a drop of fear in his heart..."

Paul stood from his chair and walked toward the window. Fairchild didn't seem to notice; she just kept on babbling and making that ticking noise.

"...driving back the gathered hordes of the south. A hundred men he slew, and then a hundred more; barely pausing when one of the savages tore out his eye..."

Paul shook his head and stared out the large window at nothing in particular. This Fairchild girl was going to spin her wild tales and make a hero out of him, and there was nothing he could do about it. Listlessly, he wandered back to his seat.

"Surely an example to which all soldiers should aspire." Fairchild giggled.

"I'm not a soldier," Paul said weakly, "I'm a conscript." Fairchild didn't seem to notice.

Barnes turned away from the door to the white room and walked back to join Lord Wingate by the stairwell. "How's Bowman doing?" Lord Wingate asked.

"He's squirming," Barnes said with a devilish grin.

"Good," Lord Wingate matched Barnes's look, "Let's head for

the bridge and let the captain know we're ready to raise ship."

"My lord," Barnes said as he followed Lord Wingate down the stairwell, "might I ask a question?"

"Speak your mind, Barnes," Lord Wingate responded.

"Why him?" Barnes asked, "Why let Bowman get all the glory?"

Lord Wingate stopped at the bottom of the stair, and sighed heavily. "Well, he certainly wasn't my first choice, but that Fairchild girl was promised an interview, and Bowman's the only one we can give her."

"Rubbish, my lord!" Barnes spat, "You're a much better candidate than him, and you know it!"

"Don't be naïve, Barnes," Lord Wingate said ruefully, "I lost my ship and lived to tell the tale. If I am the face of this story, I'll be branded a coward and a fraud, and you can bet the rest of the crew won't be far behind. The reputation of the ARAF will be irreparably tarnished."

"My lord, you did everything you could!" Barnes protested, "You followed protocol to the letter, and probably won the day to boot!"

"I still lost my ship," Lord Wingate grumbled, "Fairchild is a civilian. Worse than that, she's with the press. I've never known her sort to deal in nuance or subtlety."

"Good point," Barnes admitted.

"Besides," Lord Wingate said darkly, "we lost people today."

"It was only three engineers," Barnes said, "Given what happened, it could have been much worse."

"Three engineers is still three too many," Lord Wingate locked eyes with Barnes.

"My lord, I hardly think—" Barnes was about to speak, but shrank from Lord Wingate's glare, "Y-yes my lord, I understand."

Lord Wingate went on... "Fairchild can't have you, or anyone else from the *Celsius,* as that would eventually bring the issue back to me. *Albion* and *Fearless* weren't present for the action, so she'll want to interview someone who was on the ground. This Leftenant Stuart sounds like he would have made an ideal candidate, but corpses give poor interviews. And as for Wilmont..."

Barnes nodded. The memory of Lord Wingate's vicious dressing-down of Captain Wilmont was still fresh in his mind.

"...I refuse to let that obnoxious blundering fop win even a shred of glory for this action," Lord Wingate concluded.

"I see," Barnes said, "And that only leaves Bowman."

"Precisely," Lord Wingate said, "whether he deserves it or not."

"Can anything be done about it?" Barnes asked.

"Not much to be honest," Lord Wingate said, "The man's hardly a proper soldier. He was just in the right place at the right time. Still, he didn't violate any regulations or anything else we could conceivably punish him for. We can only hope Bowman gets decorated and promoted to some other job, maybe an ambassadorship or a low-level peerage. Anything, just as long as he's out of active duty and we don't have to deal with him."

"I understand, my lord," Barnes agreed. He was young and idealistic, but he would learn in time.

"Come," Lord Wingate started off towards the bridge, "let's get airborne."

"Right behind you, my lord."

Chapter III

A Hero's Welcome

PAUL perked up when he heard three rings of a mechanical bell somewhere in the bowels of the airship. He still didn't know what it meant, but he could feel the ships reactor drawing down. *We've finally arrived.*

"Do please try not to move overmuch, Mister Bowman," the footman droned in a nearly lifeless voice.

Paul tried his best not to move as the footman fiddled with his new uniform. It was a ridiculous green-and-gold thing, like the ones he had seen worn by other officers, and it was the most uncomfortable thing he had ever worn in his life. The fabric was rough and rigid, and he could feel more than a few loose ends of embroidered gold wire scratching at his skin through the white tunic underneath the coat. Paul doubted this uniform was anywhere near the right size for him.

"Why do I have to wear this damn thing?" Paul grumbled.

"There is to be a ball at the Dawn Palace," the footman said, "during which you are to be honored for courage by Her Majesty, the

Queen. A certain measure of decorum is to be expected."

"What about her?" Paul gestured across the cargo bay to where Batu sat against the side of the hull, flanked by two guards. She was wearing the same patterned robes she had worn since her capture, and her wrists were bound behind her back. The golden hoops that had once hung from her ears were conspicuously absent. "Why don't you fuss over her outfit for a change?"

The footman didn't look up from his work, "Because *she* is a savage. It is not to be expected of her."

"Right," Paul said, and felt the airship begin to descend. He glanced back over at Batu; the woman was outwardly calm, but he couldn't help noticing how her eyes darted frantically back and forth. *This must be a completely new sensation for her,* Paul thought. Paul had spent the majority of the five days since the battle shut up in the small cabin that had been set aside for him. He imagined Batu had been treated with much less courtesy.

The footman ducked away for a moment, and returned with the reins of a tall brown horse. "Now then," he droned, heedless of the change in altitude, "you need only mount up, and all will be ready."

Paul stared blankly at the beast, "I've never ridden a horse before."

"That shan't be a problem," the footman said, "I shall lead your mount by his reins. All you need do is sit atop him."

Paul shrugged and unsteadily mounted the horse. Batu was being hoisted atop a horse of her own by two guards. They looked as if they were lifting a sack of potatoes.

"And do please mind your spurs," the footman said. Paul glanced down at his new boots; he hadn't even noticed the gleaming brass spurs mounted on his heels. "Try to keep those away from your mount," the footman continued, "I'd much rather not have to chase after your horse if it can be avoided."

"I'll try," Paul grumbled.

After a few moments, the loading ramp at the front of the cargo bay opened, and the chaotic noise of a restless crowd filtered through. The horse trembled and whinnied, causing Paul to grip the top of the saddle for balance. That was what you did, wasn't it? Luckily, the footman knew what he was doing; he held the reins steady and probably kept the horse from throwing Paul off. Once the horse was calm, the footman led it forward down the cargo ramp and off the airship.

Once Paul's eye adjusted to the early afternoon sunlight, he looked around. The airship had come to ground in the middle of a wide, red-brick street that stretched at least a mile toward a grand palace in the distance, the Dawn Palace. On either side of the boulevard, great stairs rose up at least ten feet to a higher level, giving the illusion that the brick street had been carved into the mountain. The stairs ran the length of the boulevard, and they were packed full to bursting with cheering spectators. Beyond the crowd, Paul could just see the roofs of the houses—good, modern tin roofs by the look of them. This part of the city must be pretty well-off; even the wrought-iron lampposts that lined the boulevard had the look of luxury about them.

Paul looked out across the crowd. They seemed to be gathered from all walks of life, rich and poor, young and old, men and women. Especially the women—more than a few ried to force their way through the picket of soldiers that held the crowd back. Paul raised his hand to wave at the crowd, and the cheering exploded into a frenzy. *They've all come out to see me,* Paul thought, forcing a smile. He wasn't entirely sure if he liked the idea.

Absently, Paul glanced back at the airship. A second horse was following about twenty paces or so behind him with Batu sitting awkwardly atop it. The crowd's reaction to her was much different. At first they stared, not knowing what to make of a woman like her; Paul supposed that few, if any, of the spectators had ever seen a person with her dark complexion before. Eventually, the crowd took notice of the two soldiers flanking her mount, as well as her bound wrists, and determined that she was a prisoner. Then they began to scream insults and curses at her.

Paul turned his gaze back to the crowd. Wherever his eyes fell, people cheered him on and jostled to catch his eye. Then as soon as he passed them by, the crowd began hurling vicious insults at Batu. The fact that she clearly didn't understand what the mob was screaming only made them scream louder. It was an ugly sight.

"A magnificent sight, is it not, Mister Bowman?" the footman said, "A welcome worthy of a hero."

"Not for her, it isn't," Paul looked back at Batu. She was as stoic as she had ever been, but her eyes quickly stole glances at the mob. She seemed to understand the intent of their insults, if not their literal meaning.

"I should think not," the footman droned, "but she is an enemy and a savage. It is as she deserves."

"She is a queen, you know," Paul said. He wasn't entirely sure how accurate that statement was, but judging by the way Batu carried herself, it seemed right.

"There's naught but one queen I recognise," the footman droned, "and that barbarian wench is not her."

Someone in the mob hurled a small rock at Batu. She barely flinched as it struck her squarely in the forehead. Paul noticed a thin streak of red dribbling down her face.

"Turn around," he told the footman, "I want to go to her."

"I cannot allow that," the footman droned, "It wouldn't be proper."

"I don't give a damn what's proper," Paul snapped, "Turn around."

"I'm sorry, Mister Bowman," the footman droned—*was this man capable of any human emotion at all?* "but I cannot allow that."

Paul dug one of his spurs into his horse's side. The beast whinnied and tried to bolt. The footman was barely able to restrain the creature. The crowd cheered wildly, ignorant of what was actually going on. Paul locked eyes with the footman. "Turn. Around."

"As you say," the footman sighed and turned the horse around.

The men leading Batu's horse slowed as Paul neared, and eventually they came to a halt. As soon as Paul could reach Batu, he rolled up the sleeve of his jacket and wiped the blood off Batu's face with the white tunic underneath. "Sorry about the crowd," Paul muttered softly, ignoring the fact that Batu couldn't understand the words. The crowd fell silent as Paul wiped. He barely noticed. When he was done, Batu looked at him strangely, and then she gave a gentle nod—the first real sign of approval Paul had ever seen from the woman.

Paul looked down at his footman. "Let's continue."

"Yes," the footman gave him a disapproving look, "Do let's."

The procession continued onward up the boulevard. Confusion stilled the crowd for a minute or two, but soon they returned to cheering Paul and flinging curses at Batu just as before. In the distance, the Dawn Palace loomed closer every second.

Lord Wingate watched from inside the cargo bay as Bowman's procession moved along the promenade. The crowd dissipated after him; some of them wandered away to return to their daily lives, while others followed the parade towards the Dawn Palace. Once the crowds were mostly gone, Lord Wingate saddles the last remaining horse, and rode down the cargo ramp and onto the empty boulevard below.

Once he was clear of the ramp, Lord Wingate looked up at the bridge of the airship *Fearless*. Through the sun's glare, he could just barely make out her captain standing at the window. The captain saluted, and Lord Wingate returned the gesture as best he could while mounted. A few seconds later, he felt the reactor come to full power, and the airship *Fearless* lifted off into the afternoon sky. Lord Wingate watched as it floated away like a dream and vanished into the distance.

I have no ship, Lord Wingate thought suddenly. It had been five days since the loss of the *Celsius,* but only now did it really hit him. For the first time in more than twenty years, he was completely earthbound. It was a bitter thought. *I wonder if I shall ever command another airship again.* Lord Wingate shook his head and spurred his horse down a back street; there was no sense in dwelling on that which could not be helped.

As Lord Wingate rode, he considered what would become of his crew. He might have to restrict himself to administrative duties for a while to preserve his reputation, but there was no reason to punish the rest of his crew like that; Hanscom maybe, but not the rest of them. They would need to be transferred to other postings throughout the fleet. Lord Wingate shuddered at the thought of all that paperwork. This was going to take weeks to sort out.

Eventually, the buildings parted and the Dawn Palace came into view. Lord Wingate had come around the back to the horse-gate so as to avoid the crowds that were sure to be massing outside the front entrance. In contrast, the vast palace stables were deserted, apart from a pair of stable boys and a dozen or so horses. That was good —Lord Wingate had never been fond of crowds and he didn't completely trust anyone who was. He handed the reins off to one of the stable boys, along with a silver shilling for each of them, and slipped quietly into the palace.

Even from this back entrance, walking into the Dawn Palace was like stepping into a whole other world. The floor was tiled with white Analerian marble and covered with a fine Illyrian carpet that likely ran the full length of the hallway. The walls were paneled with dark oak and hung with portraits depicting grand scenes from Aurora's history. The sweet aromas of incense and whale oil burning in the lamps hung thick in the air. It reeked of luxury. Lord Wingate sighed; this was the life he had been born to, for better or for worse.

"Orpheus!"

Lord Wingate turned about at the sound of his name, and there she was: the love of his life, "Amelia!" He rushed over to his wife and scooped her up into an embrace.

"I saw your ship's name mentioned in the news journals," Amelia said as she buried her face in her husband's chest, "They said you crashed, but they didn't say who survived or how many..."

"It's alright," Lord Wingate said, gently stroking her smooth auburn hair.

"We prayed for you every night," Amelia whispered, "I know you don't really believe, but we still prayed for you."

Lord Wingate didn't mind. He had never spared much thought for the One God, or the Great Truth, or whatever the Church called its nonsense. He fancied it a pack of frivolous old superstitions at best, and a dangerous reactionary doctrine that stood firmly against progress at worst. Still, if it gave his family hope while he was away on assignment, who was he to spoil it for them?

"Well, I've returned safe and sound," Lord Wingate said, "and I believe I shall be staying for a good long while."

Amelia looked up into his eyes and smiled one of her beautiful smiles, "That's good. Mary and Sophie shall like that. They're always asking after news of their father whenever you're away. You'll get a hero's welcome from them."

Lord Wingate smiled; that certainly sounded like his girls. Marion and Sophia adored him, and they amazed him more and more with every passing day. Marion was sixteen, and had already begun helping Amelia manage the family estate. And at only ten, Sophia had just announced her intention to join the WAVE when she was old enough, just like her mother had done. Lord Wingate was immensely proud of the two of them.

"Where are the girls now?" He asked.

"They've gone off to the front entrance," Amelia said, "They want to see this Bowman fellow up close."

"I see," said Lord Wingate with a father's disapproval.

Amelia giggled lightly at her husband's sudden severity, "They've been reading all about his heroics in the news journals for the past few days. The man is becoming quite a sensation. Have you read what the broadsheets are printing about him?"

"I've been somewhat indisposed," Lord Wingate grumbled.

Amelia walked past Lord Wingate to the door and poked her head out to speak with one of the stable lads. A moment later, she returned with a copy of *The Queen's Messenger* which she presented to Lord Wingate, "This is the article."

HEROIC VICTORY AT THE SOUTHERN GAP!

taken from the account of Mdlle. Isabelle Fairchild esq.

Paul Bowman is the latest hero of Aurora! In the face of certain death, this gallant fellow rallied his troops to beat back a brutish invasion from the savage realm of Isafar! Such a daring and noble action is surely deserving of the highest adulation and praise!

Good readers, can you imagine the scene? A torrent of black-skinned barbarians pouring through the Southern Gap and threatening to visit unspeakable atrocity upon all good and decent folk! The Mountains of Dawn echo with shouts in their horrid tongue, and the earth trembles with their many footfalls! Only Bowman and his meager force block the way into the fair Auroran heartland! What is he to do?

Option one: he can retreat with his men and let the Isafari menace sweep into the land of his forefathers. No! What man can stand idly by while his countryfolk suffer? Or option two: he can fortify his position and let the savages fall upon him instead. What a choice! To let his blessed homeland burn, or to stand and die!

For any lesser man, such a choice would surely break his resolve. But Paul Bowman is not a man to accept defeat! With urgent purpose, he spreads the message to all his loyal men: "No surrender! No turning back!" Sure enough, his soldiers form up their ranks, and when the Isafari menace finally comes into view, Bowman raises the standard of the Queen, and with a tremendous shout, he leads his men forward in a great charge!

Captain and hireling alike amongst the savages quake with terror as Bowman and his force make their attack! The barbarian hordes of the south, driven forwards like beasts by their nefarious overlords, hold their ground. But not long can they stand against Bowman and his heroic company! Oh, what a sight! Six-hundred men charging across the open field towards the foe, standard of the Queen blazing above them in the dawn and not a drop of fear in their hearts!

But all is not well, for the cunning Isafari horde has taken captives! The airship Celsius, *the pride of the Auroran Royal Airborne Fleet, has crashed, and her surviving crew has been made prisoner! Now Bowman and his band of heroes must rescue their captive countrymen as well!*

Must I paint you a picture of the glorious scene that now unfolds? Bowman and his brave companions charge back into the fray with renewed purpose! They fight like warriors of legend! Their numbers are few against the massed hordes of the south, but they fight without regard for numbers! One of the savages rips out Bowman's eye, but he barely notices —such is the strength of his conviction!

Be heartened, dear readers, for all storms must pass. As the ferocity of his resistance is made clear, the barbarians begin to lose their resolve! Their ranks falter, and they flee from the fray, their hearts given over to fear and cowardice! Bowman and his companions raise the cry of victory! They are beaten and bruised, but they have triumphed!

Convinced of the final and utter defeat of her armies, the Queen of the Savages herself surrenders to Paul Bowman and makes herself his prisoner. With the surrender of their queen, the hordes of the south follow suit and lay down their arms. At last, the terrible force that laid low the airship Celsius *is no more!*

Speaking of the Celsius, *what has become of the survivors from her crew? Have they fallen victim to the malice of Isafari torturers? Have they been flayed alive, as the savages are known to do to their prisoners? Or have they simply been slain out of hand and left to rot for carrion birds? Oh, have no fear! All the surviving crew has been rescued from torture and death by Bowman's heroic action; they may be worse for wear, but they are safe!*

About two thousand menacing Isafari warriors now lie dead at the Southern Gap, and ten thousand more have been taken captive! Surely this is a tremendous blow to the nefarious designs of the vile southern menace!

Airships Albion *and* Fearless *soon arrive to help set everything in order after the battle. Bowman is whisked away to give his account of the battle, and it is at this point that our valiant hero sits down to give an interview with a humble reporter. Despite his heroism, Bowman is a remarkably modest chap. He is well spoken, respectful, and prays twice every day at the least, but most of all, he loves his country! Surely he represents an example to which all soldiers should aspire!*

Good Queen Cassandra has called for a great celebration in honour of Sergeant Bowman and his magnificent victory at the Southern Gap. Bowman is to receive a special commendation of merit from Her Majesty at a grand ball in four days' time.

Plan for large crowds if you wish to attend; an occasion such as this is sure to draw thousands!

Lord Wingate grimaced. *That Fairchild girl surely knows how to sell a story!* He roughly folded the journal and handed it back to his wife.

"So?" Amelia enquired, "What do you think of it?"

"It's rubbish," Lord Wingate grumbled, "A complete tissue of lies."

Amelia's mouth quirked into a clever smile, "Yes, I suspected the account might have been a little embellished in places."

"*A little embellished?*" Lord Wingate spat, "Why it's a complete fabrication! And what was all that nonsense about the survivors from the *Celsius* being tortured and flayed alive? My god, it reads like one of those goddamn penny dreadfuls!"

"Orpheus!" Amelia snapped, "Mind your tongue! Do you want the girls hearing such vulgar speech?"

"Forgive me," Lord Wingate said quickly; his wife was always wary of rough language. "It's just..." His voice softened, "We lost people that day. Three engineers from my ship and nearly fifty men on the ground. That story, that"—he searched for a suitably forceful expression that wouldn't offend his wife—"that pile of rubbish! It cheapens everything they fought for, everything they *died* for!"

He paused for a moment and then added in a low voice, "And the public has to believe it. I don't like it, but that's the way it has to be."

Amelia nodded solemnly, "Politics?"

"Quite so," Lord Wingate sighed, "If the public hears the raw details, reputations will be ruined, starting with my own. Right now, I need to keep my head low and let Bowman soak up all the attention. Hopefully, that'll be enough."

Amelia slipped her arms around him, "I understand, my love," she whispered. Lord Wingate smiled and put his arms around her as well. *I will love this woman until the day I die.*

Somewhere in the distance, the sound of a great shout filtered through the palace. Bowman had arrived. "Come," Amelia said with a fond smile, "There is a ball going on after all."

"Yes," Lord Wingate said resignedly, "Let us have this nonsense over with."

"And while we're at it"—Amelia wrapped her arm around Lord Wingate's elbow as the two began to walk toward the noise from the

Great Hall—"you can tell me what *really* happened at the Southern Gap."

Lord Wingate grinned, "I've missed you so much."

Paul had seen the Dawn Palace several times before, but always from the air; seeing its sprawling immensity from ground level was another thing entirely!

The individual pieces of its gleaming white stone exterior interlocked so tightly that it looked almost as though it had been carved out of a single piece of rock. Six brilliant white towers pierced the sky, three on each side, with a vast dome in the middle. All were capped with gold, and each one flew a green banner showing the golden eight-pointed Star of Dawn. It was an incredible sight to behold!

Slowly, the horse came to a stop in front of a tall set of stairs that led up to the palace. When Paul looked down, the footman met his gaze and announced, "We have arrived at the Dawn Palace, Mister Bowman. Would you care to dismount?" Bowman nodded and dismounted as easily as he could.

The footman started up the steps to the palace, and Paul was about to follow, but he stumbled violently the moment he tried to take a step. He looked down at his boots; the heels were raised almost an inch off the ground. Paul hadn't noticed his raised heels while he was riding, but now that he was back on the ground, they messed with his balance. Paul forced down a curse and began to climb the steps. Slowly.

At the top of the steps, Paul turned back to look out over the vast square. It was packed to the brim with people, as far as his eye could see, and each one was cheering wildly for him. Some small children had even climbed atop the great bronze statue of some old queen that stood in the middle of the fountain in the center of the square to catch a glimpse of him. Paul smiled and made a casual two-finger salute at the kids atop the statue. He couldn't help it—he liked kids.

"Mister Bowman," the footman called back. Paul turned away from the crowd and followed the footman through the tall arched doorway of the Dawn Palace.

Paul could hardly believe what he saw. The hall was vast enough to house a whole airship inside it with room to spare. Tremendous columns of smooth white stone stood like trees along the sides of the hall, supporting the vaulted ceiling that had to be at least three stories above the floor, maybe higher. The ceiling itself was painted with fantastically detailed scenes, each one edged with rivers of gold that flowed like vines down the columns.

At the back of the hall, there was a raised platform with steps leading up to it. At the center of that platform sat a wooden chair. A vast banner hung above it, green with the golden eight-pointed Star of Dawn, like the banners flying from the palace. *The Seat of Dawn.* A great crowd of well-dressed people milled about in front of the throne, a dull hum of conversation coming off them, and a soft elegant music floating unobtrusively over everything.

The footman cleared his throat, and in a tremendous voice that Paul had never suspected the man might have, he announced, "Sergeant Paul Bowman of the Forty Second Regiment of Infantry in Her Majesty's Royal Army."

Before the footman had even finished his announcement, a great scream erupted from the crowd, and they charged toward him. Instinctively, Paul reached for his rifle, and he panicked for a moment when he remembered that it had been taken from him. With difficulty, Paul reminded himself that this crowd wasn't hostile, though he found himself sorely wishing that they were.

Within moments, Paul was surrounded. Men and women (mostly women) pressed up against him and shouted questions over each other. "How did you feel when you charged the Isafari lines?" "Were you scared?" "How many of the savages did you kill?" Paul tried to answer the questions as best he could, but they came on so fast, Paul could barely keep up. Still, the questions kept on coming. "How long was it before the barbarians surrendered?" "Were the savages really led by a woman?" "Did it hurt when they ripped out your eye?"

"Everyone!" A loud voice from behind Paul cut through the babble, "Please step back and give the poor man some breathing room. Rest assured there will be time enough for all your enquiries."

Sure enough, the crowd of women thinned. Paul turned about to see a balding white-haired man somewhat shorter than himself. His face was wrinkled with age, and there was a distinct air of authority about him. "Sorry about the rabble," the man said with an inviting, but somehow false smile; it was the same voice as before, "You've become quite the sensation, Mister Bowman."

"Thanks," Paul said, "uh... milord?"

The man extended a welcoming hand. "Lord Barnabas Obadiah of the House of Franklin, at your service," he introduced himself, "but you may address me as 'Lord Franklin' or 'my lord,' if it please you."

"Paul," Paul took Lord Franklin's hand and shook it firmly, "Paul Bowman."

"It's a most excellent pleasure to make your acquaintance, Mister Bowman," Lord Franklin said with a slight bow, "We're all rather impressed with your exploits."

"I can tell," Paul said, glancing at the crowd of women waiting off to the side. Their enthusiasm hadn't changed.

Lord Franklin threw back his head and made a terrifying sound that was probably supposed to be a laugh, "I'll bet you can, at that!" He leaned closer, "Now, tell me Mister Bowman, I've always wondered: what is it exactly that makes a man like yourself want to become a soldier in the first place?"

Paul laughed awkwardly, "I'm not a soldier. I'm a conscript."

"Aha!" Lord Franklin said, as if trying to make a clever point about something or other, "So you didn't choose the life of a soldier, did you? I understand. You know, I'm something of a conscript myself, after a fashion." Paul blinked in surprise as the man went on, "The burden of nobility was thrust upon me at my birth. I certainly didn't choose it out for myself. Still, we must play such parts as we have been dealt as best we can, would you not agree?"

Paul's jaw almost dropped open. He couldn't believe how out of touch this Lord Franklin was. Even Lieutenant Stuart hadn't been such a hypocrite.

"My Lord Franklin?" A woman's voice said from behind the elderly man, "What sort of nonsense are you putting into this poor man's head?"

The woman stepped out from behind Lord Franklin. She was tall, taller than Franklin, and nearly as tall as Paul himself. Her long, wavy hair was dark brown, and her piercing blue eyes had a clever glint to them. Paul could feel the woman's gaze measuring him like a thing she was considering buying or selling. "Paul Bowman, I presume?"

"Yes, milady," Paul said as he made a bow. That was what you were supposed to do when addressing a lady.

The woman laughed, "*Milady?* Dear me! That's awfully courteous of you, sir! *Awfully* courteous!" Paul blinked. Had he said something wrong?

"This woman," Lord Franklin said, "is Miranda Babcock, head of the Auroran Trade Consortium. She is a much respected and celebrated gentlewoman of the court, yet, she is common-born—not a lady."

"Not *yet*, Lord Franklin!" Miss Babcock said with a playful edge to her husky voice, "But I'll be raised to the nobility in time. You mark my words!"

"I have been marking your words for the past nine years, Miss Babcock," Lord Franklin said, with another empty smile, "The way I see it, if your accomplishments are as worthy as you say, you would have already been raised."

"Oh! Is that so?" Miss Babcock said, turning her attentions to Paul, "Perhaps we should hear Mister Bowman's thoughts on the matter!"

"Capital idea!" Lord Franklin turned toward Paul as well, "Mister Bowman, what say you?"

"About what?" Paul had been trying his hardest not to pay attention.

"Miss Babcock is of the opinion that her achievements warrant a place among the nobility," Lord Franklin explained, as if to a child, "I on the other hand, am of the opinion that Miss Babcock, esteemed and celebrated though she may be, has not earned such a place."

"And you what to know that I think?" Paul said.

"Precisely!" Lord Franklin said with a smile.

"I think you're an idiot," Paul replied. A smile grew on Miss Babcock's face, and vanished from Lord Franklin'.

"Mister Bowman!" Lord Franklin spluttered, "I'm shocked that —"

"I mean it!" Paul cut off the old man's protests, "Weren't you just bangin' on about the 'burden of nobility' a minute ago? If being noble really is such a pain, I think you'd want to spread it around as much as possible to lighten your share of the load! But now you want to keep the *burden* all for yourself?"

Miss Babcock giggled, "Dear me, my lord! I do believe this rube has gotten you in a bit of a fix!"

Paul glared at Miss Babcock. She didn't seem to notice (or care) that she had just called him a rube. She had turned back to Lord Franklin who was frantically trying to preserve his reputation, or so it seemed. Paul sighed and slipped away while the two of them bounced their egos against each other.

For a time, Paul wandered through the Great Hall, weaving around people here and there, stopping every so often to answer a stupid question for someone who recognized him. He found himself staring at the extreme luxury of the place. He counted five crystal chandeliers hanging from the ceiling, each one with too many candles to count. The large columns throughout the hall were of a strange kind of stone, mostly white but with flecks of gray and black suspended in the stone like waves. Even the tiled floor was made of the same sort of stone, polished so that he could almost see his reflection in it. Paul had never seen its like before, but it looked expensive as hell.

Eventually, Paul noticed a table standing at the side of the Great Hall. There were a number of tall glass bottles on the table with an array of shimmering crystal glasses standing beside it. Paul made his way over to the table, snatched a glass, and downed the entire thing in a single gulp, barely noticing the well-dressed young man standing behind the table who stared at Paul with shock and disgust. Paul winced at the extreme sweetness of the drink, but he forced it down. There was alcohol in it; that was what mattered. *It's probably wine,* he supposed, *that's what fancy people drink, isn't it?*

Leaning back against a column beside the table, Paul looked out across the crowd. He didn't think he had ever seen so many people dressed in such fine clothes. All the men wore jackets that didn't quite reach their waists, each one with good brass buttons and gold stitching up and down the sleeves, and some covered in medals. Many of the men wore spurs on their spit-shined boots, and those who did had tucked their trousers into the tops of their boots, causing them to bunch up like sacks of grain. It looked uncomfortable, and Paul should know; he was dressed in the exact same way.

The women were another matter entirely. They all wore tooled leather corsets, most of which had brass gears sewn onto them in bizarre patterns. What was the point of that? The gears clearly didn't do anything. It was as if the women had just stuck them on because everyone else was wearing them, and nobody wanted to be left as the odd one out. They all looked ridiculous.

Just like that Fairchild girl, Paul thought. She was the first woman he had ever seen with those strange gear-patterns sewn onto her corset.

"Paul! Paul is that you?" A woman's shrill voice cried over the murmur of the crowd.

Speak of the devil.

"My word!" Fairchild giggled as she slid through the crowd toward him. She was dressed exactly as he remembered her, with a jacket that left her bosom exposed, the corset with gears sewn into it, and that ridiculous pinstriped skirt, "Don't you look ever so dashing in your uniform!"

"Miss Fairchild," Paul grumbled, trying not to look up at her.

"Oh, do call me Isabelle," Fairchild said as she leaned against the column beside him, "All my friends call me Isabelle"

"We're not friends," Paul said without missing a beat.

Fairchild laughed, "Oh, I have greatly missed your capital wit, Paul!" Paul ground his teeth. It would be a miracle if he could keep from strangling this girl. "Now then," The girl—she was *not* a woman whatever anyone said—leaned closer to him, "I don't suppose you'd be willing to sit for a follow-up, would you?"

"A what?"

"Oh, you know, a follow-up," Fairchild said as the boy behind the table handed her a glass of wine, "Another interview to see how your newfound fame and glory are treating you! You know, my first piece on you was such a sensation; I'm quite sure the general public would be most fascinated to hear your—"

"You already got one interview out of me," Paul interrupted, "you're not getting another."

"Oh, you *wound* me, Paul," Fairchild said with mock-sadness in her too-eager blue eyes, "You're really going to make me wait until you save the day *again* before you let me have another interview?"

"There isn't going to be another one," Paul said more loudly this time.

"I shouldn't think so!" There was a glint in Fairchild's eye, "I'm certain there are more heroic deeds yet to be done in your future, Paul!"

"No, I mean I'm not going to give you anoth—Oh, forget it!" Paul sighed and walked back to the table to get another drink. He was in no mood for this girl's stupid little games.

"Mister Bowman!"

Paul froze in his tracks. It was the only other person he wanted to see less than Fairchild. He turned around and stood at attention. "Captain, sir."

Captain Wilmont stood before Paul with a broad smile on his face. It looked horribly out of place on the man, "Don't stand so stiff, Bowman, old boy! We're both off duty. You can call me 'Sir

Alphonse,' if you please!"

Paul frowned. Was this man actually trying to be *friends* with him? The same man who had very nearly had him flogged during an inspection because his eye patch wasn't part of the standard uniform? The same man who not five days ago had tried to have him flogged again? Why was this bastard suddenly trying to make nice? What was his game?

"Why the dour look, old boy?" Wilmont said, "Not still brooding on poor old Stuart are you? Chin up now; the leftenant died a hero! We must all hope to fall so gloriously when our time comes." Paul frowned even deeper.

"Excuse me, sir," Fairchild butted in, "I cannot help but overhear. Are you by any chance a friend of Sergeant Bowman?"

"Am I?" Captain Wilmont boasted, "Why my dear, I was his commanding officer at the Defense of the Southern Gap!"

"Truly?" Fairchild simpered, "Oh, how marvelous! You simply *must* give me your account of that glorious day!"

"I suppose I must," Captain Wilmont said with a grin. "Boy!" he shouted at the young man standing behind the table, "A glass of wine!" The young man jumped, and quickly poured a glass of wine for Wilmont, who snatched it up and began blathering away to Fairchild.

"...was like nothing I'd ever seen before!" Wilmont was saying while Fairchild stared with wide-eyed wonder, "Thousands upon thousands coming for us. I could feel the very earth shaking with every step they took!"

Paul grabbed another glass of wine from the table and downed it in a single gulp, just like before. He didn't know how much more of Captain Wilmont's bragging he could stand...

"...too far back to join the fray myself, but I knew straight away that something had to be done to stop them! So I jumped on the radio and ordered the front to hold. 'Bowman,' I said to him, 'you steady that line and hold your position if it's the last thing you do!' And the rest as they say is—"

Finally, Paul had heard enough. "Oh, would you please shut up!"

"Calm yourself, Mister Bowman," Wilmont said, his trademark haughtiness beginning to creep back into his voice. He turned back to Fairchild, "It's the artillery shells, you see. The pressure from the blasts jostle the brains about, thereby causing madness. It's really quite a pitiable—"

"No! I'm sick of listening to you!" Paul refused to back down,

"None of what you just said is true in the slightest!"

"Watch yourself, Mister Bowman," Wilmont threatened, "I'll thank you to remember that I outrank—"

Paul ignored Wilmont and turned toward Fairchild, "You want to know what really happened? This idiot didn't even *know* about the battle until two hours after it was over! For all I know, he probably slept through the whole damn thing!"

"Is that true?" Fairchild's eyes lit up, and she hastily produced a pencil and small book and began to scribble down notes.

"Oh yeah, and you know what else?" Paul added, "When this idiot found out what happened, the *very first thing* he did was try to have me flogged for breaking position! Don't believe a word he says!"

"Dear me!" Fairchild giggled excitedly to herself as she continued taking down notes, "What a scandal!" Paul didn't like the girl in the least, but she was nothing compared to Wilmont.

"Mister Bowman, are you calling me a liar?" Wilmont's face was starting to turn red.

"Yes," Paul shouted, "Yes I am!"

"Right! That does it!" Wilmont grabbed another glass of wine and threw its contents in Paul's face. Paul staggered back from the shock of it, and Fairchild shrieked as some of the liquid splashed on her dress.

"Mister Bowman, you have impugned my honour for the last time," Wilmont said, "I'll grant you one final opportunity to retract your accusations, or I shall be forced to challenge—"

Paul tackled Wilmont to the floor before he could finish his sentence. The two of them went careening over the table, landing in a mess of wine and broken glass. Paul loomed over the portly man, hurling a vicious barrage of punches against his face, "Impugn this!" Paul screamed in between blows, "You stupid, miserable, lying piece of—"

"Mister Bowman!" A voice shouted behind him.

Paul whirled around furiously, "What?!?"

It was the same footman from before. He flinched at Paul's shout and took a step back. As the man regained his composure, Paul noticed that the entire hall had gone silent, and almost everyone was staring at him. Even the music in the background had stopped. Finally, the footman straightened and cleared his throat.

"Her Most Royal Majesty the Queen."

Chapter IV

An Audience with the Queen

THE Queen was a tall woman, almost as tall as Paul was himself. She stood at the top of the raised platform at the front of the Great Hall, looking out across the silent crowd. Her dark brown hair was twisted into an ornate braid, atop which sat a glittering golden crown studded with emeralds. She wore a shimmering purple dress with a green-and-gold sash across her chest, long purple gloves, and more jewelry than Paul had ever seen a woman wear at once.

"Her Most Royal Majesty Queen Cassandra the Second, Beloved of God, and Supreme Ruler of Aurora and All the Provinces," the footman announced.

It was about that time that Paul realized he was still crouching over Captain Wilmont with his fist poised to strike again. Sheepishly, Paul picked himself up and straightened out his uniform. Captain Wilmont also picked himself up and dabbed at a thin trickle of blood from beneath his nose. "You'll pay for that, Bowman," Wilmont growled under his breath.

"I will murder your lying ass!" Paul hissed back.

"Would Mister Paul Bowman please come forwards," the footman said.

Paul glanced up at the sound of his name and discovered, to his horror, that the Queen was looking directly at him! He swallowed and began to make his way toward the front of the Great Hall. The crowds parted before him, and soon he found himself standing before the Queen at the base of the steps that led up to the throne.

"You are Sergeant Paul Bowman of the Forty Second Infantry Regiment?" Her voice was clear and refined.

Paul quickly saluted. "Yes, sir," he said instinctively, and then corrected, "Ma'am! ...Milady! ...Your Highness!" For a moment all was silent. *Crap! Did I just insult the Queen?*

The silence was broken by the sound of the Queen failing to hold in a laugh, "Oh my!" she managed to say in between giggles, "He's so rigid!" A wave of laughter sprang up from the crowd. Paul felt his face redden with embarrassment. "Oh, do relax Mister Bowman," the Queen said as she started down the steps toward him, "This is a ball, and you're the guest of honour!" Paul got a sinking feeling in his stomach. This woman was just as silly and airheaded as that Fairchild girl. *And just as young too,* Paul noticed, *maybe even younger.*

As the Queen reached the bottom of the steps, she held out a purple-gloved hand to Paul. *Hadvari silk,* Paul recognized immediately, *colored with purple dye from Isafar and perfumed with ambergris from Western Illyria.* Just one of those gloves cost more money than Paul could make in a lifetime of freighthauling. He took her hand and kissed it lightly. Paul knew that much at least about how to behave toward noble ladies; he had transported a few during his time working on airships.

The Queen jerked her hand away from Paul and let out an earsplitting shriek! A small army of guardsmen with pistols drawn and dashed out of the crowd surrounded the Queen. "Why, Mister Bowman!" the Queen trembled, "there's blood upon your sleeve! You've been wounded!"

Paul glanced down at his left hand, and sure enough there was a small splotch of red on the cuff of the white tunic beneath his jacket sleeve. "Oh right," he said sheepishly as he tucked that hand away behind his back, like he had seen other noblemen do, "Don't worry about that. It's nothing."

"Mister Bowman, this is no time for boasting," the Queen said with concern, "We must have your wound closed at once, or it shall fester. Summon my personal physician!"

"Please, don't make a fuss over it," Paul said frantically, and then added, "It's... it's not actually *my* blood."

"What do you mean *it isn't your blood?*" the Queen said with confusion. Then she seemed to take Paul's meaning, "Why Mister Bowman," she ventured suspiciously, "you haven't been... *brawling,* have you?"

Paul was about to answer when another voice cut him off, "Indeed he has, Your Majesty!"

It was Wilmont. The portly man had ploughed his way through the crowd and was now standing right beside Paul, "My Queen, I am Sir Alphonse Wilmont, *Captain* of Company Baker of the Forty Second Regiment of Infantry in Your Most Royal Army," he said, making a fancy bow, "And I am most loath to interrupt Your Most Royal Majesty, but I can be silent no longer," He pointed a thick sausage of a finger at Paul, "This man, my subordinate, has given grave personal insult to me, and when I called him out and demanded satisfaction, he assaulted me! Like to a drunkard in a tavern!"

"I sincerely hope you can present a suitable explanation for this most uncivilised behaviour, Mister Bowman," the Queen said.

Paul glared at Wilmont. He wanted to strangle the bastard, and if it weren't for the Queen and everyone else watching him, he might just have done it! Still, he was among fancy people now, and he had to play their game. Now then, how would a fancy gentleman like that Lord Wingate handle a situation like this?

"My Queen," Paul began with a bow, "this man has... impugned the honor of the army," *Impugned,* that was a good word. A *fancy* word. Then Paul added, "*Your* army, my Queen," That was clever. It would make Wilmont's insults seem directed at her personally!

"Oh dear," the Queen said with exaggerated dismay.

"Bah! Poppycock!" Wilmont spat, "Majesty, I know this man very well. In truth, I was his commanding officer at the Defence of the Southern Gap—"

"Which you *missed entirely,*" Paul interrupted "I seem to remember that you spent the entire battle lurking in the officers caravan, a *mile* behind the front lines!" A sudden wave of gasps rippled through the crowd, and Paul grinned. *It's working!*

"Is this true, Sir Alphonse?" The Queen said, now firmly in

Paul's camp.

"My Queen," Wilmont protested, "we can quibble over tactical minutiae until winter comes again, but we are avoiding the larger point! This man called me a liar and I demand—"

"I don't know how things are done here," Paul interrupted, "but where *I* come from, when a man says things that are *known* to be lies, that makes him a liar!" More gasps from the crowd.

"There! You see?" Wilmont shrieked and waggled his meaty finger at Paul, "He's gone and done it again! Mister Bowman, you have gravely insulted my honour, and I must have satisfaction! I demand you retract your accusation at once!"

By now, the crowd was clearly on Paul's side. "I retract nothing!" Paul said firmly, "You are a lying..."

Paul tried to come up with a good word; a nice fancy word, but for some reason he couldn't think of a good one. Hell, he couldn't think of any. It was as if every word in the Auroran language had evaporated right out of his head in an instant.

"...lie-telling..."

The words came out before Paul could stop them. And yet, as stupid as they sounded, Paul didn't think he could have picked out any others. There simply were no other words in his head.

"...teller-of-lies," Paul finished clumsily.

There was an awkward silence. *That was a terrible finish,* Paul thought, *What a disaster!*

Then, laughter from the Queen! "Oh dear me! But you do have a way with words, Mister Bowman!" she cried through fits of laughter. Paul was very confused, and even more confused when the rest of the crowd began to laugh along with her! He even heard some of the crowd repeating the phrase: "Lying, lie-telling, teller-of-lies!" They seemed to genuinely find it funny! Eventually, even Paul began to laugh! He barely noticed Wilmont vanishing into the crowd, red as a tomato and just as round.

"You are most certainly a shining wit, Paul," the Queen said as the laughter finally subsided, "May I call you *Paul?*"

"Yeah, sure," Paul said absently, still laughing a little.

"Thank you, Paul," the Queen giggled, "I seem to be growing rather fond of you," The Queen turned aside, trying, and failing, to hide a deep crimson blush. Paul felt all of his mirth evaporate in an instant. *That's right,* he reminded himself, *That girl might be a queen, but she's still a complete idiot.*

"And who is *this?*" The Queen gasped dramatically as she strode past Paul. A pair of overdressed guards escorted Batu up to the Queen. Her wrists were still bound behind her back, and her face remained as unreadable as ever. The rest of the crowd drew aawy from Batu and her escort, and many began to exchange fearful whispers.

One of Batu's guards stepped forward, "May it please Your Highness," he announced, "The Lady Batu of the Sultanate of Isafar."

"Ooh! This must be the Queen of the Savages!" the Queen said, "The one whom you took prisoner!"

"Yeah," Paul sighed, "that's her."

"My word," the Queen said awkwardly, "whatever has she done with her hair?" Batu's head was covered with a thin black fuzz; no doubt the result of going five days without a razor. Paul had noticed as much on the ride to the palace. For all he knew of Isafari customs, that thin covering of hair was probably more of an embarrassment than being taken captive and paraded through the streets like a criminal.

"We bid you welcome to our fair kingdom," the Queen said to Batu, making a grand gesture with both arms. There was a moment of silence. Batu's expression did not change.

"Umm..." Paul whispered to the Queen, "she doesn't speak our language."

"Of course," the Queen giggled, "How foolish of me. Summon a translator who speaks the Isafari tongue!"

"That won't work either," Paul said quickly.

"No?" the Queen looked at Paul, "and why not?"

"Because she doesn't speak Isafari," Paul explained.

"A woman of Isafar who does not speak the Isafari tongue?" The Queen seemed confused, "Curiouser and curiouser."

"We had to use two translators when we brought her in," Paul said, "One of 'em was just a kid."

"Did you now!" the Queen's eyes lit up with exaggerated amazement, "Oh you are just full of marvelous tales! I simply must hear more!" The Queen turned to one of her footmen, "Escort Sergeant Bowman to my private audience chamber. I should very much like to conduct private discourse with this most fascinating gentleman."

Paul shuddered. He didn't know how much more of this idiotic woman he could stomach, and now he was going to be *alone* with her? It would be that Fairchild interview all over again.

"This gentleman will show you the way, Mister Bowman," the

Queen said, smiling broadly and indicating the footman she had spoken with, "I'll be along in just a minute!"

"If you'd care to follow me, Mister Bowman," the footman droned. Paul nodded and followed the footman toward a side door. Paul wasn't looking forward to his private audience with that foolish girl, but he was at least glad to get away from the crowd.

Just before he passed through the door, Paul glanced back at the Queen. She waved across the hall at him, and covered her mouth with her other hand, probably to hide another giddy smile. Paul cringed.

The Queen's private audience chamber immediately reminded Paul of Lord Wingate's office on that airship. *The Fearless,* Paul remembered, *that was its name.* This room was just as luxurious, if not more so. Even the scent spoke of luxury; that sweet aroma of whale-oil and incense burning in the lamps. *The smell of money,* Paul thought, remembering those easy but lucrative runs up and down the Auroran coast, before the Auroran Trade Consortium muscled in and monopolized the market.

Two couches faced each other at the center of the room, each finely upholstered with fur of the white bear from up in Torrenberg, just on the edge of the Great Unclaimed North. Between the couches stood a short table that was almost certainly carved out of seprya wood, the kind you had to smuggle out of Hadvar by the ounce. Paul could only wonder how the Queen had gotten her hands on enough to make something as large as the table. A broadsheet sat neatly folded at the center of the table. Paul ignored that; he wouldn't be able to read it anyways.

The carpet beneath the furniture was definitely Illyrian, and the floor below that was black oak from the Great Northern Forest of Analeria. The wall hangings were Hadvari silk, much easier to smuggle out of Hadvar than seprya wood but still expensive, and they were colored green with Halcivine dye *(locally grown for once)* and gold with... wait, was that actual gold? Paul walked up to the tapestry and gently brushed his fingers across it... It *was* gold! The tapestry actually had gold wires woven into the silk in the pattern of the Banner of Dawn. That was just ridiculous!

Paul glanced back at the footman, who was standing between the liquor cabinet and the door. The footman was watching his every move with an empty expression on his face. Paul looked closer... yep, that was the exact same footman who had led his horse up the boulevard, and who had stopped him from beating Wilmont to a bloody pulp!

"You got a name?" Paul asked.

"As a matter of fact," the footman droned—*Definitely the same man*—"I *do* have a name."

There was a pause.

"...Well, what is it?" Paul asked sharply. For a moment, Paul could have sworn he saw a grin flash across the man's face. Had the man actually managed a *joke?*

"Barnes, Mister Bowman," the footman said. "Harold Barnes, esquire."

Barnes? That name sounded familiar. "...Do you have a family member in the fleet?"

The footman actually looked surprised, "Yes, in fact. My nephew, Theodore. He is executive officer to Lord Wingate aboard the airship *Celsius.*"

The Celsius, Paul noted, *That's the ship that crashed.* Did he know yet? "I met him," Paul said, "He survived the crash. He's alright."

"I hadn't heard," the footman said unsteadily, the first real emotion Paul had seen from the man, "Thank you."

"He seems like a good officer," Paul said, "Bit of a prick though."

"I shall give him your compliments," the footman droned, back to his usual composed self again.

At that moment, the door burst open, and the Queen strode through, all smiles and cheer. "Oh, my dear Paul," she sighed, "Already I find my self sorely missing your pleasant company." Paul winced, bracing himself for another round of painfully idiotic conversation.

The footman bowed, "Shall, I give you the room, Majesty?"

"Do please." The Queen didn't even look in his direction. She had already opened the liquor cabinet and was busy pouring a pair of drinks. "Why don't we have our little discussion out on the balcony?" she said merrily.

"Are you sure, Your Majesty?" Paul said awkwardly, "You wouldn't prefer to stay inside where it's... comfortable?"

"Oh, tish tosh!" the Queen said, "It's a lovely evening and the air shall do us good." She turned around to face him, with a crystal glass in each hand. "Lead the way, Mister Bowman," she said with a smile.

Paul walked over to the doors and began fiddling with the latch. By the time he managed to get the doors open, the Queen was standing at his side, giggling like an idiot. "Here, hold my drink," she said, handing the glasses to Paul, "I'll close the doors behind us."

Paul took the glasses and stepped outside. The twilight air was cool, and a gentle breeze blew across the balcony. It carried the scent of the pine trees growing on the high mountain slopes, mixed with the faint smell of animal dung and coal-fired machinery from the city below. The sky was cloudless and the sun had vanished behind the Mountains of Dawn to the west. It was going to be a beautifully clear spring night.

The Queen walked up beside Paul and took back her glass. She held a deep breath for a second or two, then breathed out a heavy sigh. She met Paul's eye and gave him a crooked smile.

"Sorry about the show back there in the Great Hall," she said with a distinctly lower voice, "I do so tire of playing the part, but appearances must be kept up."

Paul looked down at the glass in his hand. The liquid wasn't wine. It was cloudy white, and it smelled of raisins and anise.

"Aren't you going to enjoy your drink?" the Queen said, "Surely you could use something to calm your nerves."

"I thought Illyrian dog ale was illegal," Paul said nervously. Several old acquaintances of his had been dragged off to prison for smuggling this very substance.

"And yet you seem familiar with it," the Queen said in between sips, "Do you disapprove? Don't tell me you're one of those wretched god botherers from the Church."

The Queen had transformed a completely different woman. The giggling little trollop from before was gone, replaced by someone much more intelligent, perceptive, even majestic. For the first time since meeting her, Paul actually felt as though he was standing before a queen.

"No. No, not at all," Paul grinned and started drinking, "I just thought you might prefer... wine or something fancy like that."

"Oh?" the Queen said playfully, "Is this not *fancy* enough for you? Drinking contraband liquor out of fine crystal glasses and hobnobbing with royalty?"

Paul laughed, "Yeah, I guess so." A moment passed in silence between the two figures sharing a drink on the balcony.

"So," Paul asked, "what's with the act?"

"I've told you," the Queen said frankly, "Appearances must be kept up."

"But it doesn't make sense." Paul pressed further, "Why go to all the trouble of making yourself seem like a fool in front of all the nobility?"

"Are you suggesting that I let on that I'm actually a perceptive and intelligent woman who is fully capable of matching wits with anyone the nobility can put forth?" The Queen laughed, "My god! I'd be assassinated before the week was out!"

"But they don't respect you!" Paul raised his voice, and he would have continued, but the Queen quickly raised a finger to her lips.

"Not so loud," she said sternly, "there's a listening device in the bottom of the liquor cabinet." Paul glanced back through the glass doors. The dark stained-oak cabinet was right where it had always been, as if nothing had changed.

"I don't need them to *respect* me," the Queen said, "I need them to think me a suggestible little nitwit whom they can manipulate."

"But why?"

She grinned as if presenting a pearl of wisdom, "So that I can control *them!*"

Paul blinked, "I don't get it."

"Power is curious thing," the Queen said, "Everyone wants it, but nobody wants to be *seen* to want it."

"Not me," Paul said, "I can do without all that trouble."

"Oh, I very much doubt that," the Queen said with a malicious smirk, "You present yourself as a simple man of simple ways. You might even believe it a little. But can you honestly say that when you were down in the Great Hall making fools of the nobility, you didn't feel a certain sense of pride?"

"N-no..." Paul stammered, caught off guard.

"No?" The Queen leaned closer, her grin growing wider by the second, "Not even a little?"

Paul could feel beads of sweat sprouting on the back of his neck, "Well... maybe a bit," he admitted, nervously scratching at the back of his neck.

The Queen stepped away, "You don't have to be so embarrassed about it," she said, "It's just the way things are."

"Maybe..." Paul muttered into his drink.

"And there's another thing about power," the Queen continued, "It breeds jealousy. The more power one accumulates, the more people desire to steal it away from you, especially here at court," the

Queen turned to face Paul, "That's the ugly truth about civilised society. It's a pyramid. A great writhing pile of human flesh, each wretched soul scrambling to reach as high as it can before it is crushed beneath all the rest," she sighed, "and I am the luckless cunt sitting right at the very top!"

Paul stared. He had never heard such a word come from a woman like her before. "Well, when you put it like that..." Paul chuckled.

"But there's a way to make it work," the Queen said, "If I come off as intelligent or perceptive, then the rest of the nobility will regard me as a threat. But if I seem like a bit of an idiot, like someone who can be manipulated and persuaded, then that's exactly what they'll try to do. I'm no longer a threat, but a potential asset to whomever can persuade me the best," The Queen leaned against the edge of the balcony, seeming very satisfied with herself, "And while they're trying to manipulate me, I can do the exact same thing to them without them even noticing! And if those manipulating me don't get what they want, then it's not my fault—I was probably being manipulated by someone else!"

"That still doesn't really make sense," Paul said with a shrug.

"I can't really blame you," the Queen said, "I don't suppose you have to deal with this sort of thing on an airship."

"Well, it's definitely not as bad as—" Paul blinked, "How did you know I used to work on airships?"

The Queen smirked, "Your accent. A touch of Longview, if I'm not mistaken."

"Now hang on," Paul protested, "Longview's a pretty big town. There's more to it than just airships."

"True," the Queen said, "but you were also familiar with Illyrian dog ale, despite it being an illegal substance as you said. That indicates a passing familiarity with Auroran trade regulations. Specifically the ones pertaining to the Illyrian markets, which are primarily serviced by airships."

Paul stared into his now-empty glass, "Yeah, I guess that makes sense."

"Furthermore," the Queen said, "I would hazard a guess that you didn't just work on an airship. You also traded in contraband goods. I would also guess that you were caught smuggling and agreed to military service in lieu of trial and sentence," the Queen's grin widened, "...which would technically make you a *conscript!*"

Paul laughed, "That's incredible! What else can you tell about me?"

"Well, let's see..." the Queens eyes scanned him up and down, measuring him, "The news journals are all saying that you lost your left eye during the Defence of the Southern Gap."

"Well, I've never much trusted the broadsheets," Paul said.

"Good, because they're wrong," the Queen said casually, "The injury is much older than that."

"And how do you know?" Paul ventured warily.

"Well, first of all, it hasn't yet been a week since the battle," the Queen said, "If you had really just lost your eye, I suspect you'd still be in bandages."

"Not necessarily," Paul shrugged, "Maybe it was a small wound and it's already healed up?"

"True, but there's also the matter of your eye patch," the Queen went on, "It appears to be rather worn and weathered, suggesting that you've owned it for some time already."

"Maybe I got it used," Paul shrugged deeper, "Cheaper that way."

"And there's one more thing," the Queen grinned, "When you look at an inanimate object, you twist your head slightly. I'd guess you do it to centre the object in your field of vision. But when you talk to a person, you look at them head on, without twisting your head."

Paul stared blankly, "...Really? I do that?"

"It's subtle," the Queen assured, "But it's clear enough if you know what to look for. Behaviors like that don't come along right away. I'd say six months at least—longer if it was your dominant eye, as I suspect it was, given that you favour your left hand."

My left hand? Paul thought for a moment. "Back in the Great Hall, when I kissed your hand, I used my left hand. *That's* how you knew."

The Queen shook her head, "Earlier than that, when you were assaulting Sir Alphonse."

"Oh, right," Paul had completely forgotten, "Sorry about that."

"Oh, please. I could thank you for it," the Queen rolled her eyes, "The man is a frightful bore. He spent nearly an hour blabbering at me during the Coronation Ball. *Glory of this! Honour of that!* My god, I thought my bloody ears were going to drop off."

Paul laughed awkwardly, "You don't think he's going to... y'know, try to get back at me or anything?"

"Don't worry about him," the Queen said, "Oh, sure, he'll complain to whomever can stand to listen to him long enough, but he's been put in his place, and he knows it."

"So he's not going to challenge me to a duel or... whatever fancy people do?"

"Of course not!" the Queen laughed, "Wilmont is far too much of a coward to even dream of that. Besides, duels aren't especially frequent. They're generally reserved for matters of last resort."

"That's a relief," Paul sighed.

The Queen was silent for a moment. "You know, I've never actually ridden on an airship before."

"Really?"

"I've never had the opportunity," she sighed, "I've always wondered what it might be like though."

"It's incredible," Paul said, "It's like nothing else in the world."

"Tell me more," the Queen said.

"Look out there," Paul said, pointing out beyond the balcony, "Look at that view."

The sky was still light blue behind the mountains in the west, but the stars had begun to twinkle in the gathering dark. Below the balcony, the city shone brightly. Many of those buildings had apparently been fitted with electric candles, and light was spilling out of them like water through a sieve. It was like a second sky to match the first. Far below the city, the southern countryside stretched for miles upon miles until it vanished beyond the horizon.

"Imagine that you could go anywhere," Paul said, "Absolutely anywhere in the world. You could cross the widest oceans, leap over mountains, soar just above the treetops of the largest forests. And everywhere you go, you'll find a view just like this."

"It sounds breathtaking," the Queen said.

"There's nothing else I'd rather do with my life," Paul said.

"You still could, you know," the Queen said.

"Yeah, maybe," Paul sighed, "Once my term of service is up perhaps." *Assuming I'm still alive by then.*

The Queen turned to face Paul, "What if I told you that you could be commanding your own airship before the week is out?"

Something stirred inside Paul. A half-forgotten dream. *An airship of my own!* "I..." Paul stammered, "You... What do you mean?"

"It is within my power to reward you for your heroism in one of three ways," the Queen explained, "I can pin some garish decoration on your chest and send you back to the ranks to finish out your service. I can grant you a peerage of nobility, thus condemning you to spend the rest of your life surrounded by people who think they're better than you. Or I can award you an officer's commission and an airship to command."

"An officer's commission?" Paul stammered, "And an airship?"

"Personally, I think that would suit you the best," the Queen grinned, "Wouldn't you agree, *Captain* Bowman?"

Captain Bowman! Paul could feel his ambition growing by the second, *And a ship of my own!* It was everything he had ever dreamed of! *It's too perfect...* "What's the catch?"

"There's no catch," the Queen said, "You get your airship, and I get another captain serving with distinction in the skies of Aurora."

Paul didn't believe it. It was too good to be true. There was more to it that the Queen wasn't saying, no doubt about it. There was also the problem that Paul didn't know a thing about commanding military airships. But at that very moment, he honestly didn't care. *I am the wind!*

"So what do you say?" the Queen asked.

"I'll take it!" Paul said confidently.

The Queen beamed, "Excellent!"

Amelia's musical laughter echoed through the tight hallways, "*Choice words!* You got that one from papa, didn't you?"

"Sir Arthur Belmont was a most striking man," Lord Wingate smiled, remembering his late father-by-marriage, "I'll always recall, whenever he was mad at someone he would say: *'I've some choice words for you.'* And then he'd pull the poor idiot aside and shout him down until he got back in line."

"Which is what you did to that oaf Wilmont?" Amelia laughed again.

"I learned from the very best!"

"Ah, I miss father," Amelia sighed fondly.

"Me too," Lord Wingate said as the two of them rounded a corner and stepped into the Great Hall. Lord Wingate shuddered at the sight of the crowd. He and Amelia had deliberately taken their time making their way to the Great Hall. They had even made a point of using a side entrance so that they would not be announced, but despite their best efforts to get lost along the way, they had still managed to arrive. Lord Wingate sighed and waded into the crowd with his wife.

"Papa!" A shrill voice pierced the murmur of the crowd. No sooner had Lord Wingate heard it than a young girl joyfully rushed towards him.

"Sophie!" Lord Wingate knelt down and caught his younger daughter in an embrace, "I've missed you so much. How have you been?"

"Papa, you'll never guess who we just saw!" Sophie was practically jumping up and down with excitement.

"*Whom* did you see?" Amelia asked. She never could help correcting her children's grammar.

"The Hero of the Southern Gap!" Sophie squealed, "Paul Bowman himself!"

"*The Hero of the Southern Gap?*" Lord Wingate tried his best to hide his disdain. *Bloody hell, the man's already crafting epithets for himself.*

"Is your sister about?" Amelia asked.

"Mary's with some friends," Sophie giggled, "They went to see Sergeant Bowman up close! She *likes* him!"

"I'll put a stop to that," Lord Wingate grumbled. His wife stifled a laugh.

"Orpheus, old boy!" Lord Wingate recognised the voice, and his heart nearly stopped. *Not this pompous old gasbag.* He turned around and forced a smile, "Barnabas, my old friend, what a pleasant surprise."

The balding, white-haired man bowed, and Lord Wingate returned the gesture, "And this must be your lovely wife!" He stretched out a bony hand to kiss Amelia's gloved fingers. "I don't believe we've yet been introduced, my lady. I am Lord Barnabas Obadiah of House Franklin. But you may call me Barnabas."

"Enchanted," Amelia said, clearly squirming to get away from the man. Lord Wingate couldn't blame her; he sorely wished he could do the same.

"I don't suppose I might borrow your husband for a spell?" A chill ran down Lord Wingate's spine.

"By all means!" Amelia forced a smile and turned to Lord Wingate, "We'll just find Marion and catch up with you later," She slipped off into the crowd with Sophie following close after. Lord Wingate watched them go. *Please don't leave me alone with this tedious buffoon!*

"You just missed Sergeant Bowman, Orpheus," Lord Franklin

said, "He caused quite a stir."

"Yes," Lord Wingate said, "I can imagine."

"And atop that," Lord Franklin went on, "he was granted an audience with the Queen. A *private* audience. I suspect there are great things on the horizon for our Mister Bowman."

"I agree," Lord Wingate said, *just as long as those great things have nothing to do with the military.*

"I understand you know Sergeant Bowman," Lord Franklin pried, "Is that correct?"

"Indeed it is," Lord Wingate responded, "I debriefed him personally after the action at the Southern Gap."

"Where you lost your ship," Lord Franklin said casually.

Lord Wingate's blood froze, "Come again?"

"Am I wrong?" Lord Franklin continued, a malicious grin sprouting on his face, "Or does the good airship *Celsius* still patrol our fair skies?"

"She was..." Lord Wingate groped for a suitable bunch of words, "...disabled due to enemy action, at which time I saw fit to evacuate the crew and scuttle her, as dictated by protocol."

"You know, I was always told that it was tradition that the captain goes down with the ship," Lord Franklin said with accusation in his voice, "And yet here I find you."

"Fancy that," Lord Wingate muttered, desperately looking for a way out. *My reputation is already beginning to suffer.*

"Am I to understand that you fled the scene of the greatest military disaster in the history of our fair kingdom?" Lord Franklin said, now openly castigating, "And for what purpose? To save your own hide?"

"You're one to talk, aren't you?" said a voice from behind Lord Franklin, "Exactly how many duels have *you* backed down from in your time?"

"That's hardly the point, Theobald!" Lord Franklin turned to address Lord Theobald Paracelsus Newton who had appeared behind him, "I am referring to actions carried out by our esteemed Lord Wingate, which by dint of cowardice cast aspersions upon us all!"

"And you think you could have done better, is that it?" asked Lord Perseus Hiram Stolos, who had materialised beside Lord Wingate, "Have *you* any military experience, besides playing with toy soldiers as a child?"

Lord Franklin wheeled about, his face red with indignation, "Now just a minute, young Perseus! I am simply asking legitimate questions! You've no call to go bringing personal history into this!"

By now, Lord Wingate had gotten his footing back, "I followed the dictates of protocol, and I stand by my actions."

"But surely tradition—" Lord Franklin insisted.

"Tradition is for the parade ground and nowhere else," Lord Wingate interrupted, "In battle, you follow protocol, or people die."

"But it's a matter of honour!" Lord Franklin was grasping at straws.

"I think you should leave, Barnabas," Lord Wingate said firmly. Lord Franklin spluttered for a moment, but eventually he slipped into the crowd and vanished. Lord Wingate breathed a sigh of relief. "Thanks for having my back."

"It was an honour to do so, my lord," Lord Stolos said with a humble bow, still addressing Lord Wingate as if he still weren't a lord himself. Lord Wingate shook his head fondly; the sandy-haired man had only just recently been raised to lordship with the untimely death of his uncle, and old habits had a way of lingering. *It took me nearly a year to break those habits myself,* he remembered.

Lord Wingate turned his attention to the older man, "Theo!" Lord Newton grinned broadly, and the two of them exchanged a firm handshake. They had each been best man at the other's wedding, and they were as close as brothers, "How have you been?"

"Great," the tall, wiry man said, "The laboratory has been keeping me very busy."

"What have they got you working on now?" Lord Wingate asked.

Lord Newton adjusted his half-moon spectacles, as was his habit before starting off on one of his rants, "Well, the other day I was conducting an experiment on a number of different materials, and I happened to notice an inverse correlation between the heat of a substance and its electrical conductivity! So, I took an assortment of conductive metals, cooled them to successively lower temperatures, and measured their electrical resistance. And I have discovered that when lead is immersed in liquefied helium gas, all electrical resistivity drops to zero!

"Amazing, isn't it?" Lord Newton's pace quickened as his excitement grew, "Common lead, a perfect conductor. Think of the applications! Why I could generate an electric potential in my laboratory and conduct it all the way to Torrenberg without any loss of strength. And to think that common lead is what shall make such miracles possible!"

"You are insane, Theo," Lord Wingate laughed.

Lord Newton smiled, "So I have been told." He had always been something of a mad dreamer, and his mad dreams had a habit of coming true.

"I think it's a wonderful discovery," Lord Stolos said, "It shall enable us to spread the blessings of electricity throughout the kingdom, improving the lives of the common people."

"Everything always comes back to the common people with you, doesn't it Percy?" Lord Wingate said. Lord Stolos was full of wide-eyed idealism, as younger men generally were, but with him it was practically an obsession.

"And why should it not?" Lord Stolos retorted, "The common folk are full of promise, yet we consistently ignore them. Take our Mister Bowman for example. A sterling example of excellence, yet we had to wait for him to distinguish himself before we even bothered to glanced in his direction. Think of all the other prime specimens we must be overlooking at this very moment!"

"*A sterling example of excellence?*" Lord Wingate struggled to contain a laugh.

"Oh yes," Lord Stolos continued unaware, "Mister Bowman presents a perspective that differs quite starkly from the conventional wisdom hereabouts. I'm certain he will become an invaluable statesman in time."

"I very much doubt that," Lord Wingate said, still suppressing a bout of laughter.

"See? Right there!" Lord Stolos brandished a finger at Lord Wingate, "That is precisely my point! It is this corrosive system of thought that has pervaded our national discourse over the past six hundred years. Mister Bowman has distinguished himself remarkably, and the nobility scoffs at the poor man simply because he can't be bothered to trace his lineage back to the Founding. It is utterly preposterous, and it shall have to be done away with. It's a new day, my friend!"

Before Lord Wingate could respond, a small voice beside him said, "Excuse me, my lord?" Lord Wingate turned to see whom had spoken, and found himself looking at a young woman a WAVE uniform. He could have sworn he knew her face. "My lord, I don't suppose you'd remember me. I'm—"

"Miss Halford!" Lord Wingate recognised the young woman who had been serving tea on the bridge of the *Celsius*. He excused himself from Lord Stolos and Lord Newton's conversation and turned his full attentions to the young woman, "To what do I owe the pleasure?"

Halford paused for a moment and produced a small folded letter, "I... My lord, I'd like to submit a formal request for a transfer."

Lord Wingate chuckled, "Miss Halford, we're at a ball. Whatever this is, I'm sure it can wait until tomorrow morning."

"I understand, my lord," Halford stammered, "But I really would prefer that this matter be taken care of now."

"Oh, if you insist," Lord Wingate took Halford's letter and began to read...

"Wait a minute," He muttered as he scanned the document, "this can't be right. There must be some mistake."

Halford shook her head stiffly, "No, I've checked. It's accurate."

"But..." Lord Wingate said, "the *Dreadnought?* You're requesting a transfer to the airship *Dreadnought?*"

"Yes, that is correct," Halford said.

"Do you know what that ship is?" Lord Wingate whispered emphatically, "We dump our incompetents there! It's where careers go to die!"

"I... am aware of its unsavoury reputation," Halford's voice was growing unsteady.

"It's not a reputation," Lord Wingate insisted, "It's the entire point of the ship! It just sits idle in port and never sees any action!"

"I am also aware of that," Halford said.

Lord Wingate was about to list some more reasons why this was a bad career move when something occurred to him... "You're trying to avoid combat!"

"I..." Halford's lip trembled. She looked to be on the verge of tears, "Yes."

At that moment, Lord Wingate could have easily launched into a furious rant about cowardice in the face of the enemy, but he stopped just as he opened his mouth. Something about the frightened young woman triggered a memory: a young boy about the same age as her, assigned to a post he was completely unprepared for, and terrified that he might get blown out of the sky at any moment. *I was exactly the same way when I was her age.*

"I understand," Lord Wingate said, gently placing a hand on her shoulder. He took the letter and tucked it into his jacket, "I'll file your request first thing in the morning. You should receive orders within the week."

"Thank you, my lord," Halford curtsied and vanished into the crowd. Lord Wingate sighed and turned back to Lord Stolos and Lord Newton.

"Who was that young lady?" Lord Newton asked.

"One of my crew," Lord Wingate said, "She's requesting a transfer."

"A transfer to where?" Lord Stolos enquired.

"The *Dreadnought*," Lord Wingate said.

"Isn't that the ship your son is serving on?" Lord Newton asked.

Lord Wingate hesitated. The *Dreadnought* was indeed the ship where his son was serving, his son that he didn't particularly like talking about. Wolfram Howard Wingate, his firstborn, had entered the Auroran Military Academy at South Sands a year early at fifteen and graduated a year late at nineteen. Not only that, but his time in the academy had been beset by low marks, disciplinary troubles, and all manner of scandals. A thorough disappointment. Lord Wingate himself had recommended his son for the dead-end position as the *Dreadnought's* tactical officer. He hadn't told Amelia or his daughters.

"Yes," Lord Wingate said carefully, "Wolfram is serving on board the *Dreadnought*. How did you know?"

"My nephew Hudson is the *Dreadnought's* chief engineer," Lord Newton said cheerfully, unaware it seemed of the significance of his nephew's assignment, "He writes about your boy quite a bit. I think they'll both make fine young officers."

Lord Wingate laughed awkwardly. He didn't have the heart to tell his lifelong friend that his poor nephew was languishing in such an ignominious posting—and worse, that he had probably deserved it.

All of a sudden, the dull murmur of the crowd exploded into cheers and applause. Lord Wingate looked up at the raised dais at the head of the Great Hall. The Queen had emerged, and Bowman was at her side. Lord Wingate watched as the Queen strode to the very front and centre of the dais and raised a hand to still the crowd.

"Sergeant Bowman has given us his personal account of the heroic action at the Southern Gap," the Queen addressed the room, "And we have seen fit to reward his uncommon valour and gallantry by appointing him an officer of the Auroran Royal Airborne Fleet with the rank of captain,"

Lord Wingate's jaw dropped open. Paul Bowman, a captain in the fleet? He couldn't imagine a more disastrous role for the man.

"My god, that woman is a fool," Lord Stolos whispered, "It

makes sense to grant the man a peerage, but to raise him to captain? That girl will be the ruination of this kingdom!" Lord Wingate shuddered; those words were highly seditious, but he couldn't help agreeing with them. If Paul Bowman was made a captain, it would be a disaster.

Unless...

Lord Wingate began to make his way through the crowd. He just might be able to contain the damage if he could only get to the Queen in time. Finally, he pushed through the last layer of people and stood before the Queen and Sergeant Bowman (He didn't care what anyone said; the man was *not* a captain!) Lord Wingate locked eyes with Bowman, and they shared a look of sheer hatred.

"My Lord Wingate," the Queen turned to address him, "You are one the most auspicious commanders of the Auroran Royal Airborne Fleet, are you not? What do you think of my latest captain?"

Lord Wingate swallowed his pride and put his plan into motion.

"I think it's an inspired choice, Majesty!" Lord Wingate forced a smile as he spoke, "I'm certain that he will do us all proud in his new capacity as captain! Of course, he'll need an airship to command."

"Oh!" the Queen exclaimed, "Dear me, I've completely forgotten. A captain without an airship is no captain at all! This must be remedied at once."

"Not to worry, Majesty," Lord Wingate assured, "I'm certain that a... *suitable* ship can be found for our newest captain," his false smile broadened, "In fact, I think I know just the one."

Chapter V

What the Future Holds

THE gentle warmth of early spring from the morning sun wafted off the surface of the boulevard as the three riders departed the Dawn Palace. The crowds were much thinner than they had been three days ago, but a few spectators had turned out to witness their departure. Paul rode on the right, Batu on the left, with another man in the middle acting as a translator. Paul was relieved that someone had finally been ferreted out who could actually speak Batu's language, though he was also a little uneasy to learn that most of what Batu had actually been saying was completely different from what everyone had thought.

"So she *didn't* surrender to me?" Paul asked.

"I'm afraid there isn't an exact translation for the word she used," the translator explained. He was a tall, broad-shouldered, stallion of a man with a full mane of silver hair and a thick silver mustache to match it, "It would be more accurate to say that she... accepted your offer of stewardship and protection in exchange for her co-operation. Your Isafari translator must have chosen a more conventional translation."

"So, she thought I was going to protect her?" Paul laughed awkwardly. Batu had been treated like a criminal ever since her capture at the Southern Gap. "I bet she's pretty sore at me."

The translator turned back toward Batu and spoke to her in a voice that might have been stolen from a native speaker. Batu listened intently to the translator, her face expressionless as ever. Her Isafari garb had been replaced by a fine green silk robe with gold stitching (a gift from the Queen), and her golden hoops had been recovered (or more likely, replaced), but most notably, her head was freshly shaven. When the translator was done, she considered for a moment and gave a response.

"The Lady Batu understands that you were doing the best you could under trying circumstances," the translator said, "and she appreciates the lengths to which you have gone in order to protect her dignity."

Paul breathed a sigh of relief, "That's very... diplomatic of her."

"It's hardly surprising," the translator said, "The Masada are a very conciliatory race. Diplomacy is written in her blood."

"Masada?" Paul repeated. The word sounded familiar, "That's a part of Isafar, right?"

"Well, it's a complicated thing," the translator said, "Isafar isn't exactly a country. It's more of an alliance between tribes with a limited degree of central control. Not so much a nation, but a conglomeration of many smaller entities, each with varying degrees of commitment to the larger body."

"So... nobody from Isafar is actually Isafari?"

The translator laughed lightly, "As I've said, it's complicated. The Isafari themselves are merely one tribal group amongst many others, but as they tend to dominate the central government, we have taken to simply calling the entire country *Isafar.*"

"Right, I think I understand," Paul nodded.

Batu leaned over to the translator and asked a question. "The Lady Batu wants to know to which tribe you belong," the translator said.

My tribe? Paul had never thought about it that way. Was that like the difference between growing up in one city or another? He'd been born in a whorehouse in Two Lakes up in the Analerian Highlands, but he had never felt any particular connection to that city. Even Longview had only really been a temporary lodging for him whenever he was between crews (though apparently he had stayed long enough to pick up an accent!) *What about a family?* That wasn't much help either; he had no brothers or sisters, he had never known his father, and he barely remembered his mother. Besides his old uncle Howard, he'd never had a real family.

"I..." Paul shrugged, "I don't really know how to answer that question."

The translator relayed his answer to Batu.

"The Lady Batu says she is sad for you," the translator said, "She says every man should know his tribe so that he can follow the traditions of his father and great-fathers."

"Is that why she shaves her head?" Paul asked, "Because of tradition?"

The translator leaned over to ask Batu, "She says that she shaves her head so that all the world can see her pride," he said, "It's a very common thing amongst the Masada, especially those of higher social standing."

"Pride?" Paul muttered. That didn't make sense. She was *proud* of being bald?

"I have my own theory on how it may have originated," the translator said, "In many parts of Isafar, long hair is seen as a mark of a great warrior, particularly among the Ngori tribe. However, the Masada generally abhor violence and conflict. I suspect that the shaving of the head began as a symbolic gesture of pacifism, and its original meaning may have been embellished over the generations."

"You seem to know quite a bit about Isafar," Paul said.

The translator grinned broadly, "I've spent more than half my life in the subcontinent, getting to know every last tribe and enclave I could find." The man blinked and held out a hand, "Forgive me. Where are my manners? The name's Malavar, Corvin Malavar. Retired captain in Her Majesty's Royal Army."

Paul shook the man's hand "Paul. Paul Bowman, Sergeant—" *No, now it's captain!* Paul smiled and sat a little taller, "Captain. Captain of the airship *Dreadnought*." It felt good to say.

Malavar looked off into the distance, toward the airship that waited at the end of the boulevard, "This will be my first time riding in one of those contraptions, if you can believe it. This should be an interesting trip."

"You're going with Batu?" Paul asked.

"Of course!" Malavar beamed, "Her Majesty summoned me out of retirement so that I may serve as special ambassador to the Sultan of Isafar. According to the Lady Batu, they've gone through quite a few Sultans since I was last there. I can tell you all about my travels during our journey to the south."

"I wish I could," Paul said, "but I'm not going with you. After this, I'm hopping on a train to Norvell to join up with my new command."

Malavar reined in his horse and dismounted at the foot of the airship's cargo ramp, "In that case, Captain Bowman, here is where our ways must part for now," He offered his hand again, and Paul shook it, "I'll look you up once I return; I'm certain I'll have plenty of new stories to tell this time!"

"I'd like that," Paul grinned, "Good luck, Ambassador."

"And the same to you, Captain," Malavar said.

Paul glanced at Batu. She was struggling to dismount her horse. Should he wish her luck as well? "Hey, how do say 'good luck' in her language?"

Malavar responded without a moment to think, "*Shoje'chebakwu* —" he finished with a loud click of his tongue. "It means *may you walk peacefully.*"

"Oh boy..." Paul laughed nervously, "That's... quite a mouthful."

"I can tell her for you if you want," Malavar offered.

"No," Paul shook his head, "I want to say it myself," He stepped up to Batu, who had finally managed to dismount. "Batu..."

She turned to face him... Dammit, he couldn't remember the words!

"*Shoje*" Malavar whispered.

"Uh... Show jay," Paul fumbled through the words...

"*chebakwu*"

"...chay back woo..."

Malavar clicked his tongue, "***click***-et."

Paul hesitated for a moment, and clumsily tried to imitate the sound. "***clock***-eyt."

For a moment, Batu stared wide-eyed at Paul. Then she smiled broadly for the first time Paul had ever seen, and then clasped her hands together and bowed deeply.

"*Jashe'chakwabu****click****at, Polboman.*"

It sounded beautiful. Paul had never noticed it before, but Batu's way of speaking was so smooth and gentle. Each syllable flowed gracefully into the next. Even those strange tongue-popping sounds —in her mouth, they sounded almost delicate. There was no doubt, Batu was a highly refined woman. Perhaps not in a way that was obvious to ordinary Aurorans, but it was there all the same.

Malavar leaned to whisper in Paul's ear, "She wishes you all the same. Even used your proper name. It seems you've earned yourself a friend in Isafar."

Paul watched the two of them ascend the ramp and vanish into the bowels of the airship. The ramp lifted to a closed position, and the airship's reactors roared to life. He could feel the vibrations, first through his feet and then on his face, as the impact coils came alive and the ship lifted off into the morning sky. Paul watched as the airship floated away like a dream and vanished into the distance.

And I've got a ship just like that one, Paul thought with a grin, *waiting for me in Norvell!*

He turned around. Now which way was it to the train station from here?

From high up on a balcony of one of the palace towers, Queen Cassandra the Second watched the newly minted Captain Bowman depart the Dawn Palace. Lady Batu was with him, and Ambassador Malavar. She had always been fond of Corvin Malavar; he was like a dear old uncle to her. Some of Cassandra's fondest childhood memories were of Malavar dandling her on his knee and spinning marvelous tales of the mysterious and exotic land of Isafar. No doubt he would have plenty more stories by the time he returned.

The door opened and closed behind her. She raised her empty silver goblet to check the reflection, "Harold," she said as the serving man came to her side. Servants were always addressed by their given names.

"Majesty," Harold Barnes said, "shall I refill your glass?"

"Later perhaps," Cassandra nodded towards the three figures down on the boulevard, "Paul Bowman—what do you make of him?"

"He is..." Harold bit his lip, clearly groping for diplomatic words, "...a most singular man."

"So I have noticed," Cassandra said.

"He is quite headstrong," Harold continued, "and more perceptive than he lets on."

"You think so?"

"When he was waiting in your private audience chamber," Harold said, "I noted him looking at nearly every little trapping of luxury. But he did not dwell on the luxury of it, as one might expect of a man unaccustomed to such things. It was as though he were merely cataloguing them and then moving on to the next item. Given his experience with commercial skyfreighters, I'd wager the man could identify every last piece of finery in the palace, along with their place of origin, and perhaps even put a price to them."

"You would credit the man with such an intellect?" Cassandra asked.

"Perhaps not an overabundance of schooling," Harold said with a shrug, "but he is most certainly a man of great intellect. And of principle as well. The man holds a number of firm convictions."

"By which you mean he is stubborn," Cassandra said.

"Obstinate to a fault," Harold said, "Do you know that when I was leading him to the Dawn Palace, he stopped the entire procession in order to tend to a superficial injury received by the Lady Batu. He *insisted* on it."

"That was good of him," Cassandra said, "She is a queen, you know."

"There's naught but one queen I recognise, Majesty," Harold said.

Cassandra smiled. It was good of him to say that. She already knew it of course, but it was nice to be reminded every now and again that not everyone in the Capitol was scheming against her.

"Do you know why Aurora has a queen?" Cassandra said after a moment.

Harold shrugged, "I suppose someone needs to be in charge."

"But why a *queen?*" Cassandra pressed, "Aurora used to have Kings you know. Then 342 years ago, Queen Helen the First assumed the throne. And in all the time since, Aurora hasn't had a single king. Did you not ever question why that might be?"

"I don't believe it's my place to question such things," Harold said.

"It's a number of factors," Cassandra explained, "but mostly due to the military. Kings tend to take war into their own hands, meddling in the minutiae of campaigning and the like. Conventional wisdom holds that a *mere woman* doesn't have the stomach to meddle in military affairs."

"You are no mere woman, Majesty," Harold said.

"Oh, shut up," Cassandra rolled her eyes, "The military has been right more often than not. Nearly every one of Aurora's queens was content to leave military matters to her generals completely, and history reflects it."

"The Three-Hundred-Year War against Hadvar," Harold inferred.

"Precisely," Cassandra grumbled, "It started in the fifth year of Helen the First's reign and dragged on for 297 more. The war officially ended only forty years ago, and less than a dozen years later we started up another one."

"And you believe that Aurora has favoured queens over kings primarily because queens turn a blind eye to the military?"

"My mother did," Cassandra said, "She only started paying attention to the military during the last two months of her reign."

"Might I enquire as to what happened?"

"Oh, I'm sure you read about it in the broadsheets," Cassandra said, "She organised a peace conference with a number of Hadvari representatives and began a series of negotiations to create a lasting peace between our two nations."

"She died before the negotiations concluded," Harold said, "As I recall, you postponed your own coronation to complete the negotiations. I believe she would have been proud."

"She was assassinated," Cassandra said, keeping her voice level. It took less effort than she would like to admit; she hadn't been especially close to her lady mother.

"I..." Harold faltered, a rare thing for the man, and a sign of great shock, "Are you certain?"

"It's hardly unprecedented," Cassandra shrugged, "Queens have been assassinated before. She was poisoned slowly with sulfate of thallium. As far as the rest of the world knows, she fell tragically ill and died of exhaustion while working tirelessly for peace." Cassandra's eyes narrowed, "But I know what really happened."

"Have you... found the culprit, Majesty?"

Cassandra shook her head, "I have people working on that. The important thing is that some person, or persons, unknown, tried to sabotage the negotiations," she sighed heavily, "And they bloody well succeeded!"

"But you still achieved peace, Majesty," Harold assured.

"What I *achieved*"—Cassandra rolled her eyes—"was a glorified cease-fire. Give it a year or two and we'll be right back at each others throats again," She turned to face Harold, a look of determination burning in her eyes, "And *this* time, I intend to be prepared."

"Is that what Captain Bowman is for?"

"Exactly," Cassandra said, "The military is plotting something, and our Mister Bowman is just the man to smoke it out."

"Majesty, I rather think..." Harold began unsteadily, "Well, it is hardly my place to question—"

"Speak your mind, Harold," Cassandra said.

"I think it's a bad idea," Harold said, dropping all pretense, "I don't think Paul Bowman is the right man for the job."

"You don't?"

"I'll grant he has a keen mind," Harold said, "but he lacks the patience and finesse required of covert agents. Frankly, the man is a bungler."

Cassandra laughed, "Good! This country is full to bursting with clever agents, all of them scheming and counter-scheming. Perhaps a bungler is just what is needed to shake things up!"

Harold stiffened, "If you say so."

Off in the distance, the airship lifted off into the sky. Cassandra smiled; all the actors were taking their places. Soon the show would begin. She held out her silver goblet, "Refill that for me, would you?"

"Warrant Officer Matthew Hagan."

Lord Wingate paced back and forth across the fine Illyrian carpet of his new office in the War Ministry. *Matthew Hagan...* The name sounded familiar, but Lord Wingate couldn't quite put a face to it, "Which one was he again?"

Commander Barnes checked the duty roster, "Deputy supply chief, my lord."

"Hmm... deputy supply chief," Lord Wingate still couldn't quite picture the man. It didn't help that the *Celsius* had only just left port when she was shot down, not to mention a good number of the crew were on their first posting. There hadn't been nearly enough time to familiarise himself with the vast majority of his crew. Lord Wingate shrugged and moved on to the crucial question: "Is he related to anyone important?"

"I don't recognise the name," Barnes said, "and I doubt he comes from nobility given his lack of a commission."

Lord Wingate hated having to ask that question; he'd much rather simply ask if a man was competent, but too often, politics got in the way. Sending the wrong man to the wrong posting (even if it was the right posting for that man) could make powerful enemies.

"Put him on the list," Lord Wingate grumbled, and Barnes scribbled the name on a list of people to be assigned later by the ARAF Personnel Department (likely to random postings throughout the fleet). The list was growing at an unsettling rate. "Who's next?"

Barnes moved down to the next name, "Louise Halford, WAVE."

"She's already been taken care of," Lord Wingate said.

"Where did she go?" Barnes asked as he crossed her name off the duty roster.

"The *Dreadnought*," Lord Wingate said.

Barnes paused, "Was it because she dropped that teapot on the bridge? I don't think much of the WAVE myself, but exiling her to the *Dreadnought* is hardly—"

"She *requested* it, Barnes," Lord Wingate interrupted, "She tracked me down at the ball, and all but begged me to accept her transfer request."

Barnes shook his head, "And you *approved* it, my lord?"

"We can't all be heroes, Barnes," Lord Wingate said, "The poor girl was barely three days into her first posting, and she had to make a parachute jump into a combat zone. She needs a nice, quiet posting to recover, and I doubt she'll see much action on the *Dreadnought*. We'll give her a few months to calm her nerves, and then fetch her back out again. No one else need ever know."

"Very well," Barnes moved on to the next entry, "Commander William Travis Hanscom."

Lord Wingate half sighed, half growled; if there was anyone on his ship who deserved reassignment to the *Dreadnought*, it was Hanscom. Of course, if he actually sent Hanscom there, his career would be over before lunch. Hanscom's father, His Excellency High Admiral the Lord Cecil Robert Hanscom, was commander-in-chief of the ARAF, and therefore Lord Wingate's immediate superior, as well as his long-time rival. If Lord Wingate didn't give his son the best posting he could find, the consequences could be dire.

A sudden knock at the door shook Lord Wingate from his contemplation. Barnes was about to get up from the dark mahogany desk that technically wasn't his, but Lord Wingate stopped him with a raised hand. Lord Wingate opened the door and found himself standing face to face with the last person he wanted to see at that moment.

"Lord Hanscom sir," Lord Wingate saluted. Lord Hanscom saluted back. He wasn't a tall man, but he didn't need to be; his presence was intimidating enough without the need of extra height. His face was dominated by a long, aquiline nose and capped with a head of dark brown hair that stubbornly refused to grey with age, despite being nearly a decade older than Lord Wingate. His piercing blue eyes darted past Lord Wingate to scan the interior of the office and focused squarely on Barnes who quickly jumped to his feet and saluted. Lord Hanscom's mouth quirked into a brief sneer before snapping back to its usual scowl.

"Wingate," Lord Hanscom said as he strode into Lord Wingate's office, "I heard you'd just moved in. I thought I'd drop by and see how you're settling into your new office."

"I can't complain, sir," Lord Wingate said, trying not to grit his teeth with frustration.

Lord Hanscom looked about, "It looks rather stark, don't you think, Wingate?" He was right; beyond the desk and carpet, which had come with the room, Lord Wingate's office was still largely bare. There weren't any other chairs in the room aside from the one that came with the desk. There were no bookshelves or liquor cabinets lining the walls, as in most other offices. There was even a number of conspicuous dark patches on the walls where portraits had once hung.

"I've only had the room for a day," Lord Wingate explained, "and I'm busy with something else at the moment."

"Transferring your former crew to other positions in the fleet?" Lord Hanscom said.

"Indeed," Lord Wingate nodded.

"My son, William, was on your crew, was he not Wingate?" Lord Hanscom said, as if happening upon the thought by chance. Lord Wingate knew better. *He's come by to remind me to give his boy a good posting or else!*

"He was indeed, my lord," Lord Wingate said, forcing a cheerful expression, "and I must say, young William has the makings of a fine officer in him."

"Interesting," Lord Hanscom's voice grew dark, like an oncoming storm front, "Because he told me you threatened to transfer him to the *Dreadnought*."

Lord Wingate sighed and dropped all pretense, "Your boy was hungover on duty, and he caused a disturbance on my bridge. The boy has no sense of self-discipline."

"A *disturbance on the bridge?*" Lord Hanscom barked a laugh, "As I understand it, one of those clumsy little WAVE trollops emptied a pot of tea over his head! And when William complained about her conduct, you sent him away and pulled the little chit aside to *soothe her ego.*" Lord Hanscom practically sneered those last few words.

Lord Wingate maintained a calm expression, but inside he was seething with rage. *I should have known young Hanscom would run crying to his father.* "William suspects that you were sweet on the girl," Lord Hanscom went on, "I can only imagine what your *wife* would think if she knew."

"I should think she would approve," Lord Wingate said with a slight grin, "My Amelia served in the WAVE, and I doubt she would have appreciated your boy's behaviour." Was Lord Hanscom actually trying to *blackmail* him? If so, he'd have to do better than that; Amelia was much too smart to believe anything so outrageous.

"Still, threatening to transfer William to the *Dreadnought?* That is rather drastic," Lord Hanscom matched Lord Wingate's grin, "Are you concerned that *your* boy might be getting lonely? I understand Wolfram is serving on the *Dreadnought.*"

Lord Wingate bit his lip to keep from screaming. Lord Hanscom had watched with glee from afar over the last few years as Wolfram's spectacular ineptitude all but ruined the future of the Wingate family name, and now he delighted in rubbing Wolfram's failure in Lord Wingate's face whenever the opportunity presented itself. Lord Wingate had never gotten along with Lord Hanscom, but in the last few years their relationship had degenerated into a game of "whose son is the bigger failure." It was a game Lord Wingate was likely to lose.

"Forgive me, my lord," Barnes spoke up, snapping Lord Wingate out of his rage, "It was most gracious of you to come by, but we really do have quite a bit of work beginning to pile up."

"Yes, I suppose I should let you go," Lord Hanscom said, turning to leave. He stopped halfway to the door and paused, "Commander Barnes, was it?"

"Yes my lord."

"You know, Captain Alverson of the *Dawn Spear* is in need of a new executive officer before the exercises next month," Lord Hanscom said, "Shall I give him your name?"

"That is a very kind offer, my lord," Barnes said, "I will consider it."

Lord Hanscom grinned, "Good. Very good," He closed the door behind him as he left.

Lord Wingate breathed an audible sigh of relief. "Impeccable timing there, Barnes," he said after a moments pause.

"I thought you could use an escape, my lord," Barnes said, taking his seat again.

"Good instincts," Lord Wingate groaned. Lord Hanscom was tedious, petty, and arrogant, but worst of all, he was competent. He had been the architect of a number of major victories during the Analerian campaigns of the war against Hadvar that had only just concluded two months earlier. Hanscom had been particularly upset when the peace was declared; he had been putting the finishing touches on a massive invasion plan that now would never see the light of day.

"*Dawn Spear* is a fine ship," Lord Wingate said after a short pause, "And Richard Alverson is a fine captain."

"I'm sure that's true," Barnes said without looking up from the duty roster.

"You should take Lord Hanscom up on his offer," Lord Wingate said more emphatically.

"I probably should," Barnes still didn't look up.

"...It would be a good career move," Lord Wingate added, "especially with the exercises coming up in—"

"I told him I would consider it," Barnes interrupted, still not looking up from the duty roster, "and I've considered it."

"Barnes," Lord Wingate sighed with exasperation, "Just take the damn offer!"

Barnes was silent for a moment. Then he stood and said, "I cannot do that, my lord."

"Barnes, think about what you're doing!" Lord Wingate said, "You'll be throwing your career away if you refuse Lord Hanscom's offer!"

"Not necessarily," Barnes said, "You could give the position to Lord Hanscom's son instead. It'll placate the man and give me an excuse not to take his offer. I suspect that is what he intended by making the offer in your presence, anyhow," his mouth twisted into a devilish smirked, "Besides, I'm certain there will be plenty of opportunities for Commander Hanscom to disgrace himself during the exercises."

Lord Wingate chuckled, "You're quite a devious young man, Barnes!"

Barnes smiled, "I learned from the best, my lord."

"But I still don't understand why you're refusing Lord Hanscom's offer," Lord Wingate said.

Barnes shrugged and coloured slightly, "I am your man, my lord."

Lord Wingate smiled. Some people were just loyal like that, "You know, I think you'd make a good husband for my daughter Marion," Lord Wingate said.

"Y-you think so, my lord?" Barnes laughed awkwardly.

"Oh yes," Lord Wingate said, "just as soon as I can get her to stop mooning over Bowman."

"Right..." Barnes rolled his eyes.

"I'll be sure to introduce you to my family when we head south," Lord Wingate said as he walked over to look out one of the windows.

"My lord, you..." Barnes paused in the middle of his thought, "We're going south?"

"Yes," Lord Wingate's eyes narrowed, "I need to examine the remains of that Isafari artillery battery up close."

"This is about Lady Batu's debriefing, isn't it?" Barnes asked as he came to Lord Wingate's side.

"Precisely," Lord Wingate said, "We need to know exactly how Isafar got their hands on our own military equipment." The Lady Batu had been debriefed extensively the day before; Lord Wingate had made absolutely sure to get as much information as possible before sending her and her people back to Isafar with Ambassador Malavar. This time, the interview had been a much smoother affair, what with Malavar acting as translator, but a number of unsettling revelations had also come to light.

Aside from the anticipated cultural misunderstandings and confusion about who was really in charge, much of Lady Batu's new information directly contradicted her old statements. She claimed to know nothing at all of the artillery in the salt flats, despite claiming to have given the order to fire in her first interview. She also insisted that the Isafari scouts that had attacked the Auroran trenches weren't under her command, despite declaring in her first interview that she had ordered a raid. It was as though she had become a completely different woman.

"We had to use two translators for her first debriefing," Barnes said, "and I rather suspect that the Isafari gentleman was doing more than just translating. Something is afoot in Isafar."

"You think the Isafari translator we employed may have been a political operative with an agenda," It was hardly a question—Lord Wingate had reached the same conclusion.

"It smacks of conspiracy, my lord," Barnes said.

"It may very well be," Lord Wingate agreed, "but on what scale? We know precious little about the internal politics of Isafar. Even Malavar admitted that most of his knowledge is woefully out of date. We have no idea if we're looking at the persecution of a dissident or just some factional pissing contest. Hell, for all we know, the translator may have simply been scapegoating his mistress in order to secure better treatment for himself," Lord Wingate shrugged, "It is also possible that the Lady Batu could be putting on a guise of victimhood in order to win our support."

"You think she could be playing the damsel in distress to provoke a foreign intervention?" Barnes said.

"We must consider *every* possibility," Lord Wingate said.

"Yes, I suppose we must," Barnes furrowed his brow in thought, "I suppose... she could be in league with Bowman."

Lord Wingate laughed, "Now that I very much doubt!"

"But it is still possible," Barnes insisted.

"It's not possible. The man is an imbecile of the highest order," Lord Wingate shook his head, "In any case, I wouldn't be too worried about our Mister Bowman. He's well on his way to irrelevance."

Paul walked through the doors at the top of the stairs and entered the grand interior of the Capitol's railway station. It was like a miniature version of the Great Hall in the Dawn Palace: great columns rising up out of the floor to meet the vaulted ceiling and fine stone tiles polished so that he could nearly see his reflection staring back up at him. At the back wall was an array of booths, each with a line of people trailing back nearly half the length of the room, and looming over the ticket booths was a large sign displaying the rail schedule.

At least, that was what Paul thought it said. He couldn't read the words.

Paul had never actually learned how to read. He had never needed to. Loading and offloading cargo didn't require any real skill beyond a good grip and a strong pair of legs. Paul could recognize numbers and he had a basic understanding of arithmetic, which allowed him to handle some engineering jobs (and make sure he wasn't being cheated out of his pay), but when it came to actual words, Paul was completely flummoxed.

Paul set his suitcase down beside him and fished into the pocket of his uniform jacket to pull out the yellow scrap of paper that was his ticket. It was covered in the same unintelligible symbols. The only thing he could make out was a set of numbers: *8:15*, which Paul recognized as the time his train was to depart. *Well, it's a start.*

There was a large wrought-iron clock sitting atop the board with the rail schedule. Paul squinted. The big hand was on the eight, and the small hand was almost on the two. Just shy of 8:10. *I only have five minutes to figure out where I need to go.* Paul looked back down at his ticket, and then back up at the rail schedule. He could probably figure out which train was his if he compared the letters, but that would take time, and he was rapidly running out of time.

"Are you lost, mister?"

Paul looked down at the shrill voice. It was a young boy, maybe eight or nine years old. "It's my first time going through this station," Paul said with a smile. He couldn't help it—kids always put a smile on his face, "I'm not quite sure where to go just yet."

"What happened to your eye, mister?" the boy asked.

Paul sat down on his suitcase, "Well, it's quite a story," he began, "It all started when—"

"Hey!" the boy eyes lit up and he almost shouted, "Are you Paul Bowman? The Hero of the Southern Gap?"

"Shh!" Paul frantically hushed the boy and glanced about to make sure nobody else had noticed him, "Not so loud, kid! You'll give me away."

"Oooh! Are you on a secret mission?" the boy lowered his voice, but not his enthusiasm.

Paul got an idea, "Yeah," he said with a grin, "I'm on a secret mission, so you can't tell anyone I was here. But I *could* use your help."

"Really?" the boy was almost bursting with excitement.

Paul beckoned for the boy to lean in closer, "You seem like a smart kid. Now I need to catch a train, but I've never been in this station before, and all I have to go on is this ticket," Paul pulled out his ticket and held it out for the boy "So I need *you* to help me figure out where I need to go next."

"Wow!" The boy leaned in to examine the ticket. He read slowly, sometimes stumbling over the larger words, "Royal Railway Company... One way... Capitol to Norvell!" The boy looked up with a broad, toothy smile.

"That's right," Paul nodded, "That's the train I need to catch. But what else does it say?"

The boy looked again, "Uh... 8:15... And I think that's today's date..."

"Does it say anything about where the train is boarding?" Paul asked more urgently.

"I don't know," the boy said, "I don't think it says here..." Paul's gaze flicked nervously up to the clock.

Paul was about to speak again when a shrill whistle cut him off. He leaped to his feet and reached over his shoulder for a rifle that wasn't there. He panicked for a moment when he couldn't find it. *What the hell am I thinking?* Paul blinked, *This isn't the Southern Gap!* Paul took a deep breath to calm his racing heart and bring himself back to reality.

A few more blasts of the whistle, and a metallic voice filled the station, "Attention. The 8:15 running express to Norvell will be departing in five minutes. All passengers please report to platform six."

"Hey! Norvell," The boy perked up, "That's your train! Platform six!" He pointed to a wide arched doorway beside the ticket booths, "Right up there!"

Paul breathed a sigh of relief. He picked up his suitcase and ruffled the boy's hair, "Thanks, kid, you've been a big help!" He fished into his coat pocket, pulled out a gold crown, and tossed it to the boy. The boy caught the coin, and his jaw dropped at the value of it.

"Remember," Paul said with a wink, "It's a secret mission."

The boy stiffened and made what he probably thought was a salute, "Yes sir!" he turned around and dashed back to the line in front of the ticket booth. Paul hurried through the arched doorway. Out of the corner of his eye, Paul noticed the kid tugging the sleeve of one of the men in the line, "Papa! Papa," he could hear the kid say, "you'll never guess who I just met!"

Paul emerged onto a walkway looking down over a wide array of train platforms. A stairway led down to each platform with a sign hanging over each one. Luckily, those signs had numbers so Paul could tell which was which. Paul hurried down the stairway to the platform six where a train waited.

This passenger train was completely different from the cargo train that had transported Paul and the Forty Second Infantry to the Southern Gap. For one thing, this train was painted a deep crimson, and there was real glass in the windows. Through the windows, Paul could see well-dressed people sitting in finely upholstered seats, being waited on by uniformed attendants. Paul showed his ticket to the conductor standing by the door and stepped inside the train.

Once inside the train, another man in uniform approached him and asked for his ticket. The porter's eyes widened as soon as Paul showed the ticket. He frantically bowed and motioned for Paul to follow him. Paul followed the man down the aisle and into another train car. This car was vastly different; the corridor was much narrower, with windows on one side and doors to private compartments on the other. The porter opened one of the doors and motioned for Paul to enter.

The interior of the private compartment instantly reminded Paul of the Dawn Palace. The walls were varnished wood with gear patterns worked into the panels. Gears seemed to be the latest fashion nowadays; supposedly they symbolized the industrial might of Aurora. A pair of benches upholstered with fine leather faced each other along the walls with the window in between. Thick red carpet covered the floor, and a pair of wire-and-glass electric candles hung from the ceiling.

Paul sat on one of the benches and opened his suitcase. It had been packed for him the night before his departure by palace servants. Inside was a spare uniform, a leather purse with a few hundred gold crowns inside, and a small green book. Paul couldn't read the title, but he knew what it said well enough. He had seen Lieutenant Stuart reading a book that looked exactly like it. *Her Majesty's Guidebook of Military Regulations.*

Paul reached into his jacket and pulled out his letter of orders, given to him by the Queen. Not that it mattered, since he wouldn't be able to read it either. *A fine captain I'm shaping up to be,* Paul thought with a sad laugh, *I can't even read my own orders!* Paul stuffed the letter back into his jacket pocket and closed his suitcase. He couldn't bear to look any longer.

The door of the compartment slid open, and Paul looked up to see a woman wearing a tooled leather corset with brass gears sewn into it, a too-short jacket that left the top of her bosom exposed, and a ridiculous pinstriped skirt.

"Paul!" Isabelle Fairchild squealed with delight, "It seems we shall be sharing a cabin for this journey! How auspicious!"

"Right," Paul groaned, "very suspicious," There was no way in hell this was a coincidence.

Fairchild laughed, "Dear me! How very clever!" Paul blinked. Had he said something funny?

Fairchild flounced into the cabin and plopped herself down onto the seat right beside Paul as a pair of uniformed men wheeled a large trunk into the cabin after her, "So Paul," Fairchild leaned uncomfortably close, "The latest gossip has it that you have been made up to captain! Are you off to assume your new posting?"

"Yeah," Paul mumbled, trying his hardest not to meet her eyes.

"Oh how exciting!" Fairchild giggled, "Did I not say that there were more heroic deeds yet to be done in your future? I don't suppose you could give a little hint about what the future holds for the Hero of the Southern Gap?"

Paul glanced nervously down at his jacket to the pocket that held his unopened letter of orders. "I... uh," Paul stammered, "It's a secret."

"Oooh, right," Fairchild blushed, "military secrets and all that. Do please forgive me for being so forward with you!" she brushed away a stray lock of wavy red hair that had slipped out from beneath an outrageous feathered hat. Paul blinked. Was the girl actually *flirting* with him?

Off in the distance, a steam whistle shrieked, and Paul felt the train lurch into motion. Paul stared intently out the window as the train rolled out of the station; it was as good a way as any to ignore Fairchild. Apparently this was one of those new trains, the really fast ones that were always bragging about speed records in the broadsheets. The twelve-hundred mile journey to Norvell would take just under sixteen hours. *Sixteen hours locked in a room with this insufferable little trollop.*

The train left the station by way of a large dark tunnel that had been bored directly through the mountains to the north of the Capitol. After a few minutes, the train emerged on the other side, and Paul's view was replaced with the high slopes of the Mountains of Dawn in the west.

For what seemed like hours, the high mountain slopes marched past the train, and with them, the gaping entrances to the numerous mines that riddled the mountains. Those mines were the only known source of fulgurite ore in the world, and they were a vital resource for the airship industry, as well as the Auroran military. Many of the mines looked abandoned.

It was hardly a revelation. Paul had long heard rumors about the increasing cost of fuel, and it wasn't hard to figure out what was behind those rising prices. But it was a different thing to actually see all the abandoned mines. Sooner or later, the fulgurite deposits would dry up completely. Sure there was the occasional talk about synthetic fulgurite or reprocessing spent fuel, but those rumors never amounted to anything real.

What's going to happen when it all runs out? Paul wondered. It would be the end of the airfreight industry—that much was obvious—and probably the ARAF as well. *That'll definitely be a problem,* Paul thought. He knew as well as anyone that Auroran dominance of the sky was what had kept Hadvar from crushing Aurora by sheer weight of numbers during the war. Without airships, Aurora's largest strength as a nation would vanish overnight, and if Hadvar attacked again...

"Our land cannot possibly fail with you watching over us!" Fairchild sighed. Paul glanced back at the woman. Had she been talking this whole time? "Why you've already donned your uniform in anticipation of your new command! Such dedication to duty!"

Paul looked down at his uniform. It had been custom fitted for him, along with his spare in the suitcase, which meant that it was slightly less uncomfortable then the temporary one he had worn several days earlier. It was a brilliant green with polished brass buttons and a golden braid over his left shoulder. Supposedly that braid marked him as a captain. Or was it the four golden bars on his cuffs? Paul shrugged, "I don't actually have anything else to wear."

"Really?" Fairchild gasped dramatically, "To abjure civilian garb completely! Truly you are an inspiration to us all!"

Paul slouched into his seat. Fairchild continued to babble about heroism and duty and other nonsense. After a while, she opened up her trunk and pulled out her typesetting machine, and that awful ticking began once again.

It was strange, but Paul didn't hate Fairchild. He certainly didn't *like* her—she was annoying as hell, and she had a miraculous talent of hearing the exact opposite of what you told her—but try though he might, Paul couldn't bring himself to hate the poor girl.

She honestly believes that I'm some amazing hero of legend, Paul thought. *What will she think when she learns the truth?*

Chapter VI

The Dreadnought

LIEUTENANT James Butler sat outside the Norvell Train Depot, reading his pulp novel by the light of the streetlamp. *Penny dreadfuls* most people called them, and not without reason; each chapter usually cost one copper penny, and most of them weren't worth the cheap pulp they were printed on. Then again, a few gems were always hidden among the rubbish heap, and it was well worth slogging through the mire of mediocrity to dig them out.

This story was certainly not one of them.

Butler didn't mind; they were just so much fun to read! This one took place in one of those bleak post-disaster futures that had become so popular lately. The hero was the same lantern-jawed titan with a heart of gold and a mysterious past from a thousand other stories. He and his annoying kid sidekick were hounded all across the land by a cadre of nameless villains with inconsistent motivations. And to top it off, it was full of ham-fisted and poorly executed religious symbolism. It was a bloody masterpiece!

A steam whistle sounded inside the station, and Butler checked his pocket watch. 23:55. *Right on schedule.* He folded back his current page and tucked the book into his jacket pocket. There would be time to enjoy it later. Plenty of time. Nobody on the *Dreadnought* lacked for free time.

Taking his time, Butler climbed the steps to the main entrance of the station. He was there to collect two new crew members who would be arriving from the Capitol. One of them was a new WAVE girl, and the other was their new captain. *And not just any captain!* Butler reminded himself, *Paul Bowman himself!*

Butler certainly didn't believe the wild tales about Paul Bowman that had been filling up the news journals. The broadsheets were just as much fun to read as pulp novels, and sometimes nearly as accurate! But the Queen herself had raised Paul Bowman to captain, and the Queen did nothing without good reason, right? That had to count for something.

It would be good to have a captain aboard the *Dreadnought* again. The ship had never been a bastion of discipline, but since Captain Hannegan's retirement a few months ago, the *Dreadnought* had descended into near anarchy. Officially, Lieutenant Commander Vaughn was in charge, but hardly anyone on the ship took their beleaguered executive officer seriously—at least, when they could afford not to; Vaughn could be... intimidating.

That was probably why Butler had been sent to collect Captain Bowman; as the *Dreadnought's* supply chief, he was the only person who had a good relationship with every individual department. Anyone who needed anything on the ship had to go to him for it, and he was usually able to get it. Even if it was... less than legal. If the crew saw Captain Bowman arriving with Butler, the new captain would likely reap some of the goodwill the crew held for Butler, thereby making his job a little easier. Besides, sending Vaughn to collect him wouldn't exactly be putting their best foot forward.

At the top of the stairs, Butler looked up to check the arrivals board. The 23:55 from the Capitol would be coming in at platform two. Butler shrugged and plopped down onto a bench beside the entrance. The passengers would have to come this way, so why bother chasing them down? Butler smiled a self-satisfied grin; one of his talents was the ability to do as little work as possible.

Soon, the passengers from the train began to trickle into the foyer through the arched doorway that led to the train platforms, the dull hum of conversation following with them. Butler's eyes scanned each passenger. Most were well dressed and evidently well moneyed.

The men all wore three-piece suits, and the women they escorted wore long dresses that they had probably been told were elegant. Butler ignored the women, of course; women were pretty, but *men* were beautiful.

Butler's fingers brushed across the two golden bars on the cuffs of his jacket. Not too long ago there had been three bars, back when he had been a full commander. Before he and his lover had been caught in the act. *Before the bastard sold me out to protect his damn reputation!* The flash of anger was gone as quickly as it had come. *If I had been the one with noble connections,* Butler surmised,*I probably would have sold him out as well.* Besides, he couldn't stay angry at a pair of shoulders like that.

Among the passengers, Butler noticed a pair of men in featureless black robes with shaven heads that marked them as clergy. He smirked maliciously at them; a pack of arrogant moralizing hypocrites. And to think that he had actually wanted to join the Church at one point during his youth. Of course, his local vicar had put a stop to such dreams after a young James had confessed his... unconventional desires. *A good thing too,* Butler noted, *given all the recent rumors about vicars buggering young boys.* Butler was a lecher through and through, but children—that was just disgusting.

A young woman in the crowd caught Butler's notice; she was of average height for a woman, which was to say she was about even with Butler's height, with a soft blue-eyed face and blond hair tied back in a ponytail. She was probably very beautiful. Of course what he was really looking at were her clothes: a bright green jacket with a silver pair of wings embroidered over the left breast, an ankle-length skirt, and a green scarf tied neatly around her neck. The uniform of the Women's Airborne Volunteer Echelon.

The WAVE girl flagged him down, apparently noticing his uniform. Butler stood and crossed the foyer to meet her, "Excuse me, miss," he said as soon as he was close enough not to shout, "Are you here for the *Dreadnought?*"

"Yes, I am," the girl said, setting a small suitcase at her feet.

"I'm Lieutenant James Butler," he said, extending a hand, "I'm the supply chief on board the *Dreadnought.* I've been sent to collect you."

"Louise Halford," the girl curtsied, but didn't shake his hand. She didn't even seem to *notice* it, "of the Women's Airborne Volunteer Echelon."

Butler pointed to her suitcase, "Is this the only luggage you brought with you?"

"Yes," Halford nodded, "This is everything."

"Excellent," Butler picked up the suitcase, "One more thing: have you seen a tall man with an eye patch?"

"Uh, n-no, I've not," Halford stammered, no doubt picturing someone truly frightening.

At that moment, Butler noticed a figure emerging from the arched doorway with a small suitcase. He was tall, he wore an eye patch, and if that wasn't enough of a clue, he wore the uniform of a captain. "Nevermind," Butler said, setting the suitcase back down, "I think that's him."

Bowman looked like he was moving in a hurry, but Butler intercepted him and struck a salute, "Captain Bowman, sir!"

Bowman looked up suddenly and started toward Butler at an urgent pace, "You with the fleet?" he asked urgently.

"Y-yeah," Butler said, awkwardly lowering his salute, "I'm Lieutenant Butler, supply chief of the *Dreadnought*."

Bowman walked past him, "Good. Nice to meet you. Let's get going."

"Why the rush, sir?" Butler said, struggling to keep up with the man's pace.

"I just want to get out of here before—" Bowman started, before a shrill voice cut him off from across the foyer: "Paul! Oh Paul!"

Butler looked back to see a young woman hustling down the stairs as fast as her ridiculous pinstriped skirt would permit her. "Ah hell," Bowman groaned, and suddenly Butler understood his haste.

"An admirer?" Butler said.

"Worse," Bowman responded, "a journalist."

"God help us," Butler sighed.

"Paul," the woman said as she caught up with them, "I was worried you were going to leave before I could wish you farewell!"

"Yeah," Bowman grumbled, "wouldn't that be a shame." Butler suppressed a laugh.

"And is this one of your new crew?" Fairchild turned to Butler, "Are you not going to introduce me, Paul?"

"Right," Bowman said, "Miss Fairchild, this is... What was your name again?"

"Lieutenant James Butler," he said and made a respectful bow, "I'm to be Captain Bowman's supply chief."

"Enchanted," Fairchild giggled and extended a hand which Butler kissed, "My name is Isabelle Fairchild. You can call me Isabelle. All my friends call me Isabelle!" Butler noticed Bowman rolling his eyes (well, eye *singular*) at that last sentence.

"I understand you are a journalist, Isabelle," Butler said, affecting an air of cordiality.

"Indeed I am," Fairchild's eyes lit up with enthusiasm, Perhaps you read the piece I wrote about Captain Bowman's heroic victory at the Southern Gap? It made the front page of the *Queen's Messenger* as I recall."

"That was *yours?*" Butler said, remembering an absolutely uproarious pack of jingoistic nonsense.

"My proudest work to date," Fairchild beamed, "In fact, I've only just now finished *another* piece touching on our Mister Bowman." Her eyes traced Bowman up and down, as though admiring a statue in a gallery.

"I can hardly wait to read it," Butler said; judging by the first article, this new one would be just as fun!

"I offered to show Mister Bowman my final draft, but would you believe it? The man *refused* to read it," Fairchild said, her voice full of fond exasperation, "He says it wouldn't be right for him to read it before it is published. Such integrity!"

"Well now, Isabelle," Butler said, "it was lovely to meet you, but I'm afraid we must be on our way."

"Yes, I understand," Fairchild sighed in a manner she probably thought was romantic, "The call of duty waits for no man! I'd best be off as well. I must get to the wire office if my story is to make the overnight edition." She twirled about and scampered away toward the exit; a poor bellhop followed after her with a cart of luggage, "Farewell, dear Paul!"

"My god," Butler whispered as soon as Fairchild was out of earshot, "How can you stand that woman?"

"I have no idea," Paul said, watching Fairchild vanish out the doorway into the street. "...Butler, was it?"

Butler saluted, "Yes sir, Lieutenant James Butler, supply chief, the *Dreadnought.*"

Bowman saluted back, "I'm Paul. Paul Bowman. I guess I'm your new captain."

"So you are," Butler smiled. It looked like Bowman was going to be a laid-back, easygoing sort of captain, a perfect fit for the *Dreadnought,* "Well then Captain, if you would care to follow me."

Butler led Captain Bowman over to Halford. The girl had taken her suitcase over to a small stone bench at the side of the foyer, "Captain, this is Louise Halford of the Women's Airbourne Volunteer Echelon. She will be joining us on the *Dreadnought.*"

Halford jumped to her feet and curtsied, "How do you do, Captain?" Bowman gave a slight bow, "Pleased to meet you, Miss Halford."

"Right," Butler said as he picked up Halford's suitcase, "Let's get going!"

Butler, Bowman, and Halford trooped out of the station and into the street. It was about a mile walk to the aerodrome where the *Dreadnought* waited. A few scraps of dirty winter snow still lingered on the streets, but otherwise the night was clear and warm for the season.

"Forgive me for asking sir," Butler said, "but it doesn't sound like you come from nobility."

"Not in the slightest," Captain Bowman said, sounding almost proud, "What about you?"

"No sir," Butler said, "at least not quite. My father is head of logistics for *Newton and Sons*; the Fleet's chief civilian contractor. He's got a fair bit of pull, but it's not quite on the same level as nobility." *If it weren't for him,* Butler thought ruefully, *I would have probably been drummed out of the service altogether. Maybe even jailed for buggery,* "Do you have any family, Captain?"

"None left, as far as I know," Captain Bowman said.

"Did you lose 'em during the war?"

Captain Bowman was silent for a moment, "Yeah, I guess you could say that. How about you? You must have lost a few friends during the war."

"Not really," Butler said awkwardly, "We didn't actually see a whole lot of action on the *Dreadnought*. Hell, *you* probably saw more action during the war than we did!"

"I wasn't *in* the war," Captain Bowman said.

"Really?" Butler said, "But... you're the most famous soldier in the realm!"

"I was only recruited after the war was over," Captain Bowman explained, "And I wasn't a soldier, I was a conscript."

The journey to the aerodrome took about twenty minutes. The aerodrome was a colossal building with a number of wide berths carved into its side at regular intervals; most of them were occupied. Butler pointed toward the airship in the nearest berth, "Right there.

That's your new command."

The *Dreadnought* wasn't a very large airship, just under fifty meters long with only three-and-a-half decks. Guns peeked through an outer shield-hull on her side, mimicking the broadside batteries of a surface warship—a spectacularly useless configuration given that the Auroran monopoly on air power made airship-to-airship combat a thing of the imagination. The emblem of the ARAF, a pair of wings spreading out from the golden eight-pointed Star of Dawn on a field of green, was painted on the shield-hull and illuminated by arrays of bright calcium lamps from the aerodrome.

She was a piece of junk.

Butler glanced back at Captain Bowman. The man was staring at the *Dreadnought* with wonder twinkling in his eye. "I am the wind," Butler heard him say. *What did he mean by that?*

Butler shrugged. Captain Bowman's wonder would wear off in good time, "Follow me, Captain."

A single glass candle on the ceiling lit the bridge of the *Dreadnought,* casting large pools of shadow behind the monitors and exposed piping inside the walls. In one corner, a large metal bulkhead that really should have been installed by now had been propped over the heating vent so as to direct the flow of warmth towards the centre of the bridge where five men sat playing a game of cards. The men were officers: three lieutenants and two ensigns. A full house.

"Fifteen for two," Lieutenant Junior-Grade Malcolm Barlowe announced as he laid the five of flags on the empty fuel drum that had been repurposed as a table. Everyone nodded as he took his points on the ivory pegboard.

Lieutenant Junior Grade Archibald Hakefeldt considered his hand for a moment before playing the six of coins, "One-and-twenty for three."

"Hey, wait a minute! You can't do that," young Ensign Powell Wagner cried out, "This isn't blackjack. One-and-twenty doesn't earn any points."

"He's not getting points for one-and-twenty," Ensign Marius Noel Hamilton said, "He's getting the points for a run of three." He pointed to the seven of pikes that Wagner himself had played before Barlowe's five of flags, "See there? Five, six, seven. Run for three."

"But they aren't in order," Wagner insisted, "It goes seven, five, and then six; that's not a run."

"They don't have to be in order, Wagner," Lieutenant Wolfram Howard Wingate said, slouching in the captain's chair and not looking up from the cigarette he was rolling, "We're not playing by army rules. Runs scored during the count don't need to be in sequence, just consecutive." He looked up, "Take your points, Archie."

"Sorry, kid," Archie shook his head at Wagner as he took his three points. Wagner was just about at that age where boys want to prove themselves worthy to be considered men. Unfortunately, Wagner had never attended the Auroran Royal Military Academy at South Sands, which marked him as something of an outsider, and a favored target of abuse from the rest of the bridge officers. He was also, in no uncertain terms, an idiot.

"Nine-and-twenty for four," Hamilton said with a grin as he played the eight of wings for a run of four.

Everyone looked at Wagner. The kid scratched behind his ear; a habit of his when he was embarrassed. "Go," he mumbled without playing a card.

"Go," Barlowe said with a nod, followed by Archie.

"One for the go," Hamilton said, taking his point as the count was reset. The game continued.

"You think we'll get orders soon?" Wagner asked after a few moments.

"Nope," Wolfram said bluntly while smoothing out the tobacco in his cigarette.

"God, I hope not," Barlowe laughed and took a swig of something from a small hip flask in his jacket, "The war's finally over, and I'm not sorry I missed the whole damn thing."

"Me neither," Hamilton said.

"Yeah," Archie said, "I don't see us getting orders any time soon."

"What about this new captain we're getting?" Wagner said, "I heard he's supposed to be a big hero from the war."

"He can't have been much of a hero if he got himself shuffled off to this dump," Barlowe laughed again, stowing the hip flask back inside his jacket.

"Why are you so eager for orders anyways kid?," Wolfram said, "Learn to enjoy your downtime. God knows we've got plenty of it."

"You never know," Wagner shrugged, "we *could* get orders."

"We're a *peacetime* fleet now kid," Archie said, "What could they even order us to do?"

"Well, what about these fleet exercises coming up next month?" Wagner said, "That should be pretty exciting,"

"Yeah!" Archie laughed, "Like *we're* getting into those exercises." He glanced down at his empty hand and then around the table, "Is everyone out?" Barlowe, Hamilton and Wagner nodded, "Right. Show your hands, and call your points."

The four players collected their cards, while Wolfram continued rolling his cigarette. Since he was on the dealer's left, Wagner showed his hand first. "Six, seven, eight, nine, and a three on the deck. Run of four, and two fifteens. Eight points." Wagner took his points, and Barlowe showed his hand.

While Barlowe called his points, Wingate leaned forwards to borrow Archie's matchbook. As he lit his cigarette, he whispered in Archie's ear, "Muggins. Flush on Wagner."

Archie didn't react right away, but discreetly glanced at Wagner's hand. Sure enough, all four cards matched the suit of the three of pikes on top of the deck. A flush, and Wagner had neglected to claim the four points he might have earned from it. Archie nodded subtly at Wingate, who leaned back casually in the captain's chair to enjoy his cigarette.

"Muggins!" Archie called out as soon as everyone else had declared and taken their points. Barlowe and Hamilton immediately glanced down at their hands, frantically checking to see if they had missed any points. Wagner just looked confused; this was probably the first time he had encountered the Muggins rule. Archie continued, "Wagner had a flush."

"W-what?" Wagner glanced down at his hand.

"All your cards are pikes," Archie said, pointing out the suits of the cards in Wagner's hand, "Deck card too. That's a flush. Four points."

"So I get four extra points?" Wagner's eyes lit up.

"No," Barlowe nodded his head to indicate Archie, "*He* gets four extra points. *You* didn't declare your flush when you had the chance."

"Oh come on!" Wagner protested, but Wolfram cut him off.

"You can forfeit if you want, but if you want to keep playing with us; you play by our rules. Clear?"

"Alright," Wagner said resignedly. Archie took his stolen points and let his free hand wander down out of sight of the other players to exchange a secret handshake with Wingate.

He had been Archie's best friend since the first day they met at the South Sands Academy. Wolfram was one of the most brilliant people he had ever met; he had a quick mind, a good eye for tactics, and an inexhaustible reserve of charisma. Paradoxically, he also had incredibly low marks in almost every class. It hadn't helped that during the bi-annual South Sands war games, he had regularly disregarded the established objectives, usually leading to mass confusion. If he hadn't been the son of Lord Orpheus Chester Wingate himself, Wolfram probably would have been expelled several times over.

Archie had been almost the exact opposite: a well-organized model student, but, he freely admitted, one without the same spark of brilliance that Wolfram had been born with. He was also common-born; his father was a fisherman and his mother worked in a textile mill down in Newport. They had spent years saving up the money to send Archie to South Sands. Of course, once he got there, Archie quickly noticed that being common-born instantly put him at the bottom of the social hierarchy. All of the other cadets at South Sands saw him as little better than a jumped-up pauper.

All of the other cadets, that was, except Wolfram. For whatever reason, Wolfram had never treated Archie as anything less than an equal, and Archie had reciprocated in kind. They had rigged wagers together, they had raided the commissary after hours together. Wolfram had even helped Archie shed his native thick Newport accent, and in return Archie had helped Wolfram cheat on his final examinations.

When Wolfram had been given his current position as tactical officer of the *Dreadnought* (by his lord father no less), Archie had immediately requested a position on the *Dreadnought* as well. *If I had known what this ship was,* Archie thought...

...He glanced at Wolfram; he'd had the worst of the deal by far. Archie had just made a foolish mistake out of loyalty to a friend; Wolfram had been *betrayed*, and by his own father. That had to hurt worse than anything Archie had suffered. He sighed, *Hell, if I had known what this ship was, I still would have requested a position here.* He smiled. It was the least he could do for a friend.

The sound of footsteps coming up the stairwell to the bridge brought the game to an abrupt halt. Five pairs of eyes turned to stare at the door, and then with a flurry of motion, the cards and ivory pegboard vanished from sight. Archie saw Wolfram extinguish his cigarette with his thumb and forefinger and wave his free hand to disperse the smoke. If the wrong person caught them slacking off... *If Vaughn catches us like this...* Archie shuddered.

Finally, a figure entered the bridge, and everyone breathed a sigh of relief. It wasn't Vaughn; it was just one of the WAVE girls. "Good evening officers!" the girl said cheerfully as she approached.

"And a very good evening to you, my darling," Barlowe said with a broad and inviting smile, "It's Jesslyn, isn't it?"

"Yes, sir," The girl curtsied, "Jesslyn Meyers of the Women's Airbourne Volunteer Echelon. And you, sir?"

Barlowe made an exaggerated bow, "Malcolm Barlowe, leftenant junior grade," he said, "And I have the particular honour to serve as the boatswain of this noble vessel."

Archie, Wolfram ,and Hamilton sniggered at Barlowe's act. There wasn't any honour to be had on this dump of an airship and there never would be. That was the point.

"Oh, how ...exciting!" Meyers giggled and then composed herself, "Would any of you gentlemen care for anything from the commissary?"

"Well now," Barlowe said, still working his charms, "I suppose that would depend on what you're offering, wouldn't it?"

Meyers blushed, "Oh yes, of course. There's tea and coffee. I believe the kitchen is closed for the night, but I think I could fix something light from the pantry..." She trailed off awkwardly, blushing like a rose.

"I could go for coffee," Barlowe said, "I think we could all use a little something to keep us warm."

"Yeah," Hamilton said, "coffee sounds good."

"I'll take coffee too," Archie said.

"One for me as well," Wolfram said.

"None for me, thanks," Wagner said. The kid still hadn't managed to pick up a taste for coffee. Archie shook his head. That boy was going to make a terrible officer.

"You think you can manage four coffees, darling?" Barlowe grinned.

"Of course!" Meyers curtsied eagerly, "I'll be back before you know it!"

Barlowe watched the WAVE girl scurry back down the stairwell, and then sauntered back to his seat and plopped down with a devilish grin. His eye gleamed mischievously, "Ten crowns says I can give her a fat belly by week's end," he said.

Archie and Hamilton laughed uproariously, and Wagner quickly followed suit. Archie fished into his open jacket to produce his purse,

"I'll take that bet!" he grinned.

"I'll double you," Hamilton said; he was a relative newcomer to the crew, but he was quickly earning a reputation as a gambler, "Twenty crowns!"

Barlowe's eyes lit up at Hamilton's offer, "I like the sound of that!"

"Gentlemen!" Wolfram's bellow cut through the merriment like a gas-torch through butter, "You ought to be ashamed of yourselves!" Everyone fell silent, and Archie was suddenly acutely aware that his best friend was also the only full lieutenant in the room, and therefore the ranking officer on the bridge. According to regulations, his word was law.

"In all my days," Wolfram continued in a deadly serious tone, "never have I seen such an amateurish wager!" His mouth quirked into a broad grin and a round of laughter burst up around the table, "I'll draw up a ledger," Wolfram said, producing a small book with a mocking flourish, "and we'll establish this wager like gentlemen."

Archie slipped his purse back inside his jacket as Wolfram drew up the book. "Alright," Wolfram began, "we will each lay money on how long we think it will take for our esteemed Mister Malcolm Barlowe to seduce Miss Jesslyn Meyers. Mal, I assume I can put you down for one week?"

"That's right, twenty crowns on one week," Barlowe said, meeting Hamilton's eye with a smirk.

"Ten on two weeks," Archie fired right back, "Nobody works that quickly."

"You haven't seen how quickly I can work," Barlowe's eyebrows danced lasciviously.

"Put me down for twenty crowns on *three* weeks," Hamilton said.

Barlowe sighed with mock-indignation, "I am surrounded by sceptics."

"I'll wager ten crowns on one week," Wagner said, producing his purse.

"There. At least someone believes me," Barlowe said, fondly ruffling Wagner's hair, "Put your purse away, kid. That comes later."

"So," Wolfram said as he reviewed the book, "Barlowe bets twenty on one week, Wagner bets ten on one week, Archie bets ten on two weeks, and Hamilton bets twenty on three weeks," He looked up, "Is that accurate so far?" Everyone nodded.

Wolfram made one more note in his book, "Right then, I suppose I'll play devil's advocate and bet twenty crowns that you won't be able to manage it at all."

"Not you too," Barlowe laughed, "I can't believe you would doubt my skill."

"Oh, I'm not doubting you," Wolfram said, playfully matching Barlowe's mock-offended tone, "Your skills are very much known to me. It's Miss Meyers whom I am doubting. She represents an *unknown quantity,*" he emphasised the phrase with a comically overdone flourish, "I've no clue how susceptible she may prove to your charms."

"She seemed pretty *susceptible* from where I was standing," Barlowe grinned.

"Perhaps she was merely putting on a congenial face," Wolfram said, "But what is she *really* like? She might be an alehouse lightskirt or a sanctimonious little churchmouse," He leaned forwards and continued in a hushed tone, "Or worse yet: a *tease!*"

"Well I guess we'll find out soon," Barlowe said.

"But not too soon," Hamilton butted in.

"Everything looks to be in order," Wolfram said, and dramatically closed the ledger, "Gentlemen, the book is closed. All bets stand as they are." There was a murmur of approval.

At that moment, the sound of footsteps began to trickle up the stairwell. "And not a moment too soon," Barlowe grinned. A round of mischievous chuckles passed between the men.

"Quiet," Wolfram held up a hand to silence the group. For a moment, the approaching footsteps were the only sound on the bridge, "Officer!" Wolfram whispered. Archie knew he was right; the footfalls were much too heavy to belong to one of the WAVE girls. Not just that, but Archie also thought he could hear another set of footsteps following close after the first.

An air of tension settled over the bridge; Wolfram was the third-highest-ranking officer on the ship, after Lieutenant Commander Vaughn, and Lieutenant Butler who was senior to him. If it was any other officer, Wolfram would outrank them, and Butler was usually laid-back enough to let them be. But if it was Vaughn... Five pairs of eyes stared at the door in dread silence.

Finally, a man emerged onto the bridge whom none of them had ever seen before. He was a little taller than an average man, with brown hair and an eye patch over his left eye. His uniform bore four golden bars on his cuffs and a golden braid over his shoulder. Wolfram jumped to his feet and announced, "Captain on deck."

Archie and the others quickly followed Wolfram's lead, standing to attention and saluting. The new captain stared blankly for a moment, then awkwardly returned the salute as Lieutenant Butler clambered out of the stairwell after him.

"Right then," the captain said unsteadily, "I, uh... I'm Paul Bowman... and I'm your new captain."

Archie shuffled nervously while standing at attention. Something was supposed to happen, right? There had to be some sort of ceremony involved with a transfer of command, but Archie didn't know it. And it looked like this Captain Bowman didn't know it either. Archie glanced at Wolfram; he was usually the one who took charge in situations like this. The taller man's face was a blank mask. Archie had seen that look before, whenever Wolfram was about to be dressed down by a superior officer.

Finally, Lieutenant Butler broke the silence, "Line up and present yourselves to the captain," All five officers scrambled to form a line, clearly relieved at having something to do.

Wagner went first: "Ensign Powell Eugene Wagner!" he shouted like some parade-ground grunt, "Communic—"

"Dammit—calm the hell down, kid!" Captain Bowman raised a hand to silence Wagner, "I'm standing right here! You don't have to wake up the whole ship."

"Sorry sir," Wagner lowered his voice, but stood even more rigid as he continued, "As I said, I am the communications officer aboard the *Dreadnought,* sir."

"That's better," Captain Bowman nodded and moved on to the next officer.

"Ensign Marius Noel Hamilton, helmsman, sir," Hamilton was much calmer than Wagner had been. Captain Bowman nodded and moved on.

"Leftenant Archibald Warren Hakefeldt," Archie said, "I'm the navigator, sir."

Captain Bowman looked at Archie oddly, "What was your rank again?"

Archie jumped, "Sorry, sir. I meant Leftenant *Junior Grade,* sir," Captain Bowman must have recognised the insignia on his shoulder boards that marked him as junior grade.

"...Right," Captain Bowman nodded slowly, and moved on to Wolfram.

"Leftenant Wolfram How—"

"Okay, seriously," Captain Bowman interrupted, "why the hell is everyone saying it that way? It's pronounced *lieu*tenant!"

Archie blinked. Wolfram had taken great pains to show Archie how to mimic the speech patterns of his noble-born classmates at the academy. Archie no longer noticed when he used upper-class pronunciation; it had become almost second-nature to him.

"Sorry, Captain," Wolfram said slowly and deliberately, with a tone that told Archie that he meant nothing of the sort.

Captain Bowman sighed and waved a dismissive hand, "Go on and introduce yourself, kid."

"*Lieu*tenant,"—he emphasised every syllable of the word —"Wolfram Howard Wingate, tactical officer, sir."

Captain Bowman's eyes traced Wolfram up and down, "Is somebody in your family a lord?"

Wolfram's eyes lit up, "You've met my lord father?"

"Yeah, I met the guy," Captain Bowman nodded, "Bit of a prick."

Archie barely managed to choke down a laugh. He had only ever met Wolfram's lord father once in passing, but his reputation was nothing short of legendary. To hear that uncompromising paragon of duty and discipline described as *a bit of a prick,* was the most hilariously subversive thing he had ever heard! The sudden furrowing of Wolfram's brow told Archie that his best friend did not share his mirth in the slightest. He could already tell that Wolfram and Captain Bowman were not going to get on very well.

Meanwhile, Captain Bowman had moved on to the last man in the lineup: "Lieutenant Junior-Grade Malcolm Barlowe, bo'sun, sir," Captain Bowman nodded with approval, "Alright. Stand at ease, people."

At that moment, a figure emerged onto the bridge from the stairwell, carrying a porcelain teapot and a number of mugs on a silver tray. It was Miss Meyers, returning with their coffee. Her eyes met Barlowe's and she blushed, "I've brought your coffee, gentlemen!" She started across the bridge to deliver her coffee and stopped when she noticed Captain Bowman, "Oh! Captain?"

"Jesslyn Meyers," Butler said stepping forward to make introductions, "this is Captain Bowman. Captain Bowman, this is Miss Jesslyn Meyers of the Women's Airborne Volunteer Echelon."

Meyers curtsied carefully so as not to upset her tray, "Can I get you anything, Captain?" Captain Bowman bowed slightly, "No, I don't need anything right now."

Meyers curtsied again and scurried over to deliver the coffee. Archie and the rest of the officers had returned to their seats around the fuel drum. Barlowe eyed Meyers's posterior greedily as she leaned over to pour the coffee.

"Excuse me, Captain," said a woman's voice from behind Captain Bowman.

"I said I don't need anything right now," Captain Bowman said.

Archie was about to take a sip of coffee when Wolfram frantically tapped his arm and nodded at the woman who had spoken. Archie glanced up at her, and nearly choked on his coffee.

She was a very tall woman, almost as tall as Captain Bowman. Or maybe Captain Bowman was almost as tall as her? Archie couldn't tell which, but it was definitely one or the other. Her uniform wasn't anything like that of the WAVE; she wore a much narrower skirt that only reached her knees, and the double-breasted jacket of an officer. Her dark brown hair was tied back in a tight bun, and a pair of narrow spectacles were perched on the bridge of her nose.

"Captain..." she began again. This time, Captain Bowman raised his voice, "I already told you I don't need anything right now! Go bother someone else. Dammit, you girls are useless."

By now, a terrified silence had settled over the bridge. Barlowe had even stopped trying to flirt with Meyers, who was almost cowering with fear. Captain Bowman glanced about the bridge awkwardly, "What is it?"

Butler cleared his throat, "...Captain Bowman, may I present Lieutenant Commander the Lady Fiora Marie Vaughn. Your XO."

Captain Bowman was silent for a moment. He stared at Vaughn, no doubt trying to take stock of her. After a moment, he glanced over at Butler, "Wait, she's my what?"

"Your, *executive officer*," Butler reiterated.

"Right," Captain Bowman said, nodding slowly, "and... what does that mean?" Archie could practically hear everyone's jaw drop.

"She..." Butler began awkwardly, "she handles the... administrative responsibilities of the ship."

Captain Bowman considered for a moment, "So... like a secretary?" Vaughn's left eye twitched irritably. Elsewhere on the bridge, someone squeaked in terror; Archie couldn't be certain that it hadn't been him.

"Eh..." Butler rubbed the back of his head awkwardly, "not quite. It's more like... like a..."

"She's your *first mate*," Barlowe said uneasily.

Captain Bowman glanced at Barlowe and shrugged, "Yeah, I think that makes sense," He turned back to face Vaughn, "So... you, uh... you were gonna say something?"

"I was going to introduce myself, Captain," Vaughn said in a perfectly neutral tone.

"Yes," Captain Bowman said and awkwardly extended a hand, "Well, good to meet you... Lieutenant Commander."

Vaughn looked at Captain Bowman's hand for a moment, then shook it. The three golden bars on her cuffs gleamed brightly in the low light, "Likewise, I'm sure, Captain," she said, her voice still terrifyingly neutral.

"Right," Captain Bowman glanced around the bridge, "Is that everyone?"

"For the moment, sir," Butler said, "It's past midnight, I'm afraid. Most of the crew is asleep."

"Well then," Captain Bowman said, "I guess I can meet the rest of the crew in the morning."

"Good idea," Butler said, nervously glancing at Vaughn, "We can assemble the entire crew for you tomorrow morning in the mess hall. If you'll follow me, Captain, I'll show you to your cabin." Captain Bowman followed Butler off the bridge. Vaughn watched them leave in silence.

"Miss Meyers," she said after a short tense pause, "you may retire for the evening."

Meyers jumped suddenly, "A-are you sure, mistress?"

"I think these gentlemen have enough coffee to see them through the rest of their watch," Vaughn's dark blue glare swept over to the five young officers huddled around the fuel drum, "Besides," she said, "it looks like they have a bulkhead to install."

"Very good, mistress," Meyers said as she picked up her tray and scurried off the bridge.

"*Ma'am*, girl," Vaughn corrected half-heartedly as she followed the girl down the stairwell.

Archie glanced around the makeshift table. Any semblance of merriment had long since vanished. After a moment, Hamilton reached down and picked up his ivory pegboard. All the pegs had fallen out in his haste to stow it. Hamilton shrugged—"Another match?"

Paul stepped through the doorway and into the captain's cabin. *My cabin.*

"If you need anything, just ring the bell,"—Butler pointed to a small hook on the wall—"and they'll send one of the WAVE girls to check on you."

"Right..." Paul nodded, and Butler slipped out the door.

Paul was no longer as awestruck by the luxury as he might have been; three days in the Dawn Palace had broken him of that. The walls were paneled with the same dark lacquered wood, and another expensive carpet had been flopped down on the fine hardwood floor. There was an ornately carved wooden desk standing to one side of the door; it looked like it had been made from the same wood as the wall paneling.

In the far corner of the room, lay a bed that was much too large for one person. Paul walked over and sat on its edge; it was soft. Too soft for comfort. People weren't supposed to sleep on things that were this soft; it would be like trying to bed down in a swamp.

Paul looked about the room to see what else there was. A small table, a finely upholstered sofa with a few chairs to match it, two smaller doors; probably a private washroom and a wardrobe (or was it a *closet?* Apparently there was a difference between the two.), a large cabinet. Paul looked closer; it looked just like the liquor cabinets in the Dawn Palace.

Is there a listening device in that one too? Paul thought suddenly. He jumped off the bed and rushed over to the cabinet. He frantically opened every compartment from the top to the bottom, but he only found glasses and an odd collection of alcohol. *What does a listening device even look like?* Paul wondered. He sighed and snatched up a bottle of something that smelled like whiskey; a stiff drink would help him sleep more easily.

There was a soft knock at the door. Paul quickly put the bottle back and called out, "Who is it?"

"Maid service," a tiny voice responded. Paul blinked. *Maid service?* he thought for a moment. *Right, I have that now.* "Come in," he called.

The door opened and the girl stepped through. Paul recognized her soft blue-eyed face, she was the girl who had followed them from the train station, the one from the Women's Volunteer something-or-other. "Halford, right?"

"Yes, Captain," She curtsied, "Louise Halford, of the Women's Air—"

"Yeah, yeah, I know," Paul interrupted, "What do you need?"

For a moment, Halford just stood there, watching Paul with a strange expression. Finally she spoke, "I was at the Southern Gap."

"You were?" Paul turned to look at her.

"I was on the airship *Celsius*," Halford said, "It was my first posting."

"...And you were shot down," Paul said softly, "That must have been frightening."

"It was. Very," Halford nodded, "We had to jump from our burning ship with parachutes."

Paul had never made a parachute jump before, and with any luck, he would never have to. And he was a grown man; this poor girl couldn't be much more than half his age. He could only imagine how terrified she must have been.

"But we all landed and got away safely," Halford smiled, "...thanks to you."

Paul blinked, "Thanks to *me*?"

Halford nodded, "Your charge on the Isafari lines. I read all about it in the newsjournals; how you led your men against all odds to stand against the enemy, how you kept fighting even after one of them tore out your eye..."

Fairchild! Paul groaned and shook his head, *What kind of lies has that damn girl been putting in everyone's head?*

Halford continued, clearly having misunderstood his expression, "I understand this must be terribly ordinary for you by now, people congratulating you for your heroism and all. But I just wanted you to know how much I appreciate what you did for all of us," She paused before adding, "And if there's anything I can do to make you more comfortable here, please don't hesitate to ask it."

Paul didn't know what to say to that. He was no hero. All he had done was try to save his own skin the only way he could. He might have blundered into a bit of fame and fortune along the way, but that didn't change anything. In the end, he was still just an ordinary, past-his-prime freighthauler who couldn't even read.

Paul glanced down at his jacket pocket where the letter of orders was still tucked away, unopened, and he got an idea.

"Actually," he said, "there is something you might be able to help me with."

"Really?" Halford's eyes lit up.

"Yes," Paul took out the letter of orders, "But I need you to keep this an absolute secret."

Chapter VII

A Demonstration

THE sudden ring of the alarm clock lanced into Lieutenant Commander the Lady Fiora Marie Vaughn's brain and roused her from a short, dreamless slumber. Fiora rolled over with a groan and silenced the alarm. It was six thirty; the officers mess would open for breakfast in half an hour. *Just enough time,* she thought as she picked herself up out of bed.

A trickle of orange daylight filtered through the blinds to illuminate her bedchamber. The executive officer's cabin was noticeably larger than the other officers quarters, but it was hardly luxury. The wooden paneling on the wall was stained and cracked in places, and one of the glass candles in her ceiling fixture didn't work; probably just a faulty electrical contact, but whatever it was, it hadn't been attended to in the two years she had occupied this cabin.

Fiora's eyes alighted on a large sliding curtain that divided her cabin in half. It had been installed for her as a courtesy, one of the only nice things anyone had ever done for her during her two years in this dump (or really in her entire career). Its purpose was to preserve her decency if she was forced to change her outfit or undress while she was entertaining guests in her cabin (which she never did). Of course, Fiora had found another, more practical use for it.

Fiora stood beneath the curtain rod, grasped it firmly and lifted herself up to a resting position. The strong brass pole trembled slightly, but it held firm; Fiora weighed only two-and-eighty kilos, nowhere near enough to break the sturdy pole. Slowly, Fiora lifted herself up so that her chin was level with the brass curtain rod; then holding her position there, she tucked up her legs so that her knees were almost level with her chin. After a count of three, she slowly let her legs down, and then the rest of her body, to return to the resting position.

Four more times she performed the exercise; then she changed the position of her hands and performed a further five repetitions. Once that was done, Fiora planted her feet back on the floor again, relishing the soft sensation of the carpet between her bare toes. Not wasting a moment, she dropped to the floor and performed a set of thirty press-ups. Once that was done, she walked over to the wardrobe to collect her uniform.

As Fiora gathered up the pieces of her uniform, she caught a glimpse of herself in the tall mirror that lined the interior door of the wardrobe. She squinted; it was difficult to see without her spectacles, but the muscles in her arms and shoulders were much larger and more defined than she remembered them being. Fiora grinned and gave a small flex into the mirror. At last her morning routine was starting to show some results!

Fiora turned away from the mirror and donned her uniform. She started with her dark polished false-silk stockings, cheaper than real silk but more durable and almost as comfortable. Then came her green uniform skirt, knee length with a small triangular fold running up the back—a *kick pleat,* her tailor had called it. Then her blouse and necktie, which she tied perfectly without the aid of a mirror. Finally, she pulled on her boots and her double-breasted officer's jacket, noting with some relief that the sleeves of her jacket were wide enough to conceal the contours of her arm muscles.

Fiora looked herself up and down in the mirror. Everything looked to be in perfect order with her uniform, but somehow... wrong. It fit her as well as a military uniform could be expected to fit, but still... Fiora squinted, and for a second she could see someone else in the mirror: a beautiful lady in the flower of her youth, impeccably mannered, and graceful despite her height. In her mind's eye, she saw the girl in the mirror twirl about and spread her skirts into an elegant curtsy. Fiora could still do it; the muscle memory was still there.

No! Fiora tried to tell herself as she pried her eyes away from the mirror, *That girl is gone, and good riddance to her!* She didn't know if she believed it or not. Nobody could endure so many years of never being taken seriously by her peers without thinking that they might be right somehow.

With her uniform in order, Fiora planted herself in the chair before her small desk to fix up her hair in front of her smaller table mirror. She gathered her dark brown hair into a long thick braid which she wrapped upon itself into a bun and then secured in place with five hairpins. There was a box of makeup supplies tucked away beside the mirror; Fiora hadn't touched it in well over a year.

Beside the box of cosmetics was a small gilded picture frame. Fiora put on her spectacles and smiled as the hand-colourised photo-portrait of the young officer came into focus. Her father, Bartholomew Felix Vaughn had been of a lighter shade of hair hair than her, and it had been even lighter by the time she had known him, but their eyes were the same. *Gunmetal blue,* that was what he had always called them.

She sighed sadly. Ten years gone, and she still missed him terribly.

Fiora stood and took one last look in the mirror to check that everything was in its place and then slipped out of her cabin and into the hallway. None of the other officers were awake yet; they were never awake at this hour. Vaughn shook her head at the gross lack of discipline and continued down the corridor.

The officer's mess was smaller than the regular mess hall, but it was a much nicer space. The tables were oak instead of steel, and a number of paintings hung on the walls. The scent of incense and whale oil from the lamps mingled with the aromas that wafted forth from the kitchen. It was an intimate little place, designed to foster an air of camaraderie amongst the officers. Not that Vaughn cared; she rarely ate with the rest of the officers anymore.

The dining room was deserted apart from a pair of WAVE girls gossiping in the corner. As soon as they noticed Vaughn, they stopped chatting midsentence. One of them slipped back into the kitchen and the other dashed up to Vaughn and quickly curtsied, "What will you have for breakfast this morning, mistress?"

"Two eggs, fried," Vaughn said, "sausage, and coffee, black." The eggs, sausage, and milk would all come from the ship's new ice box; unsurprisingly, the kitchen was the only part of the ship that had kept apace with technology over the past four decades.

"Very good, mistress." Vaughn watched as the girl curtsied and scurried away to deliver her order to the kitchen. The WAVE girls always seemed a little uneasy whenever Vaughn was about. They were always respectful, at least on the surface, but there was something else to it. As though something was terribly wrong, but there was nothing that could be done about it. Vaughn shook her head; it was bad enough that the WAVE girls insisted on calling her *mistress* instead of *ma'am*, no matter how many times she corrected them.

For her part, Vaughn didn't think much of the WAVE. As far as she saw it, the organisation was just a way for silly young daughters of noble and wealthy families to meet young officers who might one day ask their hand in marriage. Any services they might actually render along the way were merely incidental.

After a few minutes, the girl returned with her breakfast on a tray. Vaughn watched the girl's expression as she set the tray down before her on the table. There it was; that look she always got from the WAVE girls, no matter how they tried to hide it. It was a look that said Vaughn was something unnatural. Something perverse. Women weren't supposed to be officers. That was what *men* did.

Fiora watched the girl retreat to the kitchen before she picked up her tray and slipped back out of the officers mess. She usually took her meals in her cabin. It was easier that way.

On her way back to her cabin, she noticed that one of the doors to the officers rooms was open. Inside, two people were having a conversation.

"...so you see," Leftenant Wolfram Wingate, the tactical officer, was saying, "I stand to gain sixty crowns if all goes as planned. And if you play along, thirty of those sixty crowns will be yours."

"*Thirty crowns?*" The second voice giggled. It was one of the WAVE girls. Meyers, that was her name.

"It's a good deal," Wingate said with a playful lilt to his voice, "You should consider it."

"I suppose I should!" Meyers matched Wingate's tone.

Fiora picked up her pace and hurried past the open door as quickly as she could without spilling her tray. She couldn't stand to hear any more of Wingate's wanton lechery. What would Wingate's lord father say if he knew the sort of things that his son was getting up to? And Miss Meyers was just going along with him, like some wretched alehouse strumpet! Fiora couldn't decide which of the pair was more revolting.

Finally, Fiora got back to her cabin. She set the tray down on a table beside her desk and pulled out the stack of paperwork that remained from the night before. There was never a shortage of paperwork for her to look over and authorise, or scratch logs to transcribe into the official record book. Fiora ate her breakfast with her left hand while signing off on supply orders and expense reports and whatever else needed her attention.

Fiora looked closer. There was something odd about one of the items in Leftenant Butler's latest expense report...

1Cr 2s 5d – 127mm high explosive, 2 crates.

Shells? Why would the *Dreadnought* need to order any replacement shells? It had been decades since the last time the *Dreadnought's* guns had roared in anger. And one crown, two shillings and fivepence? That was an awfully high figure (not to mention a terribly irregular one) for two crates of ordinary high explosive shells.

A thought occurred to Fiora: those *shells* were probably twenty centimetres tall, made of glass, and full of alcohol.

It was an old trick, hiding personal expenditures in official expense reports so as to avoid paying for them personally. Someone was trying to get drunk on duty and have the ARAF foot the bill. It was probably Bellman, the gunnery chief—an infamous drinker and a known associate of Leftenant Butler.

Vaughn circled the line item and set the form aside. She would need to have words with Butler later on about slipping things like that into official expense reports. Vaughn allowed herself a smug grin. It was a small victory, but a victory nevertheless. If Warrant Officer Michael Bellman wanted to get shitfaced-drunk at his post in the gunpit, he could bloody well pay for it out of his own purse!

Vaughn glanced up at the chronometer above her wardrobe; it was now quarter to eight. Soon it would be time for the all-crew briefing in the mess. She gathered up the finished paperwork and slipped it into a folder; she could pass it off to Ensign Wagner once the briefing was done. Vaughn tucked the folder under her arm and departed her cabin once more.

The hallway was much livelier now; a few of the officers were still getting prepared, and WAVE girls were weaving carts of linens and laundry in between them to tidy up their cabins. The thin corridor was packed from wall to wall, but for whatever reason, everyone parted to let Vaughn pass.

The mess hall was, in comparison to the officer's dining room, a purely functional space, with little thought given over to comfort. The tables and benches were steel, just like the floor and walls, and harsh electric candles replaced the low whale oil lamps on the walls. The hall was already filled with people, and more were trickling in every second. This was the only space on the *Dreadnought* that could accommodate the entire crew, and even then, only just.

If only we could have gotten a public address system installed, Vaughn thought, before reminding herself exactly which ship this was again.

Vaughn looked out over the crowd. She spotted Warrant Officer Bellman (hung over of course, as was his habit of the morning) having a conversation with Leftenant Butler. Vaughn reminded herself to have words with the two of them after the briefing. She noticed Leftenant Barlowe with Ensign Wagner and shook her head sadly; Barlowe's influence was going to be the ruination of that poor lad. She moved on and spotted Leftenants Wingate, Hakefeldt, and Newton; those three were all but inseparable. Miss Meyers was on the other side of the hall from Wingate chatting with some other WAVE girls; at least the girl had managed to get away from Wingate's lascivious intentions!

Eventually, Vaughn glanced down a side hall, and there she saw Captain Bowman. *my Captain,* she reminded herself, *even if the man confused my position with that of a blasted clerk.* Vaughn looked closer: Captain Bowman was engaged in close conversation with a young WAVE girl. She groaned and rolled her eyes; even this new captain was a bloody lecher.

Vaughn cleared her throat to get Captain Bowman's attention. He looked up suddenly, and the girl did the same. "It's time for the briefing, Captain." Captain Bowman nodded and quickly whispered one final thing to the WAVE girl, who nodded, curtsied, and scurried away. Vaughn didn't recognise the WAVE girl; she must have been a new one. She was blonde though. Typical. It was always the blondes. What was it about blond hair that turned men into sex-crazed pigs?

Perhaps if I was blonde? Fiora thought. A mixture of ammonia and hydrogen peroxide, that should do it. She could acquire those ingredients easily enough from the cabinets in the medical bay. Doctor Pratt would certainly never miss them. It would have to be applied in increments, of course; doing the treatment all at once would be much too sudden a change... *Dammit,* Vaughn thought furiously, *I'm thinking like a bloody schoolgirl! Next I'll be tying ribbons in my hair and fluttering my eye-lashes at everyone.*

Vaughn brought her attention back to Captain Bowman as the man casually straightened his uniform.

"Right," he said, "let's get on with this. It's Fiora, right? Fiora Vaughn?"

Vaughn suppressed her sudden flash of indignation; Captain Bowman was almost certainly common-born, which made it a grave insult for him to address her, a noblewoman, by her given name.

"...Or is it *my lady?*" Bowman asked, probably trying to sound courteous.

"*Leftenant Commander* will suffice, Captain," Vaughn said, keeping her voice as neutral as she could manage. Nobility or not, Vaughn was not in command of the *Dreadnought*, nor did she hold flag rank. Thus she was not entitled to be addressed by her title of nobility while on duty.

"Good," Captain Bowman said, "and you're my... *executive officer.*" The way he said the word, Vaughn could tell it was still unfamiliar to him.

No, I'm just your bloody secretary, remember?! Vaughn thought furiously. And she might have said as much, had she not replied with an automatic, "Yes, Captain."

"Good," Captain Bowman repeated, rubbing his hands together, "good. Well, let's get to it."

"Yes," Vaughn said, "do let's."

Captain Bowman stepped into the mess hall, and Vaughn followed close behind. Bowman strode to the front of the mess hall, (there wasn't really a *front* or *back* of the mess hall, but that was beside the point.) Bowman finally stopped at the head of a long steel table that ran the length of the hall. He looked about awkwardly. "Okay... how are we gonna do this?"

Without hesitating, Vaughn snatched up a metal tray and banged it four times against the table. Every conversation in the room ceased instantly, and Vaughn shouted into the silence: "All hands! Attention!" Every eye in the room was now on her.

Vaughn glanced at Captain Bowman. The man shrugged and stepped forwards, "Take a seat, everyone."

After the sound of shuffling stools had subsided, Captain Bowman continued, "Alright... I'm Paul Bowman, and I'm your new captain."

There was an awkward silence.

Captain Bowman shrugged and reached into his uniform jacket. "Orders," he said, producing a letter, "from Her Majesty the Queen." He pulled a folded piece of paper from the envelope; it had already been opened. Vaughn glared with disapproval; it was tradition that a captain did not open his letter of orders until officially briefing his crew. Captain Bowman had clearly peeked.

"Her Most Royal Majesty Queen Cassandra the Second, Beloved of God, and Supreme Ruler of Aurora and All the Provinces," Captain Bowman began reading, "does hereby enjoin the honourable Captain Paul Bowman (that's me) to assume command of the airship *Dreadnought* and, having done so, to proceed to the city of Longview, there to oversee the application and enforcement of customs regulations upon all airship commerce passing from Analeria into Aurora via the Gates of Dawn."

Vaughn blinked. She still didn't know much about Captain Bowman, but that sentence seemed entirely too eloquent for a man like him. He had obviously read it directly off the paper of course; but even so, he hadn't stumbled once, nor had he mispronounced a single word. Not even the uncommon words like *enjoin*.

"Right..." Captain Bowman continued unsteadily, his sudden eloquence vanishing in an instant, "So, uh... we're going to be raising ship in a bit and heading for Longview."

Another awkward silence. Someone coughed.

"And, uh... during the trip, we'll be—I mean, *I* will be... touring the ship to, uh... to... get to know all of you."

Yet another awkward silence.

"I, uh..." Paul glanced about the mess hall, "I think that's about it." He turned to Vaughn, "Anything to add?"

Vaughn cleared her throat, "Leftenant Butler, and Warrant Officer Bellman, I'd like a word when this is over." Out of the corner of her eye, she saw the two men turning pale as milk.

"Right, then, I guess we're done here" Captain Bowman shrugged, "Dismissed."

Vaughn watched Captain Bowman depart. The man was clearly unfit for his position. Any serious captain would have prepared a great deal more for his introduction to the crew—a few words about discipline perhaps, or an encouragement to do one's best, or some other trite cliché like that.

Vaughn shrugged; it made little difference. Old Captain Hannegan had been much the same, not incompetent exactly, but elderly, senile, and long overdue for retirement. (And something of a leering pervert in his old age, but that had hardly been a quality unique to the man.) Vaughn had really been the one running the ship for the last two years, and she expected Bowman's tenure as captain would be little different.

"Commander?" Leftenant Butler appeared beside Vaughn with Bellman at his side. Behind the two men, the rest of the crew had begun to filter out of the mess. "You... wanted to see us?"

"Yes," Vaughn began, "I'd like to have a word with you two about this latest expense report."

Lord Perseus Hiram Stolos stood considering the map of Aurora and Analeria that hung on the wall of the corridor outside the Southern Audience Chamber of the Dawn Palace. It was a magnificent piece of work; every stitch of the tapestry supposedly represented a single square kilometre. It must have taken years to complete. Lord Stolos's eyes traced up and down the eastern coast of Aurora. His eyes paused on each city in turn, from Torrenberg up in the north, all the way down to South Sands. The cartographer had managed to capture every last kink in the Auroran coastline along the way.

His eyes wandered west, across the Mountains of Dawn to the Analerian Plateau. Analeria had always been a bit of a conundrum for Aurora. On the one hand, it was a place of great natural resources; the ground was rich with iron, copper, coal, and other valuable minerals, the Great Northern Forest produced a steady supply of timber, and the fertile fields of the Western Basin provided excellent farmland. On the other hand, it was extremely close to Hadvar, and its abundant resources had made it a tempting lure for invasion after invasion from the west.

The land to the south of the plateau was a completely different story. There was nothing of value there; Analerian prospectors had combed the region and found no mineral deposits worth exploiting, and the soil was too poor to support any agriculture aside from a dwindling population of stubborn ranchers. Even so, that swathe of flat, useless land stretching from the Mountains of Dawn to the shores of the vast, empty Illyrian Sea had become a hotly contested region in the months leading up to the cease-fire, so much so that people had taken to calling it the Analerian Disputed Zone.

Hadvar claimed the land was theirs by right, of course, but at the moment they lacked the ability (or more likely, the economic incentive) to enforce their claim. Aurora, recognising the danger of a direct lane of invasion into the Auroran heartland via the Southern Gap, and seeking to cover their southern flank, had been trying for months to convince the local Analerian government to expand to the south. The Analerians however, saw no clear profit in it and had only committed token resources to the venture. And now that Isafar was beginning to make noise down south, Lord Stolos had little doubt that they would try to muscle their way in at some point.

Lord Stolos frowned; the entire thing was a disgustingly cynical ploy. Analeria was being treated like a proxy, a buffer state to check Hadvari aggression. It had always been like that; Analeria had borne the brunt of Hadvar's invasions for centuries, and the advent of airship warfare had only made the destruction worse. All the while, the poor Analerian people were being mercilessly trampled underfoot from both east and west. The little people always suffered the most.

There was a simple solution of course: bring Analeria into the fold as a full-fledged province of Aurora. At present, Analeria was managed by a royal governor based out of Two Lakes, and its people were not considered full Auroran citizens. But if Analeria were inducted as a full province, then the people could enjoy much closer economic and cultural ties with the Auroran heartland, as well as the full protection of the Auroran military, which would no doubt dissuade Hadvar from any future invasions.

And really, Hadvar wasn't the threat it once might have been. The motivation for all their sabre-rattling was clear as day: Hadvar was looking to secure enough resources to support its burgeoning population. That was why it had begun establishing colonies south of the Illyrian Sea along the western coast of Isafar instead of pressing its fruitless claim on the Analerian Disputed Zone. No doubt the resources flowing in from the *Samedvar,* as it was called in the Hadvari tongue, would keep Hadvar appeased long enough for diplomacy to run its course and solidify the situation.

Lord Stolos smiled at his tidy summation of the situation. The solutions to these things were always deceptively simple.

The sound of footsteps resounded through the hallway, and Lord Stolos looked up to see Lord Theobald Paracelsus Newton making his way down the hall towards him. Lord Stolos bowed respectfully as the nobleman approached, "My Lord Newton," he said.

Lord Newton laughed softly, "Stand up straight, Percy. And my name is Theobald. You're no less a lord than I am now."

"Y-yes," Lord Stolos said, standing up straight again, "Forgive me, my lo—" He caught himself again, "Heh, sorry."

"Oh, don't you worry about it," Lord Newton said, "It always takes a while to break those old habits. It took me nearly six months when I was raised."

"So I hear," Lord Stolos nodded gratefully.

"So, Percy," Lord Newton said, "what brings you before Her Majesty today?"

Lord Stolos straightened his back and said, "I've come to propose that Analeria be inducted as a province of Aurora."

Lord Newton blinked, "Is that so?" Clearly the man would take some convincing.

"Absolutely," Lord Stolos said, "They've been close trade partners to us for centuries, and we've defended them against Hadvari encroachment for nearly as long. It's high time we inducted them as a province in their own right, with all the rights and responsibilities that entails."

Lord Newton tugged at his chin in thought for a moment, "Hmmm... yes, I... I think that could actually work."

A broad smile settled across Lord Stolos's face, "I thought you might agree."

"Oh yes," Lord Newton said pensively, "It certainly presents a number of benefits. The military would be able to keep watch along the border with Hadvar directly, heavy industry would stand to profit tremendously from the closer link to Analerian mineral resources, and Hadvar would likely see the move as... Yes... yes, that could definitely work."

"And what about you?" Lord Stolos asked, "What brings you before Her Majesty?"

Lord Newton glanced back down the hallway where a number of servants were pushing a heavily-laden cart. He turned back to Lord Stolos and beamed, "A demonstration! I'm to present the findings of my research before Her Majesty."

"Really?" Lord Stolos had always been fascinated by science. He had a poor grasp of the mathematics involved, but he marveled at the results. Less than a century ago, electricity was all but unknown, and powered flight was beyond the scope of imagination; yet science had unlocked both of these secrets and changed the face of Aurora for the better. Scientific discovery was the great engine of social progress.

"I'm certain the court will be most amazed by my discoveries," Lord Newton said as the cart rumbled past the two lords. Lord Stolos had little doubt. Lord Newton was always dreaming up the most wonderful experiments.

The grand double-doors to the Southern Audience Chamber began to swing open. A servant stepped through them and announced, "Her Majesty's court is opened for the day." The cart rumbled into the audience chamber and the two lords followed after it.

The Southern Audience Chamber was much smaller than the Great Hall, but no less luxurious. Brilliant sunlight poured into the chamber through wide windows to glitter off the tiles of Analerian marble set into the floor. It's ceiling was painted with ornate scenes of the glorious history of Aurora; and below it, the Queen sat the throne.

Lord Stolos didn't quite know what to make of this new queen yet. Cassandra the Second was a lively young lady with a romantic soul, but she was terribly naïve. Of course, she was a nearly decade younger than Lord Stolos, so it could only be expected of her, but it was dangerous. It was one thing for an ordinary woman to be foolish, silly, and impressionable, but a queen could afford no such luxury. *She needs an honest counsellor to guide her,* Lord Stolos thought, *Someone like me.*

At the moment, the Queen was engaged in close conversation with a much older man wearing the uniform of an officer of the ARAF. The man wasn't especially tall, but his iron face and powerful shoulders more than made up for his lack of height. Lord Stolos recognised him as Lord Cecil Robert Hanscom, the Lord High Admiral of the ARAF. Lord Stolos frowned; the man was a relic, a holdover from the wars against Hadvar that had plagued the realm for centuries. But those wars were over now, and good riddance to them. Men like Lord Hanscom, Lord Franklin, and alas, even Lord Wingate whom he respected very much, would have to accept that the world was changing. It was a new day, and all who weren't willing to change with the times would have to step back and let a new generation take the lead.

As Lord Stolos crossed the threshold, the servant announced, "His Excellency, the Lord Perseus Hiram Stolos."

No sooner had the servant announced him than the Queen broke off her conversation with Lord Hanscom and looked squarely at Lord Stolos. "Percy," She said with an unmistakable touch of fondness in her voice, "Fancy seeing you here!"

Lord Stolos smiled and bowed respectfully, "Majesty. It is both an honor and a pleasure." The Queen appeared to be rather sweet on him; it was hardly a proper thing to think about a queen, but it was evident in the way she behaved in his presence, and he could no doubt use her affection to his advantage.

"It's good that you've come," the Queen said, "I've something to show you," she picked up a small sheaf of paper and handed it to one of her servants, "I'm interested to hear your opinion on this article," she said as the servant crossed the throne room to deliver the broadsheet.

Lord Stolos took the journal and bowed respectfully, "I'm certain I will find it most intriguing, Majesty." He tucked the sheaf of paper under his arm; he could read it later when he had a moment.

Lord Stolos cleared his throat, preparing to begin his Analerian proposal. Before he could get a word out however, the Queen cut him off, saying, "Well, go on then."

Lord Stolos blinked, "Sorry?"

"Are you not going to have a look?" The Queen smiled, "It really is a most wonderful article."

"N-now, Majesty?" Lord Stolos stammered.

"No time like the present," The Queen giggled, "Go on, give it a look."

Lord Stolos shrugged. It was best to give the Queen what she wanted. He slipped away to a back corner of the audience chamber and opened the broadsheet.

PAUL BOWMAN PROMOTED TO CAPTAIN!

taken from the account of Mme. Isabelle Fairchild esq.

Paul Bowman has been named Captain! In honour of his most heroic action at the Defence of the Southern Gap; Her Most Royal Majesty Queen Cassandra II has seen fit to rewarded the gallant Mister Bowman with the commission of a captain in the Auroran Royal Airbourne Fleet!

Can wonder never cease around this amazing man? The newly minted Captain Bowman has departed the Capitol with Her Majesty's blessing to assume his new command. No doubt he shall prove himself just as valiant a captain as he was a sergeant!

Not only this, but it has been revealed to this most humble journalist that the airship of which Captain Bowman has been entrusted the commandership is none other than the mighty Dreadnought; *one of the most auspicious of airships in the entire fleet! Tales abound of her many ferocious battles and daring victories. And with Paul Bowman as her new captain, a new chapter is sure to unfold in her story of greatness!*

Read on and you shall glean a taste of the glory that surely awaits Captain Bowman and his loyal crew!

But who exactly is Paul Bowman? What sort of man is the Hero of the Southern Gap, and what twists of fortune set him on the fateful path that led to glory and fame eternal? Alas, there seem to be precious few details known for certain about this most fascinating gentleman.

Still, a number of things may be inferred about the fascinating Mister Bowman. For one thing, the accent of his voice tells of a childhood spent in Longview. And since Mister Bowman had, by the time of the Defence of The Southern Gap, attained the rank of Sergeant, it can be deduced that he was a veteran of the recent wars against the vile Hadvari menace. One can only surmise that Paul Bowman was the driving force behind the great victories of the Analerian campaign.

Able and willing to serve though he may be, no man can climb as high as Captain Bowman has without attracting enemies. Not the least amongst these enemies is Captain Sir Alphonse Wilmont. Long has this particular officer watched Paul's valiant career with bitterest envy in his heart.

To say that this Captain Wilmont despises Paul is an understatement of criminal magnitude. This most unscrupulous villain has long been Sergeant Bowman's commanding officer, and long has he envied the glory that his subordinate heaped upon himself. Fortunately for Paul, Wilmont is as lazy as he is covetous, having slept through the Battle of the Southern Gap entirely; and when this layabout attempted to punish Sergeant Bowman for his own sloth, his devious designs failed utterly!

Lead shall float upon air before this contemptible knave shall purge his heart of wickedness!

Will the vile villain Wilmont continue to menace good Captain Bowman? Fear not! At the ceremony where he was honoured by Her Majesty, Paul Bowman denounced the miscreant before the court of Aurora, naming the man a 'lying lie-telling teller-of-lies,' a title that surely cannot do justice to the magnitude of his mischief! Wilmont has since fled the court in disgrace.

Keep heart, though, and all shall be well. For Paul Bowman has allies. His Excellency Admiral the Lord Orpheus Chester Wingate, for example, appears to have taken a particular interest in his career; it was he who personally gave Captain Bowman his new command. Captain Bowman may have enemies in high places, yet he also has friends!

Watching the continuing adventures of Paul Bowman and his new command is sure to bring excitement and diversion to the masses! Rest assured, this humble journalist shall endeavour to keep abreast of his exploits, and when his next exciting adventure takes off (as there is little doubt that it shall), the world shall know of it as soon as possible!

As Lord Stolos perused the cringeworthy article, his gaze periodically darted up to the centre of the chamber where Lord Newton was preparing to give his demonstration. Other nobles were slowly beginning to trickle in.

"Majesty," Lord Newton began as the servants manhandled a number of large objects from the cart, "I wish to present a most astounding phenomenon which I have recently discovered."

"Oh my," the Queen gasped, "What is it?"

"Observe," Lord Newton said as two servants placed four large metal plates on a sturdy wooden crate before him, "These"—he indicated the metal plates—"are magnets, made out of an alloy of nickel, cobalt, and aluminium. They are the strongest magnets presently known to modern science."

"How wonderful," the Queen cooed.

"And this," Lord Newton said as a servant handed him a small grey block of metal, "Is a block of common lead. Aside from being moulded into shape, it has not been modified by any chemical or physiological process."

"Fascinating," said the Queen.

Lord Newton handed the block of lead back to the servant as another one produced a large thermostatic flask with a narrow spigot on the top, "And this," he said, "is liquified helium gas; the coldest substance known to modern science."

"Ohhhh," said the Queen, and she was not alone; nearly every person in the audience chamber, servant and noble alike, was staring at Lord Newton with awe. The only people who weren't were Lord Stolos himself, who still had the article to finish, and Lord Hanscom, who never showed any enjoyment.

"Now," Lord Newton said as a pair of servants produced a pair of tongs and suspended the block of lead above the magnets, "I am about to cool this sample of lead using this liquified helium. Observe what happens."

Lord Newton removed the stopper from spigot of the thermostatic flask and began to carefully pour a colourless boiling liquid into a small well at the top of the block of lead. "Note how the liquified helium boils instantly upon contact with the substance!" Lord Newton said.

For over a minute, Lord Newton poured the frothing liquid over the block of lead, never spilling a drop. The crowd gasped with wonder as crystals of frost sprouted upon the surface of the lead block and crept like ivy up the tongs towards the servants' (fortunately gloved) hands.

"Right, that should do it," Lord Newton said as he stopped pouring and capped the spigot, "Now, watch closely." The two servants holding the tongs nodded and released their grip on the tongs, leaving the ice-covered block of lead suspended in midair over the magnets!

All at once, the chamber erupted with gasps of amazement, which quickly gave way to delighted applause, "This humble material lead, when sufficiently cooled to the point of perfect conductivity, rejects all magnetic fields, thus causing it to levitate above magnets." Lord Newton passed his hand beneath the block of lead to show that there was no invisible matter supporting it, and then quickly withdrew his hand, muttering, "Dear me, that is cold."

Lord Newton motioned for his servants to clear away the experiment, and they lifted the crate back onto the cart. The lead block was still floating above it, eliciting more oohs and aahs from the courtiers. "It is my intention to study this phenomenon in greater detail," Lord Newton said, "I am also reasonably certain that other substances can be found which manifest this most intriguing property at much more manageable—"

"Oh please!" A gruff voice cut him off. All eyes turned to Lord Hanscom, who continued, "What you've demonstrated is nothing more than an expensive parlor trick. What use is there in levitating a block of lead if it must first be frozen in ice? Your time would be better served if you would stick to more practical sciences, and not these wasteful fripperies."

"My Lord Hanscom," the Queen moaned, "What a horrid thing to say! And after such a wonderful demonstration."

"Oh, it's quite alright, Majesty," Lord Newton said graciously, "One cannot expect all people to share a common interest," He wandered back to the cart and picked up a small sheaf of paper, "Perhaps Lord Hanscom might find my collection of high-strength, light-weight alloys more to his interest."

Lord Hanscom's face didn't change. He simply nodded to the door to a side chamber. "Come with me," he said, "Let's see what you're peddling."

"I suspected as much," Lord Newton said with a clever grin. He bowed deeply before departing the chamber with the sheaf of papers tucked under his arm.

When Lord Stolos had finished the article, he stepped forwards once more; hopefully this time, he would be able to present his ideas without any more distraction.

"Well?" the Queen said before Lord Stolos could open his mouth, "what did you think of it?"

"It was a fascinating demonstration," Lord Stolos said, "Anyways, I have a—"

"Oh not that," the Queen giggled, "the *article,* of course! What did you think of it?"

"Oh right," Lord Stolos said, "*That.* It was... interesting."

"Wasn't it?" the Queen giggled, "I knew Paul Bowman would make a good Captain!"

"Yes..." Lord Stolos said uneasily. He had no idea what the Queen saw in Mister Bowman, but he certainly couldn't see any use out of making him an airship captain. What did an infantry sergeant know about commanding an airship? The man would be completely out of his element; would he not be of more use in court, where his commoner's insight and intuition could be of direct use to the realm?

And besides, that article had been a tangled, meandering mess of vague nonsense without any actual substance to it. He recognised the author, Isabelle Fairchild, from her article about Mister Bowman's Defence of the Southern Gap. While that article had at least been informative about a significant event, this article presented no new information of any use, aside from a few bits of trivial gossip about Lord Wingate and whomever that Wilmont fellow was.

"So," the Queen said, "what was it you wished to present before me?"

Lord Stolos shook his head. The Queen had changed to his sight; she no longer appeared as an earnest, but innocently misguided monarch. She was an idiot, a dimwit of the first order. There wasn't a drop of sense in that head of hers; it was instead stuffed with romantic delusions of her own eloquence.

"I... was going to ask you about Captain Bowman," Lord Stolos lied, "but it seems I have my answer."

The Queen laughed. It was no longer an amusing sound. "Dear me, how convenient."

"Yes, very," Lord Stolos said, "And now I must beg your leave to depart."

"Farewell," The Queen waved as Lord Stolos slipped out of the audience chamber.

Lord Stolos breathed a heavy sigh as the doors closed behind him. His eyes had been opened in the worst possible way. The Queen, the woman to whom he owed his allegiance, was a complete fool. She wasn't just a stumbling block on the path to progress; she was an outright obstruction.

As Lord Stolos started walking down the hallway, he paused for a moment to glance at the map once more. He had such grand visions for the future of his beloved Aurora, and none of them could come to fruition while that little twit sat the throne. And it wasn't just her; it was also those lords who sat beside her, whispering in her ear, feeding her exactly what they wanted her to think and do.

Something would have to be done to fix it all.

"Are you serious?" Paul groaned as he stalked up the stairwell.

"I... I don't understand," Lieutenant Junior Grade Hakefeldt said.

"How in the hell am I supposed to run an airship without loudspeakers?!" Paul said, "What happens when we need to talk to the engine room?"

"I don't know," Hakefeldt said sheepishly "We've... never really needed to."

Paul shook his head. He couldn't remember ever being on an airship without loudspeakers. How could anyone forget a thing like that? It was like building a house without a front door! And even if it had simply been overlooked, why hadn't any of the previous captains thought to install them? Just how old was this ship anyways?

Paul reached the top of the stairwell and stepped out onto the bridge. Everyone appeared to be at their post. That was good; Paul was itching to get airborne again, "Sparks," he called across the bridge.

Over by the radio, Ensign Wagner jumped to attention, "Captain, sir!"

"Talk to Aerodrome Control," Paul said, his old instincts kicking in, "and get us clearance for departure."

"Aye, sir!" Wagner sat back down at the radio and—

"Belay that, Sparks," Commander Vaughn's level voice cut across the bridge and for a moment, everyone stopped moving. Paul glanced over at the woman; she was glaring at him and holding a small leather-bound book, "Captain," she said, in the same neutral voice that seemed to terrify the rest of the crew, "there are procedures we must follow."

Paul bit his lip for a moment. Did Vaughn always insist on following some damn checklist? No wonder the rest of the crew didn't like her. *And a good thing too,* Paul thought, *The crew is supposed to hate the first mate. If they do like her, she's not doing her job!* "Alright," Paul said with a slightly annoyed tone (you had to play along with this sort of thing,) "What do we do first?"

"First," Vaughn said, glancing down at the book, "we need to start the reactor."

"Right," Paul said, and was about to pass the command on to Wagner before he remembered that there were no loudspeakers. *We'll have to send a runner,* Paul shrugged, "Barlowe!"

Barlowe, the bo'sun, was leaning against the wall beside the radio. He looked up, "Cap'n?"

"Get down to engineering and tell them to fire up the reactor."

Barlowe blinked, and for a moment he looked like he was about to protest, but he stood up and slunk off the bridge with a mumbled, "Aye, sir."

Paul turned back to Vaughn, "What else?"

The woman consulted her book again and said, "Next, we need to check the combat systems."

"Guns!" Paul shouted across the bridge to where Lieutenant Wolfram Wingate slouched in front of a large panel covered with lights and switches. The kid turned back and said, "Weapon systems are in order, Captain."

"Anything else?" Paul turned back to Vaughn.

"We should make sure our course has been plotted."

"Navi?" Paul turned to Hakefeldt, who was bent over a map chart.

"Course plotted and ready, sir!" Hakefeldt responded without missing a beat.

Once again, Paul turned to Vaughn, "What else is there?"

"Just one more thing," Vaughn said, "We need to note our departure for the log."

Paul blinked, "For the what?"

Vaughn held up her book, "The *log*," she said again, "The step-by-step account of our actions for the record."

Paul was silent for a moment, "...And who's in charge of that?"

"I am sir," Vaughn said, "But it is tradition to defer to the—"

"I don't care about tradition," Paul interrupted, "Handle it yourself. It doesn't look like you're doing anything useful anyways."

Vaughn's eyebrow twitched, and her lips tightened "As you say, Captain," she said and started scrawling something in that damn book.

Right, Paul thought, *now that she's taken care of...* "Sparks, clearance for departure."

"Aye, sir," Wagner said as he finally started operating the radio. As he began working the knobs and dials, Paul felt a familiar vibration welling up from beneath his feet. He closed his eyes for a moment and let out a long-repressed breath. *Damn, I've missed this feeling!* Paul walked toward the helm at the front of the bridge, savoring every vibrating step he took.

"Ready to get airborne, kid?" he said to Ensign Hamilton.

"Y-yeah. Yes, of course Captain," Hamilton said. He was sitting forward with his shoulders hunched over the controls. His fingers were trembling as he gripped the main control stick.

Nerves, Paul thought, and he took a knee beside the boy, "Have you flown this ship before?"

"No, not as such, Captain," the kid responded, a little too quickly.

Paul's eye quirked, "Have you *ever* flown a ship before?"

"N-no," the kid admitted, his face turning bright red.

"Alright," Paul said as he reached down to tap at a small lever beside the kid, "Vertical thrust. Always keep an eye on your vertical thrust, so you don't clip any rooftops or trees by accident." Paul tapped at the tall lever between the kid's legs, "Center stick. Keep this level unless you need to turn. That button at the top is your all-speed override. Don't touch that unless I tell you." He pointed to a pair of foot-valves, "Acceleration. Right side is forward, left is reverse." He pointed to a small panel with a few dials and lights, "And that's your compass, gyroscope, engine order switch, landing gear, and air pressure monitor. You get that so far?"

"I think so..." Hamilton said unsteadily. Paul could hardly blame the kid. He remembered the first time he had ever taken the helm of an airship. Hamilton was even younger than Paul had been at the time.

"Captain," Wagner called from over by the radio, "Aerodrome Control has cleared us for departure, sir."

"Thank you, Sparks," Paul called over his shoulder. He turned back to Hamilton and gave the boy a reassuring pat on the shoulder, "Don't worry kid. I'll walk you through this."

"Thanks, Captain," Hamilton said. Paul thought he saw the kid's shoulders relax just a bit. That was good, it was best to be relaxed when flying an airship.

"Alright," Paul said, and pointed at a three-position switch below a trio of small lights, "first, put your engine order in the middle position."

Hamilton reached up and flicked the switch. A few moments later, the green light above the switch was replaced by a yellow one to indicate that the reactor was operating at full normal power. The low vibration from the floor grew to a deep rumble. It was a wonderful sound.

"Okay," Paul said, "now, slowly open up the vertical thrust."

Hamilton gripped the vertical thrust lever, and pulled back slowly. The low rumble of the reactor was joined by the soft purr of the impact coils firing up. Paul felt the deck pitch slightly as the *Dreadnought* lifted up and out of its berth, like a mighty animal rising from hibernation after a long winter.

Hamilton jumped at the sudden movement and lowered the vertical thrust lever, causing the ship to drop slightly, "Steady now," Paul said.

"Sorry, sorry, Captain," Hamilton stammered, "I'll keep it steady."

Paul smiled at the boy. He didn't quite have the feel for it yet, but he was trying, and that was all that mattered. Everything else would come to him in time, "Trust the wind, kid," Paul said, "She'll take you where you need to go."

A smile spread across Hamilton's face as he pulled back on the lever, coaxing the mighty airship higher and higher into the sky.

Chapter VIII

A New Enemy

"**A**LRIGHT, now level her off nice and easy," Paul said, "And don't forget to pull in the landing gear."

Hamilton nodded and eased off on the vertical thrust lever as the *Dreadnought* came to an appropriate cruising altitude. Paul looked out through the forward window. The helm controls were situated at the extreme front of the bridge, and the forward window was bent back to give the helmsman as wide a field of view as possible. Hundreds of feet below, the city of Norvell looked like it had been built by ants; the earthbound people were barely visible as they went about their little lives.

I'm back in the air again! Paul smiled. It was a great feeling.

Paul quickly tucked away his excitement. There was still a job to be done. "Navi," he called out, "what's our course?"

"West by north, Captain," Hakefeldt called out, "bearing two-eight-oh."

So, west by north, Paul thought. He had a basic understanding of numbers, but he had always found the cardinal directions to make more sense when trying to hold a course. "Now," Paul said as he came back to Hamilton and indicated the right foot-valve, "accelerate forward..." he tapped the main stick, "...and turn to the left..." Paul had docked at the Norvell aerodrome many times before; he knew from the layout of the city below that west was on the left, "...until your compass dial points west by north."

"Aye, sir," Hamilton said, confidence beginning to build in his voice.

The airship began to creep forward and bank ever so slightly to the left as Hamilton worked the controls. Finally, the deck leveled out again, and Hamilton reported, "I've got the heading, sir."

"Take us a little higher," Paul said, "You always lose a bit of altitude when you pull a turn like that."

"Aye sir," Hamilton said as he corrected the issue, "What now?"

"Now we get going," Paul said, "Open up the accelerator, and let's fly!"

"Aye sir!" Hamilton stepped down hard on the forward accelerator, and the *Dreadnought* leaped forward on a burst of speed. Paul's instincts took over, and he stepped backward gracefully to balance himself against the acceleration. Behind him, Paul could hear at least one officer falling over.

"Good job, kid," Paul said giving Hamilton a reassuring pat on the shoulder, "Keep an eye on our altitude, and keep our speed steady until someone tells you otherwise."

"Aye, sir. Thank you, sir," Hamilton said.

Paul walked over to Hakefeldt, who had fallen over when the ship accelerated. He reached down to pick the boy up, "You alright there?"

"Y-yes sir, I believe I'll be alright," Hakefeldt stammered as he brushed some dust off his jacket. He checked the map chart in front of him, "Course is set and holding, sir. Three hundred and nineteen klicks; we should arrive by"—he checked a brass pocketwatch—"two hours past noon, sir."

Paul blinked, "What the hell is a *click?*"

"Oh, sorry," Hakefeldt stammered, "three hundred and nineteen *kilometres,* sir."

"Okay," Paul nodded without understanding, "...what's a *kilometer?*"

"Oh god," Hakefeldt stared as though Paul had just asked what color was the sky.

"Ah, nevermind," Paul waved a dismissive hand, "I'll figure it out on my own time." He looked out across the rest of the bridge. Wolfram (Paul couldn't bring himself to think of the kid as *Wingate* without being reminded of his father) was back to slouching in his chair by the weapon controls, while Wagner still hadn't released his death grip on the radio. Vaughn had managed to keep herself upright with a single hand on the back of the captain's chair. *She has experience,* Paul noted.

Paul noticed a section of exposed piping and wiring on one of the back walls. A large steel bulkhead leaned back against the wall next to the exposed section. Paul frowned, wandered over to Vaughn, and asked, "Why hasn't that bulkhead been put in yet?"

Vaughn looked up from her book, "I'm afraid you'd have to ask Mister Barlowe when he returns, Captain."

"The bo'sun," Paul nodded, "Of course," Be it military or civilian, you could always trust a ship's bo'sun to vanish whenever there was hard work to be done. Paul shrugged; it didn't really matter as long as the bulkhead was eventually installed. He started for the stairwell.

"Where are you going, Captain?" Vaughn spoke up as Paul reached the stairwell.

"I'm going to tour the ship," Paul said.

"Captain, is this really the best time to do that?" Vaughn said.

"I said I was going to tour this boat during the trip," Paul said, "No time like the present."

As Paul reached the stairwell Vaughn came back with, "If you must go, Captain, at least say who has the bridge."

"Fine," Paul said, trying to tamp down his annoyance at the woman, "you're in charge until I get back."

"I shall note it for the log, Captain," Vaughn said as she made another note in that damn book.

"Okay, you do that," Paul groaned, and stepped into the stairwell and down the wrought-iron steps. Vaughn was beginning to get on his nerves. Of course, some of that was alright; there was supposed to be a little healthy antagonism between a captain and his first mate, but Vaughn was taking it a little too far for his liking. *Maybe I'm overthinking this,* Paul shrugged, *It's been a little while since I was last on an airship. I probably just need to give things time to settle down.*

The first stop on Paul's tour off the ship was the supply office, a small room in the cargo hold, near the bottom of the stairwell. Much like the hold itself, the room was filled with crates. There was barely enough room for the small desk, behind which Lieutenant Butler sat, pouring over a series of papers.

Butler stood and saluted as Paul entered, "Captain sir!"

Paul saluted back, "At ease, Butler."

Butler took his seat once more, "What brings you down here, Captain?"

Paul shrugged, "Just touring the ship. Getting to know everyone."

Butler nodded and turned his head back to the forest of crates behind him, "Haskell!" he called out, and was answered by the sound of groaning wood as someone hopped off a crate. Paul watched as a scrawny red-haired youth in a ratty old uniform shuffled into view. The kid carried a small book with a magnetic clasp, which he clutched protectively to his chest.

"Haskell," Butler spoke as though to a child, "This is Captain Bowman. He's our new captain."

The kid, *Haskell*, looked up. After a moment, he quickly hid the book behind his back with one hand and made a ragged salute with the other hand. His *left* hand. "Captain," the boy mumbled just at the edge of hearing.

"Haskell," Butler said, affecting a scolding tone, "we've talked about this. You need to speak up when you're talking to people."

Haskell saluted again and said louder, though no more clearly, "Captain."

Butler quickly turned back to Paul, "Captain, I must apologize on behalf of—"

"Don't worry about it," Paul said, waving a dismissive hand, "You can get back to work, kid." The boy wandered off and vanished among the crates.

"That was Midshipman Haskell Alvis Torrenberg," Butler said as soon as Haskell was out of earshot, "He does odd jobs for me. Though I'm afraid he's... somewhat slow in the head. I can't even get him to respond to his surname."

"*Torrenberg?*" Paul said, "You mean like the city?" Paul had been up to Torrenberg many times; it was the largest producer of whale oil in all of Aurora. It was also close to the edge of the Great Unclaimed North, and as such, it attracted plenty of white bear hunters and fur trappers. Trade duties from those luxury goods had made Torrenberg one of the richest cities in the land.

"The very same," Butler nodded, "Midshipman Torrenberg is

the latest scion of the Torrenberg dynasty. His family is Old Nobility, and they have a long tradition of military service, stretching back even before the Founding." Butler glanced back over his shoulder, "Though I supremely doubt young Haskell is inclined to carry on the tradition. At least, not any more than is strictly necessary."

"The kid seems harmless enough," Paul shrugged, "What about you? What are you working on right now?"

"Oh, this?" Butler said as he sat back down behind his desk, "I'm just redoing an expense report. Commander Vaughn found one of my... one of my calculations to be in error."

"Sounds important," Paul said, turning to go, "I'll let you get back to it."

"Aye, sir," Butler nodded, "Thanks for dropping by, Captain."

The next stop on Paul's tour of the *Dreadnought* was the engine room, located at the very back of the ship, beyond a heavy steel door with planks of soft wood clumsily screwed onto the outside to soften the constant growl of the reactor. On the other side of the door, the noise swallowed every sound below the level of a shout. Half a dozen men or so swarmed around the reactor, calling out numbers from dials, opening and closing valves, and generally going about the task of keeping the core from overheating under the intense magnetic pressure that was being applied to it.

A lanky kid with glasses noticed Paul from across the room and hurried around the bulk of the reactor to meet him. Halfway across the room, he tripped over a chain that hadn't been stowed properly, but he picked himself up and continued on until he stood before Paul, "Captain, sir," he wheezed as he saluted and accidentally hit himself in the head with a wrench that he had likely forgotten he was holding.

"You okay, kid?" Paul raised an eyebrow as the young man began nursing the spot on his forehead where the wrench had hit him.

"Forgive me, Captain," the kid stammered, "I am Chief Engineer Leftenant Hudson Lowell Newton, at your service, sir. Have you come to make an inspection?"

"I'm touring the ship," Paul said, "Just getting to know how things work around here."

"Ah yes, of course," Lieutenant Newton said drawing himself up to his full height, "You know, my grandfather designed this reactor, and my uncle is presently working on the latest designs. I suppose you could say engineering runs in my family."

"Newton!" a man with a thick Newport accent shouted from directly behind him, "Get back and watch those goddamn meters! We're running too close to the induction limit."

"I can fix that!" Lieutenant Newton called back and hurried back to his post, tripping over the exact same chain as before as he went.

Meanwhile, the man who had spoken approached Paul and saluted, "We can speak outside, Cap'n," he shouted over the noise of the reactor. Paul nodded, and the two of them stepped back through the door.

"I'm Warrant Officer Stan Thatcher," the white-haired man said as soon as he didn't have to shout, "I'm the assistant chief engineer. Anything you want to know about engineering, you talk to me."

"*Assistant* chief?" Paul said warily, "Lieutenant Newton told me —"

"Newton's a goddamn idiot," Thatcher spat, "Look, sonny boy, I don't think you get it."

"What don't I get exactly?" Paul narrowed his eyes. Nobody had called him *sonny boy* in a long time.

"You know what this ship is?" Thatcher growled, "It's a goddamn leper colony. This is where high command dumps all their politically toxic fuck-ups. Every single sorry sonofabitch on this tub pissed off somebody more important than them, with only *one* exception..."

"You?" Paul finished the man's sentence.

"You're a goddamn genius," Thatcher rolled his dull brown eyes, "I've been on this ship from the very beginning. I was there when they laid down her keel in the Marburg shipyards, and I'll be there when they finally break her up and sell her for scrap. I remember when this ship was the pride of the fleet, when a bungo like you would have sold his mother to a whorehouse to get himself onto this boat.

"And I watched over the years as all the competent professionals on this ship slowly got replaced by a pack of clowns and inbred Old Nobility nerks. Now half of these bungos are drunk on duty, and the other half can't tell an intake valve from a fuckin' shrimp cocktail!" Thatcher brandished a finger at Paul, "I don't care who the hell you think is in charge. Down here, everyone answers to me."

"You know," Paul said, fighting the impulse to strangle the cranky old man, "I could have you thrown off this ship for mouthing off at an officer."

"Fat chance," Thatcher laughed, "That's a first-generation reactor in there. No safety valves, no cutoff switches, no nothing. You think any of those bungos have the slightest idea how to run a monster like that? There ain't nobody else in the whole goddamn fleet can do what I do. So unless you want to open up the hull and put in a brand spankin' new reactor yourself—"

"Get the hell back to work," Paul interrupted. Thatcher shot him a satisfied smirk and vanished into the engine room. *First Vaughn,* Paul thought, *and now this asshole. Every other person on this ship has a goddamn attitude problem.*

Fortunately, the rest of the tour went fairly smoothly. Directly above the engine room was the sick bay, a small room with four beds at each corner and the rest of the walls obscured by cabinets and counters covered with sinister-looking surgical devices. Doctor Dirk Alexander Pratt, a thin man with long dark hair and a large triangular beak of a nose, introduced himself to Paul with an ordinary handshake, not a salute. "I'm a *civilian volunteer,*" Doctor Pratt insisted, "I'm no officer, just a working man."

Next came the two gunpits on either side of the ship, where Warrant Officer Michael Bellman and his gunnery crew had prepared a very warm reception. Paul's initial suspicions that the stocky man might be drunk were confirmed right away when Bellman offered to pour Paul a crown glass of potato spirits. "The good kind," Bellman was quick to add, "imported from Hadvar. Not like that shit they brew down in Riga.   " Paul accepted the glass. He could tell already that he and Bellman were going to get along just fine.

Finally, Paul came to the galley. Supposedly this was the headquarters of the Women's Volunteer whatever-it-was. As he entered, Paul was greeted by the sound of laughter and lively conversation. The room was filled with young ladies all gathered in a circle around...

"Barlowe?!?" Paul blinked. Barlowe was indeed at the center of it all.

The hum of conversation stopped instantly as half a dozen pairs of eyes all locked onto Paul. Barlowe shrugged and got to his feet to make a salute, "Captain on deck," he said with a casual smirk.

"What are you doing here?" Paul asked, "I sent you to start up the reactor."

"So you did, Captain," Barlowe said, "But I figured once I was done..." He gestured to the young ladies clustered about him.

"Did you get lost on your way back to the bridge?"

Paul's jab sent a wave of giggles through the crowd of girls. Barlowe tried to laugh it off, "Not quite, Captain. I know where the bridge is, I just—"

"Good," Paul cut him off, "then get back up there. You've got a bulkhead to install."

Barlowe sighed dramatically, "Well ladies," he said, "we'll have to continue our conversation at a lat—"

"Now!" Paul shouted. Barlowe jumped and scampered out of the room without another word.

As Paul watched Barlowe leave, he thought about what Thatcher had said. He had been an ass, but he had been right just the same. The *Dreadnought's* crew was rotten to the core. If this were a civilian freighter, Paul would probably have just fired everybody and started over.

They might be a piss-poor crew, Paul shrugged, *But they're* my *crew.* The *Dreadnought* was his ship now, and the crew came with it. He would just have to deal with them as best he could.

Paul turned back to face the uniformed ladies as they curtsied with a single motion. One of the girls was Halford. Paul locked eyes with her for a moment, and an understanding passed between them. She had spent hours with Paul the previous night helping him commit his orders to memory. It was good to know that among his crew, one person at least was competent.

Maybe this wasn't going to turn out so bad after all.

The Gates of Dawn was a narrow gap in the mountains, just under a mile wide at its narrowest where the city of Longview sat, straddling the pass like a saddle on a horse. Directly to the north and south of the city, the impossibly high peaks of the Mountains of Dawn towered above everything. Even airships couldn't cross those mountains; if the thin air didn't suffocate the crew, then the extreme cold would cause impact columns to ice over and fail. The Gates of Dawn was one of only two spots where the mountains dipped low enough to allow a viable path into and out of the Auroran heartland. The perfect spot for a trade hub like Longview.

"We've arrived, Captain," Hamilton said, "Um... now what?"

"Just bring us to a halt for now," Paul said, "You've done a good job so far, kid."

"Aye, sir," Hamilton said as he reached up to his console and pressed a small button three times. Each time, a mechanical bell rang out.

Paul jumped at the sound, "What the hell was that?"

Hamilton blinked. "...it's the acceleration bell, Captain," he said, "to alert the rest of the crew before we move or change course. Commander Vaughn reminded me about it after you left to tour the ship."

"Did she now?" Paul turned back to glance at Vaughn over his shoulder. The woman was idly making a note in her book. *Well, I did leave her in charge.* Paul shrugged and moved on. "Sparks," he called over to the radio console, "contact Aerodrome Control, and get us clearance and a berth."

"Aye, sir," Wagner began working the radio.

As the ship waited for clearance to land, Paul looked out the forward window. It had only been two months since he had last been in Longview, and by the look of it, nothing had changed.

Paul grinned as Hakefeldt joined him at the forward window, "Ever been to Longview before, kid?"

"No sir, I have not," Hakefeldt said, "I've only ever been to Newport, South Sands, and Norvell. This is a new city for me." The kid put a hand on his forehead, "Forgive me, Captain, but I'm feeling a little light in the head."

"Altitude sickness," Paul nodded, "A mile and a half above sea level will do that to you. Just don't move around too much, and you'll get used to it after a while."

"Thank you, Captain," Hakefeldt squinted, "Hang on... What's that?"

Paul blinked, "What's what?"

"Over there," Hakefeldt pointed at a scrap of red and brown cloth fluttering above a distant building, "Is that what I think it is?"

Paul squinted, "Oh that? That's the Banner of Hadvar. The *Nôs v'tai.*"

"I thought so," Hakefeldt squinted even harder, "But why is it flying here? Is there an enclave?"

"A what?" Paul cocked his eye, "Nah, it's a war prize. It's been there ever since I brought it back from the Siege of Two Lakes."

"Really?" Hakefeldt seemed interested, "You were at the Siege of Two Lakes?"

"Well, kinda. I used to transport supplies for the army during the war. The army used to give out immunity papers if you made regular supply runs; the press gangs couldn't touch you if you had one of those. Anyways, it was about ten years ago, when the Hadvari forces had surrounded Two Lakes. The only way the army could keep the city supplied was by the air, but the Hadvari forces had the entire shoreline under their guns. So what we did was...”

“Captain,” Wagner called out from across the bridge, “Aerodrome Control has cleared us. We are to proceed to berth twelve.”

“Good work, Sparks,” Paul called back. He turned to Hakefeldt, “Get back to your post kid. I’ll tell you the rest later.”

“Aye sir,” Hakefeldt saluted crisply and returned to his post at the chart table.

Paul knelt down beside Hamilton, who was still clutching the vertical thrust lever, his knuckles white with tension, “Alright now. We’re almost done. Just a little farther...”

Hamilton nodded and rang his little bell (*the acceleration bell*) twice. The ship lurched toward the radio tower that marked the position of the aerodrome at the exact center of the city. Paul watched the boy intently, correcting the occasional mistake here and there. Once the *Dreadnought* was directly above berth twelve, Hamilton began to lower the ship into place. It was a nail-biting process in places, but eventually the ship was back on the ground, and Hamilton switched his engine order back to the low position.

“Not bad, kid,” Paul gave Hamilton a reassuring smile as the sound of the reactor shrank down to a soft hum, “You’ll get the hang of it before long.”

“Thank you, Captain,” Hamilton sighed, finally releasing all the tension in his body for the first time in hours.

Paul turned toward the rest of the bridge, “Barlowe,” he called, “run down to the engine room and tell them to power down.”

“Aye, sir,” Barlowe slunk off toward the exit without a hurry.

“And come right back here when you’re done,” Paul added, “Remember, you have a bulkhead to install.”

“Aye, sir,” Barlowe moaned. He had managed to put off installing it during the flight because it wasn’t a *stable work environment* whatever the hell that meant, but now that the ship had arrived, he had no more excuses to hide behind.

At that moment, a thought occurred to Paul: *I have no idea what I need to do now.* Ordinarily at this point, the crew would unload the cargo, and the purser and captain would meet with whoever had commissioned the load to collect their pay. But this wasn’t a civilian freighter. There wasn’t any cargo to be unloaded or any payments to collect. His letter of orders had said he was supposed to run a customs patrol, but that wasn't a whole lot to go on.

Vaughn would know, Paul glanced at the woman. She was still scribbling in that damn book of hers, like she always was. Paul crossed the bridge to stand beside her. "Alright," he said in a low voice, "what happens next?"

"First," Vaughn said without any expression, "we need to note our arrival for the log."

"Yeah, yeah," Paul groaned, *You and your damn log.* "Then what?"

"You need to report to the local fleet outpost," Vaughn continued, "and present yourself to the local fleet commander."

"Okay," Paul nodded, "Anything else?"

"Make sure you leave someone in charge while you're away."

Paul glared, but Vaughn didn't look up from her book. Her voice was neutral as always, but her disdain for him was impossible to miss. Paul shrugged and started for the stairwell. "I'm going groundside for a bit," he announced as he reached the doorway, "Vaughn has the bridge until I return."

As Paul made his way down to the cargo hold and off the ship, he wondered what Vaughn's problem with him was. Was she angry at something he said? Something he did? Was it something he was supposed to do but hadn't done yet? At least that asshole Thatcher down in the engine room had made it very clear why he didn't like Paul. Vaughn wasn't being nearly so talkative.

She might just be jealous that I'm in command and she's not, Paul thought. There wasn't much he could do if that was the case. *She is a noblewoman,* Paul remembered, *Maybe this is her way of looking down her nose at a commoner like me.* Or maybe Vaughn was just a naturally unpleasant person. Hell, there were plenty of people like that in the world.

Paul strolled down the cargo ramp and banished all thoughts of Lieutenant Commander Vaughn from his mind. He was probably overthinking it anyways. They had known each other for less than a day. If he could just stay out of her hair for a while, things were bound to settle down. Paul stepped out into the bright cold streets of Longview without a care in the world.

The streets outside the aerodrome were packed full of people. This was the market. Not the official one of course—that was off in Market Square on the other side of the city—but all of the local merchants peddled their wares here, next to the aerodrome. It was illegal to set up shop here, something about the width of the streets plus some nonsense about *zones* or something, but the local constables had long since given up trying to kick out the merchants. Nowadays they just shook a few people down for a bribe or two and left well enough alone.

Paul stopped for a moment in front of a small clothing vendor and looked at a fine heavy coat. *Deerskin from the Great Northern Forest,* Paul noted, *with gray seal-fur lining on the inside.* He had owned a jacket like that once, but one of his former crewmates had probably walked off with it after he was conscripted. A coat like that would do much better at keeping him warm than the scratchy uniform jacket he was wearing now. Paul noted the vendor's location and moved on.

He made his way through the winding alleys and broad streets, until eventually Paul found himself standing before an intimidating wrought-iron gate. Beyond it stood an ornate stone building at the center of a cobblestone yard. *The Longview Fleet Outpost,* Paul thought, swallowing hard, *I've spent most of my life trying to stay away from this building.* He almost jumped out of his skin when the two polished guards at the gate saluted him with clockwork precision. Not too long ago, Paul would have crossed the street to avoid them.

As he stepped inside the building, another officer approached Paul and saluted, "Captain," the officer said rigidly, "what can I do for you sir?"

Paul saluted back, "I'm Captain Paul Bowman, and I'm here to..." *How did Vaughn put it?* "...present myself to the ...local fleet commander?" Paul didn't quite understand what it meant, but the officer apparently did, as he nodded and beckoned for Paul to follow.

The interior of the building was just as luxurious as Paul had come to expect. Paul marched past fine oak paneled walls, with portraits hanging between the whale-oil lamps. Every person that passed him in the hallway stepped aside and saluted. *That's right,* Paul thought as he returned each gesture, *I'm important now!*

Finally, Paul stood before a dark varnished oak door at the end of a long hallway. The officer who had led him there tapped lightly on the door, and not a moment later, a loud voice called from the other side: "Come!" The officer opened the door, and Paul followed him inside.

What struck Paul about the office was its size. The room itself was nearly twice the width of the hallway outside, and at least forty feet long from front to back. At the far end of the room, a nearly bald small man sat at an expensive mahogany desk, "Give us the room please, Harrison," the man said sternly, and the other officer vanished back through the doorway.

The man looked up from a ledger, "Well? Are you going to make me shout?" His voice carried the familiar tone of a nobleman talking down to a commoner, "Come closer, damn you," Paul obliged.

"Well now, *Captain Paul Bowman*," the man leaned back in his chair and looked Paul up and down, "I am Commodore Horatio Garfield Wilmont, and I have the honour to serve as fleet commander here in Longview. You shall take your orders from me for the duration of your posting here."

Wilmont? Paul perked up at the name of his old captain.

"I understand you served under my cousin-by-marriage during the Defence of the Southern Gap."

Paul nodded warily, "Yes sir, I did."

Commodore Wilmont's mouth flashed into an empty smile, "Alphonse talks about you quite a bit. It seems you made an impression on him... particularly when you humiliated him in front of Her Majesty, and the entire court of Aurora."

Shit.

"I believe the phrase you used was 'lying, lie-telling, teller-of-lies,'" Commodore Wilmont continued, his empty smile giving way to an arrogant scowl, "It seems your lack of decency is matched only by your lack of wit."

"Look, Commander," Paul began, "I don't think—"

"*Commodore!*" the man leaped to his feet as he shouted, "It's 'Commodore,' not bloody 'Commander!' "

"Sorry, sir!" Paul stiffened quickly.

Commodore Wilmont's light brown mustache danced irately over his bloated cheeks as the man sat back down. "Now then, *Mister Bowman*," he said, deliberately leaving out Paul's rank, "You and your crew are ordered to conduct patrols for smuggling activities on the Analerian side of the mountains. In addition, you are authorised and required to carry out customs inspections upon all commercial trade passing through this city." Wilmont paused for a moment, "Did you understand all that? Or must I use smaller words?"

Paul clenched his jaw, "No, sir, I understand."

"Good," Wilmont snorted, "Now then, I'll keep this as brief as I can. You're an amateur, *Mister* Bowman. A jumped-up conscript playing at being an officer. At present, you have the love and adulation of the public at large, but soon your celebrity will fade. Once that happens, I'm afraid you will find that there's more to being an officer than just swaggering about and making noise. Personally, I rather doubt you will be able to manage it, but we shall see." Wilmont leaned forward and returned to his paperwork, "Now get out of my bloody office."

Paul breathed a heavy sigh as soon as the door closed behind him. He hated that man and Wilmont almost certainly knew it, but he didn't care. There was nothing more frustrating than having to deal with someone who knew that people hated him and didn't care. Captain sir Alphonse Wilmont had been the same sort of officer. Perhaps it ran in the family.

Paul slipped out the front gate and back into the street. The two guards saluted again, but he paid them no mind. *He called me an amateur.* Paul tried to ignore it, tried to tell himself it was just Commodore Wilmont being an asshole, but something about it... *And he's right!*

It hurt to admit, but it was true. When it came to actually being an officer, Paul was the least experienced person on the *Dreadnought*. Hell, even that Hamilton kid who had never flown his own ship before today was more experienced an officer than Paul.

Paul shrugged. If an experienced officer was what that gasbag Wilmont wanted, then that was what he would give him! He would become the most experienced officer in the entire fleet! He would become so experienced it would make Wilmont's head spin!

Paul smirked as he turned an alley the Headquarters vanished from sight. *I'll show them!* Paul thought, *Wilmont, Vaughn, Thatcher, whoever the hell else comes after them! I'll show them all!*

As Paul entered the market outside the aerodrome, he reached into his pocket for his purse. He didn't need that fine deerskin coat. No, what he really needed was a pistol.

In the west, the setting sun splashed red light all over the underside of the clouds. It was the kind of scene that lasted only a few minutes until the last rays of daylight winked out beyond the horizon. A cool breeze wafting through the mountains carried the aroma of the Great Northern Forest, and ran its fingers through the thick black hair of the man trudging up the slope.

If there was any beauty in the scene, it was lost on Dagan. He hated this land and everyone in it. Were it left to him, he would rather be in the *Samedvar,* bringing wisdom and civilization to the lives of the savages. Or maybe in Illyria; there was still plenty of work to be done in Illyria, pacifying the population and breaking them of their barbaric ways. If the choice were his, Dagan would have even chosen guard duty at one of the frigid prison camps on Far Island; anything but *this* mission. But he had his orders, direct from the Elders of the First Land, and he knew his duty.

Sometimes, Dagan reminded himself, *one must plumb the depths of dishonor to defeat a greater foe.*

Dagan reached the lip of a low ridge and turned back to gaze upon the sunset. That was one thing he could appreciate about this land: the combination of the blood-red western sky and the brown mountain soil, like the *Nôs v'tai,* the banner of Earth and Blood that had carried Dagan and his comrades to victory time and again across the plains of Analeria. It was a welcome reminder that Hadvar would soon control all of this land.

Dagan turned away from the sunset and slipped down into the valley toward the large shape hidden beneath the ragged camouflage net. It was a thing like a large boat, except made out of metal, not wood, and made to sail in the sky instead of on the ocean. Dagan shuddered at the thought; it was an unnatural thing, a blasphemous thing. Man was not meant to climb inside a metal box and fly about among the clouds.

The enemy called them *airships.* Ordinarily, Dagan despised those nonsense sounds the people of this land strung together in mockery of the First Tongue, but in this case, he was content to use their lan-guage. *Better to dirty my own mouth with their words,* Dagan supposed, *than to pollute the First Tongue with a word to describe such mechanical abominations.*

The Sazodvar, those lands beyond the Far Eastern Mountains that the locals called 'Aurora' were awash with all manner of wicked machines. Iron engines that lumbered along roads of steel, mechani-cal weavers that belched out cloth faster than a million seamstresses could make them into clothes, vast webs of wires that reduced the glorious gift of language to simple electronic shrieks, and of course, the hated airships. The machines had taken over the lives of the na-tive people, cheapening the labor of their hands, and corrupting the collective soul of their society. Time-honored traditions and knowl-edge passed down the generations had been sacrificed upon the altar of industrialization and the false-progress of plenty. It was almost tragic.

But that would all be remedied soon. Once the armies of the Sazodvar were broken in battle, and their people subjugated, all of their infernal contraptions would be gathered up and melted down for scrap or cast into the deepest depths of the sea. There would be no way for future generations to know that such vile devices had ever profaned their lands. They would be a people humbled at last; grateful to have been blessed with the gift of civilization. Well, the ones who survived at least.

Dagan slipped beneath the camouflage net and walked up a ramp into the cavernous interior of the airship. This vessel had belonged to some merchant before it had been purchased by Hadvar (through a proxy of course), but now the only cargo it carried in its iron belly was a small squad of Hadvari troops, and two heavy field guns with ammunition. Dagan climbed the ladder at the back of the cargo hold and stepped out into the metal corridor at the top of the ship. Rooms sprouted off from either side of the narrow hallway as Dagan strode toward the front of the ship, where the flight controls were situated.

He paused for a moment to peer through one of the steel doors, into a room where the *Môlsôde* sat, meditating in silence, clearing their minds and steeling their resolve for the coming battle. Dagan had never worked with one of the death squads before, but he had heard tales about them ever since he was a boy; the *Môlsôde* were the elite troops of Hadvar, superior in blood, in training, and in honor. It was their charge to lay down their lives in service to the Elders of the First Land, and wherever they went, glory was sure to follow. Dagan pulled himself away from the Death Squad and continued on toward the bow; by the time this mission was done, he was sure to have a tale of his own to tell.

As Dagan stepped into the control center, a local woman turned about in the seat that was supposed to be reserved for the captain. Her thin lips quirked almost into a smile, but her blue-green eyes never lost their disinterested glaze. "Anyone find us yet?"

Dagan frowned. The woman's speech wasn't halting or stilted, like most of her countrymen, but it was marred with an accent. Some of the younger soldiers might have found her exotic, and Dagan had to admit, there was a certain foreign-ness about the woman that was intriguing, in much the same way that an undiscovered tribe of barbarians might invite study. However, any sexual attraction Dagan might have felt was more than offset by her appearance. Women were not supposed to look like that, with skin the color of cooked chicken meat, blue-green eyes like pond scum, and long red hair that was almost certainly not its original shade.

Unnatural though her face might be, her clothing was even worse. This wretched local woman was wearing the red tunic and brown trousers of a Hadvari soldier, a horrible disgrace to the uniform. His orders from the Elders of the First Land were the only thing preventing him from strangling the woman where she stood. The woman for her part seemed to find Dagan's barely suppressed rage amusing. She had even claimed that the reason for the tunic being red and the trousers being brown was so that the enemy could not see if a soldier had been shot, or had soiled himself out of fear. Her tale had evidently been meant as a joke. Apparently that was the sort of thing these savages found funny.

The only thing Dagan knew for certain about this woman was that she was an assassin. She had come with the airship when Dagan had been given his assignment, and supposedly she was connected to the mission at hand, though exactly how would be revealed later. Those orders were sealed, not to be opened until they passed through the Gates of Dawn, five leagues to the south, which they were not to attempt until they received a signal from the Elders of the First Land themselves. Dagan sorely wished the Elders would get on with whatever was keeping the from sending the signal, so he could be done with this insolent foreign bitch for good.

"You're sitting in my chair, assassin," Dagan said. He had never asked after her proper name, and honestly he did not care to know it. It wouldn't be much use anyway; the assassin would probably just give him a false name. Dagan had heard a rumor that every child in this country was given two names at birth; these people took in duplicity with their mothers' milk.

The assassin gave another smile that never touched her eyes. "I'll check for myself," she said, and with a single fluid motion, the woman leaped up out of the chair to grasp some exposed piping on the low ceiling, and slipped feet-first through a hole in the roof to vanish in a flash of red hair.

"*Sûnba!*" Dagan spat as he took his seat.

Brotherless. It was like calling someone a savage. Worse even— savages as yet untouched by civilization could not be blamed for their ignorance, no more than an infant could be blamed for soiling its linens; they were to be pitied, not hated. But the brotherless, the *sûlbari,* they *chose* to remain ignorant in spite of their own knowledge, be it for the sake of greed, lust, pride, or wickedness of the soul. There was no insult in all the sundry tongues of men more greivous than to be named brotherless, but that foreign bitch had more than earned it.

"How are you managing the controls, Paku?" Dagan turned his attention to the young man sitting at the helm.

"I-I don't like it, *Bazi*," Paku said hastily. Officially he was just their translator, but since the crew for this mission was smaller than usual, he was doubling as a reserve pilot, "I think I'm getting used to the controls, but I still don't like it." He gestured all around at the airship, "This... this thing is a tool of the enemy."

"Sometimes it becomes necessary to use dishonorable methods to defeat a greater enemy," Dagan said, trying to take the tone of a tutor to his valued pupil.

"This I know," Paku said, and then hastily added, "but don't misunderstand, *Bazi*. It still feels wrong."

"It should," Dagan said, "Dishonor is sometimes necessary, but it is not something that should ever feel comfortable." Dagan took solace in that. This ship was only a temporary assignment for him; there would surely be more honorable postings in his future if he just did his job and did it well.

"Yes, of course," Paku laughed weakly, "You know, before we left I heard a rumor that the Elders were trying to assemble a whole fleet of these airships, to match the enemy fleet."

"That will never happen," Dagan scoffed. *And thank the Elders for that!*

"You think not?"

"Just think about it," Dagan explained, "How would we fuel them? We only need this airship for one mission, yet the fuel alone cost over nineteen thousand jades."

"That much?" Paku gaped at the sum. The boy had been raised on a mulberry farm, and he was still trying to wrap his head around the notion that there were numbers *above* ten thousand, "I had no idea."

"And besides," Dagan continued, "all of that fuel is made over there in *Sûbadvar*," he gestured over his shoulder, toward the kingdom of the enemy, *the land of the brotherless*, "All they need to do is cut off our supply of fuel, and our entire fleet has been defeated without firing a shot."

Paku shrugged, "But what if we learned how to make the fuel ourselves? Then it would just be a matter of acquiring enough of the necessary resources. And surely the cost in jades would decrease if we did not have to purchase—"

"You're missing the point," Dagan said, "It does us no good if we defeat the Brotherless by embracing their wicked machines. We would have become the very thing we set out to vanquish."

"But what other choice is there?" Paku said, "How else can we defeat the enemy fleet if not by matching them with—"

"I think we have discussed this topic enough," Dagan narrowed his eyes suspiciously at the boy, "I trust I have made myself clear, *Balû*." Dagan took special care to address the boy as the inferior that he was, and conspicuously fingered the long dark braid hanging over his left shoulder that marked his rank.

Paku blinked and hastily bowed his head, "Forgive me, *Bazi*. I forgot myself for a moment."

"See that it doesn't happen again," Dagan said, relieved that order had been restored. Paku was much too intelligent for his own good. Soldiers were not supposed to be clever; that sort of thing could easily lead to low morale, confusion in battle, or even mutiny. Not only that, but Paku had no doubt been exchanging conversation with that assassin woman. Who could say what sort of poisoned ideas she was pouring into Paku's ears?

The assassin popped her head down through her hole in the ceiling, "One of the scouts is returning," she announced, "and it looks like he's been running pretty hard."

Dagan and Paku leaped out of their seats and rushed out into the hallway and down the ladder to the cargo hold, with the assassin following after them. A young man huffed and puffed his way to a stop in front of them at the bottom of the cargo ramp.

"What news?" Dagan asked.

"*Bazi*..." the scout wheezed frantically, "in the... the pass... it's..."

"Pace yourself," Dagan said, putting a calming hand on the scout's shoulder. The man's thin tunic was soaked through with sweat, and he was panting like a stray dog, "Now, tell us what you have learned."

"A new enemy has arrived at the Gates of Dawn," the scout managed, "He is a captain of one of the Auroran airships. They call him 'Paul the Archer.' He is said to be a great hero."

"Paul the Archer..." The assassin perked up at the name, "Do you mean Paul *Bowman*?"

"Yes," the scout nodded, "Paul the Archer. That is what they call him."

"Interesting..." the assassin purred like a mountain cat.

"What do you know of this man?" Dagan demanded of the assassin.

"Not very much," the assassin said, "He's someone new."

"Do you think he's likely to cause problems for us?" Dagan pressed further.

"It's difficult to say" the assassin shook her head, "But the broadsheets have been raving about his heroism."

Dagan considered for a moment. A new enemy at the Gates of Dawn, and one about whom very little was known. That was trouble; no matter what his sealed orders contained, he would first need to get past the Gates of Dawn, and past this *Paul the Archer*. What if the signal from the Elders arrived the very next day? What was he to do?

"*Bazi?*" Paku said, "What are your orders?"

Dagan shook his head to clear his mind of empty contemplation. "Return to your duties, everyone," he announced, "In the morning we will dispatch more scouts to observe this new enemy." *And please, let the signal from the Elders come soon!*

Chapter IX

An Old Friend

A warm westerly wind rushed through the trees, playing with the young leaves that had begun to cover the branches. The steady swaying of the boughs cast ripples of shadow down onto the dry forest path that barely a week ago had carried an Auroran regiment to battle at the Southern Gap. Now, the path was all but deserted, the only traffic a pair of riders ambling their way west at an easy trot.

"So," Lord Wingate broke the silence, "what did you think of her?"

Commander Barnes looked up from his reins, "Sorry?" His voice wobbled slightly as he bounced about in the saddle; he didn't yet have Lord Wingate's sense of balance.

"My daughter, Mary," Lord Wingate smiled, "What did you think of her?"

"Ah yes, of course," Barnes stammered, "well, she's... quite a... romantic young lady."

Lord Wingate chuckled, "She certainly is at that!" His elder daughter Marion Elizabeth Wingate had been the unquestioned centre of attention for the entirety of the two-day carriage ride from the Capitol. She had blossomed into a lively and passionate young woman, but she still exhibited a childlike naïveté. Mary seemed to think of herself as though she were a character in one of those penny dreadfuls that she enjoyed so much. Lord Wingate found it endearing. Barnes evidently did not.

"All girls are like that at her age," Lord Wingate said fondly, "Not to worry though. Marriage is just the thing to put some sense in her."

"Marriage?" Barnes nearly fell off his horse, "My lord, you... you cannot be serious!"

"Why not?" Lord Wingate was puzzled by his protégé's outburst.

"My lord, your daughter is barely sixteen!" Barnes protested, "That's far too young to be considering marriage! And anyways, I'm five years her senior; surely the difference between our ages is too great."

"Amelia was sixteen when we married," Lord Wingate said matter-of-factly, "and I'm *seven* years her senior."

"I... But I..." Barnes's protests spluttered out like a dying candle, "W-what?"

"Your family is young to the peerage, aren't they?" Lord Wingate said.

"We are, my lord. I'm only the first in my family to wear the title from birth," Barnes admitted, still confused as to what the social standing of his family might have to do with anything.

"Ah, that explains it," Lord Wingate said, "The nobility have never had very many qualms about age differences between spouses."

"Evidently not," Barnes said, and hastily added, "if you'll forgive me for saying so, my lord."

Lord Wingate laughed, "You should see some of the other matches the nobility come up with! Lord Newton's first marriage was to a woman twice his age! And Lord Franklin's last two wives were young enough to be his granddaughters! Compared to them, Amelia and I are downright ordinary!"

Lord Wingate's thoughts drifted to his wife. His marriage to Amelia Belmont Wingate may have been conventional as far as their ages were concerned, but in one way at least, their marriage was completely unheard of: they loved each other.

Most noble spouses were on very good terms with each other, of course, but hardly any could truthfully say they actually *loved* one another. In fact, most of the nobility considered marriages based on love to be horrible liabilities. Why risk scandal, annulment, and ruination of family names and estates for generations, just for a few nights of romance? Passion was a thing best set aside for lovers and affairs. Still, Lord Wingate had to admit, there was a certain romantic thrill about marrying for love that he doubted a simple affair could match.

It had all been Amelia's idea of course. Like Barnes, she had also been the first in her family to be born to the peerage, and to her, marriage without love was simply inconceivable. Young Commander Orpheus Chester Wingate had protested for months, throwing out all the old arguments against marrying for love, but young Amelia Belmont of the WAVE would have none of it. Finally, Orpheus brought up the old 'half your age plus seven' rule. Without missing a beat, Amelia solved the equation and demanded to know if Orpheus would still love her in five years' time, when he was eight-and-twenty and she was one-and-twenty. That had been what finally convinced him to give in. One month later, they were married, and in the two-and-twenty years since then, their love for each other had deepened with every passing day.

The two riders rounded a bend in the path and found their way blocked by a deep trench, the remnants of the earthworks from the battle that was now being called 'the Defence of the Southern Gap.' There was no bridge across the trench, but that didn't matter to Lord Wingate. He coaxed his horse to a run, and man and beast soared over the trench with a single graceful bound.

Lord Wingate turned to wait for Barnes to follow him over the trench, and fought to stifle a laugh when his protégé's horse reared back and refused to make the jump, sending the stocky young man tumbling into a pile of soil beside the trench. Lord Wingate dismounted and tied up his horse on an exposed root sticking out of the trench wall while he waited for Barnes to climb over the trench, "We'll go on foot from here."

The path led further through the trees, sloping gently upward until the trees vanished abruptly at the top of the ridge. Lord Wingate and Barnes paused for a moment to take in the sight. The ground sloped down to a thin strip of ragged grass at the edge of the endless salt flats, where a great host of Isafari had once made camp. On either side of their position, the Mountains of Dawn marched away, north towards Analeria, and south towards Isafar.

This is where I lost my ship, Lord Wingate thought bitterly, as his eyes alighted on a jagged black scorch mark half a kilometre into the salt flats. Twisted fragments of blackened metal debris littered the desert as far as the eye could see, like the desiccated bones of some long-dead beast. It was all that remained of what had once been the pride of the ARAF. *And my career.*

Closer to the edge of the salt flats lay the warped remains of seven large artillery pieces. Lord Wingate's eyes narrowed; that was their mission. Wordlessly, the two men slipped down the slope and into the salt flats.

"What are we looking for?" Barnes asked as the two men reached the junked guns.

"Anything," Lord Wingate said, "Whatever we can learn about these guns. The slightest detail could prove significant." And they set to work.

The guns themselves were clearly Auroran; Lord Wingate had noted as much from the *Celsius*. Their muzzles still carried the shredded remains of the recoil compensators that would have redirected the hot propellant gasses off to the sides when the gun was fired, thereby reducing blowback, so the gun could be fired at the same target with minimal re-aiming. Hadvar didn't make guns with those; the hot gasses would burn any soldiers standing beside the muzzle of the gun. Hadvar much preferred to fit their heavy guns with blast shields, so that gun crews could operate under direct enemy fire. Aurora and Hadvar had very different ideas about artillery; Hadvari doctrine favoured lighter, more manoeuvrable guns that could operate alongside infantry for direct support, while Auroran commanders preferred to set up their guns miles behind the lines and rain down devastation with mathematical impunity.

Knowing that the guns were Auroran was a start, but not enough. Having spent his entire career with the ARAF, Lord Wingate was woefully unfamiliar with current models of Auroran artillery. He knew the basics—muzzle length, bore diameter, and projectile type— but that was about all he knew. *Theo would know more,* Lord Wingate thought. His old friend Lord Theobald Paracelsus Newton was the head of Newton and Sons, the Auroran military's chief civilian contractor; he would be able to identify these guns and hopefully help them trace back their origins to reveal how they had been acquired by the Isafari.

"My lord," Barnes called, "I think I've found something."

Lord Wingate hurried over to find Barnes crouching beside a charred corpse that had once been one of the gun crew. As Lord Wingate arrived, Barnes lifted the body and flipped it over. The dead man was clutching an artillery shell close to its chest; apparently his body had been enough protection to keep the propellant inside the shell casing from igniting.

It was a shell just like this one, Lord Wingate thought, and then quickly admonished himself for wallowing in self-pity. There was work to be done.

"A good find," Lord Wingate said, and then ventured, "I don't suppose you can identify what kind of shell this is?"

"I can try, my lord," Barnes hoisted up the shell and rotated it to one side, then the other. His eyes narrowed, "That's... odd."

Lord Wingate leaned closer, "What is it?"

Barnes held the shell forward for Lord Wingate to see, "This shell should be labelled. It's standard protocol: all heavy ammunition must be clearly marked with its calibre, length, and filling type for ease of access during battle." Lord Wingate blinked, and Barnes, sensing his commander's confusion, added: "I had a friend who was with the supply corps. He told me all about it."

Lord Wingate nodded, "Maybe they were burned off by the explosion?"

"I don't think that's likely," Barnes shook his head, "Any blast powerful enough to burn off the labels would have also set off the propellant, and probably the explosive filling as well."

"The operators could have removed them manually," Lord Wingate supposed.

Barnes ran his fingers across the metal surface of the shell, "hmm... I don't see any paint residue. I don't think these shells ever had any labels to begin with," Barnes squinted, "Come to think of it, I don't think I've ever seen a shell like this before."

"What do you mean?" Lord Wingate raised an eyebrow.

"Just look at this," Barnes pointed to the metallic cone that formed the top of the shell.

Lord Wingate shrugged, "It looks like a regular impact fuse."

"It does not, my lord," Barnes protested, "Look at it. Impact fuses are supposed to be rounded and blunt, so that they can collapse upon impact. This one is tapered to a point. And furthermore, impact fuses are supposed to be made from a soft, malleable metal, usually copper or brass, but this—" Barnes flicked at the silvery-grey cone, producing a sharp ringing sound—"I think this is steel."

"So..." Lord Wingate was trying to follow along, "what does that mean?"

"I'm not sure," Barnes said, "I'd guess that this shell is designed for ...penetration? Perhaps for use against fortifications?"

A terrible thought occurred to Lord Wingate, "Or airships."

It all made sense; a shell like this could punch through an airship's outer armor and probably a few internal bulkheads as well, before exploding *inside* the ship itself. A direct hit to the reactor would mean instant death for all hands, and even a glancing blow could still leave a ship severely crippled. It was perfect. Horribly perfect.

"That..." Barnes shook his head, "That can't be it. No, no, no, it-it's not possible. They must be made for use against enemy fortifications. It's the only—"

"Hadvar doesn't build fortifications," Lord Wingate said, "Hadvari doctrine holds that the best defence is a strong offense. And Isafar doesn't have the industrial capacity to build large fortifications. There's nothing else for it: this shell is a ship-killer."

"But..." Barnes spluttered, "but why? Hadvar has no airships of their own. Why would we build a weapon that can only be of use *against* us?"

"I don't know," Lord Wingate said, "But there has to be some sort of explanation."

Lord Wingate noticed a small pattern of scratches carved into the surface of the shell cartridge, "What's that there?"

Barnes looked and shrugged, "Oh, that's just the production serial number. They imprint them on the propellant casings so that in the event of a misfire—"

"—They can be traced back to the factory!" Lord Wingate grinned as he completed Barnes's thought. Barnes matched the grin and nodded. The *Newton and Sons* assembly plant records would contain not only the design and overall type of the shell but also where they had been shipped and who had ordered them in the first place. It was everything they needed to unravel the mystery. At last, they had a lead.

"Good work, Barnes," Lord Wingate clapped his young protégé on the shoulder, "Let's see how many more of these ship-killer shells we can find."

Barnes set the shell down, and the two men began to scour the rest of the wreckage.

Lieutenant Wolfram Howard Wingate leaned against a hydraulic ram at the top of the cargo ramp of the skyfreighter *Sunset Lake*. He was getting grease on the back of his uniform, but he didn't care; that was what the WAVE girls were for. He was in a foul mood. Dammit, he was the tactical officer! The fourth-highest ranking officer on the *Dreadnought.* And he was being employed as a bloody strong-arm thug! If some WAVE bitch had to get her fingers dirty removing a few poxy grease stains from his jacket, well, too bloody bad for her.

He shut his eyes for a second, and wondered what his lord father was doing at the moment. *Probably something important,* he supposed, *Too important to spare any time for me.* Wolfram hadn't seen, written, or spoken to his father for nearly two years now. They had never really been close; Lord Wingate had always been distant and aloof from his family, always away on one important assignment or another. Still, Wolfram admired his lord father tremendously and, for the longest time, had wanted nothing more than to earn his father's approval.

When Wolfram's father approved his request to begin his training at the Royal Military Academy a year early at fifteen, he thought he had earned that approval, or at least had been well on the way to earning it. Unfortunately, the subsequent four years of humiliation, failure, and disgrace had evidently soured any approval Wolfram's father might have felt for him. When his father had recommended him for the tactical officer position on the *Dreadnought,* he thought his father might have given him a second chance. He had been quickly disabused of that notion.

Wolfram still wasn't exactly sure how he felt about his lord father. Of course he resented the man for shunting him away to this ignoble posting, but a part of him, a large part, still longed for his father's respect and approval. There was even a part of him that suspected that his father had been right to send him here; he had taken four years to complete a programme that most cadets managed in two, and thought he hadn't been at the very bottom of his class, he was still a pretty poor excuse for an officer.

As Wolfram loitered at the top of the cargo ramp, he watched the workers in the berth across from him. They were carrying large steel drums of liquid fulgurite fuel up the ramp to refuel their ship for another voyage. They talked amongst themselves as they carried the drums, two men to a load. Wolfram envied those men their ordinary, simple lives. They weren't soldiers or nobility, just honest men doing honest work.

That could be me, Wolfram considered. It would be simple; all he had to do was walk over to the local fleet headquarters, resign his commission, and walk away. *But what about Archie?* If Wolfram walked away from everything, his best friend would never forgive him.

Wolfram sighed. Archie Hakefeldt, a true friend who followed him into a dead-end assignment without a second thought. And Hudson Lowell Newton; Wolfram had grown up with him—they may as well have been blood kin. And Barlowe, the scoundrel who expertly juggled every vice a man could have. And Hamilton, the wisecracking cardsharp. Even Wagner, a few months shy of sixteen but so desperate to prove that he was no less a man than any other. They might be a terrible crew, but goddammit, Wolfram liked them.

Three pairs of boots beat a ragged rhythm on the steel deck panels, and Wolfram turned to see Captain Bowman, Lieutenant Butler, and another man, probably the captain of the *Sunset Lake*. Wolfram stood up straight and picked up the rifle that had slid off his shoulder and down to the ground.

"I think that's everything, Captain," Bowman was saying, "Have a safe run."

"Thank you, sir," the man bowed respectfully, "Clear skies to you as well." And he vanished back into his own ship.

Captain Bowman and Lieutenant Butler walked down the ramp, and Wolfram fell into step behind them. "Seemed like an honest trader," Butler said as he tucked the small logbook under his arm, "I hear Illyrian spices fetch a hefty price this time of year."

"That they do," Captain Bowman said, "but Illyrian liquor fetches an even heftier price all year round."

"Illyrian liquor?" Butler hurried to open his logbook, "There wasn't any Illyrian liquor listed among the ship's cargo."

"They stashed it behind one of the side panels," Captain Bowman said casually, "in the crawlspace between the inner and outer hull. It's a common hiding place. A lot of the crawlspaces on those older ships are pretty roomy. You can fit a lot of contraband in there."

"I'll mark it down," Butler said, making a note in the logbook, "We'll alert the constables, and have Aerodrome Control ground the ship—"

"Ah, don't bother," Captain Bowman said, "I only counted two crates. It's probably just the crew's personal stash. Besides, the guy's clearly a small-timer. No use in raising a fuss over it."

Wolfram could barely contain his disgust. *No use in raising a fuss?* That was precisely what a customs inspection was supposed to do! Was Captain Bowman trying to run some sort of extortion scheme?

Or was he simply shirking his duties? Wolfram would admit to being a terrible officer, but when he was ordered to do something, he bloody well did it.

How had someone like Captain Bowman even managed to get himself made up to captain? Wolfram remembered reading somewhere that Captain Bowman (he had been only *Sergeant* Bowman then) had led troops to some great victory somewhere, but judging by his mannerisms, he was no career soldier. He had probably been a conscript. He also seemed to be familiar with a number of smuggler's tricks; no doubt that had been his trade before military service. So how had a former smuggler (who had probably been pressed into service after being caught in the act) managed to reach the rank of captain?

It couldn't have been simply for valour. There was no way the army would have heaped such glory on a former smuggler, not even if *Sergeant* Bowman had led his troops clear across Analeria to the foothills of the *Halgari,* the line of mountains that marked the border of Hadvar. For that matter, how had Bowman even made sergeant in the first place?

Bribery, Wolfram supposed, *He must have some secret smuggler's cache of crowns squirreled away somewhere.* It made sense; the regular army didn't have the same entrenched honour as the ARAF You could get just about anything done in the army if you greased the right palms. *And now that he's back at his old stamping ground,* Wolfram inferred, *he'll no doubt exploit his new position by extorting bribes and getting back at old rivals.*

"And this next ship," Lieutenant Butler said as the three men stopped before the next berth, "Uh... hang on, let me consult the register—"

"The freighter *Silesia,*" Captain Bowman interrupted sullenly as he stalked up the cargo ramp, "Come on, let's get this one over with." Wolfram and Lieutenant Butler followed him up the steel ramp and into the cavernous interior of the airship. The ship looked deserted; there was no sound save for their three pairs of boots, and apart from a few drums of fuel secured in a corner with heavy cords, the cargo hold was completely empty.

"Kid," Captain Bowman said, stretching a hand towards Wolfram, "Hand me your rifle." Wolfram bristled at being called *kid* (he was one-and-twenty, dammit), but he complied nonetheless.

"Records say this vessel is registered to one Captain Victor Knox," Lieutenant Butler said as he made a note in his logbook, "but it looks like nobody's here at the mome—"

He was interrupted by a harsh clanging sound as Captain Bowman bashed against an exposed pipe with the barrel of the rifle. "Vic!" Bowman hollered over the noise, "You lazy bastard! Get your ass down here!"

For a few moments, the cargo hold was filled with the fading echoes of Captain Bowman's outburst. Then another sound: heavy boots on the upper deck. A moment later, the man was clattering down a narrow stairwell. "What the hell is wrong with you army types?" He screeched in a voice like a mechanical saw, "Why do you have to always come knocking at the worst possible—" He stopped suddenly as he reached the deck. "Paul?"

Captain Bowman roughly handed the rifle back to Wolfram and stalked towards the man. Captain Victor Knox was a lanky man, just a hair taller than Captain Bowman, and nearly as tall as Wolfram himself. His narrow face looked like that of an overgrown rat, arrogant and conniving. He was of an age with Captain Bowman, maybe a year or two older, and the two men evidently had a history together. *Getting back at old rivals,* Wolfram thought, *exactly as I suspected.*

"Well, look at you!" Knox said, his voice now soft and smooth as poisoned wine, "I thought you were still locked up!"

"They let me out early," Captain Bowman said, "Good behavior."

"And what's with that uniform?" Knox laughed slightly, "You one of Her Majesty's faithful little errand boys now, Private?"

"It's *Captain*," Bowman glared

"Captain?" Knox said, with false amazement, "That right?"

Captain Bowman's voice never wavered, "It was *very* good behavior."

"Well then, *Captain*," Knox gave the word a mocking tone, "What brings you and your fine gentlemen to my ship?"

"*Your* ship?"

"Yeah," Knox grinned, "*my* ship. Now, as I was saying, what brings—"

"Customs inspection," Captain Bowman interrupted, "So, Vic, anything to declare?"

Knox smiled, "Nope."

"Are you sure?" Captain Bowman pressed.

Knox's expression didn't change, "Absolutely."

"So you're telling me..." Captain Bowman said, "That if I were to rip up these deck plates, I won't find, say, a crate or two of Illyrian Sleepblossoms?"

"If you rip up my deck plates," Knox said with a laugh, "I think the Consortium'll be coming after you for harassing their interests!"

"Shit!" Lieutenant Butler choked. Wolfram glanced over at the officer; his face wore an expression of sudden shock, "Captain, we need to go."

"Not just yet," Captain Bowman said, "I know you're hiding something here Vic, and I'm gonna—"

"*Captain!*" Butler shouted. Captain Bowman turned to look at the shorter man, "We need to leave! This ship belongs to the Consortium!"

Captain Bowman slowly turned back to Knox, "I should have figured you'd roll over for the Consortium first chance you got," There was acid on his voice.

"Yeah," Knox gave another impregnable grin, "Funny how their money is better than scrounging for independent jobs."

"And the rest of the crew?" Captain Bowman continued, "How are they enjoying their reduced share of the profits?"

Knox shrugged, "Not my dog, not my fight."

"Captain, are you listening to me?" Butler protested, but Captain Bowman cut him off.

"Yeah, I heard you the first time." He turned about on his heel, "Let's move on to the next ship." Butler nodded, and Wolfram followed the two of them towards the cargo ramp.

Just before the three men reached the ramp, Knox called from across the cargo hold: "Hey, Paul!" Captain Bowman looked back, and Knox spread his arms, "You like my new jacket?"

Wolfram squinted; it looked like deerskin with fur lining along the inside of the collar. The coat didn't look new at all, but Wolfram supposed that it was still as warm as it had ever been.

Captain Bowman scowled, "I liked it better when it was mine."

Knox gave one last grin and vanished up the stairwell. Captain Bowman exhaled roughly and stalked out of the ship. Wolfram and Lieutenant Butler followed after him.

"I take it you have a history with that gentleman, Captain?" Butler said warily, "An old friend, perhaps?"

At the bottom of the ramp, Captain Bowman turned to look back up at the ship. "That ship was mine, you know," he said wistfully, "She's a rickety old first-generation relic, but for a few precious days, she belonged to me."

"What happened?"Butler asked, "If you don't mind my asking, captain?"

Captain Bowman's eyes narrowed, "I was conscripted. It's a long story."

"Excuse me, Lieutenant," Wolfram interrupted cautiously, "I don't believe I quite follow your reasoning. Why exactly did we not carry out an inspection on that last ship?"

"That freighter belongs to the Auroran Trade Consortium," Barnes explained, "They have their own in-house body that runs customs checks, for greater efficiency. We don't step in unless there's immediate evidence of criminal wrongdoing."

"But why did you pull us away so quickly?" Wolfram protested. If it was an honest misunderstanding over jurisdiction, surely a polite apology would have been enough—not that Captain Bowman would have been likely to give one of course.

"Because the Consortium gets pissy when other people get involved in their business," Captain Bowman said, "They like to throw their weight around to make sure people respect them."

"Then why did you antagonise that gentleman, sir?" Wolfram insisted.

"Kid," Captain Bowman interrupted, "you're not here to ask questions. That's our job. You're just here to make sure nobody gives us trouble."

"Sir," Wolfram protested, "I am the tactical officer, not a mere strong-arm! It is my job to manage the weapons systems on board the ship. I—"

"Good," Captain Bowman interrupted again, "You want to manage the weapons systems? You can start with that rifle you're carrying."

"Captain, I must protest—"

Captain Bowman rounded on Wolfram, and even though Wolfram was taller by a good ten centimetres, he found himself taking a step back, "What did you call me?" Captain Bowman said softly.

"C-Captain, sir," Wolfram stammered.

A smile spread across Captain Bowman's face, "Exactly, kid. Now shut the hell up and do as your *captain* tells you." He turned away, apparently very satisfied with himself.

Wolfram fumed with rage as he fell into step behind Captain Bowman and Lieutenant Butler. How dare that man treat him so? How *dare* he? Wolfram was Old Nobility; he could trace the lineage of his family back to the Founding of Aurora! Why, if his lord father were here...

He would tell me the exact same thing, Wolfram thought sullenly. Captain Bowman might be an unpolished working-class lout, but he was his commanding officer all the same, and Wolfram owed the man his obedience. *I'll follow his orders,* Wolfram told himself, *But that doesn't mean I have to like the bastard!*

With a scowl, Wolfram shrugged his shoulders, deliberately exacerbating the grease stain spreading on the back of his jacket.

The officers mess was a much better place for card playing than the bridge. Six officers sat at the long varnished oak table, relaxing and enjoying each other's company. It wasn't that anybody was especially tired, but still, today had seen the crew doing more actual work than most of them had ever done since being posted to the *Dreadnought.*

"What a day it's been, eh?" Lieutenant Newton stretched back in his chair and raised his crown glass of rye spirits. Archie met Newton's eye, raised his own glass, and toasted, "Cheers!" The two young officers turned their attention to the game that was beginning.

"Nothing like a nice crown of rye," Barlowe said as he downed his glass, "Really sets the nerves at ease after a hard day's work."

"*A hard day's work?*" Archie laughed, "I don't know when the last time *you* did a hard day's work was, but it sure as shit wasn't today!"

"Cut him some slack," Hamilton said with a grin as he dealt the cards for the opening hand, "It must be pretty hard avoiding all that work!"

"Yeah, yeah, keep laughing," Barlowe shook his head and picked up his cards. For a moment, all was silent as the players considered their hands.

"On the subject of games," Hamilton said after a few moments, "how's our little wager coming along, Mal?"

"Miss Meyers is putting up a bit of a fight," Barlowe smirked, "But I'll wear her down in time. Just you wait and see."

"Are you sure?" Wolfram said, "Perhaps your reputation precedes you?" Archie noticed a glint in his best friend's eye. There was undoubtedly something going on there.

"Bah, she's just playing hard-to-get," Barlowe scoffed, "Women are stupid like that. But trust me, once she sees what she's missing she'll come running like a—"

Barlowe cut off suddenly as Wolfram jabbed him with an elbow and nodded towards the stairwell leading down to the rest of the ship. Lieutenant Commander Vaughn was standing at the top of the stairs with a sheaf of papers tucked under one arm. In an instant, the officers mess fell deathly silent. Her frigid blue glare swept across the room, stopping on each of the six young men in turn; her face never lost its stone-carved expression of disdain.

Finally, Vaughn made a sound that was half a groan and half a sigh and stepped into the room. Six pairs of eyes followed her as she strode around the table and disappeared into the hallway leading towards the officers' quarters. Her departure was followed immediately by six sighs of relief.

"So," Newton said after an awkward pause, "what does everyone think of our new captain?"

"I like him," Archie said, "He seems like a decent enough fellow."

"Oh, please," Wolfram groaned, "you cannot be serious!"

"Well, why not?" Archie blinked at his friend's sudden vitriol, "Sure he's a little rough around the edges, but I think—"

"*Rough around the edges?*" Wolfram spluttered, "Archie, the man is a complete amateur!"

Archie shrugged, "So he's inexperienced. The fleet exercises are coming up in a month; is that really such a problem?"

"Yes! Yes, it is!" Wolfram insisted, "Captains are not supposed to be amateurs; captains need to be competent leaders, experienced and tested!" Wolfram gestured over his shoulder toward the officers' quarters, "It's a good thing we have Commander Vaughn with us. Imagine what Captain Bowman would be like without her holding his leash. God only knows what sort of an arse he's likely to make of himself at the fleet exercises."

"You know what I think?" Barlowe leaned forwards with one of his broad smirks, "I think you just hate the guy because he called your daddy a prick." Archie stifled a laugh.

"Shut up," Wolfram groaned and weakly tried to push Barlowe back.

"See?" Archie smiled, "Mal likes him too."

"Oh, no, I can't stand him either," Barlowe laughed, "The man's a goddamn slave driver."

"By which you mean he wants you to do your bloody job?"

Archie said.

"And how am I supposed to do my job with him breathing down my neck all the while?" Barlowe moaned.

"Exactly my point!" Wolfram came back in, "A properly experienced Captain would know when to intervene and when to step aside and let us work. But since Captain Bowman lacks that experience—"

"Shut up," Hamilton suddenly spoke up, "Just shut up, all of you!" Everyone looked at Hamilton who was slouching over his empty glass with a sullen look on his face. He didn't look at all like himself.

"Guys," he said in an uncharacteristically serious tone, "I've never flown a ship before today. Not in training, not at my previous posting... not ever," he paused for a moment, "I told him just before we raised ship."

"Damn," Barlowe said, trying to affect a conciliatory tone, "I bet he was pissed at you."

"That's the thing," Hamilton said, "He wasn't angry at all, at least not as I could see. He just took a knee and showed me how everything worked. Even walked me through the whole process. Landing too. And that was it."

For a moment, a pensive silence hung over the room.

"Where was your last posting again?" Wagner ventured warily, "I don't think you ever told—"

"Not the point!" Hamilton cut the boy off, "He just showed me how to do my job and that was it. He didn't get mad, didn't yell at me, didn't threaten to knock me back to midshipman third-class," Hamilton laughed weakly at that last one, "You can keep complaining for as long as you want. Say that he's inexperienced, or not a proper officer, or a bit of a prick, I don't care. He's alright in my book."

Hamilton leaned back in his chair and all of a sudden noticed the pile of cards in front of him. "Are we still playing or what?"

Carrying a tray of food up a spiral stairwell was no easy task. Louise Halford took the steps slowly and deliberately, only moving on to the next once she was absolutely certain of her footing. It took her nearly two whole minutes to climb all eleven steps, but at least she kept her balance.

At the top of the stairwell was a door of varnished wood. Louise gingerly shifted the tray onto one hand and knocked on the door.

Barely a moment later, Captain Bowman called out "Come in."

Louise didn't know if the captain's cabin of the Dreadnought was particularly rich or humble for the Fleet, but either way, it was the most luxury she had ever seen on an airship. The walls were paneled with dark lacquered wood, and the floor, made of the selfsame material, was covered with a soft carpet. At the far end of the chamber stood a fine feather bed, large enough to hold Louise and her four sisters all at once. At the foot of the bed, stood an ornately carved small table with a few chairs, and there sat Captain Bowman.

Paul Bowman wasn't at all like the sort of person Louise envisioned when she imagined an airship captain; not at all like her image of Dick Blunt, the dashingly heroic officer and gentleman from the penny dreadfuls that Louise would not admit to reading. Captain Bowman's speech was rough, and his voice carried the telltale accents of the lower class. His uniform, barely two days since new, was already showing the subtle early warning signs of neglect. He looked like the sort of man her mother would have warned her about, were she a few years younger. And that eye patch! No matter how she struggled, Louise could not keep her gaze from darting back to that scrap of black cloth, nor her mind from concocting all manner of grotesque deformities that might lurk beneath it.

Of course that wasn't to say that Captain Bowman was at all a bad man. He was unpolished in his ways, to be sure, and a little intimidating on the surface, but now that Louise had known him for a day, she found herself feeling much more at ease in his presence. That he had saved her life barely a week ago helped as well. Even despite his tragic illiteracy, there was a certain shrewdness, a certain cunning intelligence about Captain Bowman that she doubted any schooling could truly replicate; there was more to this man than perhaps even he himself was aware of.

Louise curtsied as deeply as she could while still holding her tray, "Your dinner, Captain."

Captain Bowman looked up and smiled, "Good. Bring it over here." Louise crossed the chamber, set the tray on the table before Captain Bowman, and lifted the cover, filling the chamber with the tempting aroma of shepherd's pie. "Take a seat, kid," Captain Bowman said as he began eating.

"W-what?"

Captain Bowman gestured at the tray, "The other plate is for you." Louise looked down; there were indeed two plates of food.

"Go on, sit down."

"I..." Louise was flummoxed. She ought to obey her captain, but was it really right to be so... informal? She was, after all, little more than a chambermaid with a uniform, "I... I don't believe it's proper to sit in the presence of my betters."

Captain Bowman laughed and shook his head. Louise flushed red in the cheeks; had she said something wrong? "Kid," Captain Bowman said, "I was a freighthauler for eighteen years. I'm nobody's *better*." He gestured at the empty seat across from him, "Sit down."

Louise paused for a moment and then took the seat. Surely nobody could fault her for being familiar with a superior officer if it was a direct order.

Suddenly, a thought occurred to Louise: if Captain Bowman, or any officer really, could order her to be familiar with him, what *else* could he order her to do? She was a young woman, and he a man of considerable experience; just how far did his power over her extend? Louise shook her head. It wasn't right to thing such awful things about her captain, especially after how wonderful he had been to her thus far. Still, she couldn't completely banish the thought from her head...

"It's okay," Captain Bowman said, between mouthfuls, "You can start eating."

"I..." Louise stammered, "Thank you, Captain, but I'm not hungry." That wasn't precisely true; she hadn't eaten her dinner yet, and she was famished, but this was hardly the time. Servants were not supposed to eat in the presence of their betters.

"Yes you are," Captain Bowman said, without a moments pause, "I never met anyone your age who wasn't hungry all the time."

"Thank you, Captain, but I've already eaten my din—"

"Louise," Captain Bowman said with a sigh. Louise perked up at the use of her proper name, "I see what you're doing. Trying to stay professional and all that. But it's starting to get a little ridiculous. Do yourself a favor, and loosen up a little."

Louise blushed; perhaps she was making too much of it after all. She picked up the fork beside her plate and paused for a moment, "You... won't tell anyone, will you, Captain?" It would not do for other people to learn how familiar she was with her captain.

Captain Bowman chuckled, "I'll keep your secrets if you keep mine," he said. Louise smiled back, and began eating. The shepherd's pie, as it turned out, was very good. It wasn't her creation, of course; she wasn't nearly skilled enough with an oven to produce a dish of this quality.

"You settling in alright?" Captain Bowman asked after a while.

"Yes, of course," Louise said as soon as she could swallow her food, "It may be some time before I have a proper schedule, but lodgings have been found for me, and I have already been assigned several miscellaneous duties."

"That's good, that's good," Captain Bowman nodded and shoveled another mountain of shepherd's pie into his mouth.

"I..." Louise ventured warily, "I understand you spent the afternoon performing customs inspections."

"Yeah," Captain Bowman groaned.

"I hope..." Louise stammered. How exactly should she phrase her question? "That is... you didn't... require my assistance, did you? I mean, with regards to..."

"You mean reading?" Captain Bowman said through a mouthful of potatoes, "Don't worry, I let Butler handle all that stuff. I just give it a glance once he's done and agree with whatever he says."

"I see," Louise nodded and took another bite.

"Besides," Captain Bowman chuckled, "it's all lists and ledgers and manifests. You don't have any experience with that sort of thing, do you?"

"A little," Louise said, "Not nearly as much as Leftenant Butler, I'm sure, but I used to manage inventory for my father. My sisters and I always liked to help out with running the family business, you see, and father approved because it kept operating expenses down. But I should hardly think that..." She looked back up, and trailed off awkwardly when she noticed that Captain Bowman was staring at her; his face frozen with vacant surprise. "Oh," Louise realised sheepishly, "you were... making a joke, yes?"

"Huh, I might be able to use you after all," Captain Bowman muttered. He shrugged and leaned back in his chair, "What's your story, kid?"

"My what?" Louise blinked.

"You know what I mean," Captain Bowman said, "What is it exactly makes a girl like you want to join up?"

"Well..." Louise began. She supposed Captain Bowman deserved to know, "...it wasn't so much a matter of wanting, but a matter of what was best for the family. Father's business has always been rather short on funds, you see, so father decided that I should join the WAVE when I came of age, in order to find a wealthy young husband who could provide our family with the raw capital needed to continue expanding."

Captain Bowman nodded slowly, his face an unreadable mask, "So... you're here to marry someone rich?"

"And noble, if at all possible," Louise added.

"Of course," Captain Bowman rolled his eyes—his *eye*, "Where was your mother in all this?"

"Oh, she approved of course," Louise said, "It was her idea to begin with, actually."

"And what about you?" Captain Bowman asked.

"W–what?"

"How do you feel about it?"

"Well..." Louise struggled to find the best words "It is... a sound business decision."

"That's not what I asked," Captain Bowman said, "I asked how you *feel* about it."

"I..." Louise was flummoxed. Nobody had ever asked how she felt about anything. Not ever. "I... I don't..."

"You're not sure, are you?" Captain Bowman said gently.

"No," Louise admitted, "I mean, I'm sure I'd like to get married someday. But I... I just don't know yet."

"I see," Captain Bowman gave an understanding nod.

"Forgive me Captain," Louise said, "I do wish I were more articulate on the matter, only I've not really given much thought to—"

"No, no, it's alright," Captain Bowman said, "I understand completely," A moment of silence passed between the two of them. Finally, Captain Bowman changed the subject, "So... is *every* girl on this ship here to get married?"

"I suspect so," Louise said, and quickly added, "well... except for Mistress Vaughn probably."

"Right, her," Captain Bowman groaned. That was a bad sign. Were Captain Bowman and Mistress Vaughn not getting on well?

After a short pause, Captain Bowman sat forwards, "I think it's time I got to the point of all this. I don't know this crew. I don't know anything about any of them. This conversation right here?" Captain Bowman gestured back and forth between them, "This is the longest I've ever spoken with anyone on this ship." Louise started to speak up, but stopped herself; their time spent memorising his letter of orders the night before probably didn't count. Captain Bowman continued, "And if I'm going to run this ship the way it oughta be run, I need to fix that as soon as possible."

Louise blinked, "Do you intend to have conversations like this with every single crewman?"

"I don't need to," Captain Bowman grinned, "I have you girls."

"I... I don't believe I understand," Louise said.

"Sure you do," Captain Bowman leaned back again, "A bunch of young women on a ship full of soldiers all looking to get married? I bet there's quite a bit of gossip going around. Am I right?"

"Well..." Louise blushed slightly. She had never really indulged in gossip all that much; she had always been shy and reserved around people to whom she was not related. But Captain Bowman was exactly right—the other WAVE girls spent almost all of their time caught up in gossip; even when they were engaged with their duties, still they gossiped like so many clucking hens. The WAVE girls on board the *Celsius* hadn't been nearly so undisciplined, "I try not to get involved with it," Louise protested, "It's not a very proper thing—"

"I don't think you understand," Captain Bowman interrupted, "You girls have the run of the ship. You can go anywhere, hear anything, talk to anyone. And all of it gets carried back to you girls. You can find out everything there is to know about this whole crew without them even suspecting a thing," there was a gleam in Captain Bowman's eye, "and *you* will bring the best of it back to me."

"You want... to listen to our gossip?" Louise ventured.

"Ah, ah, ah," Captain Bowman waved his finger, "It's not gossip anymore. From now on, it's *intelligence.*"

Louise considered Captain Bowman's proposal. It just might work; she was still new enough to the ship that she could still make first impressions with the other WAVE girls. And as the new girl, she had a ready alibi for her inquisitiveness. Of course, she would probably have to double- and triple-check everything she heard to make sure she didn't report anything spurious by accident. She would also be playing a delicate balancing act to make sure she didn't betray her true purpose to her unsuspecting comrades. It would be a lot of work.

"Captain," Louise ventured one final question, "do you really believe I'm the right person for this task?"

Captain Bowman chuckled softly and shook his head, just like her father used to do. "You know," he said, "there was a kid I knew at the Southern Gap. An innkeeper's son from down south who ran off and joined the army so he could see the world. A real bright kid. I never told him, but he was probably the smartest person I ever met."

Captain Bowman was pensive for a moment, and then continued, "You remind me of him. A young kid, not too sure of herself but definitely smarter than the people around her, just trying to figure out where she fits in this crazy world."

"With respect Captain," Louise said, "you've not known me for very long."

"I've known you long enough," Captain Bowman's mouth quirked into a smile, "You're not the sort of girl who'd be content to spend the rest of her life changing other people's bedsheets. You've got the makings of someone great in you. I know you can handle this job."

Louise blushed deeply, "You flatter me Captain."

Captain Bowman set his knife and fork back onto his now empty plate, "Take the rest of the night off and get a good night's sleep. To-morrow, see what you can learn, and we'll meet back here to see what you've found out." Louise nodded and collected the dishes. Just before she slipped back out the door, Captain Bowman added, "Trust the wind, kid. She'll take you where you need to go."

Louise couldn't keep the giddy smile from off her face as she descended the stairwell. She greatly appreciated Captain Bowman's confidence in her, even if it was misplaced. Or was it? there was a part of her that wasn't entirely sure about that.

If nothing else, Louise told herself, *this should be fun!*

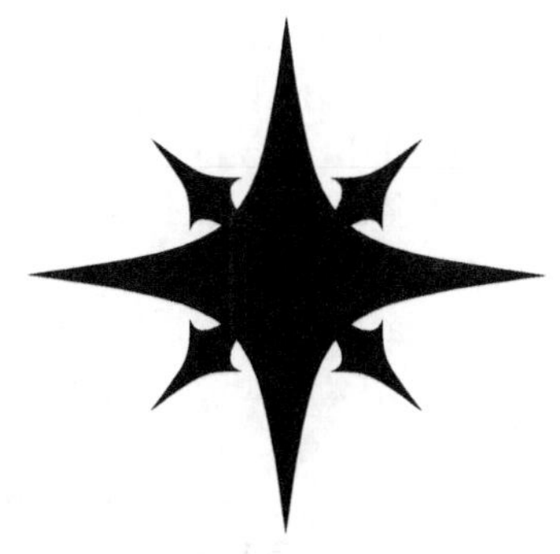

Chapter X

A Place Where I Fit

THE mechanical ringing of the acceleration bell filled the bridge. A moment later, the deck plates began to vibrate with the familiar sensation of four impact columns coming to life. Finally, the *Dreadnought* began to rise up into the sky to begin her patrol.

"So," Paul said in a low voice for only Hamilton to hear, "you have to ring that damn bell every single time the ship makes a move?"

"Yes, sir," Hamilton said, "Once when starting, twice for short movements, and thrice when coming to a halt."

"We never did anything like that on civilian freighters," Paul glanced over his shoulder at Vaughn, "The army's got a damn procedure for everything."

"How does a civilian ship usually alert its crew about movement, sir?" Hamilton asked. He seemed to be gaining confidence.

"We don't," Paul shrugged, "Usually the crew just keep close to a bulkhead so we have something to grab onto. If it's something really serious like a rainsquall, then we'd alert everyone over the..."

That's right. No loudspeakers on this ship. Paul clenched his jaw. He would really have to do something about that. Honestly, how the hell was he supposed to run a ship without loudspeakers? No wonder this ship had earned such an awful reputation.

"Alright, I think that's high enough," Paul said, bringing his attention back to Hamilton, "You can level us off now."

"Aye, sir," Hamilton nodded and eased off on the vertical thrust.

"Navi," Paul turned toward Hakefeldt, "What's our heading?"

"North-by-west, Captain," Hakefeldt called out, "bearing three-four-nine."

"You remember how to do this?" Paul whispered to Hamilton. The boy nodded back, "I think so." He bent the stick to his right and the ship tilted with his touch. Paul smiled, the kid was still sloppy, but he would improve with practice.

Paying no mind to the unnatural angle of the deck, Paul turned and walked back to his chair at the center of the bridge. Hakefeldt was gripping the map table for dear life while also trying to keep his papers from sliding off. Wingate and Wagner both had death grips on their consoles. Vaughn hadn't moved an inch.

"You've got a good sense of balance," Paul said as he dropped down into his chair, "I take it you've served on other ships?"

"I have, Captain," Vaughn didn't look up from her logbook.

"Well... which ones?" Paul asked.

"Others," Vaughn still didn't look up.

Paul glared up at the woman looming beside his chair. What was her problem? He had tried to offer a truce, but she was still as sullen and moody as ever. *She's trying to bait me,* Paul thought, *trying to get me to lose my cool and embarrass myself in front of the crew.* Paul smirked—if that was her game, he wasn't going to play it. *I'll let her stew in her own gall for a while until she's ready to meet me on my terms.*

"Navi," Paul called, "How's our course?"

"Patrol route set and holding, Captain," Archie called back. "Two hundred and fifty kilometres to the north and six hundred and fifty to the south. That's eighteen hundred in total. I estimate thirty hours round-trip time at quarter-cruising speed."

"Good work, kid," Paul acknowledged. He still had no idea just how long those *killer-meter* things were, but he could figure that out on his own time.

Speaking of time, Paul wondered, *how exactly do you spend time on a patrol?* On every other voyage Paul had ever flown, the whole point had been to get somewhere as quickly as possible. The destination had been the point, not the voyage itself. But a patrol was completely different, wasn't it? Here, the entire point of the trip was the trip itself. So... what were you supposed to do?

Paul stood up from his chair and walked slowly to the forward window. He certainly wasn't going to ask Vaughn for help with this, not with her attitude. Paul glanced over at Wolfram, slouching over his weapons console. He wouldn't ask that sulking brat either. He could ask Hakefeldt, Hamilton, or Wagner, but he doubted any of those junior officers would have an answer for him. Paul reached the forward window and shrugged; he would just have to make things up as he went along.

Paul watched as the city of Longview thinned out and gave way to the dry, cold highlands of the Analerian Plateau. Commodore Wilmont had ordered him to look for signs of smuggling activity along the edge of the mountains. That was a clear enough order, but was there a certain way he was supposed to go about it? There had to be more to the job than just staring out a window for thirty hours.

Then Paul got an idea. He turned away from the window and asked to nobody in particular, "Hey, does this ship have a top deck?"

"Of course," Vaughn was the first to respond naturally, in her almost violently neutral tone, "The officer's quarters."

"No, no," Paul shook his head, "Above that. A *top* deck."

"You mean... like a white room?" Wolfram said.

"What the hell even is a white room?" Paul snapped, "No, I mean *outside!* On *top* of the ship."

"Oh, you mean a hatch!" Wagner spoke up eagerly, "Oh yeah, sure. This ship has one of those. It's right at the top of the stars, and through the crawlspace with the radio syst—" He cut off suddenly when he noticed that Vaughn was glaring at him. "W-what? Did I say something wrong?"

"Well then," Paul shrugged, "I'm going topside for a bit."

"Captain," Vaughn said, finally looking from her book, "would you care to explain yourself?"

"Our orders are to look for signs of smuggling," Paul said as he made his way to the stairwell, "I can't see a whole lot from here, so I'm going topside to get a better view."

"Captain," Vaughn continued, "would it not be preferable to delegate this task to someone more junior?"

Paul gave Vaughn a crooked look, "Are you volunteering?"

Vaughn gestured with her damn book, "With respect Captain, I am otherwise tasked at the moment."

"Yeah, you look *real* busy," Paul continued toward the stairwell at the back of the bridge. Finally, he stopped just before the door and called back, "Wingate, you have the bridge until I get back." Paul slipped into the stairwell just as two voices squawked "What?!" He grinned mischievously, *That oughta throw them for a loop!*

Sure enough, at the top of the stairwell, there was a series of metal rungs leading up to a hatch just beneath the ceiling. Paul climbed up to the hatch, wrenched open the rusty handle, and scrambled through a narrow crawlspace where he found another hatch that opened out into the bright cold howling air above the ship.

Paul kept low as he waited for his eye to adjust to the sunlight. Nearly three decades of airship life had given him an excellent sense of balance, but he knew as well as anyone that up here, with the blinding sun and battering winds, his balance only needed to fail once. Finally, his vision adjusted enough to notice a thick wire within arm's reach that ran the entire length of the ship from prow to stern. Most ships had guide wires like this, even if they didn't have top hatches. Paul grasped the wire firmly and pulled himself upright.

With his position atop the ship now secure, Paul finally looked out across the magnificent scenery. To his right in the east, the snow-capped peaks of the Mountains of Dawn loomed over everything. And to his left in the west lay the rolling red-brown hills of the Analerian Plateau. Every now and then, a small stream would trickle out of the mountains, small farms sprouting along its path as it continued east down the slope toward Two Lakes. It was a hard country. Hard but beautiful.

Uncle Howard would have loved this view.

Paul didn't quite know why, but grand scenes like this always made him think of his old uncle Howard Bowman. He had been the closest thing Paul had ever had to a father. He had taught Paul everything he would need to know to be the best freighthauler in the skies, from how to lift heavy crates without straining your back, to how to speak Hadvari so that the Illyrian smugglers didn't cheat you blind. *I miss him.*

Paul could feel his heart sinking as he carefully made his way along the roof plating towards the stern. Thinking about Uncle Howard had always made him sad, but over the years it had gotten steadily worse. It probably wasn't helped by the realization that Uncle Howard's face was beginning to fade from his memory. Paul suspected that in a few more years he wouldn't even be able to recognize a photoportrait of Howard Bowman, not that there had ever been enough time or spare coin floating around to sit for one of those luxuries.

Finally, just before he reached the stern, Paul came upon a small dip. This was where the layout of the ship changed from three decks to two decks. *Three and a half decks,* he had sometimes heard it called. The sick bay was probably right below this, and the engine room directly below that. Up here on the roof, the missing half deck made the perfect hiding place from the howling winds. Keeping his grip on the wire, Paul slid down the slope and nearly jumped out of his skin when he realized that he was not alone atop the roof.

"Oh dear!" laughed the dark-haired, beak-nosed man who was reclining against the slope, "My hiding place has been discovered!"

"At ease, soldier," Paul laughed back, "It's Pratt, isn't it? Doc Pratt?"

"Doctor Dirk Alexander Pratt," the man said getting to his feet, "And I'm no soldier. Just a working man."

"For a working man," Paul said, "you don't look very busy."

"Well, there's not a whole lot to be done hereabouts," Doctor Pratt said awkwardly, "and there's only so many times one can organise the shelves before it starts to get boring."

Paul shrugged and sat down against the slope, "Yeah, I guess that's fair."

Doctor Pratt sat back down beside Paul and took in a deep, relaxing breath, "Besides, I rather enjoy the view from up here." He pointed a finger directly astern, "Just look at that..."

A few hundred feet astern of the *Dreadnought,* a dozen or so large birds of prey soared lazily along after the ship. They barely needed to flap their wings at all as they glided gracefully on the turbulence in the ship's wake. "Majestic, isn't it?" Doctor Pratt said.

"We used to see them all the time," Paul smiled, "My uncle and I would catch small vermin from the cargo hold, toss them overboard, and watch the birds dive after them."

"Well, so much for majesty!" Doctor Pratt laughed, "Tossing a bunch of dead rats off the back of an airship for carrion birds!"

"Oh no, they were alive," Paul said, "They had to be alive or the birds would just spit them back out and ignore you for the rest of the trip. No fun in that." That made Doctor Pratt laugh some more.

"So," Doctor Pratt managed as soon as he could breathe again, "you were raised on airships like this I take it? Does military service run in your family?"

"Nah," Paul shook his head, "My uncle worked on commercial skyfreighters. He took me in when I was a kid."

"I see," Doctor Pratt nodded, "Well, for such humble beginnings, I must say you seem to have done rather well for yourself."

"Thanks," Paul said, "What about you? The way you talk, you sound a bit like one of the nobility."

"Nope, common as dirt," Doctor Pratt said, "I was born all the way down in Last Watch, right on the edge of the Disputed Zone. You ever been down there?"

Paul shook his head, "That's pretty out of the way. Not a whole lot of air freight going through Last Watch."

"Believe me you're not missing anything special," Doctor Pratt rolled his eyes, "The town practically hibernates for months at a time. Then the ranchers bring in their cattle, and everything is chaos for a week or so until the barges can come from Riga. Then the town spends a few days cleaning up the vomit and broken glass, and everything goes back into hibernation again." Doctor Pratt laughed ruefully, "Even Hadvar ignored us. Three decades of war, and we didn't see so much as a scouting party."

Paul shrugged, "Doesn't sound all that bad actually." He was starting to get to that age when excitement wasn't quite the lure it used to be. Besides, between that mess at the Southern Gap and everything that had come after it, he wouldn't say no to a little top-quality boredom.

"Well, be that as it may," Doctor Pratt said, "one day, a bunch of travelling preachers came up the river from Riga. I managed to convince them to take me along with them, and they brought me to the seminary in Marburg."

"So you ran off to become a preacher?" Paul said, "How did you get from there to being the doctor on the worst ship in the fleet?"

Doctor Pratt laughed lightly, "Well, it's a long story. I learned a great deal in Marburg, but I never really quite fit in, so I left after a while.

I wandered around for a few years after that, worked a number of fly-by-night jobs here and there. Eventually I started working as a doctor. I picked up some of the trade in Marburg; every clergyman has to train as a reserve medical corpsman, you see. After a while, someone suggested volunteering with the fleet. But since I never actually received any formal certification, I got assigned to this lovely old dump. And here I am!"

"So you finally found a home, eh?" Paul said.

"Well," Doctor Pratt sighed, "I don't know about that. It's been almost fifteen years, but I still feel distinctly out of place here." He laughed awkwardly, "Y'know, I'm starting to think I'll never really find a place where I fit."

Paul nodded. It was funny, but he felt the exact same way. Hell, maybe everyone on the entire ship felt like that every now and again.

Life was just like that sometimes.

It was just after sundown when Fiora finally slipped back into her cabin. She carelessly tossed the logbook onto her bed, followed by her uniform jacket, gripped the brass pole, and pulled herself up into the rest position to begin her exercises. She snorted furiously, like a beast on the prowl, as her muscles clenched and relaxed. All the while, visions of Captain Bowman taunted and jeered at her through a haze of bile and bitterness.

How dare that common-born cretin treat her, a noblewoman with a bloodline reaching back to the very Founding of Aurora, with such vile contempt? How dare he shirk his duties to go sightseeing on the roof, as though this were some holiday walking party? And what was the meaning of declaring Leftenant Wingate in charge instead of her when she was clearly the senior officer on the bridge? The man was as incompetent as the day was long, but that last affront could be explained only by spite!

Fiora paused in the middle of her exercise. How many had she completed so far? She had been so consumed with her resentment that she had lost count. Fiora groaned and started again from zero. The extra exhaustion would help her sleep, and she would need to add more repetitions to her routine soon enough anyways.

With her evening exercises finished, Fiora flopped down upon her bed with a groan. What a bloody awful day this had been! *This is what it's going to be like now,* she thought, *every single blasted day from here on out.*

Fiora closed her eyes and wondered, not for the first time, if she had made the wrong decision in joining the fleet. Would she have been happier if she had simply kept her head down and gotten married when she was sixteen like a proper young noblewoman? Fiora had always been good with numbers; managing a family estate couldn't possibly be as much of a bother as running an airship. And perhaps, if she could have given her poor father some grandchildren in time, maybe he would still... *Stop that!* Fiora told herself before the tears could well up in her eyes, *You've ridden that train of thought before, and it is a dead end.*

And in any case, the past was in the past; there was no use fretting about what might have been. She was married to the fleet now, and that was that. *And what a fine bloody marriage it has been!* Fiora didn't even have the means to leave; boys like Leftenant Wingate could resign their commissions and quietly rejoin civilian life, but Fiora couldn't. She had no living relatives that she knew of, the family fortune and estate had long since withered away, and at eight-and-twenty, she had no delusions about any marriage prospects. Fiora was all that remained of the ancient and noble Vaughn bloodline, and she was all alone in the world.

Some days, Fiora wondered what was the point of it all anymore. She had thought about killing herself a few times, particularly after all that she had been forced to go through to secure the only promotion of her career, only to find herself shuffled away to the worst ship in the fleet. She had never seriously entertained the idea though. At this point, suicide would just be admitting defeat, and there was no way in hell she would give anyone that satisfaction. Fiora laughed weakly; spite wasn't exactly the healthiest motivation, but it was better than nothing.

And perhaps it wouldn't always be this bad. In a few weeks, the fleet would be holding their first ever peacetime exercises outside South Sands. Fiora had been systematically kept away from combat during the war against Hadvar, and she had little doubt that such a policy had severely hamstrung her career. But now that major combat operations were over, they couldn't possibly object to her participation. It would be the perfect opportunity to show the top brass what she was really capable of.

Of course, Captain Bowman would still be in charge during the exercises. Fiora groaned at that; whatever she managed to accomplish, she would do it in his shadow. And that was even assuming that Captain Bowman was even a skilled enough captain to bring glory to the *Dreadnought,* which he very likely was not. Still, it was Fiora's only realistic shot at reviving her career. If this failed, what would be left for her?

A soft tap at her cabin door shook Fiora from her contemplation, "Who is it?" she called out as she scrambled off the bed.

"Excuse me, mistress," a small voice answered from the other side of the door. It was one of the WAVE girls, "They said you forgot to take your supper."

Fiora blinked. She had indeed forgotten to get dinner and had barely noticed her murderous hunger. She strode over to open the door and was met with a timid looking short blonde girl holding a covered tray, "Thank you, girl. I'll take it at my desk."

Vaughn turned on her heel and marched over to her desk, then turned back around when she noticed that the WAVE girl wasn't following after her. "Is there a problem, girl?" she asked curtly.

The WAVE girl didn't move, "Shall I... put on the light for you, mistress?"

Vaughn hadn't noticed the darkness either. The dying rays of twilight had been illumination enough for her when she had first entered, and her eyes had simply adjusted to the darkness. "No need for that," Vaughn continued on to her desk, turned on her desk lamp, and adjusted it slightly so that it softly illuminated the entire cabin, "Is that good enough, girl?"

"I... believe so," the WAVE girl said as she awkwardly crossed the threshold into the cabin, "Thank you, mistress."

Vaughn took a seat at her desk as the WAVE girl set the tray down before her and removed its cover. All at once the cabin was filled with the aroma of mutton and fried potatoes. There was always some form of potatoes for dinner, but Vaughn had long since found more important things to complain about.

"Thank you, girl. That will be all," Vaughn said as she picked up the small linen napkin and tucked it carefully into her collar, "Don't bother collecting the dishes. I'll drop them off in the officer's mess when I'm finished." Vaughn picked up her knife and fork and stopped just short of carving off her first bite of mutton when she noticed that the girl was still standing beside her. That was odd; most of the girls leaped at the chance to be out of her presence. "Is there something else?"

"May I ask you a question, mistress?"

Vaughn looked the girl up and down; she was that new girl, the one who had arrived with Captain Bowman two nights ago. Halford, that was her name. She evidently hadn't yet learned the way things worked on the *Dreadnought.* Absently, Vaughn wondered what chain of indiscretions had paved this poor girl's path to the worst ship in the fleet. "You may," Vaughn said warily.

"It's about our captain," Miss Halford began a little uneasily, "What do you think of Captain Bowman?"

Vaughn bit her lip to keep herself from groaning or rolling her eyes. Captain bloody Bowman was the absolute last person she wanted on her mind right about now, but it would not do for rumors to start spreading about tensions between the captain and the executive officer. "I'm afraid I don't know him very well," Vaughn said, straining for diplomacy, "though his reputation is not inconsiderable. I suppose only time can tell what sort of officer he is."

"Yes, I suppose so," Miss Halford said, "Although, that isn't quite what I had in mind, mistress. I wanted to ask what *you* think about him, as... as a man," she paused, "I... well, I'm sure there's a more concise way of putting it, but I just wanted to know if—"

"Let me stop you right there, girl," Vaughn interrupted curtly, "He's not for you."

Miss Halford blinked, "W-what?"

Vaughn sighed; the poor girl was clearly a hopeless romantic. She was evidently looking for a husband, like every other WAVE girl in the fleet, but she was looking in exactly the wrong place. *The work of too many penny dreadfuls, no doubt,* Vaughn surmised, *they've planted false ideas of romance in the minds of a generation of young girls,* "Try Ensign Hamilton," Vaughn suggested, "or perhaps Leftenant Hakefeldt. Either of those two would make you a much better husband than Captain Bowman."

"Forgive me mistress," Miss Halford stammered, "I fear I've not properly communicated my intent—"

"I think you've wasted enough time already," Vaughn said firmly, "I'm sure you have duties elsewhere."

Miss Halford was silent for a moment, then answered with a thoroughly disappointed, "Yes, mistress." Vaughn watched out of the corner of her eye as the girl curtsied and turned to leave.

"One more thing, girl," Vaughn said, just before Miss Halford reached the door. The girl turned back about and curtsied, "Yes mistress?"

"*Ma'am.*"

"P-pardon?"

"You are to address me as '*ma'am*' or '*Leftenant Commander,*' not '*mistress,*' " Vaughn said, "You're not a chambermaid in a manor house; you're a military volunteer, and you will speak as one. Do I make myself clear?"

Miss Halford curtsied once more, "I understand mistr– *ma'am.*" The door closed behind her, and Fiora was alone in her cabin once again.

Fiora sighed heavily; goddammit, but she envied that girl. Miss Halford didn't have to deal with dirty looks, with whispers following after her like a wake on the ocean, with a crew that only begrudgingly obeyed her orders. That girl had friends; her duties made sense; she knew where she fit. Her life was simple. *Perhaps I should have gone into the WAVE instead.*

The perfect clarity of hindsight could be bloody frustrating like that sometimes.

Fiora shrugged and picked up her knife and fork. The potatoes were already starting to get cold.

Captain Bowman shook his head and prodded at his mutton with his fork, "Really? Not a damn thing?"

"I'm sorry," Louise apologised, "She wasn't very forthcoming."

"Ah, it's not your fault," Captain Bowman waved his hand dismissively, "It's just frustrating is all."

Louise could hardly blame Captain Bowman for his consternation. When he had given her this assignment yesternight, she had quickly decided to focus the lion's share of her efforts on mistre— *Leftenant Commander* Vaughn. Captain Bowman had clearly been having issues with her, and he would no doubt have been mightily impressed if Louise could have produced some pearl of insight about Commander Vaughn. Alas, the commander hadn't been in an especially loquacious mood.

"Is there anything we know about her for certain?" Captain Bowman asked.

"We know that she is a noblewoman," Louise offered, "from one of the Old Houses." It wasn't much, and the look Captain Bowman gave her said that he already knew this, but what else could she do?

"What about rumors?" Captain Bowman suggested, "Someone's got to know something about her."

Louise wasn't sure what to say. She had indeed heard a number of scandalous rumours about Commander Vaughn: She preferred women. She preferred boys. She joined the fleet to escape a monstrous husband. She joined the fleet to honour the memory of her husband. She had murdered her husband and assumed his rank. She had paid for her rank with sexual favours. She had faked her death and was living under an assumed name. She was a traitor on the run from justice. She was the rightful Queen of Aurora. There were as many rumours about Commander Vaughn as there were WAVE girls to tell them. And if one of those fanciful tales actually turned out to be true, Louise would be very surprised indeed!

"I..." Louise wondered which rumour sounded most plausible, or rather, the least outrageously implausible, before deciding to give the whole matter a miss, "I've not been able to corroborate anything."

Captain Bowman laughed ruefully, "No, I bet you haven't!"

"I don't get a sense that she really converses with anyone, at least not when she comes off duty," Louise offered, "and I can't really say I'm surprised."

"Why is that?" Paul asked.

Louise shrugged, "It's hardly a natural thing for a woman to serve aboard an airship in a man's capacity, don't you think?"

"Not really," Paul said, "I knew a few women engineers back when I was a civilian."

Louise blinked, "Really?"

"Yeah," Paul said, "I mean sure, you're not exactly tripping over 'em in the hallways or anything, but you run into 'em every now and again."

"I see," Louise nodded, "Though I was thinking more in terms of *military* airships. A woman serving on a ship like this one is hardly natural."

"Well, why shouldn't it be?" Captain Bowman shrugged, "It's not like this is a regiment of infantry. I mean, they're not marching us twenty-five miles a day with fifty pounds of kit on our backs. There's no reason a woman shouldn't be able to keep up on a job like this."

"Well... perhaps," Louise shrugged. She had to admit, Captain Bowman made a decent point, "But it's hardly traditional for a woman to—"

"Yeah," Captain Bowman interrupted, "I think you know where I stand on *tradition*." The scowl on Captain Bowman's face left no room for ambiguity.

"Let's move on," Captain Bowman said after a short pause. Louise didn't protest; they could always come back to Vaughn some other time. Perhaps a few more days would soften her attitude. And if not... well, there were plenty of other people on the ship, after all.

Like Ensign Powell Eugene Wagner. "His father is a wealthy industrialist," Louise explained, "He bought Ensign Wagner's commission without sending him to the Academy at South Sands. Apparently the rest of the fleet doesn't appreciate people jumping the queue like that, so they posted him here." Captain Bowman remarked that Wagner must be feeling rather sullen about being posted here, but Louise wasn't so certain; she'd had a brief chat with Ensign Wagner, and he had seemed rather optimistic about his career prospects. He seemed blissfully unaware of the *Dreadnought's* poor reputation.

The conversation shifted to Ensign Marius Noel Hamilton. "His father works for a mineral exploration firm in Analeria. He was originally posted on another ship but was transferred here after about six months." As to why he had been transferred, Louise had to admit that she did not know. Ensign Hamilton had evidently been very tight-lipped about his service record; Louise couldn't even ferret out the name of the ship upon which he had originally served.

Leftenant Junior Grade Malcolm Barlowe was a different matter entirely. "He is a minor nobleman from outside Kalmar, with a long family history of military service. Apparently he had a promising career ahead of him, but he fell victim to a number of vices, and so found himself posted here." When Captain Bowman enquired about which vices specifically, Louise struggled to keep from blushing as she recounted all the vivid details she had managed to gather. Barlowe had achieved a near-legendary reputation as a rogue, and everyone to whom Louise had spoken about him had been more than eager to recount scandal after scandal.

From there, Louise moved on to the WAVE girls. There was Mary Bauer who had regularly shirked her duties while serving on the airship *Dawn Spear*. There was Jesslyn Meyers who had borne a bastard daughter several months previously. There was Cecilia Hannauer whose chronic limp rendered her next to useless, but who couldn't be dismissed without offending one of the fleet's primary shipbuilding contractors. There was Ursula Ophelia Malden whose habit of casually including sensitive information in her personal letters had very nearly gotten her beheaded for espionage. And then there was Annette Brownstone who was... well, really just a bit of a twit.

As Louise concluded her report, Captain Bowman gave her a warm smile, "Not bad for your first day, kid."

"Thank you, Captain," Louise returned the expression. She had found the endeavour to be supremely diverting, and not nearly as difficult or frightening as she had initially feared. "I assume we shall be holding a similar meeting tomorrow night?"

"That's the plan," Captain Bowman said as he shoveled the last of his mutton into his mouth.

"I must say," Louise said, trying to ignore Captain Bowman's most uncouth table manners, "the crew appears to be in overall rather high spirits."

"Really?" Captain Bowman laughed through a full mouth, "That's not gonna last."

"Well, one cannot say for certain," Louise shrugged, "Perhaps the crew is feeling optimistic about the upcoming fleet exercises."

Paul blinked, "The what?"

Chapter XI

What About the Exercises

WOLFRAM was still rubbing grit from his eyes when he slunk onto the bridge. He walked over to the tactical station and gave Leftenant Zeigler a strong pat on the shoulder. "Get up, Barry. Your shift is done. I'm taking over"

Leftenant Bartholomew Zeigler awoke with a start. Wolfram wasn't surprised; Zeigler had been sent to the *Dreadnought* for sleeping on duty, so it only made sense that he would continue with that habit here. Zeigler nodded at Wolfram, got up, and slipped quietly out of the bridge.

Wolfram took his seat at gate gunboard and steeled himself for another twelve hours of mind-numbing boredom. He stared at the array of controls before him; this configuration had been obsolete for decades, but he could still identify every switch. Every dial. Every warning light. Not that he would ever need to use any of that knowledge.

Every now and again, Wolfram would daydream about battle. Waves of Hadvari soldiers would come storming out of the west like a tidal wave of red and brown to lay waste to Analeria once more, with only the *Dreadnought* standing in their way. Wolfram could see his fingers flying across the tactical controls, sending a withering hail-storm of high explosives and shrapnel to check the advance of the Hadvari menace long enough for ground troops to show up and beat them back. He could see himself being personally decorated for valour by Her Majesty the Queen. *Or maybe by my father...*

Wolfram lifted his gaze from the tactical controls and stared out the window. That was the one thing he actually liked about this position: the view. The rolling brown hills of Analeria stretched west as far as the eye could see. It made for a welcome change of scenery from the inside of the Norvell aerodrome.

As Wolfram watched the terrain go by, battles began to play out in his mind. He noted a small gap between two steep hills. *Ideal choke point. A few pre-sighted mortars and a decent lure squad would turn it into a pretty solid kill zone.* A long, gently curving ridgeline overlooking a river. *Perfect position to dig in and fortify. Maybe spread out some razorwire on the slope or possibly some of those new pressure-triggered anti-infantry bombs.* Of course Hadvar had never actually made it this far into Analerian territory; their deepest thrust had ground to a halt at the Siege of Two-Lakes, but that wasn't the point of the exercise.

Wolfram had always had a good eye for strategy, even before his time at the academy. He could still remember being five years old, sneaking into his father's study late at night, and opening up the large atlas of Aurora and Analeria to look at all the maps. Sometimes he would bring his toy soldiers and march armies across the maps in pretend wars. One night, his lord father had caught him in the act, but instead of sending him back to bed with a rough word and a spank, he sat down on the carpet beside him and recounted the story of the two Battles of Mount Blood (well, the *first* two; the other five hadn't been fought yet).

Wolfram smiled at the memory. It was one of the only happy memories he had of his lord father. Marion had been born a few months later, and Lord Wingate had showered her with attention, much more attention than he had ever given his firstborn son. He had done much the same with Sophie when she had been born six years later. Sometimes Wolfram felt like his father had forgotten about him. Or was trying to.

Wolfram had learned even more about strategy at the academy, but his time there had been watered down with less useful subjects—junk like logistics, administration, engineering, and mathematics. Wolfram resented being forced to study subjects like those; he had gone to South Sands to become a strategist and a leader, not a bloody regimental clerk. Yet the instructors had insisted that he apply himself to those useless topics as well. Had Archie not been helping him cheat during his last two years, Wolfram would probably still be stuck in South Sands, frantically trying to puzzle out the answer to some inane logistics problem.

The bi-annual South Sands wargames had been another point of frustration. Wolfram had been the unquestioned master of those games, of course, but whenever it had come time for the debriefing, the instructors had viciously castigated him for disregarding some ridiculous restriction or other. How was Wolfram supposed to have known that certain areas were out of bounds? Or that peeking at the battle plans the night before wasn't allowed? Nobody ever paid any attention at those tedious briefings anyways.

"Captain on deck," Commander Vaughn announced tersely.

Wolfram looked up. Captain Bowman stepped onto the bridge, followed by Leftenant Butler. "This is ridiculous!" Captain Bowman moaned, "How the hell am I just learning about this now?"

"What do you mean, Captain?" Leftenant Butler asked.

"You know what I mean," Captain Bowman said, "It's these goddamn exercises. Was anyone ever going to tell me about them?"

"What about the exercises, Captain?" Commander Vaughn said as she stood to vacate the captain's chair, "They were announced two months ago; surely you heard of them."

"I was still a civilian two months ago," Captain Bowman plopped himself down in the captain's chair without a whiff of decorum, "Hell, I wasn't even in the fleet until about a week ago."

"An innocent oversight, no doubt," Commander Vaughn said. Wolfram smirked, he could almost taste the sarcasm dripping off her voice.

"Well, I know about 'em now," Captain Bowman shrugged, "Navi, how long till we're back in Longview?"

"Three-hundred and eighty-four kilometers out, Captain," Archie said, checking the ship's chronometer, "About six hours."

"Good work, kid," Captain Bowman said, "Vaughn, remind me to talk to Commander Wilmont when we get back to Longview. I'm getting us in those exercises."

"I shall note it for the log," Commander Vaughn said. She started to make a note in the logbook, but paused after a moment, "...*Commander* Wilmont?"

"Yeah," Captain Bowman said, "He's the guy in charge at Longview."

"The *fleet commander*," Vaughn corrected him, "and surely it's *Commodore* Wilmont?"

"Yeah," Captain Bowman said, "He wanted me to say it that way too."

"Of course he did," Wolfram said, "That's his rank."

Captain Bowman looked surprised for a moment; clearly he hadn't expected Wolfram to join the conversation. Then he shook his head and said, "Look, kid, I'm still trying to fit my head around this whole *lieutenant-leftenant* business. I don't need another one."

"It's not some vaguery of pronunciation," Commander Vaughn said, "The man *actually* outranks you!"

Captain Bowman was silent for a moment, "Wait, *you* don't outrank me, do you?"

"No, Captain," Vaughn said through gritted teeth, "I do not outrank you."

Wolfram considered for a moment. *Captain Vaughn?* the first woman in the fleet to command a ship? It was possible; the exercises were coming soon, and Captain Bowman likely wasn't very long for his position. Vaughn was the next in line for the captain's seat if (or more likely *when*) he failed. And even despite being a woman, she was still a good officer. *Hell, she's a better officer than me!* If Vaughn could distinguish herself enough, she might even be awarded with her own command. Anything was possible; these exercises were a completely new occurrence and there was a precedent yet to be set.

If she gets her own command, will she ask for me? Wolfram wondered. He wasn't quite sure how he felt about serving under her. It wasn't just that she was a woman—he wasn't sure he was even a good enough officer to deserve her. *Will she want any of us?* She hadn't exactly been made to feel welcome onboard the *Dreadnought,* and though Wolfram hadn't personally made it worse, he certainly hadn't done anything to make it better either. Wolfram couldn't blame Vaughn if she decided to go with an entirely different command roster.

We don't deserve her, Wolfram thought, *I don't deserve her.*

"Can I go now, Captain?" Leftenant Butler asked awkwardly.

"What are you still doing up here?" Captain Bowman said, sounding a little surprised, "Get the hell back to your cave."

"Yes, sir," Leftenant Butler slipped off the bridge.

Wolfram shrugged and looked back out the window at the terrain.

It was one of the older paintings lining the walls of the Dawn Palace. Supposedly, it depicted the climactic charge at the Liberation of Riga (the first one of course; nobody was entirely certain how many times Riga had actually changed hands in the following three hundred or so years). The image showed a troop of Auroran soldiers charging out of the east with the dawn at their backs, driving before them a great host of brown-skinned Havdari soldiers. It was a glorious scene.

Lord Stolos didn't have to be a military historian to know that this painting was anything but accurate.

For one thing, all the accounts of that day that Lord Stolos had read agreed that the Auroran Royal Army hadn't even arrived at the battle until mid-morning at the earliest, and the infantry charge that was supposedly depicted here hadn't taken place until relatively late in the afternoon. The symbolism of setting the scene at dawn wasn't even subtle. Everything was always *dawn-this, dawn-that* with this bloody country.

And that wasn't the least of it. The uniforms of the Auroran soldiers were almost certainly not accurate; those men looked like they had come straight from an inspection parade, not at all as though they had been on a forced march from Two Lakes. Not only that, but each man wore the exact same face; at the time of this painting, it had been the fashion to paint all faces to a romantic ideal. Of course, over the past few centuries, this *ideal Auroran face* had fallen horribly out of fashion, leaving the soldiers looking more than a little unsettling. The Hadvari soldiers had received a similar treatment, though in a distinctly less sympathetic manner.

Lord Stolos shook his head; he found artwork like this supremely tedious, but it was only a symptom of the larger rot in the character of the Old Nobility of Aurora. Sensational historical scenes like this served no purpose beyond the aggrandisement of the nobility, lionising the comparatively trivial exploits of their ancestors while ignoring the broader historical context. Lord Stolos doubted he would ever find a painting that showed a family of refugees displaced by three and a half centuries of on-again off-again campaigns against Hadvar. Not a soul amongst the nobility ever had a spare thought for the little people.

"A glorious day, wasn't it?"

Lord Stolos turned about to see Lord Franklin coming down the corridor towards him. He was flanked by his son, Hobart Aloysius Franklin, scion of the House of Franklin, and a miserable-looking young servingmaid. "You know, one of my ancestors was there on that day. Second Leftenant Rickhard Orius Franklin, my third half cousin, eight times removed. Wasn't leading the charge himself of course, oh no. Sergeant's job, that. Still, he wrote about it in his diary, a splendid account which our house has preserved for generations." Lord Stolos tried not to listen; Lord Franklin was all the proof he needed of the degeneracy of the nobility.

"Where are your manners, boy!" Lord Franklin snapped, "Bow and show respect!"

Lord Stolos quickly stiffened and bowed, "Forgive me, my lord."

Lord Franklin threw back his head and made a terrifying sound that was probably supposed to be a laugh. "Not you, dear Perseus," Lord Stolos's cheeks coloured slightly as he straightened back up. Old habits had a way of sticking about long after they were needed.

Lord Franklin's admonishment had apparently been meant for his son. Hobart Franklin obliged and made an awkward bow, made all the more awkward by the fact that Hobart was nearly a decade older than Lord Stolos himself; Lord Stolos had rather expected to find *himself* bowing before Hobart for at least a few years before he himself was raised.

Hobart and Lord Stolos had been close friends for many years; indeed Hobart had tutored Lord Stolos in a number of subjects when he was a lad. The man was possessed of an immense intellect, but he had a propensity for disorderliness, and less-kind people thought him weak-willed and spineless. They were right of course, but Lord Stolos appreciated his friendship with Hobart all the same.

"That's better, boy," Lord Franklin huffed, "Now then... where was I?"

"You were telling me about the painting," Lord Stolos said.

"Yes. So I was," Lord Franklin grinned and puffed up his chest, "The Liberation of Riga. A most glorious day! You know, one of my ancestors was there that day: Rickhard Orius Franklin, my third half cousin—"

"Eight times removed," Lord Stolos finished the sentence, "You said as much."

Lord Franklin blinked, "Why, so I did. You'll have to excuse me, dear boy. I must confess the old brain-box is a bit off today." Lord Stolos stifled a chuckle at that; Lord Franklin's rickety old brain-box had been *a bit off today* for the better part of the past decade.

"But yes," Lord Franklin said, "I had an ancestor there, so I did. Our family has been quite active throughout the history of this glorious land. Just name any crucial turning point in our history, and nine times out of ten, there was a Franklin shaping the course of events from the background."

"I should think the events shaped *themselves*," Lord Stolos said, "The history of Aurora belongs to all the people, not just your accomplished ancestors."

"Oh, I certainly don't claim the exclusive right!" Lord Franklin said, "Surely some of *your* ancestors have helped to turn the wheel of history as well!"

"You're missing my point," Lord Stolos said, "History does not turn on the actions of a few great men. History is made by vast movements of society, great trends and paradigm shifts that individuals can influence only merely if even at all." *Well, not unless they can see the inner workings of things,* Lord Stolos thought, *like I can.*

Lord Franklin shook his head, as though he were humouring a small child, "Dear me, youngsters are always so full of amusing little ideas." He cleared his throat, "Well now, it was lovely to run into you; but we'd better be moving on soon. Important things to do and whatnot. Come now, Hobart," he admonished his son as he turned to go, "show your respect and let's be off."

"Actually," Lord Stolos said, "Hobart, I was wondering if I might have a word with you?"

Hobart rose awkwardly from his bow, "Ah... I should probably go with my lord father. It's just that—"

"Best to do as the young lord says, Hobart," Lord Franklin called back.

"A are you sure, father?" Hobart asked unsteadily.

"Don't worry about me, boy," Lord Franklin said in what was probably meant to be a conciliatory tone, "I'm certain I can manage well enough without you." And with that, he gave his serving maid a strong pat on the bottom, eliciting a startled shriek from the poor girl, and disappeared around a corner. His son sighed with visible relief.

"So... my lord," Hobart said, "you wanted to speak to me?"

"Bart, please," Lord Stolos shook his head, "My name is Percy. Let's have none of this 'my lord' business when it's just the two of us."

"But my lord father would ins—" Hobart began.

"Your *lord father* is a senile old fool who will be in his grave within a decade." Hobart seemed hurt by Lord Stolos's vitriol, and he quickly added, "I'm sorry Bart. That may have been a touch insensitive of me."

"No, no, you're correct," Hobart said quickly, "It's... it's just difficult to see him like this."

"Yes, I suppose it must be," Lord Stolos tried to affect a sympathetic tone, "I hear he was quite an intelligent man in his younger days."

"I've been told I'm rather similar to how he was in his prime," Hobart said, "Rather makes me wonder if I'm going to be just as... detached when I'm his age."

"Getting old is never a pretty thing, my friend," Lord Stolos said, "Shall we change the subject?"

"Yes, do let's," Hobart said eagerly, "You wanted to speak to me?"

"Indeed I did," Lord Stolos looked over his shoulder to make certain that they wouldn't be overheard, "I wanted your opinion on an idea that I've been working on for some time."

"Do tell," Hobart was clearly intrigued.

"Here it is," Lord Stolos began, "I believe it is time to induct Analeria into Aurora as a full-fledged province of the realm."

Lord Stolos observed his friend's expression carefully. It was always difficult to read Hobart when his brow furrowed with concentration like that. "Hmm... It's an interesting idea. But... I'm not sure..."

"It would lead to greater availability of Analerian resources," Lord Stolos explained, "and it would foster closer ties with the Analerian people, and it would solve the problem of the Disputed Zone —"

"Yes, yes, I am aware of that," Hobart waved his hand dismissively, "It's certainly a tempting economic proposal. But what about Hadvar? If we annex Analeria, it could be seen as an act of aggression."

"Pfft! Hadvar," Lord Stolos scoffed, "Hadvar isn't going to invade us over Analeria."

"Of course they will," Hobart said, "They've been doing it for the past three-hundred and fifty years."

"True," Lord Stolos acquiesced, "But that was before they acquired their holdings south of the Illyrian Sea."

"Are you certain?" Hobart still seemed uneasy, "You think their acquisition of the *Samedvar* will make up for the loss of Analeria for good?"

"Of course," Lord Stolos said, "You know Hadvar. They just want to be left alone to oppress the Illyrians in peace!"

Hobart chuckled at Lord Stolos's joke, "Okay. Well, then what about us?"

"What do you mean?" Lord Stolos asked.

"What about resistance from Auroran nobility?" Hobart explained, "This is a rather large change you're talking about. Surely you didn't think there wouldn't be any pushback."

"Like what?" Lord Stolos laughed, "Do you really think the Royal Treasury is going to put up a fight over the loss of revenue from import duties?"

"I mean"—Hobart's tone became more serious—"The Compact of the Founding."

Lord Stolos paused to consider. The Compact of the Founding was the document that had given birth to Aurora. 614 years ago, that single declaration had taken eight-and-twenty squabbling duchies and war-torn city-states and forged them into the Kingdom of Aurora. It was a feat unrivaled anywhere in the annals of history; in a single act of unity, all the lands east of the Mountains of Dawn were joined together under a common rule, a common currency, and a common glorious destiny.

Of course, six centuries had passed since those days. The Compact of the Founding had been revolutionary for its time, but now it was just a scrap of vellum gathering dust under a stack of old books in some forgotten historical archive beneath the Dawn Palace. It was an important relic of the history of Aurora, certainly, but you couldn't expect a country to go six hundred years without changing vastly. Why, Analeria hadn't even been inhabited in those days; it had probably just been poetic language to declare: *'alle landeſ ſuche aſ liye eaſt of þe Mountæneſ of þe Dawne, from þe græte norþern wæſteſ to þe ſouþern ſandeſ.'* Why let a simple oversight like that impede the path of progress?

"I wouldn't worry about the Compact of the Founding," Lord Stolos shrugged, "It shouldn't prove too much of an issue."

"The Compact expressly defines Aurora as the land east of the Mountains of Dawn," Hobart said, "And so it has remained for 614 years."

"Yes, I know," Lord Stolos protested, "but does it mean *only* the land east of the Mountains of Dawn? Or is that intended only as an absolute minimum extent?"

"Percy," Hobart said sternly, the mannerisms of a tutor beginning to slip back into his voice, "you're quibbling."

"Am I?" Lord Stolos retorted with a clever gleam in his eye, "Or are *you*? I could just as easily argue that *you* are incorrectly interpreting the will of the Founders."

"It's not a matter of whatever the Founders thought," Hobart said, "It's a matter of what the nobility of today will think. And I hate to be the one to pour cold water over your grand designs, but the nobility is not going to be very receptive of this plan."

"You really think not?" Lord Stolos scoffed.

"The nobility is conservative. It always has been," Hobart said with a sad smile, "I'm sorry Percy, but this is going to be an uphill battle for you."

"I've already spoken to Lord Newton about this plan," Lord Stolos insisted, "and he was very supportive of the idea."

"Lord Newton is hardly a representative specimen of the nobility," Hobart laughed, "Just wait until you put it before Lord Hanscom and he laughs you all the way out of court."

Lord Stolos laughed awkwardly, "I had rather hoped to leave Lord Hanscom until the last..."

Hobart shrugged, the way he did whenever he was about to pose a rhetorical question, "What about Lord Torrenberg? He's just as conservative as Lord Hanscom, if not more."

"Well..."

"And what about Lord Wingate? Or Lord Mantussian? or Lord Blackpool? Or my lord father? Do you plan to try to convince each of them individually?"

"If I must, then yes!" Lord Stolos was beginning to lose his patience. If Hobart didn't think his idea was feasible, he should just come out and say it instead of skirting about the issue by playing the bloody devil's advocate!

Hobart put up his hands, "Don't worry, Percy," he said, "I think I might have a better option."

"Alright..." Lord Stolos said, "let's hear it."

"Take your proposal to the Queen."

Lord Stolos groaned. Taking his proposal to the Queen was the last thing he wanted to do! Why couldn't Hobart see—why couldn't *anyone* see—that the Queen was a giggling little fool who would lead the kingdom down the road to ruin? Why, if someone like *him* were in charge... "I'd rather leave the Queen out of this, if it can be avoided," Lord Stolos said.

"Why not?" Hobart pressed, "She's young, energetic, at the beginning of her time. No doubt she'll be looking for some great undertaking to define her reign. This is just the thing for her to really sink her teeth into."

"But..." Lord Stolos struggled to put his thoughts into words in the least seditious manner he could manage, "Are you certain she's... well, up to the task?"

Hobart shook his head in disbelief, "Percy, she's the Queen. It's not a matter of being *up to the task*. She's the only one who can do it at all." Hobart laughed, "I'm sorry, but that's just the way it is."

Lord Stolos sighed. Hobart was right as usual; the annexation of Analeria was an initiative that had to come from the top down. "Thanks for your input," Lord Stolos said, trying his best to smile, "I'll consider your suggestions. In the meantime, you should see if you can catch up with your lord father."

"Yes, I suppose I should," Hobart glanced anxiously over his shoulder, "It was very nice talking to you, Percy." And with that, Hobart turned and slipped off down the hall leaving Lord Stolos alone.

Of course he wasn't going to put his plan before the Queen. There was no way that empty-headed chit was capable of the strong central leadership that would be required for such a task; she would in all likelihood be swayed by other parties with sinister ulterior motives. Even getting a few more of the lords on his side wouldn't be protection enough from corruption.

If I were in control... Lord Stolos banished the thought just as quickly as it had come. Wishful thinking wouldn't do any good; the Queen was the Queen, and that was that. He would just have to come up with some other way to realise his grand designs.

The deck wobbled slightly as Hamilton brought the Dreadnought into its berth. "Keep your eye on the guiding lines, kid," Paul called from captain's chair, "They put 'em there for a reason."

"Aye, sir," Hamilton responded and looked up at the white markings painted on the inside wall of the aerodrome that would guide airships into the landing cradle below. There were numbers with the markings indicating the height above the ground, as well as a bunch of other letters that Paul couldn't read, but those probably weren't all that important anyway. Eventually, Hamilton brought the *Dreadnought* to rest and set the reactor at low power, "We have come to ground, Captain."

"Good work, kid," Paul got up from the Captain's Chair and started for the stairwell, "I'm going groundside to have a chat with Commodore Wilmont. Barlowe, get the reactor turned off."

"Yes, sir," Barlowe answered lazily.

"And get that bulkhead installed when you get back," Paul said, "No excuses this time."

"Right," Barlowe groaned.

"Captain," Vaughn said without looking up from her logbook.

"What?" Paul growled.

"Who has the bridge?"

"Someone," Paul sneered as he stepped into the stairwell. *What goes around comes around, lady!*

Paul walked down the cargo ramp and off the ship, passing by Butler who was already offloading empty fuel drums. Paul stepped out into the street and made his way across the city to the military headquarters. Just as before, the gate guards saluted with clockwork precision, but this time, Paul passed them by without noticing. He had a job to do, and nobody was going to stop him.

"I want to talk to Wilmont," Paul demanded as soon as he entered the building.

"Captain Bowman, sir," Another officer approached him and saluted, "Commodore Wilmont urgently requests your presence."

"Oh..." Paul blinked, "Well, alright then, let's see what he wants."

The officer turned crisply on his heel and marched off down a corridor with Paul following close behind. Paul didn't know what to expect; he had intended to burst into Wilmont's office and demand to know why he hadn't been informed about the upcoming fleet exercises. He had even called up the memory of one particularly cantankerous captain he had flown with to try and give himself some inspiration. But the knowledge that Wilmont wanted something from him as well had rather taken the wind out of his sails. He stepped through the door into Commodore Wilmont's office without any sort of battle plan whatsoever.

"Give us the room please, Harrison," Wilmont said without looking up from whatever scrap of paper he was fussing over. The officer vanished, and Paul was alone with Wilmont.

"Mister Bowman," Wilmont still didn't look up, "Already I can tell you are going to be a wellspring of trouble for me."

"Yeah," Paul said, trying to sound more confident that he actually was, "look, *Commodore*, I've—"

"Remind me again," Wilmont interrupted, "what are your duties here?"

Paul shrugged, "To patrol the Mountains of Dawn to look for smugglers. Anyway—"

"And what else?" Wilmont interrupted again.

"Uhh..." Paul blinked. What else was there?

"What *else?*" Wilmont's pronunciation was so crisp he was practically spitting the words.

Quickly, Paul summoned up the memory of his orders. It had only been three days since he had memorized them with Louise's help. *Her Most Royal Majesty*... No, not that first bit... *does hereby enjoin*... No, not that part either, and that the hell did *enjoin* mean anyway? *Assume command of the Airship* Dreadnought... No, he'd already done that... *To oversee the application and enforcement of*—

"Customs inspections!" Paul blurted out, and then immediately wished he had been calmer about it.

Wilmont finally looked up. He stared furiously at Paul. "*Customs inspections,*" he said after a few moments of silence.

"Yeah," Paul said more confidently, "customs inspections. And as soon as you answer a few questions for me, I can get back to—"

"First," Wilmont spat, "You are going to answer a few questions for *me*. Specifically, why you permitted four-and-twenty vessels to pass through port without inspection in the past two days."

"W-what?" Paul stammered.

"*Four-and-twenty ships!*" Wilmont leaped out of his chair, Four-and-twenty bloody ships passing through the Gates of Dawn, and you just let them through!"

"We were on patrol!" Paul shouted, "What exactly was I supposed to do?"

"That is beside the point!" Wilmont shouted back, "It was your responsibility to inspect them, and you failed to do so."

"But we couldn't," Paul protested, "We were hundreds of miles away."

"I am not interested in hearing your excuses." Wilmont waved his hand, "You will find a way to carry out the inspections, or I will have your pay stopped until you do."

That threat sent a shiver running down Paul's spine. Money was always of vital importance to freighthaulers like Paul. During his military service, his regular wage, small though it had been, had taken a tremendous weight off his mind. And the thought of losing it... "I'll... see what I can do."

"I shan't hold my breath," Wilmont grumbled and sat down again, "Now then, I have a lot of work to see to. So if there is nothing else..."

"Actually there is something," Paul said.

"Yes?" Wilmont didn't look up.

"It's about the exercises," Paul said.

"What about the exercises?" Wilmont still didn't look up, "Surely you've been briefed on them."

Paul crossed his arms in front of his chest, "Well, I haven't."

"And I suppose it falls to me to fix that, doesn't it?" Wilmont shook his head and pulled a piece of paper out of his desk, "Very well. Sign this here."

Paul looked at the paper. He couldn't read any of the words, but there was a thin line at the bottom. Paul knew from his previous encounters with the Auroran legal system that he was supposed to make his mark just above that line. *No*, Paul reminded himself, *I can't just "make my mark" here*. That was what people who couldn't read did; they just made a cross and left a court clerk to fill in their name. And if Paul tried that here, it would immediately betray his secret.

"Well?" Wilmont looked up sharply.

"Right," Paul jumped, and quickly reached for a fountain pen, "Right..." Louise had shown him how to fake his signature, and he had been practicing in his free time. Paul placed the tip of the pen on the paper. *Down... Back up... One loop... Squiggle off to the right... Leave a small space... Down and back up again... Two loops this time... Another squiggle off to the right...* "There," Paul said.

Wilmont snatched back the paper and tucked it safely away into his desk, "Thank you, Captain."

"What was that for?" Paul asked, "Are the records incomplete or something?"

"What you just signed..." Wilmont's mouth quirked into an unsettling smile, "was a form-letter of resignation."

"What?" Paul's jaw dropped open, "What the hell was that for? You told me that was for the exercises!"

"I said nothing of the sort," Wilmont said sweetly, "It was merely an experiment. And I must say, I have learned something rather fascinating."

"And what is that?" Paul demanded.

Wilmont's smile twisted into a horrifying grin, "You can't read."

Paul's blood froze in his veins.

Wilmont leaned back in his chair, "You are unfit for command, *Mister* Bowman," he seemed very satisfied with himself, "I wonder if that was even your signature."

For a moment, everything was silent.

"So..." Paul said finally, fully aware of the scale of his defeat, "What happens next?"

"Oh?" Wilmont was enjoying himself entirely too much, "Shall I tell you what happens next?"

"Just get to it," Paul groaned.

"Oh no," Wilmont laughed viciously, "I shall not *just get to it!* I could very easily have you dismissed from the service, but that would be too simple." Wilmont stood, "When I am through, you'll be the laughingstock of this nation! I am going to *ruin* you, *Mister* Bowman, and there's not a bloody thing you can do about it!"

"Okay," Paul tried his hardest not to sound rattled by Wilmont's ranting, "But what about—"

"The exercises?" Wilmont sneered, "Don't worry. You already know everything you need to know about them."

"But I don't know anything!"

"Precisely," Wilmont said with a huff as he planted himself firmly back in his seat, "You will remain on patrol and customs duty until ordered to do otherwise, and that's the end of it." He locked eyes with Paul, "And you will *not* go running off to take part in those blasted fleet exercises. Are we clear?"

Paul nodded slowly, "Yes... sir."

"Good," Wilmont said, sounding not at all like someone who had just gleefully proclaimed his intent to ruin his reputation, "Now get back to work."

"Yes, sir," Paul said, and turned to leave.

James Butler manhandled the last of the fuel drums into position in the *Dreadnought's* cargo bay, and stopped for a moment to catch his breath. He had never liked this particular part of his job. He didn't have the shoulders for brute labor like this. Keeping records and filing expense reports didn't make you sweat like this. *And if they do,* Butler thought, *you're doing them wrong.*

Butler's mind wandered back to two days ago when Commander Vaughn had caught on to his latest scheme to sneak personal expenses into official reports. Damn, but that had been a tense meeting! Butler had never known Vaughn to shout or raise her voice, but she never needed to. She was more than intimidating enough already with her considerable height, her unwavering stare, and that way her lip twisted to the side with disapproval when she sensed that someone was trying to bullshit her.

It was all Bellman's fault of course! His taste for those Hadvari spirits was going to be the ruin of him. And why did that no-good drunk always have to insist on smuggled Hadvari spirits? Didn't he know the homegrown ones from Riga were cheaper?

Butler was still going to slip them into the expense reports of course. Bellman was a friend, and he wasn't going to leave that old scoundrel high and dry. He would just have to split up the costs among other items and then skim the difference out of petty cash. And maybe a little extra for his trouble as well; he could always use more reading material for his downtime.

Speaking of which... Butler hopped up on top of one of the fuel drums and pulled the penny dreadful out of his uniform pocket. This was his third re-read, but it was still fun. Every time he read it, he discovered new errors, plot holes, and other things that didn't make any sense at all. He couldn't wait for the next amazingly bad issue to come out!

"Nine-and-forty."

Butler looked up to see who had spoken. Midshipman Torrenberg was standing in front of him, his uniform as disorderly as ever, and still clutching that small journal as though someone might snatch it out of his hands at any moment. He gestured weakly to the fuel drums, "Nine-and-forty," the kid mumbled again, "Enough for 9.8 trips."

"Yes, I saw the report" Butler said, waving a dismissive hand, "Go on, get back to the office." Torrenberg shrugged and shuffled away.

Butler shuddered; goddammit, that kid was weird. He never said any more than he absolutely had to and spent all his time scribbling in that little book of his. Butler didn't even know what he was writing; he had peaked over Torrenberg's shoulder once or twice, but all he had found were a bunch of geometric symbols with some barely legible chicken-scratch text sprinkled around the page. Maybe it meant something to a simple mind like Torrenberg's, or maybe he just found the shapes interesting, but to Butler it was all nonsense.

He's right about the fuel though, Butler thought. The *Dreadnought's* horribly inefficient first-generation reactor had consumed five whole barrels of liquid fulgurite fuel in the past day and a half. At that rate, their forty-nine barrels would last less than ten round trips, barely enough for two weeks of patrols. Butler had served on other ships that could have made the same circuit on only two barrels. He had even heard rumors that some of the newer ships like the *Halcyon* and the *Dawn Spear* could have made it on just a barrel and a half.

Butler shrugged; counting barrels and comparing efficiency was important, but it was only one part of a much bigger issue. The world was running out of fulgurite. It was a fact reflected in the steadily increasing price of fuel, but numbers alone could not truly describe the magnitude of the problem it posed. The future of the entire Auroran nation depended on airships. And it wasn't just the ARAF; if the regular shipments of raw materials stopped feeding the factories of Newport, Norvell, Marburg, and Kalmar, then the entire Auroran economy would grind to a halt.

Most people preferred to simply ignore problems like that of course, but as a supply officer, Butler was confronted with that problem with every single expense report. *Independent freighters will be the first to die out,* he surmised. *The Auroran Trade Consortium might last a little while longer, but not much.* The ARAF had healthy fulgurite reserves tucked away in a few cities throughout the realm, but even that would run out after a year or two. And then? Who could say?

What about railways? Could they pick up the slack? Butler considered the possibility, but dismissed it just as quickly. Railways might serve well enough for passenger transport, and they could be run on coal or lignite which were much cheaper, but they required so much more infrastructure at all points along their routes. Rail lines had to be constructed, maintained, guarded against bandits and saboteurs. You couldn't just build a railway all the way to *Illyria*—it would get blown up by clan raiders every other Tuesday.

And even if it all went off without a hitch, in the end, all you had was a single linear route from one place to another and nowhere else. Railways were static things, tied inextricably to the land; they couldn't cross mountains, lakes, or oceans. There was simply no matching the infinite flexibility of flight.

The sound of boots coming up the cargo ramp pulled Butler's attention from his book. Captain Bowman was returning. Butler tucked the penny dreadful back into his pocket and hopped off the fuel drum. "Captain," he said and saluted.

"Butler," Captain Bowman languidly returned the salute.

"Good news, Captain," Butler said. Captain Bowman looked like he could use some good news right about now, "I had a word with one of our suppliers, and he says he can get us a PA system for the ship."

"A what?" Captain Bowman blinked.

"A *public address* system," Butler reiterated, "Y'know, loudspeakers."

"Right," Captain Bowman nodded, "That's good. How soon can we get it up and running?"

"The first components should start arriving in a few weeks," Butler said, "But it'll probably take a month or so for the whole system to get here."

"I want the system working as soon as possible," Captain Bowman said, "It doesn't have to be complete; even just one or two working circuits would be good enough. Once we get that much of the system up and running, we can finish it on our own time."

"A sound plan," Butler nodded. The exercises would be starting in about a month, and anything they could get working by then would be a tremendous boon. The army had a saying: A good plan today is better than a perfect plan tomorrow.

"I'm afraid I've got bad news for you though," Captain Bowman said, "We missed a few of customs inspections while we were on patrol."

"Of course we did," Butler said, "We were *on patrol.*"

"I know," Captain Bowman acknowledged, "But Commodore Wilmont wants us to do them anyways."

"And how exactly does he expect us to do that?" Butler laughed.

"That's the bad news," Captain Bowman said, "I need you to stay behind in port."

"Me?"

"That's right," Captain Bowman said, "You looked like you could handle the inspections well enough on your own. I need you to stay behind and continue with them. You and probably one or two other people." He shrugged, "Take whoever you want to punish."

Butler thought about it for a moment. There really should be a separate detail to handle these tasks while they were on patrol. Some officers from the fleet headquarters with nothing to do maybe. There were always plenty of those about. Butler shook his head; *maybe* and *perhaps* were no help now. It was going to be a pain in the ass, but there was no other way they could do it.

"We'll need lodgings in town," Butler said.

Captain Bowman nodded, "I'll set you up at one of the local inns."

"Alright. I can reimburse you in an expense report later," Butler cracked a half-smile. *Vaughn isn't going to be happy about that!*

Captain Bowman nodded and started for the staircase. Butler added, "Are we at least going to get someone to cover for us during the fleet exercises?"

Captain Bowman did not turn back.

"Captain," Butler called, as Captain Bowman reached the stairs, *"What about the Exercises?"*

Captain Bowman stopped for a moment, then wordlessly slipped up the stairs and vanished like a shadow.

Chapter XII

A Favor

THE sound of Paul's footsteps on the stairs was like the clanging of bells in his ears. He knew from experience that three eggs and two glasses of water was usually the best thing for a hangover, but he had only just finished his breakfast, and the cure was always slow to take effect. *I really need to stop drinking so hard.*

In the two weeks since his meeting with Commodore Wilmont, that liquor cabinet in his cabin had become a close companion. Paul had made carefully sure not to start drinking before Halford came by for their nightly meeting. *Or was it technically a briefing?* As soon as she left however, Paul would attack the stash of liquor with a vengeance and generally wake up the next morning feeling like his head was being crushed from the inside out.

Finally Paul reached the last stair. He took a deep breath to gather his nerves and stepped onto the bridge, somehow managing not to stagger as he did so. The last thing he needed was a crew who suspected that their captain was drinking himself shitfaced every night.

"Captain on deck," Vaughn announced curtly. Paul groaned softly so that no one else could hear. Vaughn was always there whenever he arrived. *She probably does that on purpose.*

"Navi," Paul called as he crossed to the captain's chair, "what's our current position?" That was how you were supposed to say it in the military. You didn't just ask: 'where the hell are we?' like you did on a civilian freighter.

"Course holding, sir," Hakefeldt reported, "eight-and-sixty klicks south of Longview heading southwest-by-south, bearing two-one-three."

"Good man," Paul said, "Guns, anything to report?"

"Nothing to report, Captain," Wolfram groaned. Paul glanced over at the lanky kid, slouching over his console. What was eating him? *Maybe I should get Halford to focus on him for a bit?* Paul considered.

"Captain," Vaughn said, "you need to see this."

Vaughn handed Paul a single sheet of paper covered with words and numbers arranged in neat rows and columns. It looked like a ledger or a manifest of some sort, not that it was much of a help to Paul who couldn't read it anyhow.

"Alright, what are we looking at here?" Paul said casually; that was usually enough to bluff someone into an explanation.

"This is Leftenant Butler's latest expense report," Vaughn explained, "He submitted it for my authorisation before we left port yesterday." She reached out with a pencil and tapped the paper right where a circle of ink had been drawn around one of the lines, "Note this item in particular."

Paul squinted. That particular line was no more comprehensible to him than any other. The only thing he could understand was a figure of twelve shillings and nine pennies, a relatively small sum of money. It could indicate any number of trivial expenses. "What about it?" Paul asked, trying not to sound nervous.

"What *about* it?" Vaughn seemed incredulous, "Captain, it is a bill for an inn! Leftenant Butler has been spending his nights in taverns, and what's worse, he is listing it amongst official expenditures."

Of course, Paul thought with relief, *The inn.* That was just Butler's bill from the inn. And only twelve and nine for three people over two weeks? Butler and his team were being remarkably thrifty!

"I've already had words with Mister Butler about his habits," Vaughn continued, "but it has clearly had no effect on his behavior. I really must insist that you have words with him when we return to—"

"It's fine," Paul handed the paper back to Vaughn, "Don't worry about it."

"Come again?" Vaughn said in her trademark neutral tone. She didn't take the paper.

"Butler's currently on customs duty in Longview," Paul said, "Him and Garseed from the gunpit, and Philpot from engineering. I told him we'd cover their expenses. I've got Torrenberg handling supply duties for the time being."

"Forgive my scepticism, captain," Vaughn said, "but this is highly unusual, and Mister Butler does have something of a history of indolence. I suspect he may be deceiving you, perhaps exploiting your inexperience to—"

"He's acting under orders from Fleet Commodore Wilmont." Paul interrupted. He gave the expense report in his hand an irritated shake. Vaughn gripped the paper, but Paul did not let go, "And if you ever question my experience in front of the crew again," Paul said in a deadly whisper, "I will shove you out a goddamn porthole."

Vaughn's face never changed. She matched his glare and, after a moment of silence, took back the expense report and said in the exact same whispered tone, "It's Fleet *Commander* Wilmont."

Paul blinked, "I thought you said he was a commodore?"

"He is," Vaughn said, "But he is also a fleet commander."

"Well which one is he?" Paul demanded, "A commodore or a commander?"

"*Commodore* is his rank," Vaughn said, sounding for all the world as if she was explaining why the sky was blue or why water was wet, "*fleet commander* is his *position*."

Paul pushed up out of the chair, "I swear you're making half this stuff up as you go along," he grumbled as he made his way to the front. He'd had just about enough of Lieutenant Commander Fiora fucking Vaughn as he could stomach.

Paul sighed and looked out the window. At first, he had been willing to accept a little rough weather between him and Vaughn but it had been two weeks, and she was only getting worse. He would need to do something about her before too long, maybe replace her or demote her or whatever you did with bad officers. Paul shrugged. At the very least, his hangover was gone.

Paul squinted at something off in the distance... a dark speck against the distant wispy clouds... An airship! "Heads up people," he called out as he looked about for a spyglass, "Airship off the starboard bow."

"I don't see anything," Wolfram said, "Wait, starboard is to the left, isn't it?"

"Right," Paul corrected.

"I thought so," Wolfram said, I still don't see anything."

"No!" Paul snapped as he snatched the spyglass off its peg beside the window, "I meant that starboard is *to the right! Port* is to the left! Didn't they teach you anything at that academy?"

"I thought port and starboard were just for ocean vessels," Wolfram protested, "Anyway, why can't you just say 'left' or 'right'?"

"Why can't *you* just say 'port' and 'starboard' like a normal person!" Paul grumbled as he fiddled with the dials on the spyglass to bring the distant ship into focus.

It was a civilian freighter. Two-and-a-half decks high, and maybe a few dozen feet longer than the *Dreadnought* herself. The mouths of four large impact columns glowed faintly blue at each corner, pushing her along at what looked like a gentle twenty-five miles per hour or so. Her side plating was caked with rust except for a small patch near the stern where someone had opened her up to replace her reactor. Paul narrowed his eyes; there couldn't be two ships like that in the whole world. It was the *Silesia*. His old airship.

Knox.

"Sparks," Paul said, snapping the spyglass closed, "Signal the airship *Silesia* and order them to come to ground and prepare to receive inspectors." *Let's see you try and hide behind the Consortium all the way out here!*

"Aye, sir," Wagner said and began fiddling with the radio.

"Hakefeldt," Paul said, "Head to the galley and ask for Louise Halford. I'll meet you both in the cargo bay."

"Aye sir," Hakefeldt nodded, and he and Paul started for the door.

"And bring Barlowe with you," Paul added.

"I'll see if I can find him, sir," Hakefeldt said.

"Don't worry," Paul muttered, "He shouldn't be too hard to find." Barlowe was in the habit of wandering off to the galley at the most inconvenient times. Louise had reported that the man had his eye on one of the WAVE girls. Paul usually didn't care too much about that sort of thing—the crew's personal lives were their own business—but in Barlowe's case it was getting to be a bit of a problem.

"Uh, Captain?" Wagner called from over by the radio, "I think we might have a problem."

Paul gave Hakefeldt a pat on the shoulder to send him on his way and turned to join Wagner at the radio, "The ship is refusing to comply," Wagner said.

Paul glanced quickly at Wolfram and then said quietly, "Tell them we have orders to open fire if they refuse." Paul grinned, *that oughta do it*. Knox was a coward at heart; the threat of violence usually put him in his place.

Wagner's face turned milk white, "Do... we actually have orders to fire, sir?"

"Nope," Paul shrugged, "but *they* don't know that, now do they?"

"I see," Wagner sounded relieved, "I shall pass on your orders, sir."

"Good kid," Paul gave Wagner a pat on the shoulder and turned back toward the stairwell, "Helm, take us closer to that ship, and then bring us to ground."

"Aye sir," Hamilton responded.

"Captain," Vaughn called from across the bridge.

"What?" Paul didn't look in her direction.

"Who has the bridge?"

"Who do you think?" Paul snapped as he slipped into the stairwell.

Paul made a quick stop in the supply office to collect two rifles. By the time he reached the cargo bay, Hakefeldt, Barlowe, and Halford were already waiting for him. Paul gave the guns to Hakefeldt and Barlowe along with strict orders not to pull the triggers. The two lieutenants both reassured Paul that they had no intention of pulling the trigger unless absolutely necessary, though they seemed a little annoyed when they learned that the real reason for Paul's orders was because the guns were missing their firing pins. Before they could protest; however, the acceleration bell chimed three times, and the ship began to descend.

It took about a minute for the *Dreadnought* to come to ground. Once the ship had touched down, Paul lowered the cargo ramp (it was a manual chain-hoist mechanism instead of a more modern hydraulic system; just another sign of how old this ship was), and the four figures marched out onto the dry dusty soil of the Analerian Plateau. The *Silesia* had come to ground about three hundred feet away. Paul grinned. His bluff had worked.

A tall lanky man with a face like an overgrown rat emerged from the *Silesia's* cavernous cargo hold. "Officers, officers," he said, his voice thick with the same false charm as ever, "I think there's been a bit of a misunder—" He stopped in mid-sentence as soon as he saw Paul. "You again!"

"Hey Vic," Paul smirked, "Fancy running into you out here."

"We've already had this little talk, Paul," Victor Knox recovered quickly, "This is a Consortium ship now. You know what that means?"

"Oh I know what it means," Paul said, "It means that you're a goddamn sellout, and you're cheating your crew out of their pay!" The Auroran Trade Consortium had been trying to buy out all the independent freighters for years. It was a slow process; freighthaulers cherished their freedom and independence, but every year, a few more captains gave in and signed over their ships to the Consortium. Sometimes it was due to rising fuel prices, other times contracts were too scarce, and other times the captains simply got greedy. Vic had no doubt been one of the third kind.

"It also means that you're not allowed to search us," Vic said, "We have our own company inspectors who handle that for us. So you boys can just go on and leave us alone." He noticed Halford, "Unless of course, *you'd* like to stick around, little lady,"

"We were in the neighborhood," Paul stepped forward, blocking Halford from view, "And there has been word of smugglers about. We thought we'd handle the inspections for a change. Maybe give your guys a day off."

Vic chuckled, "Paul, I don't think you understand—"

"No, I don't think *you* understand," Paul gave Vic a rough shove, "There is no Consortium out here. There's no rules and regulations for you to hide behind. There's only you and me. Now I'm going to inspect your ship, and you are going to let me." Paul casually let his hand rest on the brand new pistol holstered at his side, "Do we got us an understanding?"

Vic chewed at his lip and his eyes darted back and forth. Paul savored the expression; that was the face Vic had made whenever old Captain Cooper had shouted him down for drinking in the engine room, or for picking fights with other crewmen, or for sneaking off to the dogfights when he should have been on cargo duty. That was the face Vic made when he knew he had lost.

Finally, Vic turned his head and shouted, "Boy! Get the manifest!" He walked back into the cargo bay, and grumbled, "I'm filing a complaint with the fleet when we get back."

"Be my guest," Paul laughed. Nobody in the fleet office took complaints seriously anyway; everyone knew that.

The *Silesia's* cargo bay was stacked high with wooden crates all held in place with ropes and chains with narrow paths winding between them. It looked like a three-quarters load. A decent haul. At the back of the cargo bay, Vic was loitering by the staircase, no doubt waiting for someone to bring the manifest from the offices upstairs.

"So, Captain," Hakefeldt whispered, "What exactly are we supposed to do?"

"Don't worry," Paul said, "You two are just here to make sure everyone behaves themselves." He turned to Halford, "You're the one who has to do the actual work."

"What do you need me to do, Captain?" Halford asked.

Paul pointed at Vic, "That guy's going to give us the ship's manifest. It's a list of what the ship is carrying and how much it's worth."

"And you need me to inspect the cargo to make sure that the manifest is accurate. Is that correct?"

At the back of the cargo bay, a young boy clambered down the stairs a large leather folder. Vic snatched it roughly out of the boy's hand and snarled some words that Paul couldn't hear. When the boy meekly tried to protest, Vic gave him a whack upside the head with the manifest.

"Captain?" Halford asked.

Paul blinked, "Right... right. Uhh... yeah, check the labels on the crates and make sure..." Vic hit the boy again, harder this time. "...make sure they... that they match with the..." Vic hit the boy again, knocking him back into the stairs. "...with the manifest."

"I see," Halford nodded, "One last question..."

Paul was no longer listening to her, "Hey!" He started towards Vic and the kid on the stairs, "Hey!" He caught Vic's hand from behind just as he was about to let loose another blow, "*Hey!!!*"

"*What?!*" Vic snarled.

Paul was silent for a moment—he could barely form words through his anger! Beating up kids! Defenseless kids! Finally, Paul's rage simmered down enough for him to stammer, "We gonna do this, or what?"

Vic slowly nodded. He wrenched his hand out or Paul's grip and stalked off toward Hakefeldt, Barlowe, and Halford. "Dumb kid," he grumbled as he tucked the manifest under his arm.

Paul watched Vic go with a look of sheer hatred. He knew full well that Vic was a no-good, two-faced, dogfighting son of a bitch, but this! This was over the line! When Paul had started this little scheme of his, he had just intended to march about, flaunt his rank, rub Vic's face in it for a bit. But now he was really going to ruin him!

Paul turned to the kid. He looked about eight or nine years old. His skin was a swarthy brown, and head was covered with fluffy dark-brown hair. *He has the look of Hadvar,* Paul thought, *a war orphan probably.* A bruise was beginning to form on his head, and his big brown eyes were filling with tears. Paul knelt down beside the kid, put an arm around his shoulder, and whispered, *"Delû iźînĝovôu kî ŵeu?"*

"Sorry?" The boy sniffed, "I don't understand." His accent was unmistakably Auroran.

Paul shrugged. His Hadvari was rusty anyway, "You don't like that guy, do you?"

"No," the boy choked through his tears, "He yells at me, and he hits me, and he calls me a dumb kid."

"That sounds terrible," Paul said. He glanced over at Vic; he and the rest of the team had already started the inspection, "What's your name, kid?"

"Jack," the boy sniffed, "It's Jack."

"Tell me, Jack," Paul said in a low, vaguely conspiratorial tone, "would you like to help me get rid of him?"

The boy wiped his nose on the dirty sleeve of his ratty old tunic, "What?"

"I can get rid of that mean old captain for you," Paul said, "If that's what you want."

"Really?" The boy blinked, "You can do that?"

"Oh yes," Paul said, "But I need your help to make it happen. You think you're up to it?"

"Uh-huh!" The boy nodded, smiling through his tears, "I can do that!"

"Alright Jack," Paul helped the boy to his feet, "Here's what I need you to do: go find the nearest tool closet and bring me a prybar. Can you do that for me?"

"A *prybar,*" the boy repeated.

"That's right," Paul said, miming what a prybar looked like, "It's a long piece of metal with a little claw at both ends. Can you get one for me?"

"Yeah, I can do that," the boy nodded.

"Good," Paul smiled, "Now get to it."

"Right," the boy said before he scampered up the stairs and vanished. Paul watched him go with a smile and turned to rejoin the rest of his group. Halford was leading the inspection. She was a little unsteady at times, but she seemed to be managing rather well. Every now and then, Vic would make a nauseating remark about her eyes or her figure; but whenever he did, Halford would just *humbly request that Captain Knox render his full attention to the task at hand.* Damn, but that girl had the patience of a saint!

The *Silesia* had evidently just come from Illyria. About half of her cargo was goat's wool; the garment factories of Kalmar paid handsomely for every crate. The rest was the usual assortment of Illyrian goods: spices, dyes, salt, and about half a dozen bolts of Hadvari silk. It was a completely ordinary load. Nothing at all suspicious about it.

"Uh, Captain?" said a small voice from behind Paul. Both he and Vic turned around and answered "Yeah?"

It was the boy, Jack, struggling to hold up the heavy metal prybar in both hands, "I got the... y'know."

"What the hell is this?" Vic snapped at the boy.

Paul smiled, "Good work, Jack." He took the heavy bar with one hand and started toward the back of the cargo bay. That was usually the place.

"The hell is goin' on here?" Vic demanded as he hurried to catch up with Paul. Halford, Barlowe and Hakefeldt followed close after.

"You'll see," Paul said as he neared the second-to-last panel on the left side of the back wall, "You'll see." Paul slipped the claw of the prybar into the gap between the panels and wrenched them apart. The large steel plate clattered to the floor with a great resounding clang. Paul reached into the opening and pulled out a knee-high wooden crate.

"So Vic"—Paul snapped the lid off the crate and pulled out a bottle of a cloudy white liquid—"you want to tell me what this is?" The stunned look on Vic's face was absolutely sublime. *You really need to get a new hiding place.*

"Tell me, Miss Halford," Paul said theatrically, "did you by chance happen to notice a crate or two of Illyrian dog ale on the manifest?"

"I believe I would remember something like that, Captain," Halford said, weaving around Vic. Hakefeldt and Barlowe followed after her.

"I thought so," Paul turned his attention back to Vic, "Captain," he said, brandishing the bottle with delight. All of the royal inspectors he'd ever had the misfortune of crossing paths with had liked to toy with their prey, "Are you aware that importing this substance into Aurora is *illegal?*"

"I... I," Vic stammered, "Now hand on a sec, we're not—"

"We are less than sixty miles from the Gates of Dawn," Paul pressed his attack further, *That is correct, isn't it? Kilometers are shorter than miles, right?* "Do you expect me to believe that you were going to toss all of these overboard before you got to Longview?"

Vic's eyes fell on young Jack, "You! You little rat-faced gink! I'll gut you like a—"

"Ah, ah, ah," Paul stepped between Vic and the boy, "Not so fast. This fine young man has just assisted in the capture of a *known criminal,*" Paul let the word hang in the air like a fine perfume, "That entitles him to the Queen's favor and protection."

"You think you can do this to me?" Vic snarled, "*To me?!*"

"Boys," Paul said, and right on cue, Hakefeldt and Barlowe brandished their rifles. Vic's protests vanished at the threat of violence. *He always was a coward at heart.*

"By the authority conferred upon me by Her Majesty the Queen," Paul announced. *(that was what you had to say before making any sort of declaration like this),* "I am ordering this vessel impounded and placing you under arrest.

"Mister Barlowe, Do we have a brig back on the *Dreadnought?*" He hadn't seen one back when he was touring the ship, but most ships usually had one.

"I don't believe we do, Captain," Barlowe said.

Paul shrugged, "Well I guess we'll have to improvise then then. Dump him in the supply office and keep an eye on him."

"Aye, sir," Barlowe nodded and roughly grasped Vic's arm to lead him away. Vic squirmed weakly, but didn't resist too much. He was beaten, and he knew it. Paul watched Vic shuffle down the cargo ramp with a very satisfied look on his face.

"Mister Hakefeldt," Paul said, "head up to the *Silesia's* bridge and tell the helmsman to lay in a course for Longview. Advise them that they will be under our guns the whole way."

"Aye, sir," Hakefeldt nodded and started for the staircase.

Paul looked about and noticed that he was still holding the bottle of Illyrian liquor. He shrugged and tucked it into his jacket. The liquor cabinet in his room was starting to run low. "Good work, Miss

Halford."

Louise smiled and curtsied, "Thank you, Captain."

"Where are you going, kid?" Paul called over to Jack who was starting to make his way up the stairs.

"I'm going upstairs," the boy seemed confused, "To get ready for the trip to Longview."

"No you're not," Paul said with a fond grin, "You're a hero, kid! You're riding back with us!"

The coach rattled through the narrow streets of Newport. Every now and again, the driver would crack his whip to keep the horses in line, or shout at some pedestrians to make way, or stop to consult the map. Newport was large city; it was easy to lose one's way amongst the sprawling expanse of large wood-and-brick buildings.

Inside the coach, Marion Elizabeth Wingate chattered away without a care in the world. She had been going on about the latest adventures from the penny dreadfuls for the last half hour. Beside her, Commander Barnes was trying his hardest not to listen. On Barnes's other side, Sophie gazed out the window with amazement; Newport was the largest city in Aurora, and this was Sophie's first time seeing it.

On the opposite bench, Lord Wingate and Amelia watched the youngsters fondly.

"It doesn't seem like he's particularly invested, Orpheus," Amelia giggled in a low voice.

"Give her time," Lord Wingate chuckled, "She's wearing him down."

"Tiring him out perhaps," Amelia retorted, "It seems that our young Mister Barnes is rather disinterested in the doings of Captain Dick Blunt."

Lord Wingate was hardly surprised. He had managed to borrow one of those stories once, and he had found it to be spectacularly in-accurate. Whoever had written that drivel clearly didn't know the first thing about life in the army. It was almost laughable.

"They just need to find a topic of conversation which they both find interesting," Lord Wingate said. That was how he and Amelia had first kindled their romance—with long deep conversations about politics, literature, history, society, and a dozen other topics. If it had worked for them, it could work for anyone.

"Easily said. Not so easily done I fear," Amelia shook her head fondly, "Something tells me that the poor lad is rather... Disinclined to take an interest in our little Mary."

"And just what do you mean by that?" Lord Wingate cocked an eyebrow.

Amelia smiled, "I'll explain later."

The rattling and bumping of the carriage began to slow. Outside, the rhythmic clip-clop of the horses hooves on cobblestone clattered to a halt, to be replaced with the hum of a large crowd. Amelia looked about, "Is this it? Have we arrived?"

Lord Wingate pulled back the curtains and peered through the door window, "It doesn't look like we've arrived yet," he muttered to himself. The carriage was supposed to take them to the Newport Munitions Plant operated by Newton and Sons. Specifically, it was supposed to deliver them directly to the front gates of the factory. Judging from what he could see though the window, they were still a ways off. "Hang on. I'll ask the driver."

Lord Wingate opened the door to ask what was going on, but paused when he saw just what was the matter. Outside the carriage, what had been the indistinct hum of people was now the roar of a mighty crowd. They milled about a large square in front of the gates of the Newport Munitions Plant. Some carried signs and placards, but Lord Wingate couldn't read them from this angle. Every now and then, someone in the crowd would start an angry chant, and the crowd would take it up with furious enthusiasm.

"Driver?" Lord Wingate finally managed, "what's the matter?"

"Not to worry, my lord," the driver said, "It's just another riot."

"*Another* riot?" Lord Wingate blinked, "Can we go through them?"

"Not right now," the driver said, "They're mainly clustered around the main gate. It doesn't look like we'll be getting in that way for a while."

Lord Wingate racked his brain for another option, "Is there a back entrance perhaps?"

"I don't rightly know, my lord," the driver said, "But it may be worth a look. Shall I go ahead?"

Lord Wingate shrugged, "You may as well," He slipped back inside the coach.

"So," Amelia asked as the carriage started up again, "What's going on, Orpheus?"

"Just a small riot," Lord Wingate said, "The driver is going to look for a back entrance."

"*Just* a small riot?" Amelia said suspiciously.

"It's nothing to be concerned over," Lord Wingate said confidently, though that confidence was somewhat undercut a few moments later when he gently pulled Sophie away from the window and drew the curtain closed.

Newport was a... unique city. Most cities of comparable size were seats of provincial governance, and as such, they all had nobility in residence. Newport was different; at the time of the Founding, Newport had been a small fishing village sitting beside the mouth of the River Kalmar, straddling the border between two provinces. It hadn't even really been much of a port; the river was much too shallow for deep-draft cargo ships to make the winding two-hundred-kilometre trek up to Kalmar, and the surrounding farmland wasn't of much economic interest either. For almost five and a half centuries, the town had remained insignificant in every way.

Then about fifty years ago, some clever soul had gotten the idea to dam the River Kalmar and use the resulting waterwheels to power a series of small textile mills. The result was an unprecedented manufacturing boom. Tens of thousands of people from the surrounding countryside poured into the city to seek employment in the factories, and dozens of other companies moved in to exploit this sudden influx of labour. Its location, almost exactly in the middle of the Auroran coast meant that the city was perfectly poised to become a major trade hub. There had even been talk of dredging the river so that deep-draft ships could go up to Kalmar, though interest in that project had fizzled out with the advent of airfreight.

In the space of only a few decades, Newport had grown spectacularly from a forgotten backwater to the primary industrial powerhouse of Aurora. Today, one out of every five Aurorans lived in this sprawling metropolis. And with such a large population, there came an equally large set of problems.

For one thing, civil unrest was extremely common in Newport. It was to be expected; whenever there were a large number of people gathered in one place, particularly when they were mostly poor and young, there was bound to be trouble. The fledgling Newport Bureau of Public Order had been formed to address the issue of civil unrest, but more often than not, their excessively brutal methods merely exacerbated the problems.

Perhaps if there were nobility in residence, Lord Wingate surmised.

The presence of nobility could do wonderful things for a city; nobility kept the public order, maintained justice, served as an anchor for society, patronised the local arts, and brought culture to the masses. But most importantly, they put a human face to the government, an ideal to which the common people could look up to and aspire. Newport could benefit tremendously from even just a single noble family. *The Barlowes of Kalmar perhaps,* Lord Wingate thought, *That pack of delinquents and scandalmongers would probably feel right at home here!*

At present, governmental authority in Newport was vested in the office of an elected mayor. Lord Wingate shook his head—mayors and aldermen elected by the common people were all good and well when dealing with hamlets and smaller villages, but for a city the size of Newport, it was dangerously close to mob rule. Cities needed continuity of government. They could not simply trust the winds of public opinion to take them where they needed to go. That was especially true of Newport, with a fifth of the population, and a third of the industrial capacity of Aurora. Something would have to change, and soon.

The carriage rattled to a stop, and again Lord Wingate poked his head out the door to consult with the driver. "We've arrived," the man said cheerfully. Lord Wingate nodded, and all the passengers were disembarked into the rear courtyard of the Newport Munitions Plant. Amelia and the girls were garbed in simple riding dresses and light overcoats. Lord Wingate and Barnes had elected for ordinary suits and tophats in lieu of their military uniforms; there was no need to let anyone suspect as to the true purpose behind this outing.

As the procession made their way to the rear door of the plant, they were greeted by a tall, wiry man in a leather apron with half-moon spectacles. "Orpheus," he waved, "I thought you might come in by the rear entrance."

"Theo," Lord Wingate clasped his dear friend's hand with a firm shake, "It's good to see you again."

"Sorry about that business out front," Lord Newton said, "I've already sent for the Bureau of Public Order to disperse them, but they've always been slow to arrive."

"Oh, it's quite alright," Lord Wingate said, "May I present my protégé, Commander Theodore Barnes."

"How do you do?" Lord Newton nodded to the young man. Barnes doffed his hat and bowed respectfully, but did not offer to shake hands; that would have been presumptuous of a lesser nobleman like himself.

"Theobald," Amelia said with a smile, and offered her hand. "Amelia," Lord Newton took her hand and kissed it lightly, "And the girls!"

"Good morning Uncle Theo," Marion and Sophie curtsied daintily.

"Now then," Lord Newton said, "Shall we begin the tour?"

It was terribly loud inside the plant; the clatter of machines, the shriek of metal lathes, and the hiss of steam valves combined into a hypnotic cacophony of noise. It was oppressively hot and dry compared to the comfortable early spring warmth outside, and the air was filled with a fine black dust that stung the eyes and nose. "Up this way please," Lord Newton led the party up a stair to a catwalk above the work floor where the environment was slightly more agreeable.

"This is our main assembly hall," Lord Newton explained, "Here we take the components and assemble them to make the shells." On the work floor below, men in grease-stained coveralls stood hunched over two long motion belts that carried various components past them. Two other motion belts lay still and unmanned beside them. "Why does every man only have one job, Uncle Theo?" Sophie asked.

"I'm glad you asked that," Lord Newton said, "Making a single artillery shell, like most modern industrial processes, is long, slow, and rather complicated. In the old days, if someone wanted to make a shell like these on their own, they would have to learn how to construct the shell casings to an exact size and shape, how to brew both the propellants and the explosives, and how to assemble the fuses, the ignition caps, and a number of other delicate components. That's a lot of skills, and only for one type of shell. Suppose the army changes the size of their guns, and we start getting orders for lighter or heavier shells? We'd have to completely retrain our workers on the new design.

"But now," Lord Newton said, "we can take a man and train him to focus upon just one aspect of production. It speeds up the training process, and it greatly increases overall quality." He pointed to worker, "That man there is filling the shell casings with propellant," He pointed to a different worker, "and that man there is fitting the shells onto the casings."

"And those men there," Sophie pointed to the men at the end of the motion belts, "Are packaging them for transport?"

"Exactly!" Lord Newton gave the girl a pat on the head. Lord

Newton shared a warm smile with Amelia. Sophie was such a clever lass. *She gets it from her mother.*

"I notice two other motion belts," Amelia said as the procession continued along the catwalk. "Is there a reason why they are not currently in use?"

"Economics," Lord Newton explained, "A few months ago, all four belts would have been running at full capacity, but now that we are no longer at wartime production levels, we have deactivated those belts and reduced the staff to conserve funds and resources."

"Is that the cause of the present unrest outside the front gate?" Amelia said. She sounded disapproving; she may have been born a noblewoman, but she still retained a deep concern for the common people. "I can't imagine that the workers who were *reduced,* as you say, were particularly pleased."

"Possibly," Lord Newton shrugged, "Who can tell?"

The catwalk led over a wall and into a new area. "This is our brewing hall," Lord Newton pointed to the tall vats of boiling chemicals that reached almost halfway up to the ceiling, "Here we take raw chemicals and process them into explosives and propellants."

"It sounds rather perilous!" Marion said, and clutched playfully at Barnes's arm, causing the young man to squirm.

"I'll grant, it is a highly delicate multistage process," Lord Newton said, "but it's not nearly so dangerous as one might think if it is managed properly." Lord Newton pointed at two of the vats, "For example, those two are precursor chemicals. They are crucial to the process, but they are not themselves combustible." Sophie poked her head over the catwalk railing, and Lord Newton gently pulled her back, "Though I must stress that it is still dangerous in other ways."

The tour continued into other rooms. There was the area where the shells were fitted with explosives. There was the area where the impact fuses and firing caps were assembled. There was the boiler room, where great mountains of coal were fed into a vast furnace which powered the steam dynamos that turned the motion belts and heated the chemical vats. Everything appeared to be in excellent working order, with the sole exception of one incident when a firing cap burst in the eye of the worker inspecting it. Lord Newton assured the party that it was nothing to worry about; the worker would heal with time. Probably.

Finally, the tour reached a small staircase leading up to a padded door. "And this," Lord Newton said as he opened the door and led the party through, "is my laboratory!"

The space beyond the door stood in complete contrast to the factory below. The walls and floors were dark varnished oak instead of bare brick and concrete. The walls and ceiling were adorned by glass candles, though they were switched off due to the late morning sun filtering in through wide windows. The fine black dust was conspicuously absent from the air, and the noise of the factory, already lessened by the walls, faded to a distant rumble as the door closed behind them.

"And this is where you conduct all your experiments, Uncle Theo?" Sophie looked about with amazement in her eyes.

"Some of them," Lord Newton said, "This is a rather small facility. My main complex outside Marburg is a good deal larger than this. Still, there are a number of smaller experiments currently underway here." He waved over at a group of people clustered around a worktable on the far side of the room; at his signal, a tall, horse-faced young woman wearing an apron and a pair of goggles broke off from the group and crossed the room to present herself.

"This is Hildegard, one of my research assistants," Lord Newton said as the young lady curtsied, "I'm certain she will be delighted to show you what we are working on at the moment." Hildegard crossed back to the worktable with Mary, Sophie, and Amelia following behind her. Barnes was about to follow as well, but Lord Wingate quickly motioned for him to wait a moment.

"Theo," Lord Wingate said in a hushed tone, "I wonder if we could have a word in confidence?"

"I should have expected there was a hidden purpose to this visit," Lord Newton chuckled, "What is it?"

"I need a favour," Lord Wingate pulled a scrap of paper out of his jacket pocket. Lord Newton took the paper and squinted at the writing on it, "These... look like production numbers."

"This is part of an internal investigation, my lord," Barnes said, "We need these shell numbers traced. We need as much information as you can provide about them: types, dates of production, shipping destinations, who ordered them. Anything you can tell us would be greatly appreciated."

"An internal investigation?" Lord Newton sounded concerned, "Is something the matter with our equipment?"

"I'm afraid that information is being kept on a need-to-know basis," Lord Wingate said firmly. It was always difficult to keep secrets from friends, but security was paramount. Lord Wingate was not going to let the fact that it had been an Auroran shell that downed the *Celsius* become public.

"I understand..." Lord Newton nodded slowly. His lower lip curled in a way that generally indicated that he was thinking hard, "These numbers look old."

"Is that a problem?" Lord Wingate asked.

"Oh, no, not at all," Lord Newton said reassuringly, "It's just that we don't store records on site for more than a week at a time. The information you want will have been transferred to our records facility in Marburg."

"Ah," Lord Wingate nodded with disappointment.

"I can get you the records," Lord Newton said, "It's just that it might take a while to dig them out."

"That's alright," Lord Wingate said, "As long as we get them in the end."

Lord Newton tucked the parchment into his pocket, "In the meantime, may I invite you to observe our current experiment?" He motioned towards the worktable the ladies were gathered around.

"Lead the way, Theo."

"What happens now, my lord?" Barnes whispered.

"Now," Lord Wingate whispered back, "we hurry up and wait."

Barnes nodded, and the two of them joined the rest of the crowd by the experiment table. "I think you'll be most fascinated by our latest discovery," Lord Newton was saying. Outside the window, the Newport Bureau of Public Order was starting to break up the protest.

Lieutenant Butler leaned back against a pillar and watched the skyfreighter *Red River* rise up out of berth six and then turn east toward Riga. Butler and his team had just finished their inspection, and now they were back to doing nothing.

"Goddammit," Andrew Garseed moaned as he slumped to the ground, "my feet are killing me." Butler couldn't exactly fault the man; gunmonkeys like him weren't used to all this walking, though the gunpit did tend to produce the strong pair of shoulders that Butler liked on a man. Garseed wasn't for him of course; the man's whoring habits, which had originally sent him to the *Dreadnought* had made that abundantly clear. *Look, but don't touch.*

"I should have thought you'd be used to it by now," Eric Philpot groaned, "What's it been? Two weeks?"

"Just about," Butler said. His hand dipped uncertainly into his jacket pocket to pull out his latest penny dreadful, but he ultimately decided against it. The latest issue wasn't nearly as entertaining at the previous entries. The quality of the story was going up; that was no fun! Who the hell wanted to read an actually *good* story? *It's probably a new author or something.*

"Dammit, but I'm bored," Philpot sighed, "Why don't we have any more ships to check?"

"Because we don't," Butler said, "We've already done berths four through nine, and all the rest are Consortium ships, so we don't touch them."

"Why don't we?"

"Because we don't," Butler shook his head; he had already explained it to Philpot any number of times. But for whatever reason, the idiot just couldn't seem to fit his head around it. No wonder Philpot had been shuffled off to the worst ship in the fleet.

Butler looked up; the sound of the departing skyfreighter wasn't receding into the distance like it should be. In fact, it was starting to get louder. Was it a new ship? Butler shrugged and got to his feet, "Heads up. We've got another ship coming in."

"Alright then," Philpot said.

"Goddammit," Garseed grumbled.

Just as the trio got to their feet, a dozen or so local constables rushed by. Butler watched as the officers took up positions just outside berth six. That must be where the ship was set to arrive, but why the police presence? "Officer," Butler asked one of the constables, "what's going on here?"

"Sir!" the officer saluted, and Butler returned the gesture on instinct, "We have received notice that the ship due to arrive here is carrying contraband. We have orders to detain all personnel."

"Carrying contraband?" Philpot parroted gleefully, "This should be fun!"

After a few minutes, a large, rusty freighter came to ground in berth six. As soon as her impact columns and reactor were turned off, the constables filed into the berth and took up positions to prevent escape; they were overcompensating, but you couldn't take any chances with smugglers. Finally, the cargo ramp opened, and the constables moved in to apprehend the crew.

"Sir," Garseed wheezed as he waddled up to Butler, "there's another ship touching down in berth nine."

Butler nodded, "We'll hit that one next. Just as soon as we're done here."

"But sir," Garseed stammered, "it's the captain!"

Butler blinked, "!hat?"

"You heard me," Garseed said, "It's the *Dreadnought!* Captain Bowman's back early!"

Captain Bowman must have caught this ship on his patrol, and escorted her back to port! "Tell the captain where we are," Butler ordered, "and tell him to join us at the earliest convenience."

"Right," Garseed moaned and turned to waddle back to berth nine, "Oh god, my feet..."

After a few minutes, the constables filed out of the ship, escorting a dozen or so rough-looking men; the freighter's crew. They looked to be a typical grab bag of ne'er-do-wells: Newport thugs, grown-up cutpurses, a few Alanerian-born Hadvari misfits. *The usual culprits.*

"Alright now," Butler stepped forward to take charge of the situation, "which one of you is the captain of this freighter?" The collection of human filth looked about. Some of them mumbled softly, but none made any reply.

"He's with us," said a familiar voice. Butler turned about and saw Captain Bowman striding into the berth, pushing a tall, spindly, rat-faced man before him. The man looked vaguely familiar. Barlowe and Hakefeldt followed after Captain Bowman, as well as one of the WAVE girls; Halford probably. "We didn't want him trying to escape," Captain Bowman said, "so we kept an eye on him ourselves. Hope you don't mind."

"Not at all," Butler saluted, "It's good to see you again, Captain,"

"You too," Captain Bowman kicked his prisoner forward onto the concrete floor of the berth and casually returned the salute.

Two constables sprang to apprehend the captain as he scrambled to his feet. They were about to slap him in wrist irons when Captain Bowman held up a hand, "Just a moment," he said, striding forward confidently, a triumphant grin spreading across his face, "That coat you're wearing is stolen property."

The captain grumbled wordlessly as he tore off his jacket and flung it viciously at Paul who caught the jacket, and nodded for the constables to carry on.

"What was that about?" Butler asked.

"Just settling old scores," Captain Bowman put the jacket on. A few moments later he took it off again, folded it clumsily, and handed it to the WAVE girl, "Remind me to have that thing cleaned," he said to the girl.

"Anyway," Captain Bowman said as he handed Butler a leather folder, "Here's the manifest. Tear that ship apart until you find every last bit of contraband. Open every compartment, look in every crawlspace, lift every deck panel. Give her the works."

"I will, sir," Butler took the ledger.

"Good man," Captain Bowman nodded, "I'll send a few more able bodies your way as soon as I can spare 'em." He started back toward the *Dreadnought* with Barlowe, Hakefeldt, and the WAVE girl trooping after him.

By now the constables were leading the crew away. Butler turned to Philpot and Garseed, "Stand guard on this berth," he said, "nobody gets in or out without prior approval." The men nodded and took up positions at the entrance to the berth. Butler turned his attention to the ledger, and his heart nearly stopped beating; embossed on the leather were three ornate letters: *A, T,* and *C* surrounded by an equally ornate Star of Dawn—the emblem of the Auroran Trade Consortium!

Shit!

Butler turned about to alert Captain Bowman to his error, but the man and his retinue had already vanished back into the belly of the *Dreadnought.* Butler turned back to consider the Manifest. The military wasn't supposed to meddle in the affairs of the ATC unless there was immediate evidence of criminal wrongdoing. Smuggling certainly qualified, but if it could be demonstrated in a court of law that Captain Bowman hadn't been completely certain about their guilt before initiating the inspection, then the ATC's infamous legal division would tear him to pieces like so many bloodthirsty wolves. Captain Bowman's case had better be absolutely ironclad. And even if it was, Butler had little doubt that the man had just made an enemy of the ATC for life.

"Excuse me?" A woman called from the entrance to the berth, "Excuse me? Hello?" Butler turned to see a young woman wearing an outrageous feathered hat, a jacket that left part of the bare flesh of her bosom exposed, and a ridiculous pinstriped skirt. *Aww hell!* Butler thought, *You again!*

"Miss Fairchild," Butler strode toward the entrance to the berth, "What a... pleasant surprise."

The Fairchild girl jiggled with glee and would have rushed toward Butler had Garseed and Philpot not stopped her from entering the berth. "Leftenant Butler, I believe?" She held out her hand as soon as Butler was close enough for it, "We met briefly some weeks ago in the Norvell train depot."

Butler took her hand and kissed it lightly. "It is a rare pleasure, Miss Fairchild."

"Oh, do call me Isabelle," the girl said airily, "All my friends call me Isabelle."

"Yes," Butler nodded, "So they do."

Fairchild giggled lightly and batted coquettishly at a stray lock of hair, "I don't suppose you've seen Captain Bowman about, have you?"

"I'm afraid you've only just missed him," Butler said.

"Oh, fiddlesticks!" Fairchild whined, "And here I am, having come all this way, only to have arrived mere moments too late! All that effort gone to waste! Oh, but I do have the most rotten luck!"

Of course! The idea came to Butler like the dawning of the sun, *The press!* The only authority greater than a court of law was the court of public opinion. If Captain Bowman could get his story into the newsjournals, he could take the moral high ground before the Consortium had a chance to react. No doubt the ATC would have to think twice about summoning a celebrated hero before a public court of law to defend a known smuggler.

And of course, Butler thought deviously, *It needn't necessarily be Captain Bowman himself who tell the story.*

"Yes, the captain is a very busy man," Butler commiserated, "He has just returned from apprehending a crew of dangerous smugglers in fact."

Fairchild let out a theatrical gasp of childish delight, "You don't say! Oh, how exciting!" She batted her eyelashes in what she probably thought was a flirtatious manner, "I don't suppose you would be willing to share with me your account of the story?"

"Why, it would be my genuine pleasure!" Butler grinned.

And so, he recounted to Fairchild the story of how Captain Paul Bowman had heroically and shrewdly outwitted a pack of fiendish smugglers, in the name of Her Majesty the Queen. It was all a fabrication of course; Butler had no idea what had actually happened, but that wasn't important. What mattered was that Captain Bowman had caught some smugglers, that the ATC had been somehow involved. Once that was clear, the public's collective imagination could do all the rest.

    Besides, Butler told himself, *people always like a good story!*

Chapter XIII

Rumor and Hearsay

BUTLER smoothed out the roll of blue paper on the map table, and Paul placed the toolbucket on the loose end to hold it in place. "Okay," Paul said, "what are we looking at here?"

"This blueprint," Butler said, "is for the main loudspeaker control console." He pointed to a smaller sheet of blue paper beside the larger one, "And that's the design for the individual speakers."

The bridge of the *Dreadnought* was littered with small wooden crates containing the parts for the loudspeaker system. Butler had told Haskell to "just put them anywhere," and no doubt by now he was beginning to regret his choice of words. The deck was in no condition for flight, but at the moment, that didn't matter. Apprehending the *Silesia* the previous day had thrown off their patrol schedule and left the *Dreadnought* with a free day. Most of the crew were taking the day at their ease, but not Paul, Butler, Haskell, or Barlowe. The parts for the loudspeaker system had started to arrive, and there was work to be done.

"Well then, let's get started," Paul said, "looks like we have enough for the main control console, and..." he counted the other crates, "...three speakers?"

"Haskell's coming up with a few more crates," Butler took off his jacket and rolled up his tunic sleeves, "And Barlowe should be here in a few minutes. We should have enough for four speakers."

"Alright," Paul considered for a moment. He and Butler had identified at least eleven spaces where the loudspeakers were needed. There was the engine room of course; that would be the first circuit they hooked up. The starboard and port gunpits would come next, and after that... probably the mess hall. That was about as close to covering the whole ship as they could get with only four speakers. Then, once the rest of the system arrived, they would hit the cargo bay, crew quarters, sick bay, the officers mess, the supply office, and the galley. They could leave the speaker on the bridge until they had enough parts for the talkback circuits, "I'll get started on the main console. You work on putting the speakers together. Once Barlowe gets here, we can install them and start laying the wires."

"Sounds like a plan," Butler opened one of the smaller crates and got to work. Paul did the same with the large crate that held the parts for the main loudspeaker console. He had always liked putting things together; he'd never been able to read the words on a blue-print, but that had never stopped him before! It was like a puzzle!

"So, Butler," Paul said after a few minutes of fiddling with a rat's nest of wires, "how exactly did you wind up on this ship?"

"Pardon?" Butler was carefully winding a length of copper wire about a metal rod.

"You seem different from most of the other people on this ship," Paul said.

"Really?" Paul could hear the tension on Butler's voice, "H-how so?"

"You're competent," Paul said.

"Ah, I see," Butler said, clearly trying to hide his relief, "I'm flat-tered, Captain."

Paul knew why Butler was on edge; Halford had covered him a few days earlier. A number of WAVE girls, past and present, had made overtures to Butler, and he had gently declined them all. Louise's initial suspicions that the man was happily married had been thrown into question when another girl swore that Butler hadn't taken any home leave in almost three years; no self-respecting hus-band would ever leave his poor wife alone for so long. The obvious conclusion was that Butler was unsatisfied by his wife and was seeking affection in the arms of another woman, or so Louise thought. She had been utterly shocked when Paul suggested that perhaps Butler simply preferred men.

"So," Paul continued (you had to lure these things out of someone. You couldn't just walk up and ask someone if they fancied you), "how does a competent officer like you get himself shipped off to the worst post in the fleet?"

"It's a long story," Butler said. Paul frowned; that was what you said when you wanted to avoid talking about something.

"Did you sleep with the wrong WAVE girl or something?" Paul suggested. It was close enough to what Paul suspected was the truth.

"Yeah," Butler laughed weakly, "something like that."

Both men were silent for a moment.

"Was she noble?" Paul said, pressing further, but also offering Butler an escape route, "I imagine that would land you in a good bit of trouble."

"Yeah, it was one of them," Butler said, "You know how uptight those old families can be."

"Do I ever!" Paul said, noting that Butler hadn't actually specified that it was a *woman* that he had slept with. *I'm on the right track.*

"What about you, Captain?" Butler changed the subject, "What's your story?"

Paul shrugged, "You've probably read all about me in the broadsheets."

"The broadsheets aren't the story," Butler said, "I want to hear it from you."

I've been grilling him for a bit now, Paul supposed, *It's only fair.*

"I guess you deserve to know," Paul began, "I was born in a whorehouse in Two-Lakes. My uncle took me in, and I spent most of my childhood with him working on airships. I figured the rest of my life would play out pretty much the same."

"Sounds like you had everything all figured out," Butler said, "So how did you wind up here?"

"I got conscripted," Paul said, "The army used to give out immunity from conscription in exchange for making supply runs to the troops. But toward the end of the war, the Consortium came along and started to eat up all those jobs. Eventually my luck just ran out."

"Is that right?"

"Yeah," Paul said. It wasn't the whole truth of course, but it was close enough that he could say it without feeling like a liar.

"Well, that explains how you became a soldier," Butler said as he finished the first speaker coil and started on another one, "How did you become *the Hero of the Southern Gap?*"

"By accident," Paul said with a groan, "It was either retreat from a bunch of snipers and get myself shot by the provos, or charge them and maybe survive. It was basically my only option."

"You'd be surprised," Butler said, "Charging a whole army head-on? I know plenty of people who would have just turned tail and ran, provos or not."

Paul laughed, "You want to know the best part? Turns out it wasn't even an army. It was a bunch of civilians."

"Really?"

"Yeah," Paul lay down and slid underneath the console frame to connect some wires, "Apparently there was a flood or a famine or some sort of disaster down in Isafar. The people were all refugees."

"Refugees?" Butler sounded skeptical, "Didn't you say they had snipers with them?"

Paul shrugged, "Scouts probably. Could have been spooked by the airship explosions."

"I don't know," Butler said, "Seems like there's more to it."

Paul blinked. Now that he stopped to think about it, something didn't quite add up. Having scouts was all good and well, but if they were protecting a bunch of refugees, why had they attacked first? They had to know that doing so would provoke a counterattack.

And for another thing, they'd brought artillery with them. And not those old front-loading solid-shot cannons that you saw in those etchings from before the war; these were modern guns. *Modern enough to shoot down an airship!* Butler was right; there had to be something they weren't seeing.

Maybe he should have asked Lady Batu about it before she left? Or would she have just given him an excuse? He had liked Lady Batu, and she had evidently liked him as well, but she probably wasn't in the habit of giving out secrets to people she had known for less than a week. *Maybe I'll ask her if I ever see her again,* Paul thought.

"Hang on a second. Scoot over," Butler said as he crossed the bridge to join Paul underneath the console. All of a sudden, Paul was acutely aware of the smaller man lying on the deck beside him. This smaller man who preferred other men.

Paul's thoughts began to race. He had only ever known two other men like Butler, and those two only distantly. This was the first time he had ever been in such close proximity with... someone like him. Well, he had been in close quarters with other men before, but that had always been on the job. Well, they were both on the job *right now*, but... Dammit, he just didn't know!

"So, this right here?" Butler pointed to an array of electrical connections on the underbelly of the console. "This is where we hook the speakers up?"

"Yeah," Paul tried not to stammer, "you, uh... you split the wires on this end so that each one has two endings. Then you connect one to the separate circuits here," Paul pointed to another array, "And the other one to the master switch over here."

"What about these ones down here?" Butler pointed to another array of electrical connections. Paul could feel Butler's shoulder rubbing against his own.

"Those connections," Paul said, swallowing his discomfort, "are the talkback circuits. They let the people on the other end... well, talk back."

"I see," Butler said and slid back out from under the console frame. Paul tried to hide his relief. Butler went back to the map table and resumed working on the speakers. "Well, it'll probably be a while before I can get us those ones."

"Don't worry about it just now," Paul said as he got back up off the deck, "It'll be enough just to get these first four up and running."

Paul looked down at the console frame standing before him. Apart from all the wire connections, it was as complete as it was going to get. All that was left to do was... "Get over here," Paul said, "Help me move this thing into place."

"Of course, Captain," Butler set down his speaker and joined Paul on the other side of the console frame. It wasn't particularly heavy, but it was always best to move something like this with two people.

"So Captain," Butler asked as they set their load down beside the radio, "how did you find out?"

"Simple really," Paul pointed, "The wires from the top connections are hooked up to the individual switches, but the ones at the bottom are all hooked up to where the bridge speaker—"

"That's not what I meant," Butler interrupted, "How did you find out about"—he paused and lowered his voice—"about me?"

"Oh right," Paul said sheepishly, "that..." He shrugged, "Call it a hunch."

"A hunch?" Butler frowned. He wasn't buying it.

"I didn't hear it from a rumor, if that's what you mean." Paul tried to sound reassuring. At least people weren't talking about him behind his back.

Butler nodded slowly. His expression didn't change, "I trust you understand the need for discretion, Captain?"

"Don't worry, I ain't a gossip," Paul said, "Besides, you really think I'm going to risk the only other competent person on this ship?"

Butler nodded slowly; his expression still carefully neutral, "I suppose that's fair." An awkward silence settled over the bridge.

"So..." Paul ventured, "How did *you* know?"

Butler shrugged, "Well, when I was a kid, the preachers used to go on and on about how—"

"No, I mean just now," Paul interrupted, "How did you know... that *I* knew?"

"Oh, that," Butler said, "Because your breathing changed."

Paul blinked, "What? When did I—"

"Under the console frame," Butler said, "Of course you were being pretty obvious earlier, so I figured you'd found out somehow, or at least suspected it. And since you obviously don't share my tastes, I decided to—"

Paul blinked, "Wait, how do you know *that?*"

"Believe me Captain, I can tell," Butler cracked a grin, "And before you ask, don't worry, you're not nearly pretty enough for me."

Paul burst out laughing, "And here I thought I was being subtle!"

Butler started laughing as well, "Believe me Captain, you're a good deal more subtle than some."

It was strange; Paul had thought he would notice something about Butler, maybe the way he spoke, or the way he walked, or some other character tic that would have made his sexual preferences obvious in retrospect. But there wasn't anything. He was just Butler; the same good old Lieutenant James Butler as he had always been. *And why the hell shouldn't he be?*

"Sorry for giving you such a hard time," Paul gave Butler a friendly punch on the shoulder, "I don't care what any preacher has to say. There ain't a damn thing wrong with you."

Butler grinned, "Thanks, Captain."

A WAVE girl, stepped onto the bridge. "Captain," She held out a large leather bundle, "Your coat has been cleaned."

"Thanks," Paul smiled and crossed to the WAVE girl to collect his jacket. He threw it on over his uniform jacket. Damn but he had missed the feel of it. The soft seal fur on the collar... The way the deerskin held onto every last scrap of heat... Luckily Knox hadn't been mistreating the old thing too badly.

"And there is a Leftenant Harrison waiting for you outside," the girl added, "He says that Commodore Wilmont requests your presence."

"Does he now," Paul grumbled, his joy at being reunited with his old jacket suddenly evaporating.

"He does indeed," the girl said.

Paul turned back to Butler, "You think you can handle things from here?"

Butler considered for a moment, "I don't think so. I can handle putting in the speakers and running the wires and all, but that"—he pointed over at the console—"that thing has got to be riveted into place, and I don't know how to do that."

"Oh, don't worry, it's easy," Paul said, "They've already bored all the holes in the console frame. You just have to drill some more holes in the bulkheads, put the rivets in, and buck 'em from inside the crawlspaces. Barlowe can help you out with it when he gets here."

"Alright, Captain," Butler nodded, turning over one completed loudspeaker in his hands, "Come to think of it, where is Barlowe? I told him to get down here quite a while ago."

"I'll tell him to hurry up for you." Paul tucked a rivet hammer into his belt and started for the stairwell. "Thanks Captain," Butler said as he got back to work on the next speaker.

"Excuse me Captain," the WAVE girl said as she followed Paul into the stairwell.

"Don't worry," Paul called back, "I'll track down Barlowe, *then* I'll go see what Commodore Crankypants wants."

"That's not what I meant Captain," Paul stopped in his tracks and turned to face the girl. She continued in a low tone, "I think I know where Leftenant Barlowe is."

Paul turned to regard the girl who was now a few steps behind him. Rose Willingham was her name, and according to Louise, she was the daughter of some baron who had been hidden away on the Dreadnought after refusing her mother's command to marry the son of a rich merchant. If a noble girl like her was speaking in hushed tones about Barlowe, there was definitely something scandalous going on. *What the hell is he up to this time?* "Alright," Paul said, "Lead the way."

Willingham led Paul down the stairs, and toward the back of the ship. Just outside the door to the deserted medical bay, the girl pointed out a ladder and a ceiling hatch above it. *What the hell is he doing on the top deck?* Paul thanked Miss Willingham for her help and climbed up the ladder and through the hatch.

The rear top deck of the *Dreadnought* was about level with the top of the aerodrome, and the front level was even higher. Paul spared only a moment to take in the view of the rooftops of Longview before he heard voices coming from up on the higher deck.

"You're being ridiculous, darling," It was a man's voice. *Barlowe.*

"I most certainly am not!" A girl laughed, "Why, I've heard the most scandalous things said about you, Mister Barlowe. Any decent woman would want nothing to do with someone of your dishonest reputation."

"Well you know what they say," Barlowe said, "One girl's idea of dishonesty is another girl's idea of fun."

"Your charming witticisms shan't do you any good." The girl giggled playfully.

"Come on," Barlowe said, "I know you want it, girl."

"Ohoho, is that so?" The girl's voice was growing husky and thick.

"Trust me," Barlowe said, "I know what women want." And he would have leaned in to plant a kiss on the girl had Paul not come up from behind and planted a firm hand on his shoulder. "Oh! Captain," Barlowe stammered to a salute, "I... I didn't hear you coming."

"You want to tell me what the hell you're doing up here?" Paul growled.

"Captain, I..." Barlowe's charisma evaporated in an instant, "You... you gave the rest of the crew a day off. How we spend it is our business."

"I don't care what *the rest of the crew* is doing." Paul pulled the rivet hammer out of his belt and handed it roughly to Barlowe, "Butler needs you on the bridge. Get the hell down there."

"Okay," Butler said, taking the hammer awkwardly, "I'll be along in a few minutes; just tell—"

"*NOW!*" Paul shouted, "And if I ever catch you playing grab-ass up here again, I'm docking your pay!" That did the trick. Barlowe shrank back like a frightened mouse and scurried off to the lower deck and back down the hatch to the inside.

Paul shook his head. *For every half-competent person on this ship, I've got two complete morons.*

"I am in your debt, Captain," the WAVE girl said lightly, "I must offer my sincerest gratitude for helping to preserve my virtue."

Paul glanced over at the girl, "Meyers, isn't it?"

"Indeed, Captain," The girl curtsied, "Jesslyn Meyers, of the Women's Airborne Volunteer—"

"Don't you already have a kid?" Paul interrupted.

"Ah..." the girl's face twisted into shock and embarrassment, "You... heard about that..."

Paul shook his head, "Take my advice, and stop flirting, girl."

Meyers looked away and began to straighten her scarf, "I wasn't doing that," she muttered sullenly.

"Sure you weren't." Paul started back to the hatch. *Let's see what Wilmont wants to yell at me about this time.*

Commodore Horatio Garfield Wilmont was still smoothing his freshly waxed moustache when the knock came. He took one last glance in his pocket mirror and tucked the golden bauble back into his breast pocket. One had to keep up appearances once a rank such as his was reached, and since his hair was growing rather sparse, there was a need to compensate elsewhere. "Come," he shouted, not bothering to mask the contempt in his voice. He knew perfectly well who had just arrived.

Leftenant Harrison marched in, and following after him was Captain Paul blasted Bowman. The two men made their way to the centre of the room and saluted, Harrison with crisp precision, Bowman with ragged carelessness. "Give us the room please, Harrison," Wilmont said, and Harrison turned on his heel and marched back out. *The very picture of discipline.*

Wilmont turned his gaze upon Bowman. *The source of all of the Wilmont family's current woes.* Everything had started to go downhill for them right about the time when Bowman had deliberately and maliciously disgraced Cousin Alphonse before the court of Aurora, naming him a *lying, lie-telling teller-of-lies.* It was an accurate assessment of his cousin-by-marriage of course—even a little bit funny in an oafish sort of way—but that wasn't the point! Bowman had callously embarrassed one of their own, and in doing so, he had made himself an enemy of the Wilmont family for life!

After a moment of utter hatred passed between the two men,

Wilmont reached down and pulled a broadsheet from out of his desk, "I don't suppose you've read this latest edition?" It was a rhetorical question of course; Bowman couldn't read, and Wilmont had the signed letter of resignation to prove it. *A most fortuitous discovery,* Wilmont told himself, *I must make sure to put it to good use.*

Bowman made no response. That was good. A man should know when he has been defeated. Wilmont opened the news journal and cleared his throat.

CAPTAIN PAUL BOWMAN SMASHES SMUGGLING RING!

taken from the account of Mdlle. Isabelle Fairchild esq.

Paul Bowman, the Hero of the Southern Gap, and the ARAF's latest Captain, has done it again! In a stunning action, Captain Bowman has apprehended a band of vile smugglers seeking to defile our fair land by peddling their wicked wares!

Making his spectacular return to the public eye, Captain Bowman has for this past fortnight, been patrolling the Mountains of Dawn. Rumours abound of an increase in smuggling activities along the Analerian border, and valiant Captain Bowman has made it his solemn mission to stamp out this menace once and for all!

Enemies on the field of battle are easy to spot, but smugglers are much less overt in their dealings. For two weeks, Captain Bowman searched and searched but could find neither hide no hair of illegal activities. The smugglers, no doubt dreading the arrival of such a storied hero, went to ground, praying that Captain Bowman would pass them by without noticing.

Of course, Captain Bowman is not such a man to permit a wrong-doer to slip through his fingers!

Auroran law has for many years justly prohibited the importing of certain foreign goods which damage the moral fibre of civilisation. However, such laws must be backed up with great vigilance lest civilisation itself degenerate into vile barbarism. It is with this in mind that Captain Bowman has applied himself to inspecting every last airship carrying goods through the Gates of Dawn and into Aurora. It is a grueling task, one which only the most dedicated can hope to achieve, yet it is to this very task that Captain Bowman has selflessly applied himself.

Trade in prohibited goods was finally unmasked yesterday when Captain Bowman inspected the airship Silesia. *Her captain, a wicked soul by the name of* Victor Knox, *has long been fattening his purse with the profits from his expansive smuggling ring. But when a preponderance of evidence implicated him as the mastermind, Captain Bowman moved in to arrest the notorious criminal! But the plot thickens, as the vile Mister Knox has managed to associate himself with the honourable Auroran Trade Consortium!*

Consortium members are afforded special privileges by the Crown, including exemption from traditional customs inspections; an internal body carries out Consortium inspections, for greater expediency. However, it seems plainly evident that Mister Knox and the crew of the airship Silesia *have long been using the honourable Auroran Trade Consortium to mask his illegal activities!*

Could it be that the Consortium itself is merely a front for smuggling? Most certainly not! Far be it from this humble journalist to cast aspersions upon the character of so reputable an organization. But it does raise serious concerns about other associates. How many more contraband traffickers have been hiding beneath the petticoats of the Consortium? Ah, but let us not become distracted by such wild speculation, for Captain Bowman still has a criminal to apprehend!

Present arrangements with the Consortium prohibit traditional inspections without immediate evidence of criminal wrongdoing. But Captain Bowman is a man of action! He is certainly not one to sit idly by while the law of the land is openly scoffed at by wanton criminals! With justice on his side, Captain Bowman intercepts the airship Silesia *and orders Knox to submit to an immediate inspection.*

Threat after threat spews forth from Knox's lying lips! He proclaims his affiliation with the Auroran Trade Consortium and demands the privileges thereof. But Captain Bowman shan't be cowed by mere words! He refuses to take no for an answer and forthwith conducts his inspection.

Recommend against it, would you? Perhaps you are one of those who trembles at the mere mention of the Consortium? In any case, it is good that Captain Bowman is not so easily intimidated, for in carrying out his inspection, he discovers a vast shipment of contraband goods, worth nearly five thousand crowns! By far the largest smuggler's cache discovered to date!

Putting all pretense aside, Captain Bowman now orders the airship Silesia *impounded. She is returned under armed escort to the Gates of Dawn, and her crew is placed under close arrest. Once again, law and order have triumphed thanks to the heroism of Captain Paul Bowman!*

Pressure is sure to mount upon the rest of the smugglers who make their trade by flouting the law. For soon, Knox and his minions shall stand trial for their wicked crimes, after which they shall surely meet with an ignominious end upon the gallows! No doubt, there shall be more smugglers following after them in the coming weeks and months!

On another matter, it is not known what role exactly the Auroran Trade Consortium played in this sorry affair. It is evident that their special privileges from the Crown have become a target of criminal exploitation, but exactly how far does the rot extend? Was the Consortium a willing collaborator? Or merely a victim of criminal cunning? Whatever the truth, the Crown shall surely be reviewing their arrangement with the Auroran Trade Consortium before long.

Consortium representatives could not be reached for comment at the time of the publication of this article.

Wilmont theatrically closed the news journal and set it on his desk. "You've been rather busy these past few days, haven't you, Mister Bowman?" Bowman made no response, "Anything to say for yourself?"

Bowman only shrugged, "You can't believe everything you read in the broadsheets."

"How convenient for you, then," Wilmont said with a wicked grin. He doubted that he would ever tire of rubbing Bowman's illiteracy back in his face.

"Is that it, sir?" Bowman said, "...'cause I should really get back to my—"

"Of course there's more!" Wilmont snapped. Bloody hell, but Bowman had a way of working his nerves, "You executed a search on a bloody Consortium vessel!"

"Yeah," Bowman said bluntly. He seemed not to comprehend the magnitude of his blunder, "And we found seventeen crates of—"

"What you *found* is irrelevant. The *search itself* was illegal!" Wilmont spluttered, "If the Consortium doesn't agree to look the other way this one time, we could have had a serious incident on our hands."

"If *they* agreed to look the other way?!" Bowman's eye nearly popped out of his head, "We caught *them* breaking the law!"

"And in doing so, you broke the law yourself!" Wilmont pounded on his desk to emphasise the point.

"I don't understand," Bowman said.

"Of course you don't," Wilmont grumbled, "I don't know why I expected any different from you," He really should have seen it coming; the man was illiterate after all. That was what happened when officers were jumped up from the rank and file; there was just no sense of professionalism.

"If this is about their people getting dragged off to jail..." Bowman started.

"Nobody's getting 'dragged off to jail,'" Wilmont interrupted.

"What?!" Somehow Bowman seemed more upset by this news than anything else.

"Were you not paying attention?" Wilmont said, "Your search was illegal, and therefore any evidences you may have hit upon are inadmissible in a court of law. We simply have no evidence with which to prosecute a case against Captain Knox."

"The guy's a goddamn smuggler!" Bowman was practically shouting. "Give me two days, and I can dig up a dozen people who'd all say the same."

"Rumour and hearsay," Wilmont scoffed. Bowman really had no idea of the workings of civilised society, "I don't doubt the man is a most unsavoury character, but unless he informed you of his smuggling activities firsthand and invited you onto his ship to personally observe them, then I'm afraid there's not a court in the realm foolish enough to take up this case."

"So Knox is gonna walk?" Bowman folded his arms in what he probably imagined was an imposing manner, "You're just gonna let a known smuggler go free?"

"Your actions have placed me in a most unenviable position," Wilmont said, "but I'm afraid my hands are tied. There's nothing to be done."

"*Nothing to be done,*" Bowman repeated, mimicking Wilmont's upper-class accent.

"Well, there is one more thing," Wilmont fished into his desk and pulled out another small piece of paper, "A complaint as to your conduct."

Bowman's face twisted into an absolutely delicious look of horror, "Is that from who I think it is?"

Wilmont smoothed out the complaint report on his desk with another theatrical flourish, "This complaint concerns, amongst other things: false arrest, illegal search and seizure of trade goods, damage to private property, and particularly..." Wilmont paused for emphasis, "*...tortious interference.*"

"Torture-what?" Bowman evidently was not familiar with the

word, "Does he mean when I stopped him beating that kid?"

"No doubt Captain Knox is referring to how the Consortium terminated his contract," Wilmont said

"The Consortium kicked him out?"

"Yes," Wilmont said, "and he is apparently of the opinion that you were the cause."

"Well, ain't that a pity." Bowman seemed rather pleased by the news. *Much too pleased,* Wilmont thought, *We can't have that.*

"And there's one more item of note," Wilmont added, "It seems you stole something from him."

Bowman's mirth vanished instantly, *that's better.*

"What was it?"

"A jacket," Wilmont said, his eyes tracing up and down Bowman's coat. "A fine deerskin jacket with seal fur lining," It was an exact description of the garment which Bowman was presently wearing over his uniform, "He claims it was stolen."

"It's been returned to its rightful owner," Bowman said firmly.

"That's for me to decide," Wilmont said, "Now hand it over."

"What? No!" Bowman refused.

"Are you disobeying the direct order of a senior officer?" Wilmont said with an evil grin, "Or perhaps you'd like the order in *writing?*"

For a moment, Bowman just glared. Then, he slowly removed the jacket, folded it, and placed it on the desk. Wilmont took it and tucked it away into a small drawer.

"Now then," Wilmont said, "I believe some sort of punishment is called for."

"Punishment?" Bowman blinked.

"But of course! Certainly you didn't think I summoned you here only to rap your knuckles and send you on your merry way, did you?" Wilmont said, "Yes, I think a week of suspended pay ought to put some sense into you."

"A week's pay," Bowman nodded, "Alright," He seemed resigned to it. That wasn't good; punishments were supposed to be harsh...

"No," Wilmont said, "*two* weeks. For your *entire crew.*"

"What?!" Bowman squawked, "You can't do that to my crew! They were just doing like I told them."

"Then you should have considered that before you issued your orders," Wilmont said firmly, "Two weeks of crew-wide pay suspension. Am I clear?"

Bowman's indignation slowly faded back to resignation, "Yes

sir."

"Good," Wilmont said, "Now get out of my office before I decide to make it three weeks." Bowman turned and shuffled to the door.

Wilmont glanced down at the drawer that held Bowman's jacket. There was no way he was going to return that tattered old rag to Captain Knox. The man was evidently a bungler; it took an extraordinary degree of clumsiness to actually get kicked out of the ATC. The Consortium hadn't dismissed him for smuggling; it had dismissed him for being *caught* smuggling. It wasn't worth making an ally of a small man like him.

Everyone in the fleet knew that the ATC was involved in smuggling of course; it was smuggling revenue that had kept the Consortium operating at a tidy profit since the beginning of airfreight. In fact, the reason the fleet engaged in customs inspections wasn't to catch smugglers, but rather to enforce the ATC's monopoly. Contraband goods fetched a hefty premium on local black markets, and it would not do if anyone with an airship could undercut their prices.

And then there was that article—an amazingly sensational piece of nonsense. Wilmont recognised the author; Mademoiselle Fairchild had already written two other similarly grandiose articles about Bowman. The girl was clearly inexperienced as a journalist (and quite evidently besotted with Captain Bowman), but more importantly, her article had cast a heavy suspicion on the ATC. That was by design, no doubt; Bowman had almost certainly had a hand in its production. A clever move on his part.

Wilmont produced a piece of paper and began to draw up the order for suspension of pay to the crew of the *Dreadnought. Only suspension?* Wilmont considered for a moment, then crumpled the paper to begin again. Suspension was all good and well of course, but that money had to go somewhere, and the wages for two-and-ninety people was quite a significant sum. *Why let that money simply slip back into general assets,* Wilmont supposed, *when it could just as easily slip into my own purse?*

With the order drawn up, Wilmont leaned back in his chair and let out a deep sigh of contentment. What a jolly way to spend a morning! Cousin Alphonse would no doubt enjoy hearing of this battle and how the haughty Captain Paul Bowman had been taken down a peg. At last, the tide of Paul Bowman's war against the Wilmont family was beginning to turn.

Paul kicked idly at a small pebble as he shuffled down the streets of Longview with his hands in his pockets. He wondered what he was going to say to the crew. How would they react to loosing two weeks of pay? Would they understand that it was out of his hands? Would they blame him for their misfortune? *They should blame me,* Paul thought, *I screwed up.*

If the *Dreadnought* were a civilian ship, the crew would probably band together to kick him off the ship and choose one of their own to replace him as captain. But the military did things differently. Here, orders were orders, and orders had to be obeyed no matter what. If the crew started causing problems, all Paul really had to do was put his foot down. I'm in charge, and that's that; now get the hell back to work! *No, that's not the kind of captain I want to be,* Paul shook his head, *The crew deserves better.*

Would they mutiny? Paul had heard stories about mutinies on oceangoing ships, and the occasional commercial skyfreighter, but never on a military ship. *It has to have happened before,* Paul supposed, *Just because the public doesn't know about any, that doesn't mean they haven't hushed up a few incidents over the years.* Paul shrugged, even if the Fleet did have a spotless record with respect to mutinies, there was no guarantee that it would stay spotless. And if there was any ship in the fleet that was primed for a mutiny, the *Dreadnought* was it.

"Captain!" Paul looked up to see Halford hurrying toward him, as quick as her skirt would let her. She was waving a small envelope, "Captain, a letter just arrived for you!"

A letter? Halford wouldn't have tracked him down in the city for just any letter. "Who's it from?"

"Just look," Halford came to a stop in front of Paul and turned the letter over to show a green splotch of sealing wax, "Look at this."

Paul squinted at the seal. Pressed into the green wax was the imprint of the eight-pointed Star of Dawn. Above it there was a crown, and to either side there were some letters that Paul couldn't read. "I think I've seen this before," Paul said.

"It's the Royal Seal," Halford said in a frantic whisper, "Her Majesty's personal seal!"

The Queen? No wonder Halford had tracked him down all the way out here! "Let's go inside"—Paul nodded toward a small pub —"and see what Her Majesty has to say."

Halford nodded and followed Paul into the pub. Paul's brain was a flurry of anticipation. What could possibly be so important that the Queen felt the need to contact him over it? *It can only either be really good news, or really bad news,* Paul thought, *Please don't let it be more bad news.*

The steel rivet anvil shuddered with each blow of Barlowe's hammer. Butler did not envy the man his current task; he had only ever had to work in the crawlspace between the decks of an airship once, and it had been the most miserable, cramped, sweaty experience Butler could remember. Barlowe had been at this task for at least half an hour now; Butler could only imagine how uncomfortable he must be.

One final blow was struck, and the tapping stopped, "Done," Barlowe wheezed from under the deck.

"Good," Butler picked up the last rivet, slipped it into the freshly drilled hole, and placed the rivet anvil over its head, "Just one more, and then we're finished."

"Thank God," Barlowe moaned, and the tapping resumed lethargically.

Butler's mind wandered to the conversation he'd had with Captain Bowman barely an hour ago. He had never really been comfortable discussing his... situation with other people, not the least because they rarely treated him the same way afterward. Even among his own family. His father had called in all his favors to keep his *boy Jimmy* in the fleet, but Butler couldn't help noticing that his father hadn't once written to him in the three years since he'd found out.

Butler had known a fair few other men in his situation, but none of them had any advice to give; the few who had told their families were disowned soon afterward. Butler could even recall one unfortunate fellow who had vanished into a bedlam house not long after resolving to tell his family. And those were the lighter stories; if your secret slipped out through rumor or hearsay, you could just as easily find yourself murdered "in a family dispute over an inheritance" or some other excuse.

Captain Bowman isn't a gossip, Butler reassured himself. If anyone learned his secret, it wasn't going to be from Captain Bowman. But how had he found out in the first place? Butler didn't buy that *hunch* excuse for a second; he had to have heard it from someone, who had heard it from someone, who had heard it from someone, and so on. So where had that initial leak come from?

The tapping from beneath the deck stopped for a moment and was replaced by a low moan. "Hit yourself again?" Butler asked casually. Another muffled groan was all the answer he needed. After a few moments, the tapping resumed more slowly.

Finally the tapping ceased for good, and Barlowe clambered over to the open hatch that was the entrance to the crawlspace. He slumped down next to the hatch as soon as he was clear, leaning against the uninstalled bulkhead that he had managed to ignore for the past two weeks now, and nursed a trio of purple-green bruises on his cheeks. Butler decided to let him be. All that was left to do was to connect all the wires; he could handle that himself.

As Butler slid under the console to connect the wires, he heard the sound of boots coming up the stairwell. A few moments later, Captain Bowman stepped out onto the bridge. "Captain on deck," Butler said, and Barlowe managed a weak salute.

"Good work, Barlowe," Captain Bowman said as he crossed to the loudspeaker console. He seemed to be in a very good mood, "It's always nice to see my crew hard at work." Barlowe squirmed and continued rubbing at his bruise.

"What's it looking like down there, Butler?" Captain Bowman crouched just beside the console.

"Just about done, Captain," Butler said as he connected the last circuit to the master switch, "We've already put up the speakers and laid all the wires. We just need to connect everything to main power, and we should be ready for the inaugural broadcast."

"The what?" Captain Bowman blinked.

"The *first* broadcast," Butler reiterated as he twisted the last of the wires into place, "How was the meeting with Commodore Wilmont?"

"Terrible," Captain Bowman said in a tone that seemed to indicate otherwise.

Butler shrugged and closed the final circuit breaker. Something just at the edge of hearing began to hum softly. Butler slid out from under the console and got to his feet, "We're all ready, Captain," he indicated the master switch, "Care to do the honors?"

"Alright," Captain Bowman picked up the small mouthpiece and threw the master switch. A sharp pop echoed somewhere in the depths of the ship, followed by a hissing noise as Captain Bowman blew softly on the mouthpiece.

"Attention all hands. This is Captain Bowman speaking to you over our brand-new loudspeaker system," A tinny echo welled up from the stairs. *Success!*

Captain Bowman continued, "I hope you've all been enjoying your day off. I have some news for you, some good, and some bad. The bad news is, during the course of our duties we apparently stepped on the toes of some paper-pusher who has decided to have everyone's pay stopped for the next two weeks." Barlowe groaned, and Butler felt like joining him. No doubt this was the ATC getting revenge on Captain Bowman.

"The *good* news is," Captain Bowman went on, "it seems that word of our exploits has reached the ear of the Queen. Her Majesty is most pleased with our performance, and she has therefore seen fit to award a bounty of *fifty crowns* to every crewman on this ship, right on down to the WAVE girls!"

Fifty Crowns?! Butler's jaw almost dropped open; fifty crowns was more than a month's pay for him. Even to Captain Bowman, who made nearly twice as much as Butler, fifty crowns was more than enough to make up for two weeks of missing wages. Even Barlowe had managed a weak smile.

"If anyone wants to celebrate," Captain Bowman went on, "you can join me for a drink later this evening at the House of Red and Brown. Thanks again for all your hard work these past few weeks. You guys are the best crew I've ever had." Captain Bowman flipped the master switch back into the off position and put the mouthpiece back.

"We're the *only* crew you've ever had, Captain," Butler grinned. It was still a nice thing to say though. This crew might be the worst in the entire fleet, but Captain Bowman believed in them, and that was something.

"Get down to the supply office, Butler," Captain Bowman returned the grin, "There's a messenger from the Royal Treasury who wants a word with you."

The House of Red and Brown was by far the largest pub in Longview. More than half of the entire crew had taken up Captain Bowman's offer to join him for a drink. The back room was packed nearly to bursting with over fifty officers and crewmen, and even a few of the WAVE girls.

Archie Hakefeldt had just started on his first pint of the evening when a hush went around the room. At the head of the table, Captain Bowman stood up, "Well, people," Captain Bowman began, "it's been a great two and a half weeks." A murmur of approval rose up from the table.

"We haven't been together for very long," the captain went on, "but I know there are good things on the horizon for all of us. I still don't know half of you as well as I should, but I hope that in the weeks and months to come, I can..." he stumbled over the words, "Well, I hope I can... do that!" A round of laughter circled the room. Captain Bowman wasn't the most eloquent man in the world, but when he said something, he meant it.

"So," the captain raised his pint glass, "Here's to a long life, and a happy one. To a quick death, and an easy one. To a good friend, and an honest one. To a cold drink..."

"...And another one!" Everyone cheered and took a drink.

"And..." Captain Bowman added, "let us not forget Her Most Royal Majesty, Queen Cassandra the Second, whose generosity has made this booze-up possible," Another louder cheer filled the room, "Forward the Banner of Dawn!"

Archie found it a rather ironic cheer. A number of banners hung from the walls in this room, and indeed in every room in the tavern, but each one of them was the red and brown Nôs v'tai of Hadvar. Evidently, that was how the House of Red and Brown had acquired its name; the original owner had been a famous collector of war memorabilia. Every banner in the entire building had been a war prize, and a small placard beside each flag explained in great detail exactly when, where, and how each flag had been captured.

Archie downed his lager and leaned back to take everything in. Everyone was enjoying themselves. To his left, Warrant Officer Bellman, the gunnery chief, was explaining in great detail the crucial differences between Hadvari and Analerian spirits. He was just starting his third pint of the evening, but three pints of lager was nothing for an experienced drunkard like him.

To Archie's right, Warrant Officer Stan Thatcher, still on his first pint, was in a much worse condition, "I'm not saying he's bad," he slurred, "He's probably good at what he does, I don't know. All I'm sayin' is that... is that old Captain Hannegan, he never needed no fancy squawkboxes. He kept this ship running like a... like... *hic* like a... like a ship that was... running good!" His companions laughed; Thatcher didn't seem to notice, "An'... an' he never needed no fancy squawkboxes to do it neither." He took a final swig of lager, "Captain Hannegan, now there was a fine officer."

Some people were notably absent. Leftenant Commander Vaughn had declined the invitation of course; she wasn't one for social gatherings. Barlowe had stayed behind to finish installing a bulkhead on the bridge. Ensign Wagner had also stayed behind; Captain Bowman had left him with instructions to "breathe down Barlowe's neck" to make sure he carried out his job. Archie sniggered at that; Wagner idolised Barlowe; Captain Bowman couldn't have chosen a worse taskmaster.

A few seats down, Wolfram, Hamilton, and Newton stood up and made for the stairs in the far corner of the room. They were headed up to the second floor, probably to enjoy a few rounds of cards. From across the room, Wingate nodded for Archie to join them. Archie stood and waded through the crowd towards the stairs.

Archie's path took him behind Captain Bowman's place at the head of the table. Acting on a spur of the moment, Archie leaned over beside the captain. He paused for a moment to consider his words. "Thank you, Captain," Archie said at last, "for sponsoring this outing."

"*Outing?*" Captain Bowman laughed, "Kid, this ain't no outing; this here's a booze-up!"

"Of course. So you have said," Archie laughed, and then got to his purpose, "Some of the officers are heading upstairs. Perhaps you'd like to join us for a hand or two of cards?"

"Cards, eh?" Captain Bowman said.

"Indeed," Archie said, "Leftenant Wingate just won a rather substantial wager; we're going to see if we can't win some of it back."

"Well, I'm afraid my skills with a deck aren't what they used to be. But I guess I could stand to drop a few crowns." The captain stood up and finished off his pint, "Alright then, lead the way, Mister Hakefeldt."

Archie turned and led Captain Bowman up the stairs. Just before the room disappeared from view, the captain turned back to take one last look at the crew.

"Remember tonight, kid," Captain Bowman said with a proud grin, "Life is good tonight."

Chapter XIV

Hard Lessons

THE temptation was strong to lean against the pillar, but Lord Stolos forced himself to stand upright. Good posture was its own reward, and it would not do for someone to glance aside and notice him and think him uncouth. He was a lord now, and there were standards to uphold. Lord Stolos sighed, and glanced back up at the woman now presenting herself before the Queen: Miranda Babcock, head of the Auroran Trade Consortium. She had come to court today to air some grievances before Her Majesty.

Miss Babcock had evidently put a great deal of consideration into her appearance today. Her gown was of the finest Hadvari silk, but the colours were all calm, cool blues and greens; even the fur trimming on her parasol was dark. Her jewelry was all of silver, not gold, and there wasn't a single gemstone to be found anywhere on her person.

It was a balancing act; her outfit had to portray wealth and power, else she would not be taken seriously, but at the same time, she had to be careful not to express too much wealth and power.

Who could say how that petulant child-monarch would react were she confronted with someone who outshone her own meager radiance? It was an unfortunate thing that so much of politics was wrapped up in such superficial matters of appearance, but that was the way of things.

"Your Majesty," Miss Babcock was saying (it was miss, not lady, since she was not a member of the nobility) "I sincerely hope that these recent happenings shall not unduly disrupt the working relationship between the Consortium and the Crown."

"Hm?" The Queen looked up from the news journal she was reading.

Typical of the girl! Lord Stolos thought, *She makes no effort to educate herself about affairs of state in her copious free time and leaves the work of government until the very last moment!*

The Queen folded the broadsheet clumsily and passed it off to a servant, "Oh, yes," she said, "I heard all about those events. Oh, what a horrid thing, smuggling. Something really ought to be done about it."

"Indeed," Miss Babcock was being very patient with Her Majesty, "And I can assure Your Majesty that all necessary steps are being taken. The smugglers in question have been dismissed from the Consortium's employ, and a full investigation is being carried out upon all of our remaining vessels. I am certain that this is the last we shall hear of smuggling for a good long while."

"It gladdens my heart to hear so," the Queen said, "Such a rapid response stands as a credit to your organisation!"

"Majesty, if I might interject," Lord Franklin said as he stepped forwards, "I cannot help but question whether it is truly wise to simply take this woman at her word? Far be it from me to cast aspersions upon the moral character of another, but smuggling is a criminal matter. Surely it behooves us to make certain."

"I concur with his lordship," said the pale, spindly figure of Lord Armand Hannibal Blackpool, "One smuggler has already been uncovered. Who can say with certainty how many more criminal acts shall come to light? We must make certain how far this rot extends before it spreads! I recommend that all Crown contracts with the Auroran Trade Consortium be suspended at once pending a full investigation."

Lord Stolos snorted; Lord Blackpool's outrage was anything but honest. The Blackpool Group, of which he himself was the head, had been trying to expand into the airfreight sector for years. If the ATC had all of its Crown contracts suspended, the Blackpool Group would be more than willing to take on those jobs—and the profits that came with them.

"I see," the Queen said, her sentiments having been flipped back against Babcock, "It does seem that an investigation is warranted. And of course we shall need to put our contracts with the Consortium on hold in the meanwhile."

"Majesty," Miss Babcock said, "no one is keener than I to make certain of the good intentions of the Consortium's employees, but I fear I must caution against such a rash decision. Even if a mere handful of individuals are engaged in illicit activities, I believe that Your Majesty shall find that the vast majority of Consortium employees are honest, hardworking, law-abiding folk like any others. If the relationship between the Consortium and the Crown is interrupted, what shall become of these poor men? And their wives? And their children?"

"Then you had best hope that the investigation proceeds quickly," said General the Lord Wolfgang Theseus Harlocke, commander-in-chief of the Auroran Royal Army, "and that nothing untoward is discovered." The cantankerous general had spent the last ten years commanding troops just behind the front line, and his social graces had evidently suffered for it.

"My Lord Harlocke," Miss Babcock said, sounding terribly hurt, "I am shocked! Might I remind you, that during this recent war, it was the men of the Consortium who braved many perils to keep Her Majesties troops in full supply. These men are courageous and loyal, and though they might never have fired a shot, they did their part to defend their country. How can you be so callous as to cast them aside now?"

"I should also like to remind *you*, my Lord Hanscom"—Miss Babcock turned to the man beside Lord Harlocke, Lord Cecil Robert Hanscom, High Admiral of the ARAF—"That the search in question was carried out in a flagrantly illegal manner. I feel it necessary to further point out that the officer who ordered the search, one Captain Paul Bowman, is known to have a personal vendetta against the *alleged* smuggler. I question therefore whether or not the results of this search can even be considered valid, given this glaring conflict of interests?"

"I can't say that I've met this Captain Bowman in person," Lord Hanscom growled, like a beast irritated at having been disturbed from its rest, "but from what I've heard of the incident, he was following the orders he was given, and I stand by his actions."

"It is your duty to advocate for your underlings," Miss Babcock said, "and I am certain that Captain Bowman would appreciate your confidence, were he present. But the facts remain unchanged," Miss Babcock turned to face the Queen, "Your Majesty, I ask you, is it truly just for the Crown to suspend its relationship with the Consortium, causing so much upheaval and confusion, upon such an insubstantial basis?"

A wave of unimpressed grumbles went up from the crowd; evidently Miss Babcock's complaints were not being taken seriously by the assembled lords and ladies. This sort of thing tended to happen to people who were not of noble blood whenever they tried to air their grievances before the court. The nobility never took the lives of the little people seriously.

Lord Stolos decided that he'd had just about enough of this farce. He stepped forwards and cleared his throat for attention, "If I may beg your indulgence, Majesty," he announced as he took a place beside Miss Babcock, "I believe I have a solution."

"Wonderful," the Queen chirped, "Let us hear it."

"An investigation is clearly warranted," Lord Stolos began, "but not a complete cessation of Crown business. I therefore propose a compromise. The Crown shall uphold its current contracts with the Auroran Trade Consortium, but shall not establish any *new* contracts until an investigation shall have been completed to the Crown's satisfaction." He was making a conscious effort to refer to the girl as *The Crown* and not *Your Majesty*. There was no majesty to be found in this slip of a girl.

"That way," Lord Stolos continued, "we may determine *how far the rot extends*"—he allowed himself a smirk in the direction of Lord Blackpool—"while avoiding the economic panic that would no doubt precipitate from a full suspension." Lord Stolos forced a smile as he brought his attention back to the Queen, "Is this arrangement acceptable to the Crown?"

"That's a wonderful idea," The Queen said, "Do you find this an acceptable compromise, Miss Babcock?"

"Well," Miss Babcock exhaled with subtle relief, "It would mean taking a loss, but if it ensures the Crown's continued confidence in our organization, I would count it a small price to pay," She made an impeccably graceful curtsy, "I accept the compromise, Majesty."

"Oh wonderful! Simply wonderful!" The Queen turned to a court stenographer, "Let it be known that... ah... oh dear," She turned to Lord Stolos, "Remind me again, how did it go?"

Lord Stolos sighed and reiterated his proposal, "The Crown shall uphold its current contracts with the Auroran Trade Consortium, but shall not establish any *new* contracts until an investigation shall have been completed to the Crown's satisfaction."

"Yes, that was it," the Queen said, paying no heed to the court stenographer who was taking it all down, "It gladdens my heart to have this matter concluded. Now then, what is next on the day's agenda?"

Miss Babcock curtsied once more and backed into the crowd. Her business was done, and there was no need for her to remain where she was clearly unwanted. Lord Stolos bowed as well, and followed Miss Babcock out of the hall and into the corridor, "Excuse me, Miss Babcock," he called out, "Do you have a moment?"

The woman turned and made another supremely graceful curtsy, "My Lord Stolos," Her voice was dark and husky; her eyes, like smoky turquoise gemstones set in a marble face, "To what do I owe the pleasure?"

Lord Stolos bowed, "Miss Babcock, please allow me to offer my sincerest apologies for your inexcusable treatment at the hands of my fellow lords."

"You're too kind, my lord," Miss Babcock smiled warmly. Her smile was like the dawning of the sun after a century of darkness. And her eyes! A man could get lost in those blue eyes, like deep pools of calm water, yet with an energy and intelligence lying just beneath the surface, like a predator lying in wait to snare an unwitting soul.

"Erm... my lord?"

"Ah, yes, Of course!" Lord Stolos stammered; Miss Babcock, as a commoner, was not permitted to leave his presence until he dismissed her; that was the established protocol after all. "Now... where was I?" He knew he'd meant to say something... "Ah, yes, I wish to offer my sincerest apologies for your inexcusable treatment at the hands of my fellow lords."

Miss Babcock laughed lightly, "So you have said, my lord."

Lord Stolos blinked. Of course he had already mentioned that part. *Confound it all, I'm turning into Lord Franklin!* It wasn't his fault of course; what man could possibly stand before such a woman as her and fail to be distracted by her beauty? "A-and... should you ever find yourself confronted with such opposition in the future," Lord Stolos managed to spit out, "then I hope you shall count me as a friend."

"I shall endeavor so to do, my lord," Miss Babcock curtsied deeply. Lord Stolos bowed, and the two departed in opposite directions down the corridor, sharing one final backwards glance before they both vanished around a corner.

Now that he was alone, Lord Stolos's head finally began to clear. Damn, but that woman was beautiful! And well spoken too! She had raised a number of highly sensible points during her audience with the Queen. She might have even convinced the Queen on her own, had the rest of the nobility not consistently discounted her due to her status as a common-born woman.

It was hardly fair! Miss Babcock has served as head of the Auroran Trade Consortium for at least a decade, and under her astute guidance, the Consortium had risen to new heights of wealth and influence. Yet despite all her achievements, whenever she presented herself in Court, she was still treated like some unwashed peasant woman coming to air some petty grievance about a troublesome neighbour. Even a low-level peerage, of the sort the Crown handed out to just about anyone with enough crowns in their purse, had been repeatedly denied the poor woman.

There is a convenient way around all that nonsense of course, Lord Stolos told himself, *Marriage.* Miss Babcock was some years older than him, but nobility had never made much of a fuss over age differences between spouses. Personally, Lord Stolos considered marrying for social status a terribly old-fashioned thing; he would much prefer to marry someone he loved, as Lord Wingate had done. But if it was Miranda Babcock, he supposed it wouldn't be too bad. Lord Stolos smiled, *No, not so bad at all.*

The familiar vibrations began to well up from beneath the deck, and the *Dreadnought* rose from the Longview aerodrome to begin another patrol. Vaughn checked her chronometer and made another note in the logbook. *09:21 - Departed Longview aerodrome, heading north by east, bearing...* She paused for a moment before completing the line...

"Hakefeldt," Captain Bowman called out from the captain's chair, "What's our heading?"

"North by east, Captain," Leftenant Hakefeldt said, with a tone that oozed with disdain, "bearing, oh-oh-niner." Vaughn added the bearing to her line and closed the logbook for the moment.

"What's the matter, kid?" Captain Bowman said, "Not still sore about our little card game, are you?"

Gambling. Vaughn rolled her eyes. Of course that would be another of Captain Bowman's vices.

"You said your skills weren't what they used to be," Leftenant Hakefeldt grumbled.

"I never said they were *bad*," Captain Bowman said, probably thinking himself terribly clever, "My uncle used card games to teach me my sums." Vaughn glared down at the man slouching in the captain's chair. So he hadn't received formal education? Somehow she couldn't bring herself to be especially surprised.

Perhaps if he had been formally educated, Vaughn suspected, *We wouldn't find ourselves in our current situation.* Supplies on the *Dreadnought* were starting to stretch thin, despite Leftenant Butler's regular supply orders. Vaughn had little doubt that this was the Consortium retaliating for Captain Bowman's seizure of their ship; the ATC handled most of the supply shipments for the Auroran military. Diverting crucial supplies from Longview would be a trivial process.

Captain Bowman had to have known that the airship was a part of the Consortium. The ship's captain would almost certainly have informed him prior to conducting the search, and likely made a vociferous protest besides. Had Captain Bowman not known beforehand about the Consortium's arrangement with the Crown? If he hadn't, then surely a simple explanation and apology should be sufficient to smooth the Consortium's feathers. Vaughn shrugged. Captain Paul bloody Bowman didn't seem like the sort of person to apologise, even when he was demonstrably at fault.

The deck pitched as the Dreadnought turned north to begin the patrol. Vaughn steadied herself with a single bent knee. She had served for ten years and had picked up a very good sense of balance. She had never served in combat though; whenever there was a risk that some particular ship might see action, her captain had always found some excuse to transfer Leftenant the Lady Fiora Marie Vaughn to some other post. And once the danger was passed, that same captain more often than not would *generously* invite her to return and take up her old posting once again.

Vaughn had always resented being kept away from combat. Of course she had never really bought into that whole "To Die Gloriously for Aurora" nonsense, and honestly her reserves of patriotic fervor were starting to run dry. But on the other hand, it had almost certainly prevented her from gaining vital career experience. And beyond that, it was terribly patronising.

Vaughn had inquired about this policy multiple times, and not once had she received a satisfactory answer. Sometimes a captain would make it a matter of her sex, but then couldn't answer why the WAVE girls were not also being transferred. Other times captains would frame it as "keeping safe such an important member of the nobility as her," but then were unwilling to send away some other noble scion from elsewhere in his crew. Often the reply would be followed with a condescending smile and a friendly pat on the shoulder; such feigned sympathy was always the worst part of it.

"Heads up, people," Captain Bowman announced, "Airship off the port bow." Vaughn looked up. There was indeed an airship to their left, heading south towards Longview at what looked like a leisurely pace. Vaughn squinted; its rust-caked hull looked rather familiar.

"Sparks," Captain Bowman got up from the chair, "Signal the airship *Silesia* and order them to come to ground and prepare to receive an inspection party."

The airship Silesia? Vaughn's blood nearly froze in her veins. That was the same ship from before. Bloody hell, Captain Bowman still hadn't learned his lesson!

"Belay that order, Sparks," Vaughn said just as Ensign Wagner was about to signal the *Silesia*, "Captain, that is a *Consortium* vessel. If you force an inspection upon her, you will be exposing all of us to further reprisals."

Captain Bowman wagged a finger at the ship and smiled. "Oh no," he said, "that's not a Consortium ship anymore. They got kicked out after we exposed them. That right there's a private freighter now, and that makes her fair game."

Vaughn locked eyes with Captain Bowman for a moment. She didn't believe his excuse for a moment, but he was captain; if he was dead set on violating protocol again, there was nothing she could to to stop him. "As you say, Captain," Vaughn said.

Vaughn opened the logbook and checked her chronometer. *09:28 - Encountered airship* Silesia *(private freighter). Came to ground and executed inspection upon said freighter.* Vaughn hesitated for a moment, then added *against crew recommendations.* Captain Bowman was certain to catch the ire of the top brass for this action, and Vaughn would make certain she was well out of range of any reprisals.

"Message sent, Captain." Ensign Wagner reported.

"Captain," Leftenant Hakefeldt called from over by the map table, "will you be wanting me to assemble an inspection party?"

"Not just yet," Captain Bowman was a balloon swollen with pride and confidence, "Let's wait until they respond first." *Make them wait,* Captain Knox no longer had the protection of the Consortium, and Captain Bowman clearly intended to savour the final downfall of his old rival.

Six pairs of eyes peered out the forward window at the distant ship. After a minute, Captain Bowman glanced back at the radio, "Anything, Sparks?"

"No response, Captain," Ensign Wagner reported, "Shall I repeat the message?"

"Captain," Leftenant Wingate spoke up, "she's turning." Everyone looked up; the *Silesia* was indeed turning towards the *Dreadnought*.

"That's better," Captain Bowman said, evidently feeling rather satisfied with himself.

Vaughn wasn't so sure. Military protocol clearly stated that any message between ships, no matter how trivial, must be dignified with an acknowledgement, unless expressly stated otherwise. Sure, one couldn't expect civilian ships to always adhere the same rigid code of discipline, but something didn't sit right with her about this.

"Helm," Captain Bowman continued giving orders, "find us a level patch of ground, and make ready to come to ground. Hakefeldt, go to the galley and ask for—"

"Captain," Leftenant Wingate spoke up again, "I don't think they're coming to ground."

"What makes you think that?" Captain Bowman growled at the leftenant.

"Well, for one thing," Leftenant Wingate said sheepishly, "they're gaining altitude."

All eyes darted back to the approaching airship; she was indeed picking up altitude. But for what purpose? They couldn't be trying to get away; if that were the case, they wouldn't have turned *towards* the *Dreadnought*. Were they just trying to thumb their nose at Captain Bowman? If so, that was a rather petty way of going about it.

"Shit!" Captain Bowman spat sharply, as the *Silesia* drew even closer, "Vic, you bastard!"

"Captain," Vaughn said, "What's going on?"

Captain Bowman ignored her, "Helm!" he shouted, "Take us higher! Now!"

"R-right!" Ensign Hamilton stammered. The *Dreadnought* began to rise higher, but the *Silesia* still approached. "Captain!" Vaughn said more urgently, "What is going on?"

"Faster, Helm!" Captain Bowman continued to ignore Vaughn, "They're still gaining altitude on us!"

"We can't climb any faster, Captain!" Hamilton said, "I'm at maximum thrust now!"

"Goddammit," Captain Bowman hissed as the *Silesia* began to loom large over the *Dreadnought*, "Reverse! Full reverse!"

"Captain!" Vaughn shouted as the *Dreadnought* lurched suddenly backwards, "What the hell is going on?"

Before Captain Bowman could respond, there was a loud metallic crunching sound from above. The ceiling began to buckle and warp out of shape. Several electric candles exploded into flames as their glass housings cracked, and then fizzled out as their filaments caught fire and fizzled away. Almost simultaneously, the deck began to tilt forward sharply. Vaughn could also feel the ship turning, though unnaturally, as though someone had forgotten to undo a mooring chain. "Stop! Stop!" Captain Bowman shouted at Ensign Hamilton. The ensign, who was now frantically hyperventilating, released the thrust, and the deck slowly returned to an even level.

"Captain," Vaughn said through gritted teeth.

"The bastard was trying to clip our reactor," Captain Bowman pointed up at the buckling ceiling, "He just turned off his forward columns and dropped the bow of his ship on top of us. If that had hit the reactor, we'd be falling out of the sky right now."

"So what do we do now?" Vaughn said, glancing up nervously at the distended ceiling.

"Don't worry," Captain Bowman said, "I'll come up with something."

The roof began to groan from the strain. "Captain..." Vaughn said nervously.

"I said I'll come up with something!" Captain Bowman snapped.

Vaughn's mind was racing. There had to be a way out of this, some obvious solution that she wasn't seeing. Perhaps if she hadn't been kept out of combat for so long... *Stop that! There's no use fretting over maybes and never-weres right now!*

"Captain," Vaughn said, swallowing her pride and asked a crucial question, "Have you ever been in this situation before?"

"No," Captain Bowman said, "but I remember seeing it happen

once outside Kalmar."

Well, it's better than nothing, Vaughn shrugged, "And what happened there? How was the situation remedied?"

"Both ships crashed," Captain Bowman said, "Loss of all hands. Took out three city blocks." There was another loud clank from the ceiling, followed by a slow groaning crescendo of noise.

Nevermind then. "Well, what do we do now?" Vaughn demanded. Something had to be done, and soon!

"Wait," Captain Bowman held up a hand, "Wait... I think I've got something..."

Finally, a solution! "What is it, Captain?" Vaughn asked.

"Hang on," Captain Bowman said, "Just give me a moment..."

Up on the ceiling, something snapped, and a metal pipe dropped onto the deck with a clatter right at Vaughn's feet. *A few centimetres closer and...*

"We're quickly running out of *moments,* Captain!" Vaughn snapped.

"Shut up!" Captain Bowman roared, "You want to make yourself useful, lady? Jump on the loudspeaker and tell the crew to brace for a drop."

"Right," Vaughn rushed over to the loudspeakers. At least there was something for her to do now. And hopefully Captain Bowman's plan would—Wait... "Captain, what do you mean by *a drop?*"

"It means grab onto something," Captain Bowman was crouching beside Hamilton at the helm, "What do you think it means?"

Vaughn had no earthly idea what sort of mad scheme Captain Bowman was cooking up, but it was their only shot at getting out of this mess alive. Vaughn snatched up the mouthpiece and flipped the master switch. "All hands," She said, with a calmness that she certainly did not feel, "Take hold of the nearest secure object and brace for—"

Before Vaughn could finish her announcement, something terrifying happened. The deck dropped away from beneath her, and she was floating in midair. Vaughn could feel her stomach turning about in alarm at this unnatural situation. She quickly reached out and grasped the underside of the public address console before she could float away. A quick glance about the bridge showed that the other officers were doing likewise.

Barely a second later, the ship suddenly accelerated backwards. The loose bulkhead, still uninstalled after nearly three weeks, clattered about but remained relatively in place thanks to the radio console.

Vaughn was thrown violently to the side. She nearly lost her grip when Ensign Wagner collided with her after being thrown from his seat at the radio. Vaughn managed to catch the boy by his boot with her free hand, but she immediately regretted her decision as the deck suddenly rose back up and slammed into both of them. Then everything was normal again.

Vaughn carefully got to her feet and checked herself over to make sure that nothing was broken. On the deck beside her, Ensign Wagner rolled over and moaned softly, "Did we just die?" Moments later, the loose bulkhead clanged to the ground. On the other side of the bridge, Leftenant Hakefeldt vomited. Captain Bowman was still crouching beside the helm controls; he seemed not to have moved at all since the last moment Vaughn had glanced over at him.

"Captain," Vaughn demanded as she bent down to help Ensign Wagner to his feet, "what the hell just happened?"

"We cut out the vertical columns for a few seconds," Captain Bowman said, as though turning off the very thing that kept the ship aloft had been the most obvious solution in the world, "Combined with a full reverse. That seems to have disengaged us from the *Silesia* well enough." He stood up, and gave Ensign Hamilton a pat on the shoulder. "You did good, kid," he told the boy. Ensign Hamilton looked utterly thoroughly traumatised.

"And the *Silesia?*" Vaughn reached the forward window and glanced out at the sky above, "What happened to her? I don't see where she went."

Captain Bowman pointed downwards, "You're looking in the wrong place."

Vaughn lowered her gaze and saw the *Silesia,* or rather what remained of her, lying upside down on the dry mountain slope. She had split in half from the impact, and both halves were now spewing out smoke and flames. It was a grisly sight.

"She was a good ship," Captain Bowman said softly, "She deserved a better fate." He shrugged, turned about, and returned to the captain's chair. "Nothing we can do now. Let's head for home."

"Captain," Vaughn said, "Should we not at the least make an effort to search for survivors?" No sooner had the words left her lips however, then a tremendous explosion tore through the remains of the *Silesia.* The entire back half of the ship was reduced to shrapnel, several pieces of which tinkled harmlessly against the forward window. The front half of the *Silesia* collapsed from the shock wave, and soon all that remained of the ship was a smouldering pile of twisted metal belching out a thick cloud of black smoke.

"And there goes the reactor," Captain Bowman said casually as he slumped down into the chair. He gave Vaughn a tired glance, "What were you saying?"

"Nevermind," Vaughn said. There was no sense in protesting any further; at this point, it was a fait accompli.

"Alright, people," Captain Bowman sighed, "Helm, come about and bring us back to Longview. Sparks, radio Longview to let them know we're coming. Hakefeldt, Wolfram, you two start looking around the ship for anyone who's injured, and get them to sick bay. Vaughn..." The two of them locked eyes for a moment, "...do whatever it is you do."

"I shall, Captain," Vaughn tried her hardest not to groan. Captain Bowman's brazen disdain for her was getting unbearable. She didn't know how much more of this nonsense she could put up with.

"Erm, Commander?" Vaughn wheeled about, causing Leftenant Wingate to jump back slightly. The taller boy hesitated for a moment before awkwardly handing her the Logbook, "you... dropped this, Commander."

Vaughn blinked, "...so I did." She took the book, "Thank you, Leftenant." The boy nodded and slipped off the bridge. Vaughn opened the logbook, checked her chronometer, and began the daunting task of writing down exactly what had just happened.

"Captain," Ensign Wagner said timidly, "I think the radio's broken."

Wonderful. Just bloody wonderful.

Commodore Wilmont tapped his finger irritably on his desk and glared up at Captain Bowman, "So, Mister Bowman," he said at length, "how do you plan on excusing this latest blunder of yours?"

"Earlier this morning," Bowman began, "while setting out on patrol, we encountered the airship *Silesia*. Given her record as a known smuggling vessel, we ordered her to come to ground in order to receive an inspection party. Instead of heeding our orders, the *Silesia* turned and attempted to ram us, and she crashed when her attempt failed. Having sustained minor damage to our outer hull, we returned to port to await further orders."

Wilmont frowned, Bowman was beginning to acquaint himself

with the proper military terminology; the man was evidently quick of study. "Well," Wilmont said, "it looks like you've gone and done it again, Mister Bowman."

"I *defended my ship*," Bowman insisted, "Against an assault by a known criminal."

"You *destroyed* a Consortium ship!" Wilmont sprang to his feet, "My god, Bowman, are you a complete imbecile? It's been barely a week since the last incident!"

"That was *not* a Consortium ship," Bowman laughed, "The ship was dismissed after I exposed them last time, remember?"

"I think you'll find that the *Silesia* had her certification reinstated by the Consortium two days ago," Wilmont said with tremendous satisfaction.

"What?" Bowman's jaw dropped open, "How... But... That's not... Why wasn't I informed?"

"How you learn these things is your own business," Wilmont tutted, "I certainly cannot be expected to hold all my junior officers' hands. You shall have to take on the responsibility for this incident yourself."

"And what does that mean?" Bowman said, "More paycuts?"

"I don't think so," Wilmont said, "since you clearly haven't learned the hard lessons from last time, I believe a new form of punishment is in order." He considered for a moment. "You say you sustained damage during this... incident?"

"My crew is currently taking account of the damage," Bowman clarified.

"In that case, you shall have to make repairs," Wilmont said, "the costs of which *you* shall pay out of pocket."

"That's ridiculous!" Bowman exclaimed, "There's thousands of crowns of work to be done on her. I can't possibly cover all of that on my own!"

"You are more than welcome to explain the situation to your crew, and to ask them to contribute," Wilmont smirked, "Though I can make no guarantee with regards to their co-operation. Being as they are in the midst of a pay-suspension, they may not be in an especially charitable mood."

Bowman clenched his jaw, a welcome sign that he was giving in to the inevitable. "Is that everything?"

"There is one other thing," Wilmont said, "It seems your antics have attracted the notice of the head of the Consortium, Miss Miranda Babcock herself." Wilmont reached into his desk, "She has sent you a telegram. Would you care to read it?" Bowman's glare was positively delicious.

Wilmont opened the telegram, "I shall summarise it for you. Miss Miranda Babcock, founder and chief executive officer of the Auroran Trade Consortium, does herein express her deep displeasure over the actions of *certain rogue elements* within the Auroran Royal Airborne Fleet, with particular regard to the actions of one Captain Paul Bowman." Bowman gave no sign at the mention of his name.

"Furthermore," Wilmont continued, "she writes to inform all parties concerned that she is currently in transit to Longview and expects to arrive early this evening, at which point she intends to meet personally with said Captain Bowman. Hopefully a settlement can be reached which shall preclude further misunderstanding." Wilmont set the telegram down, "Need I summarise any further?"

"I understand," Bowman growled.

"Good!" Wilmont said sweetly, "Now then, I'm sure you have much to prepare for this evening's meeting, so I shan't keep you any longer. Shoo, shoo." Bowman gave one final glare and shuffled out the door.

With Bowman gone, Wilmont's mirth faded. All posturing aside, this matter wasn't nearly so open-and-shut as it might have been.

For one thing, Miss Babcock's telegram had arrived at headquarters only minutes after the *Dreadnought* had departed for the morning's patrol. Furthermore, it had been dispatched through civilian channels, which added delivery time from the telegraph office; not to mention the time it had no doubt taken to compose such a message. The implication was clear: it had been sent *before* the incident with the *Silesia*. That would complicate matters tremendously.

The incident seemed shocking on the surface, but once one got through all the smoke, debris, and lives lost, there was no question. This wasn't like the earlier incident with the *Silesia*, where the Consortium had been protected by a legal loophole. This time, Bowman had been in the right; the *Silesia* had clearly been the offending party, and the response of the *Dreadnought* was more than justified.

Of course the fact that Bowman's actions had lined up with protocol this time was very likely a fortunate coincidence on his part. Wilmont supposed he could comb through logs and expense reports to try and pick out a collection of petty violations, but he decided against it; it would be a lot of work without much in the way of a clear payoff. Besides, Bowman could very easily complain to the higher-ups about persecution, which would instantly negate all of Wilmont's efforts.

Still, the fact that Miss Babcock was coming at all would be a tremendous opportunity! Someone as highly placed as Miss Babcock could make a useful ally for the Wilmont clan. If Wilmont could send someone to intercept her before the meeting, then perhaps he could provide her with some valuable bits of intelligence. *Does she know that Bowman is illiterate?* Wilmont wondered. Such a pearl of insight would almost certainly be worth a favour in the future!

Allowing himself a malicious smile, Wilmont produced a paper and began to draw up an order for funds to effect repairs upon the *Dreadnought*. Bowman wouldn't see these funds of course—they would be conveniently intercepted by Wilmont himself and then promptly melt away into the Wilmont family purse. Now then... eleven thousand crowns? Yes, that ought to be a reasonable sum for repairs. Just need to add some digits behind it to end up with a suitably vague number...

The sun was beginning to redden as it neared the western horizon. The air was finally starting to cool down, but up here in the foothills of the Mountains of Dawn, the freezing night would bring the exact opposite problem. Victor Knox paused for a moment to catch his breath. Dammit! They'd been walking since the *Silesia* crashed; that had to be... what, eight hours ago? Nine maybe? Goddammit, his feet were on fucking fire.

"We're takin' a rest here," Vic wheezed, and the seven crewmen following after him collapsed onto the dry red ground. Vic could feel his stomach gnawing at his insides; he hadn't eaten anything since last night. He shrugged it off—he was much too angry to be hungry. Goddammit, Paul had done it again!

Paul had always had it out for Vic, ever since they had known each other. Paul was always running off to rat him out to old Captain Cooper. So what if Vic needed to slip out to the dogfights every now and again to collect his winnings? Or needed to catch a wink or two of sleep in the engine room? For someone who couldn't read, Paul had always done things by the book!

When Paul had gotten arrested for smuggling (with a little help from Vic of course) that should have been the end of it. Captain Cooper had been on his last legs, and nobody had protested when Vic took over after Cooper snuffed it. Well, they had protested, but after a few good fights they had all either fallen in line or gone off to other ships. Vic had the *Silesia,* and Paul would spend the rest of his life rotting in jail. For a few months, life was good.

And then, out of the blue, Paul fucking Bowman showed up again. And as a fucking *captain!* How the fuck had he pulled that off? It wasn't fair! And then he goes and ignores the rules and searches the Silesia, *Vic's* ship, and gets him kicked out of the Consortium! Well, Vic had managed to fix that after a few days, but still, it had been a humiliating process.

It was that fucking kid! Vic thought. Johnny, Jimmy, whatever the fuck his name was, that little fucking gink had ratted him out. *I should've never hired that little weasel!* That was the trouble with hiring kids; they were good for simple tasks, and you didn't have to pay them shit, but the little beasts could turn on you at any time for any reason. Vic hadn't seen that kid since he ratted the *Silesia* out to Paul, and if he ever saw that dirty little brat again, he would strangle him on the spot!

Vic looked up and took stock of the ragged remains of his crew. Seven people, not counting himself. They had been on the bridge when Vic had come up with his plan. While the bridge crew broke out the parachutes (as a precaution of course, you had to say things like that), Vic took the helm of the *Silesia* and made to clip Paul's ship right on the reactor. He'd seen it done once before in Kalmar; it would mean abandoning the *Silesia,* but that didn't bother him. The ship was Consortium property now anyway.

Vic had tried his best to hit Paul's ship in the reactor, and then he had jumped out an escape hatch with the rest of his bridge crew. The men had been shocked, but it was either abandon ship with him or die. The rest of the crew was dead of course; Vic had seen the explosion, and there was no way anyone could walk away from a reactor breach like that.

And yet, even after everything Vic had done, Paul had still managed to fly away! They probably wouldn't even have to be in repair for long; the Fleet would probably have Paul's junkheap back up and running within a week. Paul had managed to get away again! He'd have to get back at Paul somehow. But how?

"Cap'n," one of the crewmen said, finally breaking the silence, "what the hell are we gonna do now?"

"We're heading north," Vic said, "There's tunnels under the mountains. That's how we'll get back into Aurora." Vic had heard stories about smugglers repurposing old spent fulgurite mines, and it sounded like a load of crap, but it was as good a plan as any. He certainly wasn't going back to Longview; assault on military assets was a hanging matter, and Vic was not going to give Paul the satisfaction of seeing him twist on a rope.

"You don't actually believe those old stories do you?" another crewman butted in.

Fucking skeptics. "I've *seen* them," Vic lied, "I've been through one of them before."

"Well, if you say so," The crewman didn't sound convinced, "Alright then, how much longer do we have to go?"

"Couldn't say," Vic shrugged, he had to come up with some convenient cover story. "It might be pretty far north of here, but we could always run into a closer one."

"Are you serious?" another crewman blurted out, "I can't believe I'm hearing this bullshit!"

"It's there!" Vic snapped. *Goddammit what the hell is wrong with these new people? Why the hell did it have to be so goddamn hard to put together a good crew?*

"The hell with this," The crewman threw up his hands and turned south, "I'm heading back to Longview."

"You go back to Longview and you're a dead man!" Vic shouted, "You'll be swingin' from a rope in a week!"

"Hey, I've got family in Newport!" the crewman wheeled back around to shout at Vic, "I'd rather risk going through Longview than wandering around looking for some tunnel that ain't there!"

As the crewman turned to start toward the south, Vic reached into his jacket, pulled out a pistol, and shot the crewman in the back. The man collapsed to the ground with a terrible scream. Vic strode calmly over to the writhing mass, put a boot on his shoulder, and planted a final bullet in his head.

For a moment, everything was silent, apart from the distant cry of a mountain bird. Vic stepped off the dead man and rubbed his boot in the dirt to get rid of the blood. He glanced over at the remaining crewmen who were now all cowering in fear.

"Bury him," Vic gestured at the corpse. Nobody moved. "*I said fuckin' bury him!*" All six remaining crewmen jumped into action.

"Uh... with what?" one of the men asked warily, pointing out that they didn't have any tools.

"I don't fuckin' care!" Vic shouted, "Use your goddamn hands! Just get the fucker in a goddamn hole!"

Vic shook his head; why the fuck was it so hard to find good people these days?

As the crewmen went about digging the hole to dump the body, Vic glanced up at the mountains rising in the east. He squinted and thought he saw a person up there. Vic rubbed his eyes, and looked again to be certain. Yeah, that was definitely a person. So he'd been right all along; there really *were* tunnels under the Mountains of Dawn! "Hey!" Vic waved his hands in the air and called out, "Hey over here!"

The figure started moving down the mountain. *Yes! Things were finally starting to work out.* "We're looking for the tunnels." Vic explained, as the figure neared, "The tunnels under the mountain. We need to get back into Aurora, see? Only, we can't go through—"

"*Kulû ĝau šo!*"

Vic blinked. The figure was pointing a rifle at him. Vic stepped back, raised his hands and said, "Hey, hey, no need for that. We're all friends here, right?" The figure kept on coming; he showed no sign of lowering his rifle. As the figure got closer, several more figures with rifles emerged from the landscape and joined the first. They all had swarthy brown skin and shaggy jet-black hair, and they were all wearing the same outfit: red tunics with brown trousers. *Hadvari.*

"*Kulû ŵø uka,*" the man said. Vic didn't know the first thing about the Hadvari language; there had always been someone else to do the translating. *Paul speaks Hadvari,* Vic remembered and quickly banished the thought. The last thing he needed was to hear Paul's voice taunting him from inside his head!

"*Kulû ŵø uka!*" The hadvari said again, shaking his rifle in a threatening manner.

"Goddammit I can't understand you! Say it in in Auroran, you fucking gink!" Vic shouted. The gink in question responded by shoving the bayonetted tip of his rifle in Vic's face. Vic stepped back quickly and put his hands back up, "Alright, alright, you've made your point..."

"*Kulû ŵø uka,*" The soldier said again. More soldiers circled around the party, surrounding Vic and his crew.

"Psst! Hey you," Vic whispered to one of his crewmen who had the same hadvari complexion as the soldiers, "You speak gink, right? What's this guy saying?"

"Are you kidding me?" the crewman said, in an accent that was unmistakably Analerian, "I'm five generations out of Two Lakes! My *granny* doesn't speak the language!"

"He says he wants you to drop your gun." Vic looked up at the sound of a female voice. The short woman slipped through the soldiers. She wore the same red-and-brown uniform as the rest of the soldiers, but with pale freckled skin, blue-green eyes, and red hair, she was unmistakably Auroran. So what was she doing here with all these ginks?

"I suggest you do as he says," the woman said with a crooked smile. *The bitch is enjoying this!* Vic shrugged and slowly reached into his coat, took out his gun and put it on the ground. That seemed to placate the soldiers.

"*Jiri fa šo ehari,*" the lead soldier said, "*Šo ôhari jiri bûuxaž, śeim že ujiri. Kenkulû kí?*"

"He wants you to come with him," the woman translated, "He'll shoot you if you try to escape."

Chapter XV

A Long Overdue Confrontation

IT was about six in the evening when the Consortium airship ar-rived at the Longview aerodrome. Hakefeldt and Barlowe stood on either side of Paul as he watched the ship set down in berth six. She was a terribly large ship, two hundred feet from prow to stern perhaps, thirty feet high, and at least forty feet wide at the middle. This was about as large as you could build a commercial freighter; any larger and it wouldn't be able to lift a full load, or something like that.

Perfect for a show of power.

The ship wobbled ever so slightly as her landing gear touched down. Paul smirked at that; apparently her helmsman was not used to handling such a large ship. She eventually settled into place, and her reactor powered down. And then... nothing.

"Shouldn't something be happening?" Hakefeldt whispered into

Paul's ear.

"Relax kid. They're just making us wait," Paul said. That was how important business negotiations always started; you always made the other person wait if you could. It was a show of power, "All you need to do is stand at attention and look all professional like." Hakefeldt nodded. Barlowe groaned.

After a few more minutes, the cargo ramp finally opened, and a woman emerged. Miranda Babcock was wearing a brilliant green silk dress with gold trim and what looked like at least three pounds of golden jewelry. Her velvet-gloved hands held a green silk parasol to keep the sun off her long, wavy locks of dark brown hair. She strode confidently down the ramp, stopping just before the edge where Paul and the two officers stood.

"Ah, Mister Bowman," Miss Babcock said, clearly forcing cheerfulness, "I trust the evening finds you well."

"Captain."

Miss Babcock blinked, "Sorry?"

"It's *Captain* Bowman," Paul said more firmly.

"Why, so it is!" Babcock laughed, "Well then, *Captain*. I don't suppose you'd remember me..."

"We met in the Capitol," Paul said flatly, "A few weeks ago."

"Ah, how wonderful!" Babcock smiled sweetly, "You *do* remember!"

"I remember you called me a rube."

"Did I?" Babcock took a whiff from a small vial of smelling salts. She seemed unfazed, "My word, nothing escapes you, does it, Captain?"

"Miss Babcock," Paul said, "if you would be so good as to accompany me back to the *Dreadnought*. I'm sure we'd both like to get everything sorted out as soon as possible." Paul was in no mood for these little games; he wanted this nonsense over with as soon as possible.

"Oh, good heavens!" Babcock laughed, "I'm being ambushed! It has been a long journey, and I've not had the chance to recover. Just give me a while to make myself a little more presentable, and then we can get down to business. How does that sound?"

Paul considered for a moment. He still wanted this nonsense over and done with as soon as possible, but he supposed a slight delay was acceptable. Maybe an hour or two. "Fair enough," Paul shrugged, "How much time do you need?"

"Oh, I shan't take more than two hours, I don't think," Babcock said, "Let us meet at the Overlook Hotel at eight o'clock."

"Alright," Paul said, "eight o'clock."

"Wonderful," Babcock smiled, "I shall be looking forward to it," The woman made a gesture, and two footmen scuttled down the ramp carrying several thick rolls of clean crimson carpet which they rolled out in front of their employer. Babcock strode along the clean path and stepped into a waiting carriage that had pulled up outside the berth.

"What's the carpet for, Captain?" Hakefeldt asked as the carriage rolled away.

"Look down," Paul said, "Would you trust that dress on a floor like this?" The concrete floor of the aerodrome was incredibly dirty. Great slicks of fuel and dark lubricant collected into pools of foul-smelling sludge before draining away through a spider web of cracks. Even the parts of the floor that were mostly dry were covered in the mud and dust of a thousand pairs of boots from every corner of the earth. The smell was... well *disgusting* wasn't the right word—Paul had certainly smelled worse things in his time—but it was very strong, and very distinct.

"No," Hakefeldt said, "I suppose I wouldn't."

Paul shrugged, "Let's get back to the ship." He turned to go, and Hakefeldt and Barlowe followed after him.

"Surely that begs the question though, why did she wear such a dress in the first place?" Hakefeldt went on.

"Negotiation tactic," Paul said without thinking, "A show of wealth and power," It was the obvious conclusion. Babcock was rich and powerful, and she wanted to make sure Paul knew it.

Should I have tried something like that? Paul wondered. He *had* suggested that they conduct the negotiations on the *Dreadnought* right away. *Maybe I should have insisted?* Paul considered. She had evidently planned everything out before arriving; if Paul could have upended those plans, she would have been put off her guard. He shook his head, *She would probably have just insisted right back or something, and then we'd be forced to give up ground.*

Paul had never liked negotiations like this. Not the least because he couldn't read whatever contracts came out of them. It was all posturing, mind games, and trickery. You always had to be on your guard against an attack from every angle, even when you had the advantage. Not only that, but the revelation that *he* was going to have to pay for the *Dreadnought's* repairs himself had already put him in a bad mood.

This is going to be such a pain.

When Paul and his group finally reached the *Dreadnought* in berth nine, Butler was waiting for them at the top of the cargo ramp with a ledger.

"Captain," Butler saluted and handed the ledger to Paul.

"More supply trouble," Paul said as he took the ledger and pretended to read it over. It was starting to become second nature for him by now.

"It's been almost a week now, Captain," Butler said, "None of my supply orders have come in."

Paul didn't have to be able to read the ledger to know exactly how bad that was. The seven remaining barrels of fuel in the cargo hold, only enough for one more patrol, said it all. If they didn't figure something out soon, the *Dreadnought* would be grounded.

"I'll see what I can do about it," Paul handed the ledger back to Butler and started for the stairwell.

"Captain," Butler said, "I can't stress enough how important this is. If we don't get another load in soon—"

"I said I'll see what I can do," Paul growled without looking back.

Paul had only gotten about halfway across the cargo bay, when Wolfram emerged from the stairwell with a ledger of his own. *Great. More problems.* Wolfram handed the new ledger to Paul, "A summary of the repairs, with cost estimates, Captain."

Paul snatched the ledger with a grunt and tucked it into his jacket.

"Are... you not going to consult it?" Wolfram said.

"Later," Paul growled.

"Captain, I must protest," Wolfram said, "This is a matter of immediate—"

"You wanna shut the hell up kid?" Paul shouted, "Goddammit, I've got more than enough on my plate right now! The last thing I need is some uptight little shit who think he knows better than everyone just because his daddy is someone big and important!"

Wolfram gaped. He appeared to be trying to form words, but his mouth would not cooperate. Paul supposed this was probably the first time anyone had been so blunt with the boy in a while. *Good,* Paul thought, *the brat needs to be taken down a peg!* "I'm gonna read it when I'm gonna read it," Paul said, "Now find some way to make yourself useful before I stuff you into a goddamn ammo locker and leave you there."

Paul started toward the stairwell, and noticed Halford cowering beside it. *The poor girl hasn't seen me angry like that before.* Halford," Paul said as calmly as he could to the girl, "I'm going to be in my cabin for a while. Bring me a South Ridge Black. Strong as you can."

"Yes Captain," the girl said with a nod and scurried up the stairs after Paul.

Paul made it to his cabin, shut the door behind him, and threw the ledger across the room. The loose pages came apart and scattered across the room like dry leaves in the wind. What the hell was wrong with that kid? Wolfram seemed to think he was better than everyone. As if he were only following orders because *he decided* to! Vaughn was a prick as well, always looking down her nose at everyone, but at least she seemed to recognize that Paul was in charge.

Growling with frustration, Paul picked up the scattered sheets of paper and stuffed them carelessly back into the ledger. Then he sat down at the desk and looked them over. They were out of order of course, but given that Paul couldn't read them anyway, that was a small matter. The only thing that mattered were the numbers.

Some of the numbers were small—a few shillings here, a shilling and nine there. Those numbers didn't bother him too much; they were probably just electric candles or lengths of wire that needed re-placing. He could pay those out of pocket easily enough. Then there were larger numbers, usually several crowns. Those were probably pipes that had broken. The really scary figures were the several-hun-dred-crown items that probably represented the deformed bulkheads and roof plating from above the bridge. The total (or at least the largest figure) was six thousand four hundred and fifty three crowns, seventeen shillings, and seven and three quarter pennies. *Dammit, why do these things have to be so goddamn specific?!*

There was a soft knock on the door. "Come in," Paul said without looking up from the ledger.

Halford slipped through the door and set a tea tray down on the desk beside the ledger. "I must say, Captain," she said cheerfully, "I never pictured you as a tea drinker."

"It's better than that brown bean mud they ship out of Illyria," Paul said with a chuckle. Tea was by far the most reliable Auroran export. It was just about the only thing that Illyrian traders consistently wanted from Aurora apart from finished goods, and most airship crews had access to bulk shipments of high-quality tea for next to nothing. More importantly though, tea was one of the only major trade goods that the Consortium had never managed to monopolize. At least not yet.

Paul took his tea from the tray, emptied the shallow teacup in a single gulp, spat the dregs back into the cup, and set it back down on the tray. Paul paused for a moment. *What a weak brew that was.* He glanced up at Halford and was about to say as much, but stopped when he saw her face. She looked horrified. "Something wrong?"

Halford was holding a small porcelain bowl with a spoon. "I... was going to ask if you would like some sugar or honey with your tea," she said awkwardly, "But... I can see that you are... quite alright."

Paul shrugged and scooted to the side, "Take a seat. I need you to help me with this damage report." Louise set down the bowl and started reading.

It was exactly as bad as Paul had thought. Twenty five bulkheads and forty-six roof panels needed replacing, as well as both radio transformers; that alone was enough to bankrupt Paul several times over. On top of that, there were sixty-two glass candles, nineteen portholes, and fifty-eight "meters" (about a hundred and ninety feet according to Louise) of wire to replace. Somehow, three sections of peripheral reactor ducts had also been damaged. Paul knew better than to ignore those; you always fixed your reactor before anything else.

"And how is the crew feeling?" Paul asked, once Halford was done with the report.

"Not good," Halford said, "A lot of people were rather distressed by the encounter. There's about half a dozen people in the infirmary. Fortunately nobody was very seriously hurt."

Paul nodded, "Any word about blame?"

"A little," Halford said, "Actually, most of the blame seems to be directed at Commander Vaughn."

"Really?" Paul found that surprising.

"Oh yes," Halford said, "I suppose you know that Commander Vaughn is not well liked amongst the crew."

"She's not supposed to be," Paul said, "She's the first mate. If she *is* well liked, she's not doing her job." *Still,* Paul thought, *she could stand to tone down that attitude of hers.*

"Yes, well..." Halford continued, "it seems that her warning to brace came a little too late for most of the crew. Many are of the opinion that she ought to have made the announcement sooner."

Paul shrugged; if anyone was at fault for that, it was *him.* He had been putting that whole scheme together on the quick, and it honestly hadn't occurred to him to warn the crew until it was too late. *Well, considering that the alternative was losing the ship and everyone on it,* Paul thought, *a few infirmary cases is pretty light.*

In any case, there were plenty more things to worry about. Butler's missing supply deliveries were of a much more immediate concern. Paul was convinced that it was the Consortium's doing, retaliation for the incident with Vic the previous week. He knew from his experience as a freighthauler just how dirty the Consortium was willing to play to get what they wanted.

That raised another question: even if Paul could scrape together enough crowns to afford the repairs, how would the supplies even reach the *Dreadnought* with the Consortium's blockade in place? Butler was good at finding things here and there, but even his best would only be a drop in the bucket. This negotiation would be crucial.

Speaking of which, it was almost time to get going. Paul stood up and walked over to the wardrobe. For an occasion like this, he should probably change into his spare uniform. Paul glanced back at Halford... Well, he could probably get away with just changing his jacket.

"Will you be... needing my... assistance for this meeting, Captain?" Halford ventured.

"I probably will," Paul shrugged, "But I can't take you anyhow."

"Oh," the girl said, "yes, of course."

"Sorry, kid," Paul said as he finished buttoning up his jacket, "If I want to stand any chance of coming out of this with a good deal, I'm going to need to take one of the officers with me."

"I understand, Captain," Halford took the tea tray and vanished through the door.

Now alone in his cabin, Paul considered who he should take with him when he went to confront Babcock. His first thought was Butler, of course. But Butler was still busy with the inspections, and if they missed another one of those, the consequences with Commodore Wilmont would be severe. Paul supposed that he could order all air traffic grounded for a few hours, but he quickly decided against it; he was in enough hot water already. Butler was not an option.

Paul cycled through the rest of the officers in his head. Wolfram was out of course, and Barlowe too. There was Lieutenant Newton from the engine room, but Paul hadn't seen enough of the kid to trust him with a job like this. Archie Hakefeldt had a cool head; he might do. No, he was only a lieutenant junior grade; Paul needed someone more important than him. And of course that ruled out Hamilton and Wagner.

That left only one person.

Paul stepped out of his cabin and made his way to the bridge. Vaughn was standing beside the captain's chair, and scribbling something in the logbook. "Captain on deck," she announced as Paul stepped onto the bridge. *Just as usual.*

"You"—Paul pointed at Vaughn—"With me."

Vaughn blinked, "Excuse me?"

"Come with me," Paul said, "It's important."

Vaughn was silent for a moment. Finally she nodded and passed the logbook off to Wolfram. "Leftenant Wingate," she said, "you have the bridge."

"Aye ma'am," Wolfram took the book in acknowledgment.

"Captain?" Vaughn said as she joined Paul in the stairwell.

"Go get something to write with, and meet me at the loading dock," Paul said, "We're going to meet with the Consortium."

Miranda Babcock slipped her hand into the pocket of her gown and fished out the cheap brass fob watch. The intricate engravings on its dull, tarnished surface had long since been smudged out by years of finger grease, but its insides were still as keen and accurate as they day it had been assembled. Miranda flipped open the lid. It was almost ten minutes after eight in the evening. *Bowman is making me wait.* She closed the lid and dropped the watch back into her pocket.

Miranda had gotten the watch from her father. Henry Babcock had been a brilliant man with a keen mind for business. He had always known exactly where to invest, where to cultivate allies, and any number of other tricks of entrepreneurship. And yet, despite that demonstrably superior intellect of his, (which Miranda would readily admit to inheriting,) Henry Babcock had never achieved great financial success.

The reason for her father's lack of success was obvious to Miranda: Henry Babcock had simply never put enough thought into appearances and presentation. He had worn the same worn-out suit and bowler hat to every single business negotiation, like he had just gotten off a long shift on the assembly lines. Not only that, but he presented every business proposal in the same haphazard and disorganized manner, as though he were making up the details as he went along. And every negotiation had ended the exact same way, with whatever impresario or financier saying that although Henry Babcock was clearly a man of great imagination, his ideas were simply impractical. Of course that wouldn't stop news of a startlingly similar enterprise from trickling into the broadsheets within weeks, sometimes from the exact same financier who had ridiculed the idea before.

And so, despite his towering intellect, Henry Babcock had lived the entirety of his life just on the cusp of great success, yet never achieving a fraction of his true potential.

The lesson was clear: appearance and presentation were everything.

That was why Miranda had chosen the Overlook Hotel, the most expensive in all of Longview, as the site of the negotiations. If she was willing to spend the crowns on a hotel like this, with real Illyrian carpets in every chamber and fine silk hangings to cover every wall, for such a short visit, how much further must her resources extend? Appearances like that could make the difference between a great deal and a simply good one.

Miranda had kept her father's old watch to remind her of that very important fact; she could be possessed of the keenest mind in the land, but if she could not maintain a similarly polished exterior, true success would always elude her. And Miranda would not let that happen. Whatever she had to do, she would *not* follow in the footsteps of her wretched father.

That was the kind of relentless drive that had propelled Miranda to the height of success. She had established the Dalton Trade Consortium when she was only seventeen years old, and her small trading firm had quickly made a fortune shipping tea to Isafar and Illyria. The Dalton Trade Consortium had used those profits to expand into Marburg and South Sands, becoming the Southern Trade Consortium, and eventually into every other city east of the Mountains of Dawn, to become the Auroran Trade Consortium.

Now at thirty-eight years old, Miranda had made herself one of the richest people, and certainly the richest commoner, in the entire realm. She had used her wealth to open many doors that would have otherwise remained closed—and to make sure that those doors remained closed to others who might seek to open them. Miranda was particularly proud of the way she had negotiated the customs exemption for the ATC while simultaneously advocating for the expansion of contraband restrictions, a move which had allowed the ATC to all but monopolize the Auroran black market. Now if only she could find some way to monopolize the tea trade...

Miranda brought her thoughts back to the matter at hand. *Captain Bowman.* She considered what she knew about the man. Not one hour ago, she had received a letter from one Commodore Horatio Garfield Wilmont, revealing some rather interesting facts about Paul Bowman. He was apparently facing disciplinary issues from his superiors, and he was being forced to pay for his recent repairs out of pocket; but most auspiciously of all, the man was illiterate.

Yet that was no cause for complacency. Just because a man had received no formal education, that was not in and of itself an indication of unintelligence. *Case in point,* Miranda reminded herself, *he remembered that I called him a rube.* A momentary slight, of course, trivial in every way, and yet, Bowman had remembered it. The man was evidently more astute than he seemed.

Clever he may be, Miranda concluded, *but unrefined is still unrefined.* That was an advantage for her. Simply having a nimble mind is no substitute for a deep knowledge of the inner workings of things. And in that regard, Miranda was a master.

Three soft knocks at the door to the balcony warned Miranda of Captain Bowman's approach. Miranda had posted an assistant on the balcony outside, and two more in the corridor beyond the room. They also served as security, just in case. You could never be too secure.

Miranda stood up and smoothed out a few wrinkles in her dress. She took a deep breath and let it out slowly. She was as ready now as she would ever be.

The door opened. *And now we begin.*

Miranda turned and put on a face of pleasant surprise, "Captain Bowman! So good to see..."

She trailed off when she saw the woman following Bowman into the chamber. She was a frightfully tall woman, of an even height with Bowman himself. That was unsettling; Miranda was unaccustomed to being only the *second* tallest woman in a room. She was in uniform as well; a proper uniform, not like those WAVE girls. Oh, sure, it had clearly been adapted to suit a woman, with a narrow, knee-length skirt in place of trousers and what looked like false-silk stockings, but there was no mistaking that double-breasted jacket or the three golden bars on her sleeves. This woman held rank.

Another show of power on Bowman's part, Miranda surmised and schooled her face into courtesy, "Forgive me, but I don't believe we've yet been introduced."

"Miss Babcock, allow me to introduce Lieutenant Commander the Lady Fiora Vaughn," Bowman said without glancing back at either of them, "my executive officer, and second-in-command of the airship *Dreadnought*. She's here to get everything down for the records."

Miranda laughed lightly, "Really, Captain? Is it really necessary to bring along your secretary to take the minutes?"

"Executive officer," Bowman said, planting himself in a chair that was much too finely upholstered for the man, "And that's no way to talk to a lady."

Miranda paled. *A noblewoman?* Dammit, less than a minute and Bowman had already put her on the defensive! Miranda made a hasty curtsy to Lady Vaughn, "Please forgive my impertinence, my lady," she said with as much deference as she could muster, "I confess, I should have recognized you sooner."

Lady Vaughn made a dismissive gesture, "It's no object," she took a seat beside her captain, and that was it. Miranda shrugged and returned to her seat.

"Now then, Captain," she began, "I think you will agree, this is a long overdue confrontation, yes?"

Bowman shrugged, "That's not how I see it."

"Is that so?" Miranda raised an eyebrow, "Pursuant to the Crown Charter of the Auroran Trade Consortium, Article VI, Subsection D, Paragraph 2," she recited by rote, "to facilitate the expedience of business practices, the Auroran Royal Airborne Fleet and its personnel shall refrain from executing customs searches upon vessels—"

"—Belonging to the Consortium," Bowman matched her, word for word, "unless evidence of criminal wrongdoing shall be immediately apparent." Miranda blinked. *So he knew that one...* Bowman smirked, "Still think I'm a rube?"

"Not at all," Miranda said, "It saves me the trouble of having to explain the rules to you." *There we go,* Miranda had just turned Bowman's momentary advantage against him; now she could throw out all manner of arcane legal jargon, and Bowman would be forced to match her mastery of the art. But there would be time for that later.

"Now, then," Miranda continued, "since you are evidently familiar with the pertinent regulations, perhaps you can explain why you have been victimizing my assets?"

"Victimizing your assets?" Bowman laughed mirthlessly, "Oh, that is just precious! You know, we were attacked by one of your *'assets'*

not twelve hours ago. Did you hear about that?"

Of course. *That.* "Yes," Miranda nodded slowly, *Bowman has me back on the defensive again.* "I am aware of the incident this morning."

"*Incident?*" Bowman laughed again, "Your man tried to clip our reactor! That's assault on a military vessel—a *capital offense.*" He emphasized the phrase, evidently seeming very satisfied with his choice of words. "Why, we probably wouldn't be having this conversation right now," he went on, "were it not for the *consummate professionalism* of my crew."

Bowman leaned back, and Miranda couldn't help but notice Lady Vaughn's reaction. The woman had been diligently taking down everything in a small notebook, but at Bowman's mention of the *consummate professionalism of his crew,* she looked up for a moment and gave him an absolutely loathsome glare. Had Bowman noticed it, Miranda suspected that there would be immediate consequences.

Perhaps I can use that? Miranda speculated. Lady Vaughn was quite evidently chafing under Bowman's likely clumsy leadership. Perhaps if Miranda could make overtures to Lady Vaughn... She shrugged. It was an interesting idea, but there were more pressing matters at hand.

"Actually, I was referring to the incident about a few days ago," Miranda said, changing the subject "Where you, quite without cause, impounded a ship of the Consortium—"

"Which was carrying seventeen crates of contraband goods," Bowman interrupted again, "valued at over ten thou—"

"Mister Bowman," Miranda interrupted, consciously leaving off Bowman's rank, "I don't think you truly comprehend the magnitude of your blunder. You executed an illegal search upon one of our vessels, and I would be well within my rights to have you brought before a court of law."

"I'm sorry, are you *defending* a known smuggler?" Bowman said, and quickly added, "I seem to remember hearing somewhere that you rehired him in less than a week!"

"If you have a problem with our personnel, you are certainly free to file a complaint with our office in Dalton," Miranda said, brushing off the accusation, "but the fact remains that you have wronged the Consortium. I'd rather settle matters here and now, but I am willing to resort to litigation should it become necessary."

"Actually now that you mention it, I do have a complaint," Bowman leaned forward, "As I understand it, the Consortium is in charge of logistics for the fleet. And for the past week, our supply orders have stopped coming in." Bowman locked eyes with Miranda, "Without explanation."

"I don't know *what* you're talking about," Miranda matched his glare with a grin. *Finally, I've struck a nerve!*

"Really?" Bowman said, "Well then, allow me to explain it to you. You see, I used to work on ships that took army supply contracts during the war. That was before you guys started buying them all up, you see."

"Is that so?" Miranda said, concealing her unease. So, Bowman had worked in the airfreight industry before the army? This was new information to her. That was never a good thing.

"Yes," Bowman continued, "and if I remember correctly, tampering with shipments, or *willful failure to deliver,* was considered treason. The army took that sort of thing very seriously." Bowman's mouth curled into a wicked smirk, "I wonder if they still do?"

"You are of course welcome to read over the specifics of our contract." Babcock said, placing a subtle emphasis on the phrase *read over.* She couldn't recall off the top of her head if there was such a proscription in the ATC's charter, but even if such a clause had been omitted, any reasonably competent Crown prosecutor could easily make the case for treason. It would be better if the matter were not investigated too closely.

"I suppose I'll have to," Bowman said, calling her bluff, or perhaps not even recognizing it in the first place, "If it's going to come to legal action, we'd better make sure we have all the facts. Are you getting all this down, Commander?"

"I am indeed, Captain," Lady Vaughn said. The woman's voice was terribly neutral; she was a noblewoman after all, but Miranda couldn't help but notice the slightest hint of a smile at the side of her lips. *The bitch is enjoying this!* Miranda bit her lip and laughed softly. It was a habit of hers, whenever she found herself in a particularly bad position.

Not ten minutes in, and the negotiation had absolutely gone to pieces! There was no way Miranda could resort to legal action now. Indeed, Miranda had to do everything she could to *prevent* Bowman from taking legal action; the man's petty act of contract violation was nothing compared to a willful act of treason.

If it did come to litigation, it would be the end for the ATC. They would instantly lose all of their military and government contracts; their black-market monopoly would be broken; the organization itself might even be partitioned by the Crown and cannibalized by smaller regional companies. Personnel would have to be dismissed left and right—some would be sent to prison, possibly even to the gallows. Miranda could easily pass off responsibility to her underlings, and in so doing, she would probably escape the worst of it, but at the very least, she would be forced to take an early retirement. She would spend the rest of her life living in the same limbo between poverty and wealth as her wretched father.

No! Miranda told herself firmly, *Not that! Never that!*

Miranda gathered her wits. She had no choice now; she would have to do the one thing she hated doing more than anything else.

"Captain, this back-and-forth is getting us nowhere," Miranda said sweetly, "There must be some way we can put this dreadful business behind us." She met Bowman's eyes, "Some sort of... *gentleman's agreement* perhaps?"

Bowman locked eyes with Miranda, and for a moment, the room was deadly silent. This was it; this one moment could right or ruin the future of the ATC.

"Vaughn," Bowman said without breaking eye contact with Miranda, "put the book down for a moment."

Out of the corner of her eye, Miranda noticed Lady Vaughn look up from her book. "Captain, surely you can't be suggesting—"

"Do it," Bowman said more forcefully, "*Lieutenant Commander.*"

"As you say, Captain," the woman acquiesced.

Bowman leaned back in his chair. He was still holding eye contact with Miranda. "Go on..."

"I understand that your ship sustained rather serious damage during today's... *incident,*" Miranda said, "The Consortium might be willing to handle the repairs ourselves."

Bowman's expression never changed, but Miranda knew she had just struck a chord with the man. He slowly nodded, "To repair the damage caused by your... *asset?*"

"Precisely," Miranda smiled, "I shall summon the Consortium's very own in-house rapid-response repair crew, and they shall execute the repairs themselves. As a gesture of good faith. How does that sound?"

Bowman shifted in his seat, "We've also been trying to install a new loudspeaker system for our ship, but for some reason we can't seem to track down the parts."

"You'll have it installed by midday," Miranda said. A little generosity in a time like this would go a long way.

Bowman smiled, "That's very courteous of you."

"And of course," Miranda quickly added, "it goes without saying that, in the future you will extend the selfsame courtesy to members of the Consortium."

"Well," Bowman said, smug as a clam, "since you asked me so nicely this time..."

"So," Miranda said, bringing everything to a conclusion, "do we have an understanding?"

"I think so," Bowman said, getting to his feet, "We don't need to... draw up a contract or anything like that, do we?"

"I really don't think this is the sort of arrangement you put into writing, Captain," Miranda stood as well. She glanced at Lady Vaughn; the woman was getting to her feet as well. Her notebook had remained closed.

"Well, it was a pleasure doing business with you, but we'd best be getting back to our ship now," Bowman started for the door, "Enjoy the rest of your evening, ma'am."

"I understand," Miranda said, "I'll have my people contact yours in the morning." She turned to Lady Vaughn and made another proper curtsy, "My lady." The woman only glared. It was a supreme relief when the door closed behind her and Captain Bowman, leaving Miranda alone in the chamber again. Miranda slumped back into her chair. *What a ghastly evening!*

Why the hell hadn't she been informed of Bowman's background in the airfreight industry? If she had been forewarned about that, she wouldn't have walked straight into Bowman's trap, and she wouldn't have had to resort to petty bribery to get out of it!

Miranda absolutely hated making bribes. It was illegal of course, but that was the least of her reasoning. Bribes tended to foster a sense of exchange between equal parties. That was never good for business; a truly successful business deal should leave one partner feeling clearly subordinated. Not only that, but bribes too often begat further bribes, which could easily cross over into the realm of extortion and blackmail; at that point, only a swift, subtle assassination could prevent the inevitable collapse.

Bowman had quite evidently walked away from this meeting thinking that he had gotten the better end of the deal. He hadn't of course; the cost of a few repairs and upgrades was nothing compared to the profits the ATC stood to capture thanks to Bowman's assurance of noninterference. Why, Miranda could quite easily cover the expenses out of pocket; her quarterly bonuses would more than make up for the shortfall. It would also serve to keep evidence of the bribe out of official expense reports.

But still, Bowman had *believed* that he had won. And that sentiment could be dangerous. At the moment, of course, Bowman was still just a minor player in a game greater than he could possibly conceive. But in the future... *Should Bowman be forcibly disabused of his delusions of equality? Or should I let him keep his blissful ignorance?*

Miranda shrugged. There would be time to hammer out those answers later. She had managed to avert catastrophe; that was the important thing. Right now she had to keep her end of the bargain. She wouldn't inform Commodore Wilmont of course; the man was clearly a small character, insignificant in the grand scheme of things. Miranda had more important matters to concern herself with than a petty vendetta between two inconsequential players.

Miranda rose from her chair, smoothed a few wrinkles out of her skirt, and crossed to the entrance to the balcony. "Jensson," she called to her assistant through the opening, "come in here. I need to send some telegrams."

The rhythmic sound of two pairs of boots on the cobblestones grated at Vaughn's patience. She was positively fuming! She couldn't remember ever being so furious in her entire life!

Captain Bowman was walking beside her through the empty narrow side streets of Longview, blissfully unaware of her blinding rage. How could that man be so bloody calm after what he had just done? Bloody hell, Miranda Babcock had all but confessed to treason. By all rights, they should be measuring her for a noose. And yet Captain Bowman had let her off with a bribe. *A bloody bribe!*

"Well," Bowman finally broke the silence, his voice thick with smugness, "that actually came out a lot better than I'd hoped."

"Speak for yourself," Vaughn grumbled before she could stop herself.

"What?" Bowman laughed, "Don't tell me you think we could have gotten more out of her?"

"You let her bribe you," Vaughn said, and again wished that she had kept her peace.

"That wasn't a bribe," Bowman said.

Vaughn blinked, "It most certainly *was* a bribe!"

"No, it isn't," Bowman insisted, sounding for all the world as though he were explaining something to a particularly slow child, "A bribe is when you get some extra service in exchange for something. We're not giving the Consortium anything extra. We just have to do our jobs."

"In that case, it's extortion."

"Oh, please," Bowman scoffed, "I don't think the Consortium is going to go out of business because of a few favors." After a few moments he added, "Besides, *she* extorted us first. That makes it alright."

"It does not! It absolutely does not!" Vaughn protested, "If you were a proper officer, you'd know this! I don't know why I ever expected anything different from you!"

Fuck! she thought, too late, *Why did I let that out?*

"Alright, that's it! Hold up!" Captain Bowman stepped in front of her, trying to block her way forward, "I've had just about enough of this! What the hell is your problem with me, lady?"

"Should I put it in smaller words?" Vaughn grumbled and tried to slip around Bowman.

The man put out his arm to block her way. "Ever since I took command of the *Dreadnought,* you have been looking down your nose at me. Acting like I'm something you stepped in. Well, I'm your *captain,* and I don't think I feel too comfortable having someone with your attitude on my ship."

"And how am I supposed to feel about having *you* on my ship!" Vaughn wheeled about to shout directly in Bowman's face. The man stepped back, clearly shocked. Vaughn was shocked herself to hear her fury given voice at last. *Oh, why the bloody hell not,* she figured, *In for a copper, out for a crown.*

"Ten years!" Vaughn continued, "Ten fucking years I've served! I've gotten no respect from anyone. I've no career prospects. I've been deliberately prevented from gaining crucial experience. I've been promoted exactly *once* in my whole career, and then left to rot in this shithole of a posting. And all the while, I can't help but think that I would have been treated much more equitably were I a man.

"And then one day, you show up. *You!* An upjumped conscript, who blundered into a bit of fame and fortune. Probably the only officer on the entire ship with even less experience than I! And now I am expected to kick up salutes to you? To follow *your* orders without question? 'Yes, sir! No, sir! Shall I note that for the *fucking* log, sir?' And all while you clearly haven't the slightest idea how to do your job? How am I supposed to feel about that? How am I supposed to *fucking* feel?"

"Oh yeah!" Bowman countered, "Because you've had *such a hard life*, is that it? *'Boo-hoo! The boys won't let me play with them! My life is so unfair!'* When was the last time you went to bed hungry? When was the last time you had to steal your own food? When was the last time you had to pull a thirty-two hour shift because one of your people just lost a goddamn finger? Hell, I bet you don't even know what engine grease tastes like!"

"And just what has that got to do with anything?" Vaughn scoffed. What exactly was Bowman trying to prove? *Engine grease?* Really?

"Oh yeah," Bowman laughed, "There's the attitude again. The stuck-up Old Nobility bitch. 'Mister Bowman, you are uncouth, unrefined, ill mannered, foul mouthed, slack witted, and a bunch of other words that your feeble little peasant-brain cannot possibly understand!'

"You wouldn't be talking to me like this if I were a man!" Vaughn countered.

"I'll talk at you exactly how I want, you entitled little shit!" Bowman snapped, "You think the world's been so goddamn cruel to you? You don't even know how good you have it! I bet the hardest thing you'll ever do in your life is run back home to your dad and ask the fat old prick to straighten out your—"

If Bowman had anything more to say, Fiora never heard it. The sudden blow sent the man careening backwards into a row of garbage tins at the side of the alley. Fiora's knuckles stung sharply from the force of it. She shook out her hand; it had been a long while indeed since she had struck anyone with a closed fist.

Now I've really done it! The sheer magnitude of Fiora's blunder slowly dawned upon her. Bowman had certainly deserved the blow, and worse besides, for what he had called her father! But in the eyes of the fleet, she had just struck a superior officer.

Her career was over. She would be discharged for sure. *Discharged?* Fiora thought ruefully, *I'll be lucky to escape a firing squad for this!* And even if she somehow managed to remain on active duty, where would she go? No experience, and now a disciplinary record? What captain would even agree to take her in at this point?

The pile of garbage tins rustled slightly, and Fiora heard a low groan, "Unh... bitch..."

Fiora looked down and noticed that she was still clutching the notebook in her left hand. Overcome with disgust, she threw the thing into the garbage pile and stormed off into the night.

Chapter XVI

An Opportunity Like This

PAKU sat alone in the cockpit, running over the flight controls again. There wasn't really all that much else to do right now, but he didn't mind. He had spent the first twelve years of his life on a mulberry farm with his twenty-three brothers and sisters; until his Service to Hadvar began, he had never encountered any machine more complicated than a mule-drawn wagon. The fact that such a machine like this could even exist at all was a miracle to Paku!

He had to be careful not to express such sentiment out loud of course. Just about everyone else on this mission had served in combat. They did not speak much about their experiences, but judging from the little Paku had managed to uncover, these magnificent flying machines stirred in them memories of unspeakable horror and carnage.

Entire squadrons had been swallowed up in furious storms of

blood and steel. The strongest field guns could only manage to drive the ships to higher altitudes, from where their wrath would be only slightly less accurate. Were it not for Hadvar's advantage in numbers and logistics, the enemy airships would have carried the enemy all the way to the Halgari, the mighty eastern mountains that marked the border between the fertile eastern lands and Hadvar proper.

Paku understood these sentiments and couldn't fault the men for holding them, but surely the airships *themselves* weren't to blame. A machine was just a machine; if a man took a stick and used it to beat and rob another man, was the stick responsible? Or the tree upon which was grown?

Hadvar generally frowned upon the use of complicated machines; overreliance upon technology was said to cheapen the value of labor, and weaken the collective soul of society. Perhaps this was so; but that did not change the fact that the Aurorans were using their mastery of the mechanical arts to multiply their power far beyond what their population of meager millions could manage otherwise. Surely, embracing technology to defeat them was justified, wasn't it?

And if technology was to be shunned, then what of rifles, field guns, and radios? Should not they be shunned as well? Paku had posed the question to a number of his comrades during his Service, and he had yet to receive a satisfying answer. Some held that these things were simply honest *tools*, like a hammer or a scythe; not to be confused with the complicated machines of the enemy. Others considered them tragic necessities of war, to be disposed of once victory was secure of course. One of his old instructors has postulated that the threshold of immorality lay at the point where a single man was unable to fully repair the machine. It all sounded like excuses; if the Aurorans could use Airships, then surely Hadvar was justified in opposing them with a fleet of their own.

And besides all that, how wonderful it was to fly! Paku could remember flying for the very first time after this team had acquired the ship in Illyria, and the feeling was like nothing else he had ever known. To watch as the rest of the world, so concrete and unyielding, floated away like a patchwork quilt of lives. To soar with the birds over the tallest mountains, over the broadest rivers, over the densest forests. It was like walking in a dream!

Of course, Paku had not been the one at the controls that time. His primary role on this expedition was that of a translator; he had been identified within the first year of his Service and given special lessons as an interpreter, in addition to the usual three years of training. However, Dagan had ordered that Paku take on the role of a backup pilot for the mission. On an expedition this small, so Dagan has said, everyone took on additional duties. Except the *Môlsôde* of course; Death Squads only did duty under arms.

One day, Paku told himself, *One day, I will fly a ship just like this one!*

Paku glanced out the wide forward window, and squinted... Through the camouflage netting, he could see a group of figures backlit by the setting sun. Much too many to simply be a returning scout. Was it an enemy patrol? Had they been discovered? Had the mission already failed?

A sudden pounding at the back of the cockpit made Paku jump again. He turned to see another soldier standing in the doorway, "Paku," the soldier said, "Come. You are needed outside."

Paku nodded and leaped out of the seat, "I come, *Bazi!*" Paku followed the soldier down the hallway, through the cargo hold, and down the loading ramp. As he arrived, two figures stepped beneath the camouflage net. One of them was Dagan, the leader of their entire expedition. He was dragging the second figure roughly by the arm. The figure was clearly bound. A prisoner—and an Auroran, judging by his pink skin.

Dagan threw the prisoner to the ground before Paku, "This one was wandering around the mountains with some of his people." Dagan gestured over his shoulder, and through the camouflage net, Paku could see a group of people sitting with their hands behind their heads, surrounded by several guards with rifles at the ready, "You will talk to him, and find out what he was doing and what he knows."

Paku hesitated. He had never actually spoken to an Auroran before. He had been in training for years, of course, but he had only ever spoken with other Hadvari interpreters and the occasional heavily accented Illyrian merchant. But an actual Auroran? Was Paku really ready for this? Even that nameless fire-haired assassin woman had only ever spoken in the First Tongue whenever he had tried to practice with her.

"What about the assassin?" Paku said, snatching at a convenient excuse, "Is she not with us?"

"I have set the assassin to guarding the rest of the prisoners." Dagan grumbled. Paku glanced again at the group of prisoners, and sure enough, one of the guards was the red-haired assassin, "We don't know yet what this one knows, and until we do, I'll not trust a brotherless to find it out for us."

Paku nodded and began racking his brain to formulate his first sentence. There was a set phrase for this—how did it go again?

"I am called..." He stopped; he had been about to say 'Two Eagles,' but quickly remembered that you weren't supposed to translate names, "I am called... Paku. You are how called?"

The Auroran seemed shocked, "Finally!" he exclaimed, "It's about time they hauled out someone who can actually speak!"

Hauled out? What did that mean? he recognized *hall* of course; that part was easy. But what did it mean in this context? And *out?* Did the man mean that Paku had been summoned from out of a hallway? Perhaps it was just one of those confusing idioms that littered the Auroran tongue?

Paku set aside his rumination and brought his focus back to the Auroran, who was now babbling excitedly, much too quickly for Paku to understand. Paku held up a hand and said, "You speak slow!"

"Right, right," The Auroran seemed to calm down, and began again more slowly, "I'm Victor Knox."

Vik-tor-nak's? Was that... a profession? A title of rank? A name? If it was, it was the most ridiculous name Paku had ever heard! He shrugged; whatever it meant, it would serve as an identifier, and that was the important thing.

"You are why here?" Paku continued.

The Auroran laughed, "What does it look like, kid? I got took by your people!"

No! That wasn't what he meant! Confound it all! Why did the Auroran Tongue have to use the same word for *by what reason* and *for what purpose?* They were two completely different things! How did these people even understand each other?

There was a work around for this sort of situation, Paku recalled. How did it go again? "You... you *for what* are—"

"I know what you meant, kid." the Auroran said. He seemed to find their exchange amusing. These people found humor in the oddest of places, "We're here because we got attacked."

Got attacked? Paku had never heard that construction before. They had... *acquired an "attacked?"* Did that mean that they *were* attacked? Or had *they* been the ones doing the attacking?

"You... are soldiers?" Paku probed.

"No, not exactly," the Auroran said, "We're... merchants I guess. We work on a airship. Like the one you've got there," he nodded his head up toward the ship; it was the only gesture he could manage, bound as he was.

"Paku!" Dagan snapped, "What does this one know?"

"He says they are merchants," Paku said, "He says they are here because their airship was attacked."

"So, they aren't soldiers?" Dagan didn't seem convinced. Paku wasn't sure how much of it he believed either. This man had a dishonest face. Paku suspected that even the infamously duplicitous Aurorans would find him untrustworthy.

"I will continue," Paku told Dagan, and then returned his attentions to the Auroran, "You speak me about attack."

The Auroran gave a short moan as he began, "Well, it's all to do with this guy named Paul Bowman."

Bowman? That could also mean *Archer,* couldn't it? Bow-man? "You mean Paul the Archer?" Paku interrupted, "In City-Longview?"

The Auroran looked stunned, "You know the guy?"

Paku turned back to Dagan, "This one knows Paul the Archer!"

Dagan rushed forward, "We must hear more!"

Paku continued translating as the Auroran recounted the story of how Paul the Archer had viciously attacked his unarmed merchant airship on sight, completely without cause to do so. The merchants had put up a valiant defense, and apparently they had caused some damage, but they had been tragically outmatched. In the end, only six of his crew, not counting himself, had managed to escape with their lives.

Dagan was able to confirm the wreck; scout reports of an explosion had come in just after midday. And yet, these so-called merchants had been captured a substantial distance to the north of its reported position. The Auroran assured Paku that he and the survivors of his crew had simply been wandering for half a day, but Dagan remained unconvinced.

"But, you certain," Paku said, "ship of Paul the Archer now damaged?"

"Yes," The Auroran nodded with a satisfied smile.

Yes. What a convenient word that was! True, it could be a source of much ambiguity, and it had taken Paku a long time to truly grasp the concept, but now that he understood it, he found himself wishing that the First Tongue had a similar word.

"How... how big much damage?" Paku pressed for the details, "How long repairs?"

"I'd say about a week at most," the Auroran said, and he motioned with his head for Paku to come in closer, "Listen, I take it you guys don't like Paul Bowman either? I think we might be able to help each other out."

Paku wasn't sure what the Auroran had in mind, but he responded with a wary, "Speak..."

The Auroran smiled another of his untrustworthy smiles, "I knew we had a understanding. Now, if I'm not mistaken, you and I have a common enemy here. If you can get me to Longview, I'll point Paul out for you, and you can give that bastard what he deserves! How does that sound?"

Paku nodded, "I ask." and with that, he turned to confer closely with Dagan. "He says that Paul the Archer's ship will be in repairs for the next week."

Dagan's brow furrowed with deep thought, "We are never going to get an opportunity like this again," he said at length, "We must act immediately to exploit it."

"*Bazi,* you don't mean..." Paku began, but Dagan preempted his thoughts, "We are going to move as soon as possible. It may take the rest of the night to prepare and recall the last of our scouts, but we should be ready to go by midday tomorrow."

"*Bazi,*" Paku protested, "surely we should wait until we receive the signal from the Elders?"

"There is no time to lose," Dagan said, "By the time this new intelligence reaches the Elders and a decision comes back, it will already be too late. We must act now, or this crucial opportunity will slip away."

Paku nodded, "I understand, *Bazi.*" He still wasn't entirely certain if this was the right way to go about their mission, but Dagan was in charge, and if he said so, then that was that. An order was an order. Besides, how wonderful it would feel to be back in the sky again!

"One last thing, Paku," Dagan said, "We will need someone to carry news of this to the Elders."

"That is wise," Paku said, and then realized just whom Dagan meant to carry out the task, "Oh, but *Bazi,* you cannot—"

"I will have our scribe write an explanation," Dagan said firmly, "and *you* will carry it to the Elders of the First Land."

"Why not have our scribe carry the report back?" Paku protested. "Or one of our swift scouts?" *I want to fly again!*

"Do you think to question my command, *Balû?*" Dagan narrowed his eyes.

Paku shrank from his glare. "Of course not *Bazi*. I forget myself."

Dagan's gaze softened, "We need all of our experienced soldiers for the coming mission," Dagan said in an uncharacteristically gentle voice, "and if we send our scribe with the message, the Elders might think that he wrote it himself and dismiss it as a forgery from a deserter. For this reason, *you* must be the one to carry the message."

"It is a long way back to Hadvar," Paku said resignedly, "and through unfriendly lands."

"This is known," Dagan nodded, "We will give you supplies for your journey. There are also a number of enclaves where you may be able to find shelter along the way," He clapped a hand on Paku's shoulder, "Don't worry. You're young, and you have a long and glorious Service before you. There will be other occasions for you to show your resolve."

Paku smiled, "Thank you, *Bazi*."

The two men turned their gaze back to the Auroran, still kneeling where they had left him. "What is to be done with that one?" Paku asked.

"We cannot leave any witnesses," Dagan said.

"He offered to help us," Paku suggested half-heartedly.

"We already have the help of that assassin," Dagan spat, "One brotherless is more than enough for us." He glared at the Auroran for a moment and added, "Come the morning, we'll cut their throats and leave them for the wolves."

Paku shrugged. It was of little consequence.

"So, kid!" the Auroran called, "Do we got a deal?"

"No."

"You're kidding me!" Paul's jaw dropped, "I don't believe this!"

"Well, I don't know what else I can tell you," Wilmont said, leaning back in his chair, smug as a clam, "There are well-established procedures which much be followed in a situation like this."

"She punched me in the face!" Paul could still feel the lingering ache of the blow on his cheek. Damn, but that bitch could throw one hell of a punch. He might have been impressed if he wasn't so furious!

Wilmont waved his hand in dismissal, "Yes, yes, so you have said.

And for this insult, you wish Leftenant Commander Vaughn disciplined."

"I want her *shot!*" Paul said, "but I'll settle for fired!"

Wilmont laughed, "And as I have explained, you haven't the authority to remove her from your crew."

"Is this because she's a goddamn noblewoman?" Paul grumbled.

"No," Wilmont sounded as though he was explaining the simplest thing, "It is because an officer of the Queen is, by tradition, only permitted to dismiss officers two or more ranks below his own. This is in order to preserve some measure of accountability amongst the officer corps. So by all means, dismiss as many leftenants as you see fit. But, as Vaughn is a leftenant commander, she is only a rank and a half below you, and is therefore immune."

"A rank *and a half?*" Paul gaped, How was this nonsense possible? How could someone only have half a rank? "You're making this shit up!"

"Well, one can't really expect a man like you to understand these things," Wilmont said, "Perhaps if you had read *Her Majesty's Guidebook of Military Regulations,* you would be more well-versed on the subject."

Paul glared. There it was again, another one of Wilmont's snide remarks about how he couldn't read. That asshole just couldn't let it go. "So," Paul said, "she's bombproof, is that it?"

"Not without authorisation from a higher authority," Wilmont said, "in this case: mine."

"Alright, then," Paul said bluntly, "I want it."

Wilmont raised a disingenuous eyebrow, "You want *what?*"

"Dammit! Enough of these stupid games!" Paul snapped, "I want that bitch off my ship, and I want your say-so to make it happen!"

Wilmont shrugged, "You shall not have it."

"And why the hell not?" Paul demanded.

"I can see no reason for it," Wilmont shrugged innocently, "All I have to go on are, as-yet-unsubstantiated rumours and hearsay. Hardly the substance upon which to needlessly embarrass an officer of the fleet."

"She punched me in the face!" Paul said.

"Perhaps," Wilmont said, "But as I think we have already established, *you* quite evidently have a bias against Leftenant Commander Vaughn."

"Because she punched me in the *fucking face!*" Paul screamed.

"Mister Bowman," Wilmont did not flinch, "You are not helping your case."

After a few moments, Paul's rage simmered down enough for him to form coherent thoughts. *Damn you, Wilmont!* Paul fumed, *You fat, balding prick!* "So that's it, then?" Paul threw up his hands, "I'm stuck with the bitch. Is that it?"

"You could always demote her to leftenant, and *then* dismiss her," Wilmont said pretending to offer helpful advice, "That is... assuming you first got my approval so to do."

"Which I won't get?" Paul growled.

"Precisely," Wilmont made a vicious grin.

"I see. So there's nothing I can do to her." Paul said.

"You could *promote* her," Wilmont shrugged, "I certainly would after she put you in your place! As far as I can tell, you and Leftenant Commander Fiora Vaughn deserve one another. And I wish you a long and unhappy life together." He leaned back in his seat, "Now, is there anything else you wanted to talk about? Or should I let you go?"

Paul turned and started toward the door. About halfway there, he stopped when Wilmont called, "Incidentally, how are those *repairs* coming along? I trust you're not finding it too costly?"

Paul turned back and shot Wilmont a vicious grin of his own, "We've figured something out. It shouldn't take too long." He remained in the office just long enough to see Wilmont's own grin vanish.

Paul slipped out of the headquarters and leisurely made his way back to the aerodrome. On the whole, things weren't so bad. Sure, Vaughn was going to continue to be a problem, and Wilmont had practically made an art out of being difficult, but at least that arrangement with the Consortium had worked. The repairs were being taken care of at no cost. He had outwitted Wilmont at last!

Paul had been a little shocked that morning, when a small army of workmen complete with tools and supplies had shown up outside the *Dreadnought's* berth at the crack of dawn. They had already been working for hours by the time Paul left to confront Wilmont, and judging by the speed of their work, they would be finished soon.

That left Vaughn as the only problem. Something would have to be done about her. But what? Wilmont had already ruled out any administrative options; he couldn't dismiss her, demote her, discipline her, or anything official like that. So what could he do? In Paul's civilian days, if a captain or some department head was giving his people trouble, then the thing to do was usually to jump him in an alley with some friends after the target had spent a long night drinking in a pub. But something told Paul that such a plan was unlikely to work. Vaughn didn't seem like the pub-crawling sort. Besides, you didn't do that sort of thing to girls. *Especially not to girls who punch like she does!* Paul thought, rubbing another ache out of his jaw.

Back at the aerodrome, the crews were still hard at work. They had already replaced the deformed roof plating and the radio equipment above the bridge, and they were moving on to the rest of the interior repairs and upgrades. Soon it would be time to test the new loudspeaker system. *The full one this time!* Paul told himself with a smile, *Not just some one-way half-measure compromise.* He made his way up the cargo ramp.

Thatcher was at the top.

"Cap'n," the man said with a curt salute. He was leaning against a stack of fuel drums, and anxiously smoking a cigarette. He looked like a man whose wife had just gone into labor.

"What are you doing out of the engine room?" Paul asked, more surprised than anything else.

"Repair crews are putting in the new pipes," Thatcher grumbled, "They wanted everyone out of the engine room so they could work. I don't like it, Cap'n. That's *my* reactor in there. I don't like the idea of a bunch of strangers fiddling around with her. Fuckin' around with the dials. Leaving their fingerprints all over her. It's gonna take at least a day to clean up after 'em." He threw his cigarette to the ground, smothered it with his boot, and lit up another one. "God, I hate these pre-rolled things," he muttered.

"Sorry," Paul said sarcastically, and continued on towards the main stairwell, "I'll try not to get us attacked again."

"Hey, Cap'n," thatcher shouted. Paul stopped before the stairwell. What was it now? "Uh... thanks."

Paul blinked. That ornery Newport man hadn't said a single kind word ever since Paul had taken command of the ship!

"This old ship is alive because of you," Thatcher went on, "You did good."

Paul nodded and stepped into the stairwell. Thatcher seemed to be warming up to him. *Well, that's one taken care of.* Paul shrugged and made his way up to the roof.

As it happened, the *Dreadnought* was just was just tall enough so that the top of the roof peeked over the edge of the berth. From the top of the ship, Paul had a view of the rooftops of Longview and any ships that might be departing or approaching in the meanwhile. It was the perfect place to sit and relax while they waited out the rest of the repairs.

Paul closed his eyes and leaned back against the slope of the hull. For a moment, he was nine years old again. He could see himself and Uncle Howard sitting side by side, watching the freighters coming and going. Uncle Howard had served on most of them at some point, and he would tell stories about one voyage or another. How one ship had almost crashed during a squall, or how another ship had cut through a war zone to save fuel and been fired upon, or how one particularly shrewd captain had beaten the Illyrian traders at their own game and bluffed his way into fortune.

Old Uncle Howard always had the best stories, Paul remembered fondly, and then sadly. *I miss him.*

"Captain?"

Paul jumped and looked up as a head popped out of the hatch down to the sick bay. It was Hakefeldt. "It's alright. I can find another place to—"

"Oh, come on up," Paul waved a hand to invite the kid onto the roof with him, "There's plenty of room here."

"Thank you, Captain," Hakefeldt climbed through the hatch, plopped down against the slope of the roof beside Paul, and began to feed some loose tobacco into a rolling paper. "You don't mind if I have a smoke," he said, "do you, Captain?"

"Go ahead," Paul said.

"Thank you," Hakefeldt continued filling and rolling his cigarette, "Shall I roll one for you as well, Captain?"

"Nah, I don't smoke anymore," Paul said, "I used to for a while, but then I got careless and accidentally set half a dozen crates of goat's wool on fire." Paul laughed, "Took me three whole years to work off that debt. Figured that was as good a sign as any to quit."

"I see," Archie said, striking a match and taking a long drag on the cigarette.

"Besides, all that junk has to be imported from Illyria." Paul said, "It can get pretty expensive for us working-class folks."

Hakefeldt blinked, *"Us working-class folks?"*

Paul grinned, "You're a Newport kid, right?" This wasn't one of Louise's discoveries. This was something Paul had figured out on his own.

Hakefeldt took a long pensive drag on his cigarette, "How did you know, Captain?"

Paul reached up and tapped his ear.

"My *accent?*" Hakefeldt seemed shocked. The kid had evidently gone to great lengths to pick up the speech patterns of the nobility.

"Your *ear,*" Paul said, and Hakefeldt reached up and touched his deformed earlobe with his free hand, "You've got a fighter's ear, kid," Paul said, "I guarantee you won't see one of *those* on a nobleman."

Hakefeldt laughed, "Scarped 'er up in one 'o the bread riots a few years back," he said, suddenly switching to a violently working-class Newport accent, "Some bungo was whangin' on me with a blackjack. But I janked 'em to match, Cap'n!"

"Good man!" Paul laughed.

"My folks potted up the bread for years to send me to the book-house," Hakefeldt explained, "and then to South Sands."

"Really?" Paul said, "Well I gotta say, you've done a real good job of blending in."

"You, ah..." Hakefeldt said nervously, "ya ain't gonna yack at the rest of the crew, are ya? About... y'know, me bein' from Newport and all?"

"Why?" Paul laughed again, "Kid, you made it! You should be proud! Those other idiots—Wingate, Vaughn, Barlowe, those *noble* types—they had this life handed to 'em on a silver platter, just for bein' born. But you? You pulled yourself up out of the gutter to stand just as tall as them. You oughta be shouting it from the rooftops! Hell, that's what I'd be doin' if I were in your shoes."

Hakefeldt grinned, "Ya think so, Cap'n?"

"Trust me," Paul said, "You and I, us *gentlemen of low origins,* we gotta make ourselves known! We can be a shining example for working-class kids everywhere. There's a hell of a lot more of us than the nobility. You honestly think the future belongs to nerks like Wingate and them? Nah, kid, It's us. We're the future!"

"Actually, Captain," Hakefeldt said, switching back to his regular faux-noble speech pattern, "I've been meaning to talk to you about Wolfram. *Leftenant Wingate,* that is."

"Giving you grief, is he?" Paul said, "I'll tell the little prick to back off."

"Not at all, Captain," Hakefeldt said quickly, "We're actually quite good friends, have been ever since we met at the academy."

"Really?" Paul was surprised. Archie Hakefeldt and Wolfram Wingate were from completely opposite walks of life. How had the two of them found any common ground to build a friendship on? "I didn't think any of those noble types had the knack for making friends. They'd probably just buy 'em all with daddy's money!"

"He's a good guy," Hakefeldt said, "but he's having a lot of trouble with his father."

"Is he now," Paul shifted around, "I'm not surprised. His old man's a real piece of work."

"I've only ever met Lord Wingate once in passing," Hakefeldt said, "He is... an intimidating figure."

"Yeah..." Paul said.

"Wolfram and his father aren't on very good terms," Hakefeldt went on, "You know, it was he who assigned Wolfram to this very posting. Sometimes, I think he's trying to forget that he even has a son."

"Yeah..." Paul said again.

There was an awkward silence.

"So..." Hakefeldt ventured, "if you could see your way to... easing up on Wolfram a bit..."

"I'll see what I can do," Paul said. He wasn't sure if he would actually do anything, of course, not until Wingate did something about that uptight attitude of his. *Say what you will about the kid,* Paul thought, *He's definitely his father's son.*

"Thanks, Captain," Hakefeldt said, "By the way, were you ever going to tell me about that flag?"

Paul looked up. Hakefeldt was pointing at the distant flapping banner of red and brown. "Oh yeah," Paul said, "I never did get to finish the story, did I?"

Paul shifted a little closer to Hakefeldt, "Well like I said before, that's the banner Hadvar."

"Yes I know," Hakefeldt said, "The N'gos vi-tay."

"No no, *ŋôs v'taì*" Paul said, "It's at the back of your throat. Like you're saying '-ing' or something like that."

"Nos vuh-tie..." Hakefeldt struggled with the pronunciation. "Sorry, Captain. Languages were never a strength of mine."

"Well anyways," Paul shrugged, "It means something like *earth and blood* but also *strength and honor,* or *teamwork and individual effort,* or just *red and brown* depending on how you translate it. It's basically their battle cry."

"And you said you brought that particular flag back from the war yourself?" Hakefeldt inquired.

"Yup, that's one of mine," Paul said, "It was during the Siege of Two Lakes. You're probably a little too young to remember it, but—"

"We had at least twelve different lectures about it at the Academy," Hakefeldt interrupted. The kid probably knew more about the Siege of Two Lakes that Paul did.

"Right, well, anyways," Paul said, "Hadvar had the whole city surrounded, right? So the only way to keep the city supplied was to set down the ships just above the surface of the lakes and transfer our cargo directly into the boats from the city."

"In exchange for the wounded," Hakefeldt nodded.

"More often than not, yeah," Paul said, "but sometimes, we'd engage in a little *personal* bartering. Y'know, for booze and smokes and the like. Well, one day, just as the lakes are starting to freeze over, a soldier comes along with that very flag right there. He told me that they had taken it from an abandoned fortification, and that it was a sign the defenders were beginning to push the Hadvari forces back!"

"Operation: Second Wind?" Hakefeldt leaned forward, suddenly very interested.

"I don't know. I never learned what they called it," Paul admitted, "But sure enough, two weeks later, Two Lakes was liberated," he pointed, "and that flag has flown over the House of Red and Brown ever since!"

Hakefeldt said nothing. He simply squinted off into the distance. Paul looked closer, "Something wrong, kid?"

"There's a ship out there," Hakefeldt pointed.

Paul glanced up. Sure enough, there was an airship idling a few hundred yards away. "A small freighter," Paul said, "First or second generation by the look of her. Probably just waiting on berth clearance. We'll catch her when she comes to ground."

"Captain," Hakefeldt squinted, "It looks like her cargo ramp is open."

Paul got to his feet and looked again. Sure enough, the freighter's cargo ramp was hanging open. "...the hell's going on up there?" Paul muttered, wishing he had a spyglass on hand.

"Is it some smuggler's trick?" Hakefeldt suggested.

"In full view of the city? I doubt it," Paul said, "Maybe they're making repairs to their landing gear?" It was too far away for Paul to make out any people clearly with only one eye.

"I don't see any repairmen," Hakefeldt said.

"Captain?" said a small voice behind the two of them. Paul turned back to see Louise Halford standing at the top of the sloping roof, "They are ready for you to test the public address system."

"Right," Paul nodded and started climbing up the sloping roof toward Halford.

"*Captain?*" Hakefeldt said urgently.

"What is it?" Paul said without looking back.

"They have a gun!"

Paul stopped and turned. There was something moving on the ship's cargo ramp... it was too far away for Paul to make it out, but Hakefeldt had a good eye. Two of them, in fact. "Are you sure?" Paul asked, sliding back to the bottom of the ramp beside Hakefeldt.

"They're rolling it out onto the ramp," Hakefeldt said, without taking his eyes from the ship, "It looks like a field gun. Too small to be one of ours."

"Captain," Halford said again, "They are ready to test the—"

An explosion tore through the base of the radio tower behind Halford. No sooner had the tiny girl let out a startled shriek than she was blown forward by the blast of air from the explosion. She slid down the sloping roof, and collided with Paul who in turn crashed into Hakefeldt. All three figures collapsed into a jumbled mess on the roof.

After a moment, Paul got to his knees. You didn't just stand up when you were in combat. He reached back over his shoulder... He couldn't find his rifle! Shit! Where was it? Had he left it back at camp? Captain Wilmont would tan his hide for this! He would be back among the privates before the day was over!

Paul shook his head! What the hell was going on? He looked around. On one side, Hakefeldt was lying on his back, wheezing for breath. The fall had probably knocked the wind out of him. On Paul's other side, Louise was curled into a ball, cradling her right arm and whimpering softly. Her sleeve had been ripped open in two places and was beginning to darken with what was almost certainly blood.

Paul looked up at the ship. There was another flash from the cargo ramp, followed by another explosion at the base of the radio tower. *They're firing on us,* Paul thought furiously, *It's an attack!*

Then, there came a horrible sound; a slow rumbling and groaning, mixed with the terrible sound of rivets bursting. Paul looked up and his blood froze! The mighty radio tower was collapsing toward them! Not wasting any more time, Paul grabbed the limp forms of Hakefeldt and Halford by the shoulder, and started dragging them toward the hatch to the medical bay. Maybe if he could get there in time...

A shadow moved over the sun. *I'm not going to make it!*

The radio tower landed with a deafening crash.

The sound of the explosion startled Wilmont out of his concentration. He turned around to look out his office window, and was shocked by what he saw. The base of the aerodrome radio tower had caught fire!

Wilmont hastily fished his spyglass out of a drawer and trained it on the aerodrome. The base of the radio tower was bent out of shape, and flames were now dancing all around it. The tower wouldn't remain standing for much longer; the fire would soon weaken the steel to the point of collapse. It was inevitable.

Out of the corner of his eye, Wilmont noticed an airship idling some distance off from the aerodrome. He trained the spyglass on it; the ship bore civilian markings, of course, but her cargo ramp was hanging open, and on it, a gun crew was manhandling a field gun into position. The small gun was clearly Hadvari. After a moment, its muzzle erupted in flames, and another shell tore through the base of the aerodrome radio tower!

We're under attack!

Hadvar was behind this—there was no question. Even without any formal declaration, seeing the gun on the airship was proof enough. Besides, those raging fires at the base of the radio tower were clearly the result of incendiary shells, of the sort that made up the mainstay of Hadvar's arsenal. Those devilish ginks did love their incendiary shells!

Slowly, the greater picture dawned on Wilmont: the war was back on again! It had barely been three months since the armistice, and now it was all crumbling away! And since Aurora had clearly been caught unprepared this time, Hadvar would hold the crucial early initiative. And then there was the embarrassment that was sure to follow once the press got ahold of the story! It was terrible!

This is perfect!

Wilmont's face twisted into a devilish grin as the plan came to him. This was exactly the opportunity he needed to ruin Bowman once and for all! He had to act quickly though; he was not likely to get an opportunity like this again.

Wilmont drew the curtains closed and sat back down at his desk. He produced a paper and began to draw up the necessary orders. Once that was taken care of, Wilmont pressed the call button to summon his secretary. He could hear the sound of the buzzer from the hall beyond his office, and a few moments later, the door opened. Leftenant Harrison marched through and saluted crisply.

"Harrison," Wilmont said, as he reached down and opened the drawer that held Bowman's old jacket, "I need you to make a delivery for me."

Chapter XVII

Live Fire

THE echoes of the explosions thundered across the barren desert landscape. The first row of fortifications was mercilessly torn to pieces by high explosives and shrapnel. Six-and-forty airships soared across the early morning sky in perfect formation, dealing out ruin and destruction with deadly accuracy. The combined might of the Auroran Royal Airborne Fleet was a magnificent and terrible sight to behold.

From the rocky bluffs high above the desert, the admirals of the fleet observed the exercise from the comfortable shade beneath the awning outside the command pavilion. This was the morning's third exercise, out of a planned nine-and-fifty over the next three days. This one, however, was the first to use real ammunition.

"I still don't like this waste," Lord Malden grumbled into his second cup of tea, "We should be conserving our ammunition."

"Live-fire exercises are an essential component of training," Vice Admiral Rockport reiterated, "Would you rather have a fleet that doesn't know how to fire their own guns? Besides, we're at peace now. We may as well get some use out of all these leftover shells."

"You're a fool if you think the peace will last," Lord Malden said as he finished off his cup and motioned for another, "We can hope for the best, but we must remain prepared for the worst all the same."

"That's rather the point of a peacetime exercise," Rockport said, "Or did you think we came out all this way for a bloody fox hunt?"

Malden leaped to his feet, "Now see here—"

"Alright! Stow it, you two!" Lord Wingate bellowed. The two men acquiesced and settled into a cease-fire, but there was little doubt that they would soon be at each other's throats again.

Rear Admiral the Lord Norwalt Dannovar Malden and Vice Admiral David Rockport had been enemies ever since their days together at the academy, but their rivalry had grown even worse as of late. Rockport in particular had raised a tremendous fuss about that incident with Lord Malden's foolish niece giving away the position of his flagship in her personal letters. Lord Malden himself chafed at the fact that Rockport (who was, after all, only a baron) had consistently outranked him throughout his entire career. Had it not been for Lord Wingate keeping the two of them apart whenever possible, they would almost certainly have come to blows by now. It was like looking at a less-disciplined version of his own feud with Lord Hanscom.

For his part, Lord Wingate was terribly relieved that High Admiral the Lord Hanscom had declined to show up at these exercises. It seemed that young William Travis Hanscom had landed himself in a bit of a scandal in the Capitol and had requested his father's urgent presence to sort matters out for him. It was a surprising turn of events, given how much effort Lord Hanscom had put into organising this whole series of exercises, but if fate conspired to keep the man in the Capitol to clean up his son's latest mess, Lord Wingate certainly would not object. *At least my Wolfram has sense enough not to make a scene!* Lord Wingate thought, feeling an awkward swell of pride for the boy. He shrugged and returned his attention to the exercise at hand.

"I think it's time we stir things up a bit," Lord Wingate announced, "Barnes, give the volley signal now."

Barnes nodded and was about to tap the message into the master radio console when a voice cried out, "Belay that, Wingate!"

All faces turned towards the mountain of flesh that was Admiral the Lord Albert Cassius Bundwick. The corpulent, red-faced man could barely fit into his uniform, let alone his chair, but as the most senior admiral present, command of the exercise was his. "I must insist that the schedule be observed!" the man squealed, "The first volley from the ground is not yet due for another three minutes and seventeen seconds. The fleet will be caught unprepared!"

"Precisely the point," Lord Wingate explained, trying to remain calm as best he could, "It will catch them off guard and force them to adapt."

Lord Bundwick was everything about the nobility that Lord Wingate despised all packed into a single vaguely human-shaped container. He had coasted through his entire career relying on seniority and nepotism for advancement. He had no sense of tactics or strategy, and he was only of middling competence as an administrator. His only real skills were in following orders, which he did to the letter and no more, and in currying favour with superiors, in which regard he went above and beyond the call of duty whenever possible.

"But doing so will throw off the schedule," Lord Bundwick protested, "It will sow confusion among the fleet! The exercise will be thrown into chaos!"

"Real battles don't follow a schedule," Lord Wingate said. He suspected that this revelation was news to Lord Bundwick; the man had precious little field experience, and the few engagements he had participated in had been massively one-sided, "Any second leftenant straight out of the academy can stick to a pre-set timetable. We need officers who can adapt to fluid battlefield situations."

Lord Bundwick narrowed his eyes, a sign that the man was weighing his options. Lord Wingate felt a chill; Lord Bundwick might not have a strategic bone in his body where military matters were concerned, but the man was a genius when it came to manoeuvring for power and favour. Eventually, the man nodded, "Commander Barnes," he said, "give the signal for the ground artillery."

Barnes nodded and tapped the message into the master radio console. Lord Bundwick turned to his aide-de-camp and said, "You will note for the official log that the first barrage of ground artillery has been called"—he checked his pocket watch—"two minutes and fifty seconds early. You will note in particular that this action has been taken at the suggestion of Admiral the Lord Wingate."

All eyes turned back to the exercise at hand. Sure enough, chaos ensued. As the order went out, the ramrod-straight line of battle dissolved. Some ships kept going, keeping to the schedule no matter what. Other ships picked up speed, possibly believing that they had somehow fallen behind. Still other ships, stopped completely, paralysed with confusion. The exercise was in shambles.

"Do you see what happens when you break with schedule?" Lord Bundwick harrumphed, "The entire exercise shall have to be scrapped now. And of course, as it was *your* suggestion, Orpheus, you shall bear all the responsibility for this debacle. I hope you're satisfied."

"Very satisfied," Lord Wingate grinned, and pointed at one airship in particular. The *Dawn Spear* had very fluidly moved to a higher altitude, out of the range of any potential Hadvari volleys, and continued with the bombardment; exactly as would be expected in a real situation like this. A number of the other airships were now moving to follow *Dawn Spear's* example; the battle line was slowly beginning to reconstitute itself. "A decent recovery given the circumstances," Lord Wingate said, "Wouldn't you agree?"

Lord Bundwick trembled with disgust, his jowls shaking like a bowl of jelly. "The schedule has been thrown off," he snapped, "There is no plan for the rest of the exercise. Signal all ships to return to starting positions and rearm for the next trial."

Barnes tapped the command into the master radio console, and the fleet of airships heeled about to return to their starting positions at the edge of the desert. There would be some short time given over to resupplying and rearming the ships, and then exercise number four would begin.

With this exercise concluded, the admirals rose from their seats and retired to the inside of the pavilion to take food and refreshment. All except for Lord Wingate who remained behind with Barnes.

"My god," Lord Wingate groaned, as soon as the two of them were out of earshot, "but they're a tedious lot."

"I..." Barnes began, and quickly stopped himself before he said something untoward about his superiors, "I have no opinion on the matter, my lord."

Lord Wingate laughed, "Diplomatic as ever, Barnes!"

"It's not my place to criticise flag officers," Barnes added hastily.

"*Flag officers!*" Lord Wingate scoffed, "This fleet deserves a better high-command staff. That bickering ship of fools will be the ruination of this fleet."

"They led us well during the war," Barnes said, still trying to remain as neutral as possible.

"The fleet has faced no serious opposition for three decades,"

Lord Wingate said, "And even then, we started getting terribly sloppy by the end. This state of affairs won't last forever."

"You think not, my lord?" Barnes said.

"The Hadvari are a crafty lot," Lord Wingate said, "Make no mistake, our ancient foe will have a fleet of their own before long. And when that happens, we will need a high-command structure that can quickly adapt to sudden changes in strategic conditions. Otherwise we will be overwhelmed and destroyed."

"That's a rather dark outlook," Barnes said, "If you'll forgive my bluntness, my lord."

Lord Wingate let out a deep laugh, "Your bluntness is why I keep you around, my boy! There's a real dearth of honesty in the fleet."

"I appreciate your confidence, my lord," Barnes smiled.

"You have a long and proud career ahead of you, Theodore Barnes," Lord Wingate said fondly, "Marion speaks very highly of you."

"I'm n-not surprised, my lord!" Butler seemed flustered, "Your daughter is a... most romantic young soul."

"But not one who takes your fancy?" Lord Wingate said, picking up on the subtext of his companion.

"Alas, no," Barnes sighed, clearly relieved, "I'm sorry, my lord, but it's not to be."

Lord Wingate's mouth quirked into a clever grin, "It's certainly not because you prefer men, is it?"

"What?" Barnes suddenly stiffened, "I-I don't know what you're talking about!"

"Relax, Barnes," Lord Wingate said, "It's quite alright. I understand how these things are." *So, Amelia was right about you, my boy!*

"You..." Barnes stammered, "you won't... expose me?"

"Please," Lord Wingate scoffed, "I could name a dozen other noblemen of your persuasion right off the top of my head."

"I see," Barnes said.

"Don't get me wrong," Lord Wingate said, "It's still the sort of thing you have to keep away from the common eye, but the rest of the nobility doesn't much care one way or another. Just make sure it doesn't get all over the broadsheets, and you'll be fine."

"I must say, that is a tremendous relief," Barnes said, "So... you understand why this match with your daughter is not to be."

Lord Wingate shrugged, "Not necessarily."

"What?" Barnes squawked, "My lord, did you not hear me? I

cannot marry your daughter. She's a wonderful young lady, but I cannot love her!"

"Marriage is not about love, Barnes," Lord Wingate said, "It's about economics and society. It always has been. People have been marrying each other for money and social advancement since time immemorial. Especially among the higher classes."

"Forgive me for saying so, my lord, but that sounds terribly hypocritical," Barnes protested, "Why just look at you and Lady Wingate; you practically worship the ground she walks on!"

"Amelia and I are hardly a representative specimen!" Lord Wingate laughed, "One can hardly expect every couple in the world to be as perfectly matched as we are."

"I suppose not," Barnes said, "But even so..."

"It's hardly unprecedented," Lord Wingate said, "Don't worry, Barnes. You'll make a wonderful husband."

Barnes sank into his seat, "If you say so, my lord."

A terrific commotion erupted from inside the pavilion. Lord Wingate tried to ignore it for a few seconds, but ultimately got to his feet. "I'd better go see what's going on in there," he grumbled, "Don't let the next exercise start without me."

"Aye, my lord," Barnes nodded.

The interior of the pavilion was somewhat cooler than the sweltering heat outside. Along one side of the tent, a long table held an assortment of light refreshments, and along the other side stood a row of horses with their snouts in a long trough of water. At the far end of this makeshift stable, a raucous crowd of officers milled about, each one trying to be heard over all the others. Lord Wingate quickly made his way across the pavilion and pushed into the crowd. "Alright," he demanded, "what's going on here?"

"Orpheus! Just who I need to see," It was Lord Newton.

"This man," Lord Bundwick shrieked as the noise of the crowd momentarily subsided, "tried to gain entry to our headquarters. This is an outrageous breach of protocol! If this man were not also a lord of the land, I would have him shot at once!"

"You're being unreasonable," Lord Malden protested, "Lord Newton has every right to be here."

"I've had just about enough of you making exceptions for family!" Vice Admiral Rockport shouted, and the crowd fell to riot again.

"I'll handle this," Lord Wingate bellowed, and quickly escorted Lord Newton back through a tent flap to the outside. He could hear the argument going on, but that was no longer any concern of his. "What are you doing here, Theo?" he said as kindly as he could to his absent-minded friend, "There's a standing order: no civilians allowed on the range."

"I know," Lord Newton said, pulling a dossier out from under his arm, "but I thought you'd want to see this as soon as possible."

Lord Wingate took the sheaf of papers, "What is this?"

"It's the production records for the shell numbers you brought me," Lord Newton said, "Remember?"

Of course! The production numbers that he and Barnes collected at the Southern Gap. This would be all the relevant information about those shells. Hopefully, there would be something buried in these documents, some otherwise insignificant kernel of insight, that could shed some light on how Isafar had acquired Auroran military hardware. "Thank you very much, Theo."

"Sorry it took me so long to dig these out," Lord Newton said, "It's just that the files were suppressed."

"*Suppressed?*" Lord Wingate blinked, "Whatever for?" These were just production reports; little more than bureaucratic formalities. So why had someone gone to the trouble of declaring them top secret? This went beyond a simple leak; no, this smacked of conspiracy.

"I might have an idea," Lord Newton said, "These shells were of an experimental type. They were designed for penetration against heavy armour."

"You mean, *anti-fortification* munitions?" Lord Wingate said, trying to sound surprised. He didn't want to betray his suspicions just yet.

"Anti-*ship*, actually," Lord Newton continued, "in case the ginks somehow managed to throw together a fleet of their own."

Lord Wingate nodded, "A sensible precaution." *At least I'm not the only one who can see it!* "How many shells of this design were put into production?"

"Only about a dozen crates or so," Lord Newton said, "They were prototypes, you see, due to be tested a few months back. But then the war ended and the test was cancelled. I'd imagine that was why the records were suppressed." Lord Newton adjusted his glasses, "A shame really; I was rather looking forward to seeing how they performed."

Lord Wingate bit his lip. *Believe me, Theo, they work just fine.* "Do you know where... where these shells are right now?" He had been about to say "the rest of the shells," but only just stopped himself before giving it away.

"I'm afraid I couldn't say," Lord Newton shook his head, "I know they were moved to a staging area somewhere in the Disputed Zone, but they would likely have disappeared after the test was cancelled."

"I see," Lord Wingate said, "So they're gone?"

"Perhaps not," Lord Newton offered, "I recommend you talk to Lord Hanscom. He should know more."

"Why Hanscom?" Lord Wingate asked, reluctant to let his bitter rival catch any wind of his investigation.

"Because he gave the order to cancel the test," Lord Newton said, "It would have been his responsibility to dispose of the shells."

Lord Wingate narrowed his eyes, "Is that so?" It was all starting to become clear.

"Indeed," Lord Newton said, "I imagine he was pretty disappointed, given that he ordered the shells in the first place."

"Yes," Lord Wingate said, "How tragic for him."

That was all Lord Wingate needed to know. He slipped back into the tent, barely noticing (or caring) that the officers were still rioting. He walked over to the young ensign tending the horses and, as calmly as he could manage, said, "Saddle a horse for me at once. And when you're finished, take two more horses and escort Lord Newton off the range."

As the ensign went about his task, Lord Wingate stepped outside to where Barnes sat with the master radio console, "I need to catch a train back to the Capitol, Barnes." he said, "Carry on with the exercises without me."

"What's the matter?" Barnes asked.

"It's the investigation," Lord Wingate said, "I just found a lead."

"I see," Barnes's eyes widened, "Good luck, my lord."

Lord Wingate nodded and returned to the ensign with the horses. The boy offered him the reins to a strong white gelding. Lord Wingate led the horse out of the tent, tucked the dossiers from Theo into a saddlebag, leaped into the saddle, and spurred his mount to as fast a gallop as the beast could manage.

It was all Hanscom's doing! It was plainly evident that the man had cancelled the test and sold the shells on the local black market to recoup expenses! And that was even assuming that Hanscom hadn't simply embezzled the profits! *This is exactly why I was opposed to arming the Analerian irregulars!* Lord Wingate had argued long and hard, warning about exactly this sort of situation, but Lord Hanscom had been so enamoured of his little scheme to turn those lawless, scattered bands of thugs into a proper army. And now, whether for greed or simple expedience, Hanscom's carelessness had cost the ARAF the *Celsius!*

Off in the desert, the airships were taking flight again. Exercise number four was beginning. Once again, the desert plains thundered with the sound of explosions. It was almost enough to match the storm of fury in Lord Wingate's mind.

His ears were ringing. Everything hurt. Paul turned over and hit his head on a jagged spike of metal that had, only moments before, been part of the radio tower. It was just level with his right eye. *An inch to the right, and I'd be a blind man!*

Beside him, Halford was still whimpering softly and clutching at her right arm. On the other side, Hakefeldt was lying underneath two metal crossbeams. Paul quickly got to his feet and lifted the crossbeam just enough to pull Hakefeldt out from under it. He made no effort to resist; the kid was probably concussed.

Paul looked around. The top of the *Dreadnought* was littered with debris of all sizes. The hatch leading down to the sick bay was blocked by a twisted clump of metal that had probably been part of a ladder. Paul quickly made his way over to the hatch and shifted the debris to one side.

"What's going on up there?" one of the WAVE girls asked frantically from down in the sick bay.

"Radio tower collapsed!" Paul shouted, "Get Doc Pratt! We've got wounded incoming!"

"At once, Captain!"

As Paul turned back to lift Hakefeldt up and pass him down into the sick bay, he glanced back up at the sky. The rogue airship had passed overhead, bypassing the Longview aerodrome completely, and was now floating away to the east. Paul watched murderously as the vessel shrank into the distance before vanishing behind the mountains to the south. *I will find that ship,* Paul told himself as he slid Hakefeldt down into sick bay, *and I will blow it the hell out of my goddamn sky!*

Paul gently picked up Halford and slipped her through the hatch as well, before climbing down the ladder himself. Doctor Pratt was already in the room, directing the WAVE girls to put Halford in one of the beds, and to get some bandages and sterilized tools ready.

"How's she looking, Doc?"

"Multiple lacerations on her right arm," Doctor Pratt said as one of the WAVE girls tied a white apron onto him, "She's lost blood, but not enough yet to warrant a transfusion. No obvious exit wounds, so I'm about to check for foreign objects."

Doesn't sound too bad, Paul supposed, *walking wounded perhaps.* Paul glanced over to Hakefeldt, lying on another bed, "And what about him?"

"Captain," Doctor Pratt said heavily, "I'm sorry, but the boy's dead."

For a moment, everything was still.

"W-what?" Paul stammered, "No, no, that can't be right. I was just..." Paul rushed over to the bed where Hakefeldt lay. The kid couldn't be dead! His skin was still warm! His eyes were open! Doctor Pratt had to be wrong! Somehow, he just had to! "He looks alright to me," Paul said frantically, "He's probably just concussed. Did you check for concussion yet?"

"Captain..." Doctor Pratt said gently.

"Did you check for a concussion?!" Paul shouted.

Doc Pratt simply slid his hand under Hakefeldt's shoulder and lifted him onto his side. Right at the back of the boy's head was a small hole, no larger than Paul's little finger. A thin stream of blood dribbled out of it and collected into a small pool on the pillow underneath. "I'm sorry, Captain," Doctor Pratt said sadly, "There's nothing I can do."

The doctor let the boy fall back onto the mattress, and for a moment, Paul could have sworn he saw another face. Lieutenant Miles Anderson Stuart stared back up at him with dead accusing eyes, and a single bullet hole in his forehead. Paul quickly looked away. "Goddammit," he muttered, and slowly stalked out of the sick bay, all the while repeating softly, "Goddammit. Goddammit."

Once in the hallway, Paul collapsed against the wall. Lieutenant Junior Grade Archie Hakefeldt was dead. It wasn't fair! Dammit, the kid couldn't have been more than nineteen years old! He had a family. He had his whole career ahead of him. He was probably the most competent officer on the entire goddamn ship. And he'd been crushed under a goddamn radio tower before ever seeing action.

It should have been me! Paul could feel the tears beginning to collect in his eyes. Dammit! Hakefeldt had been killed by a random sliver of debris! *Why couldn't it have hit me instead? I'd definitely deserve it if I can't even protect my own people!*

Through the deck plates below his feet, Paul could hear the reactor turning on. Paul slowly sank to the floor, letting the vibrations from below soothe his knotted muscles. *I should have done something!* Paul told himself, *Anything!*

From below, the vibrations of the reactor swelled into a vicious shaking, accompanied by a loud groaning sound. A few moments later, there was a piercing hiss, and the vibrations abruptly cut off. Paul jumped to his feet; the sound of an emergency reactor flush was never good! Paul pushed his grief aside for the moment and hurried down to the engine room.

Thick white smoke was pouring out of the engine room as Paul reached the door. Several engine techs were doubled over in coughing fits just outside. Paul could hear a pair of voices from inside the engine room; Thatcher was swearing up a storm. "God fucking dammit! This is why I don't fucking like people coming in and fucking around with my reactor!"

Paul stepped into the engine room, leaning down low to avoid the smoke. "What's going on down here?" Paul called into the chaos.

"Ah, Captain!" Lieutenant Newton coughed, "I'm afraid we've suffered a little bit of an accident."

"I can see that!" Paul snapped, "What the hell happened?"

"Well," Newton explained, "Warrant Officer Thatcher ordered a test start of the reactor to make sure that everything was in order. I tried to assure him that such an action was unwarranted, but—"

"And it's a good thing I didn't fucking listen to you!" Thatcher growled from the other side of the room, "All my settings have been thrown out of whack! If we had come to full power, we could have lost the entire fucking ship!"

"What *actually* happened?" Paul demanded.

"Still tryin'a suss that out, Cap'n," Thatcher grumbled, "We started up the old girl, and she was fine for a minute or so. Then everything started shaking like a goddamn earthquake. So we hit the emergency vent."

"Shaking, you say?" Paul said, remembering his civilian days. *Sounds like too much coolant moving through the pipes at once,* "Have you checked the internal flow regulators for the coolant loops?"

"Could be part of it, Cap'n," Thatcher said, "but I've felt a lot of fluid hammers in my time. That wasn't just a pressure surge. There's more going on here that we ain't seein'."

Paul looked the reactor up and down. The smoke was still too thick to get a good view, "Do you think the workmen could have made some mistake?"

"Not possible," Lieutenant Newton chimed in, "The repairs were made on backup circuits. There's no reason they—"

"You wanna make yourself useful, kid?" Thatcher snapped at the boy, "Go outside and open a goddamn porthole! Start gettin' this smoke cleared out of here!"

Newton jumped, "Ah, yes, of course! Smoke! Don't worry, I can fix that." The lanky kid galloped out of the room, tripping over one of his companions outside, and scrambled to open a porthole to begin letting out the smoke.

"Freakin' Old Nobility nerks," Thatcher spat, "Just because his uncle is *Lord Theobald Paracelsus Newton,* he thinks engineering runs in his blood or somethin'."

"Stay focused," Paul snapped at the ornery Newport man, "What else could it have been?"

"Dunno," Thatcher said, "I've already ruled out a backflow. We gave the pipes a flush yesterday, so I doubt it's a blockage."

Paul thought for a moment, "Power up the reactor for a moment. Lowest possible settings, and stand by the cutoffs." A live test was probably the only way to see what was wrong with the reactor without taking it apart.

"There ain't no cutoffs, Cap'n," Thatcher said, "This is a first-generation reactor, remember?"

"Just be ready to shut everything down at my say so."

"Alright, Cap'n," Thatcher didn't seem too sure about this, but he obeyed.

By now, enough of the smoke had cleared for Paul to have a decent view of the reactor. Thatcher carefully reset the dials and closed the initiator circuit, sending a jolt of energy into the fulgurite core to start the reaction cycle.

The machine came to life, filling the engine room with the familiar rotating vibrations that were the trademark of a fulgurite reactor. At first everything seemed normal; the reaction cycle was running without any apparent problems. There didn't seem to be any faults so far.

"You seem to know your way around a reactor, Cap'n," Thatcher said as he fiddled with the dials, "If ya don't mind my sayin' so."

"Civilian freighthauler for twenty years," Paul said.

"That right?" Thatcher said sheepishly, "Shoulda said so. I mighta minded my manners a little better."

"Don't worry about it," Paul said.

The primary cooling loop engaged. Now the shaking began again. There was no doubt, this was where the problem was, "Alright," Paul called out over the sound of the shaking, "shut 'er down. All stop." Thatcher closed the main reactor feedback valve, and the mighty machine slowly fell silent again.

"I see what's wrong," Paul said, taking a closer look at the primary coolant loop, "Right here." He reached through a forest of pipes and pointed at a small pipe joint. The middle of the joint showed the brilliant untarnished metal of an improperly connected pipe link, "Loose seal on the primary coolant loop. The exposed internal flange is causing turbulence in the pipe. If we'd come to full power, the cooling system would have blown itself apart."

Thatcher looked at the problem joint, "A loose joint? Dammit, that can't be right! I remember fixing that one!"

"Are you sure?" Paul said.

"Absolutely!" Thatcher protested, "I told Behringer to check the loops! Gave the whole system the once over myself afterward to make doubly sure!" Thatcher turned to Paul, "I'm so sorry, Cap'n, I don't know how this happened. I swear this ain't gonna—"

"It's alright," Paul said, urgently cutting off the stream of apologies, "We caught the problem. That's the important thing. You guys just focus on getting everything back into working order. Double-check all systems, and make sure everything is bolted down properly."

"Aye, sir!" Thatcher saluted, much more crisply than Paul had remembered. As Paul left the engine room, he heard Thatcher screaming orders at his people. *Everything's back to normal again.*

Paul wandered down to the cargo bay and collapsed onto the stairs. Goddammit, but he was tired. *What a day!* First that business with Wilmont, and then that rogue airship fired on us, and then the radio tower collapsed, and then Hakefeldt, and now this near-miss with the reactor. *I just want this day to be over already!*

"Excuse me," someone called from the other side of the cargo bay, "Excuse me, Captain Bowman, sir!"

What is it now? Paul slowly got to his feet. "Yeah?" he growled.

The officer crossed the cargo bay and saluted with clockwork precision. Paul looked the man up and down, "Harrison right?" *Wilmont's secretary?* "What's wrong this time?"

"Nothing, sir," Harrison said quickly, "At least nothing that concerns me." The man held out a small bundle of leather, "I was told by Commodore Wilmont to return this to you." Paul took the package, and unraveled it.

It was his jacket. Paul quickly donned the fine deerskin coat, relishing the soft seal fur lining on the inside. *There's got to be something more here,* Paul thought suddenly, *Wilmont hates my guts. There's no way this is just some random act of kindness.* "What's the catch?"

"Catch?" Harrison blinked, "I'm afraid I don't know what you mean, Captain."

"Why *now?*" Paul said, "Why is he only giving back my jacket after my ship just got hit?"

"I was told that there was a matter concerning the ownership of this coat," Harrison said, "and as this matter has now been rendered moot, the coat is to be returned to its rightful owner." Harrison looked about awkwardly, "As to... recent developments, I'm afraid Commodore Wilmont was not aware of what happened before he dispatched me on this errand. The timing appears to be simply an unfortunate coincidence."

"Right," Paul nodded. *'An unfortunate coincidence?'* That sounded exactly like something Wilmont would say. "Well, thanks anyway, Lieutenant."

"Incidentally," the man said, "you don't need my assistance, do you sir?"

"Thanks," Paul said, "but I think we're managing alright as we are." *We probably could use the help,* Paul supposed, *but I'm just too tired to manage it.*

Harrison saluted and marched back down the cargo ramp.

Paul was about to sit back down to rest some more, when he felt something inside the jacket. Something in one of the interior pockets... Paul fished into the pocket; he could have sworn they were empty when Wilmont had confiscated it. Paul pulled out a crumpled piece of paper with some writing scrawled on it. In the top right corner was the eight-pointed Star of Dawn with a pair of wings spreading out behind it. The emblem of the fleet.

Unfortunate coincidence, my ass!

Paul couldn't read what was written on the paper, but even he recognized official fleet letterhead when he saw it! These were orders. *I need to get this to Halford!* he thought, *and fast!*

Paul dashed back up to sick bay, taking the stairs three at a time as he ran. He passed by the engine room, where Thatcher was hollering profanities at the top of his lungs. As Paul reached sick bay, he noticed Wolfram sitting outside the door. The kid had his head buried in his arms. *So,* Paul thought oddly, *He and Hakefeldt were friends after all.*

Paul stepped into the sick bay, and the smell of blood filled his nostrils. Doctor Pratt's white apron was now covered in nauseating splotches of blood, and the man held a tray with two sharp metal chunks. "Captain," he nodded. Behind the man, Louise was lying in bed, staring up at the ceiling with a vacant expression on her face. Paul tried not to look at the other bed, where Hakefeldt's body lay underneath a white sheet.

"How does she look, Doc?" Paul asked.

"She's stable," Doctor Pratt gestured with the tray, "I took two splinters out of her, and we've stitched her up as best we can. She's lost blood, but as long as there's no infection, she should be alright."

"That's good," Paul nodded, "You think I could maybe... get a moment with her?"

"I don't see why not," Doc Pratt shrugged, and quickly shooed the rest of the WAVE girls out of the room. Paul sat down on the bed beside Louise. It was just the two of them. And Hakefeldt. *Dammit, don't think about that now!*

"Louise," Paul said, "you doing alright?"

"It hurts." the girl moaned.

"I know," Paul said gently, "I know. This is a real bad situation for all of us."

"I'm sorry, Captain," the girl said weakly, "I'm sorry for being such a burden."

"Don't say that," Paul said, "It was an accident. It could have been any of us." *It should have been me!*

"I just..." Louise whimpered, "I just wanted to help." The girl appeared to be on the verge of tears.

"You can still help," Paul pulled out the note, "You can still help me. I just need you to read this for me."

Louise wiped her eyes with her uninjured left hand, "I... I'll try," she took the paper.

Captain Bowman, I am giving you a direct order: Take your entire crew, go after that bloody ship, and destroy her by any means necessary.
Wilmont.
P.S.: Destroy this order after reading it for security.

Halford handed the paper back to Paul, "That's all there is."

Short but succinct, Paul thought, *Hell, I've got no protests!* He gave the girl a kind pat on the shoulder, "That's all I needed, kid. You just get better now. Take as much time as you need."

"Thank you, Captain," Louise nodded sadly.

Paul stood up and looked at the letter. Wilmont had said to destroy it after reading it. But should he? Why had Wilmont delivered the letter the way he did? If he had orders for the *Dreadnought,* surely he could have just sent Harrison with orders. So why had he hidden them in the jacket? There was foul play at work here, no question about it.

"Actually," Paul said, handing the note back to Halford, "I think you should hang onto this note for a while."

"But, Captain," Halford said, "the note says to destroy—"

"I know what it says," Paul said, "but, I got a feeling... Just... just keep this thing safe, okay?"

Louise took the note and clumsily tucked it into the pocket of her jacket, lying beside the bed. "I'll do what I can, Captain."

"Thanks," Paul said, and walked out of sick bay, giving a nod to Doctor Pratt and his people. *Well, we have our orders.*

"Captain Bowman!"

Dammit, now who the hell wants to talk to me?!

Paul looked up. Standing in the hallway before him was a man he didn't recognize. He held a wrench in his hand and a cigar in his mouth. His face and clothes were stained with grease, but still he didn't seem to carry himself like one of the working class. "We have finished our repairs," the man said in a voice that was clearly unaccustomed to shouting. He was the leader of the repair crew sent by the Consortium, "We'll be leaving now."

"Not so fast," Paul called after the workman, "Before you go, I need you to clear that debris off the top deck."

"I'm sorry, Captain," the workman said sweetly, "but our purview covers only the damages caused by our agent. Any other damages are beyond the scope of our charter."

"Hey," Paul said, stepping in front of the workman to block his way down a stairwell, "I asked nicely. Now I'm telling you. You are going to clear the debris off the top deck."

"I'm afraid you don't understand the situation," the workman continued. Paul could hear just the slightest twinge of unease creeping into his smooth voice, "We have already exhausted our authority, so we must do nothing. Now on the other hand, if you wish to hire our services personally—"

Paul lunged forward and shoved the workman back against the bulkhead with his forearm. "I was just down in the engine room," Paul hissed into the workman's ear, "You know what I found? One of the pipe joints on our main coolant loop had *mysteriously* come loose! You wouldn't happen to know anything about that, would you?"

"I-I," the workman stammered, "I don't know what you're talking about, Captain!"

"You know, I still haven't tested those loudspeakers yet," Paul went on, "How about I test them right now, by telling everyone on this ship that a couple of nerks from the Consortium sabotaged our reactor?"

The workman's face turned white at the suggestion. Paul gave him another shove, "Or how about I just drag you down to the engine room? I'm sure Mister Thatcher would *really* appreciate an explanation."

"It wasn't me!" the workman squealed, "It wasn't me!"

"Oh?" Paul lowered his forearm, allowing the workman to breathe more easily. He still had him backed up against the bulkhead.

"It was Babcock," the workman wheezed, "Miranda Babcock. She told us what to do... To send a message. She said you'd know what it meant."

"I assume you know," Paul said, "sabotaging military hardware is a hanging offense."

The workman nodded and gingerly touched his neck as if he could already feel the noose drawing tight around it.

"You have fifteen minutes," Paul said, "Clear the debris off the top deck, and get the fuck off my ship."

Vaughn's footsteps echoed through the cramped corridors of the *Dreadnought*. Her mind was a frantic jumble of conflicting reports and wild speculations. The radio tower had collapsed—that much was certain. But was it an accident? Was it an attack? Who was injured? Had someone died? How many? And was something wrong with the reactor?

Vaughn had demanded answers from nearly everyone she passed, but very little was forthcoming. The officers and airmen only offered token admissions of unknowing. The WAVE girls more often than not squeaked like frightened mice and scurried away. The workmen from the Consortium simply ignored her and continued on their way.

Bloody hell! What happened to her blasted ship?!

It won't be my ship for much longer, Vaughn reminded herself. Punching a superior officer was more than enough to see her dismissed from the service, or at least transferred to another ship. *Transferred?* Vaughn thought, *He'd be doing me a bloody favour!* She couldn't imagine a worse punishment than simply being forced to continue serving on the *Dreadnought* under Captain Bowman!

Vaughn reached the top of a stairwell and almost collided with Leftenant Wingate. "Leftenant!" she demanded, as soon as there was no danger of collision, "What is going on? Report!"

"They got Archie," the leftenant said, "He's... he's..." His voice sounded terribly unsteady, and he wasn't making eye contact.

"Spit it out, Leftenant!" Vaughn snapped. Blast it all! Did they teach cadets nothing of discipline at the academy anymore?

"He's dead!" Leftenant Wingate screamed at her. Vaughn stepped back. The boy's face was red; he had clearly been crying.

"...That is unfortunate," Vaughn said, "Leftenant Hakefeldt was a..." She couldn't think of anything to say about Hakefeldt, "...a fine officer."

"Yeah..." Wingate's gaze retreated back to his boots. The boy had his father's height and strong shoulders, but these blessings were not at all apparent in the poor, broken creature slouching before her.

"His sacrifice will not be forgotten," Vaughn said as stoically as she could manage, "Carry on, Leftenant."

"Right," Wingate nodded and trudged up the stairwell to his quarters.

So we've lost a crewman after all, Vaughn thought, *and an officer to boot!* It was the worst news she had heard so far; and it was probably only going to get worse from here. God only knew how Bowman would take it.

Just at that moment, Vaughn looked up, and found herself face-to-face with the last person she wanted to see. *Speak of the devil, and he shall appear!*

Captain Bowman was clearly in a dark mood, even before running into her. This was the first time the two of them had come face-to-face since the... incident the night before. What would he do? Had he already finalised a punishment for her? Would he throw something together on the quick? Vaughn's eyes glanced down at the sidearm lurking beneath his new jacket. *Or will he just shoot me right here?*

Two pairs of eyes locked into each other, and for a moment, the corridor was deathly still.

"Captain?" Vaughn said awkwardly. *Bloody hell, say something!*

"Follow me," Captain Bowman said tersely.

Vaughn followed Captain Bowman down the hallway and through the door leading to the starboard gunpit. For whatever reason, the *Dreadnought* had been constructed with broadside batteries on each side, like to an oceangoing warship; however since most every other airship had their guns toward the bottom, this area was called *the gunpit* for the sake of convenience.

"Shut the door," Captain Bowman said as Vaughn crossed the threshold. She did as she was told and noticed as she turned back that Warrant Officer Bellman and his crew were not yet at their stations. She was alone in the gunpit. With Bowman.

"Now, then," he turned to face her. The expression on his face was ironclad. "I'm going to talk, and you're going to listen."

Vaughn nodded silently.

"I don't care that you're a woman," Bowman began, "I don't care that your career hasn't been going so well. And I don't care that you're so hung up on how *unprofessional* I am, how I'm not a *proper officer* and all, that you can't see the silver spoon shoved up your ass."

How dare you! Vaughn opened her mouth to voice her objections to Bowman's language, but the man raised his voice and cut her off, "Like I said! I don't care about any of that. It's not important right now." Vaughn simmered down, and Bowman continued, "Here's what *is* important right now:

"We're going into combat soon. Hell, it's already started! And some of us aren't gonna be coming out the other side. Now, I know you don't think a lot of me—and believe me, the feeling is mutual—but like it or not, this is my ship, and I'm in charge. But a captain is only as good as his crew. And if I'm going to get as many of us back home as I can, I need to know that I can count on every last one of us to follow orders and do their job as best they can." Bowman locked eyes with her, "And *you* most of all."

"So here's what's going to happen," Bowman continued, "Either you walk off this ship right now and we leave without you—I'll strike you from all the lists and everything, all official like, and we never have to deal with each other again. Or, you stay on, and help me get as many of our people back home as we can."

"That's your choice," Bowman concluded, "It's one or the other, and I honestly don't care which one you choose. But you need to pick one, and you need to pick *now*."

Vaughn was stunned! Wasn't Bowman going to punish her? He hadn't even mentioned any disciplinary measures. And now he was offering her the chance to walk away from it all? Why, the way he had framed that option, he made it seem like *that* was the worse choice; a coward's escape! Did he actually *want* her on this ship? After all the bile and bitterness that had passed between them?

Bowman folded his arms, "So what's it gonna be?"

It's a ruse! Vaughn thought, *He's trying to get me off the ship without any action on his part!* Well, she wasn't about to fall for his little scheme. If Captain bloody Bowman wanted rid of her, he'd have to bloody well come out and say it himself!

"I'm staying."

Bowman nodded, "Get up to the bridge and start the pre-flight rundown. We raise ship in fifteen minutes." He stepped around her and exited the gunpit.

Vaughn watched Bowman go. She'd been outfoxed again! That man had tricked her into staying of her own accord! Why? Why would anyone want someone like *her* on his ship? *What sort of game have I landed myself in?*

Vaughn shook her head and headed up to the bridge. It seemed she would be remaining on the *Dreadnought* for a little while longer.

Chapter XVIII

Earth and Blood

THE cargo hold was filled with the ringing and clattering of chains as Paul and Butler hoisted the cargo ramp into the closed position. Luckily, their fuel reserves had also been restocked. Their current full two-hundred-barrel load could see them all the way to Illyria and back at top speed if necessary.

"And you're certain you need me and the customs team?" Butler asked.

"Orders said to gather the entire crew," Paul said, "That includes you." He had no idea why, but those were his orders. If Wilmont wanted him to ignore customs inspections for the moment, that was just fine by him!

"Just making certain, Captain," Butler nodded as he and Paul moved to fasten the clamps at the side of the ramp, locking it into place.

That's it, Paul thought as he gave the clamp one final twist. The entire crew was on ship, those workmen had finished clearing off the top deck and then made quick tracks, Thatcher and his people had finally brought the reactor back into working order, and Vaughn was handling matters on the bridge. *We're ready to raise ship.*

"Take a walk around the ship, and make sure everyone has everything they need." Paul told Butler as he started back to the stairs, "And get the gun crews to run some drills. I don't know how long it's been since any of them have seen combat, but I need 'em in tip-top shape."

"Aye, sir," Butler saluted.

Paul entered the stairwell. He didn't think he could remember ever being so tired. It was barely past noon, and it had already been the longest day of his life. Getting the *Dreadnought* airborne at last would probably be the most relaxing thing he did all day.

He heard voices echoing down the stairwell. There was an argument underway on the bridge. *Just what I fucking need right now!*

"I don't care what you think!" Barlowe was protesting, "We've just been hit, and we've taken casualties! This is not the time!"

"I am *ordering* you to install that bulkhead, Mister Barlowe," Vaughn was saying, "I shan't ask you again."

"Look missy," Barlowe continued protesting, "there are more important things to do right now than making a few *cosmetic repairs.* So if you'll just lay off and let me do my—"

"Kid," Paul growled as soon as he stepped onto the bridge, "are you refusing to carry out a direct order from a superior officer?"

"Oh, Captain!" Barlowe jumped to attention, "I... uh..."

"Cause that's a shooting matter," Paul said, casually brushing aside part of his jacket to reveal the pistol sitting at his hip.

All of the color washed out of Barlowe's face in an instant. "I... It's just that..." He spluttered, "Well... is it *your* order, Captain?"

By now, Paul was standing directly in front of the man. He was only an inch taller than the Bo'sun, but the way Barlowe was cowering, Paul might have been a giant.

"Are you serious right now?" Paul said in a deadly whisper, "She told you to do something. That's not good enough for you? You *really* need me to back her up on this one, is that it?"

"W-well," Barlowe stammered, "I just wanted to... to make certain that—"

"No no, I'm serious," Paul said, raising his voice, "Is this gonna be a *thing* with you? Are you gonna make me follow you around all day, *authorizing* every order you get like some fuckin' bureaucrat? Is that how it's gonna be?"

"I..." Barlowe scratched at the back of his neck, "I don't—"

"Or maybe you're just trying to get out of doing your goddamn job"—by now, Paul was shouting right in his face—"so as you can go skarkin' off to the galley again, huh? Maybe chase the girls around for a bit?"

Barlowe didn't even respond to that one. He knew when he was beaten.

Paul shook his head, "My patience with your bullshit has officially run out. You're gonna do as you're told, when you're told to do it, or I'm gonna to weld you into a goddamn crawlspace until you fix that attitude of yours. Got it?"

Barlowe nodded timidly.

"Sparks," Paul turned his attention to Wagner, already sitting at the radio console, "Go to the supply office, and pick up a tool bucket and a bag of rivets for Mister Barlowe."

"Aye, sir!" the boy jumped to his feet, saluted, and dashed into the stairwell.

As Paul approached the loudspeaker console next to the radio, Vaughn crossed the bridge to intercept him. *Probably thanking me for backing her up with Barlowe,* Paul thought smugly, *Good to see that she's finally warming up.*

"*Senior,*" she hissed into his ear.

Paul blinked, "What?"

"I am a *senior* officer, not a *superior* officer," she said, "My commission pre-dates Leftenant Barlowe's, and I hold a higher rank. Therefore from his perspective, I—"

"Lady," Paul hissed back, "are we really having this talk right now?"

Vaughn hesitated and then nodded curtly, "Right. Nevermind."

Paul turned his attention back to the loudspeaker console. He picked up the mouthpiece and flipped the master switch.

"Attention all hands," he announced, "This is Captain Bowman." The familiar echoes from the speakers throughout the ship wafted through the stairwell. *At least this thing works.*

"Well," Paul continued, "it's been one hell of a morning, and I know a lot of you are still confused as to what's been happening, so I'll give you a quick run-down. We were attacked. Caught with our pants down by some unknown airship. One of our officers was killed: Lieutenant Junior Grade Archie Hakefeldt. And then..." He paused. The crew didn't need to know about the workmen from the Consortium sabotaging the reactor. That would raise too many questions.

"And then," Paul continued, "we received new instructions from Fleet Commander Wilmont. As of fifteen minutes ago, the *Dreadnought* has been ordered to give pursuit to this rogue airship and destroy her by whatever means necessary."

Paul hesitated. That was all there was. But should he say more? He wasn't good at giving speeches. *Why not? A few words of encouragement couldn't hurt.*

"I know most of you don't have a lot of combat experience." Paul started, "In fact, I know some of you requested a post on this ship specifically to avoid combat in the first place, and I can understand that. Hell, on any other day, I'd say that was pretty a smart move. Well, smarter than me, at any rate."

Dammit, I'm rambling! Paul thought, *I'm really not good at this.*

Paul quickly drew to a conclusion, "Look, bottom line is this: keep a cool head and do your job as best you can, and I'll do my best to get us all back home again." Paul hesitated for one last moment before adding, "Trust the wind, people."

As Paul switched off the master circuit and set down the mouthpiece, Wagner returned with the supplies for Barlowe. "Good work, Sparks," Paul said, taking the tool bucket and rivets from Wagner and shoving them roughly into Barlowe's arms.

Paul turned back to Wagner and was about to order the boy to get on the radio and ask for clearance for departure, when he remembered that the radio tower had been destroyed. And even if it hadn't, military airships en route to combat assignments always got jumped to the front of the line.

"Alright, people. Let's get airborne," Paul clapped his hands together and started for the captain's chair, "Helm, take us aloft."

"Aye sir," Hamilton responded and began to work the controls.

"Belay that, Ensign," Vaughn said. Paul glanced warily up at the woman. *What's she on about now?*

"Captain," Vaughn said, meeting Paul stare for stare, "we need a navigator."

"No, we don't," Paul huffed.

"Yes, we do," Vaughn insisted

"No, we don't!" Paul got to his feet, "We're not going from one city to another. We're chasing an enemy airship! So unless that chart over there has their course already plotted out for us, we don't need a navi to track them down!"

"And then what?" Vaughn said. Her voice hadn't changed, "This pursuit could lead us anywhere. You vowed to bring us back home again. How do you intend to do that without a navigator keeping track of our position?"

"She's right, Captain," Hamilton said, "I can't just eyeball us back to civilization from anywhere in the world."

I could!

Paul shook his head. Dammit, Vaughn made a good point. They needed a navigator, but who? Paul certainly couldn't cover it himself; if he couldn't read regular words, he certainly couldn't read a map. "Are you up to it?" Paul asked Vaughn, trying to keep his voice free from any sharpness.

Vaughn glanced down at the logbook tucked under her arm, "I regret," she said, almost sounding embarrassed, "my training lies elsewhere."

"I can do it," Barlowe muttered as he manhandled the large steel bulkhead into place.

"*No you can't!*" Both Paul and Vaughn shouted at the same time. Barlowe groaned and continued with his work, his escape attempt foiled.

Paul glanced about the bridge. Wagner was needed on the radio, so he was out. That was also true of Lieutenant Ziegler, who was filling in for Wolfram at the gunboard. And as for Hamilton... "Helm," Paul addressed the kid, "can you read a map?"

"Yes," the kid said, as though it were the most obvious thing in the world, "of course."

"Good," Paul started walking toward the helm controls, "Get up."

"What are you doing, Captain?" the boy seemed confused.

"Promoting you," Paul said as he gently nudged Hamilton out of the seat, "Congrats kid, you're our new navi."

"Captain, you're only shifting the problem," Vaughn protested, "Now who is to be our *helmsman?*"

Paul flipped the engine order switch to the maximum setting and slipped into the seat as the soft hum of the reactor swelled to a growl. "Me!" he shouted over the noise.

The deck pitched violently, and the *Dreadnought* began to rise into the air.

"Honestly, boy!" Lord Franklin burst into the chamber, "Are you a complete idiot?!"

Sitting by the window, Hobart Aloysius Franklin squirmed in the finely upholstered chair and closed his book. He couldn't stand it when his lord father yelled at him like this, "What did I do this time?" he moaned.

"Stand up when you address me, boy!" Lord Franklin snapped. Hobart leaped to his feet and made a stiff bow. His lord father always had been a stickler for protocol, even amongst his own family. "Now then, I trust you are aware that the Queen was holding an audience not thirty minutes ago."

"Of course," Hobart said.

"An audience at which you failed to present yourself," Lord Franklin said, "I was there all alone, wandering about like a lost puppy!"

"What about Lucille?" Hobart gestured toward the servingmaid following at Lord Franklin's side.

"Outside servants are not permitted within the royal presence," Lord Franklin said with exasperation, "I've explained this to you any number of times, boy. Please pay attention."

"Incidentally, my lord..." Lucille spoke up.

"You may go about your business, girl," Lord Franklin said, his voice suddenly smooth and gentle. Lucille curtsied and calmly walked to the closet to fetch the feather duster.

"Now then, boy," Lord Franklin turned his attention back to Hobart, "Would you care to explain why you were absent from today's audience?"

"Father, the audience was about *tax policy,*" Hobart groaned.

"And I suppose you think such things are beneath you?" Lord Franklin snapped, "I take it that's also why you skipped that audience about the ATC last week?"

"Finance is a terribly esoteric subject, father," Hobart explained, "I haven't anything of substance to offer on the matter."

"I don't care if you haven't anything to say, you shall attend those gatherings regardless," Lord Franklin said firmly, "The Ancient and Noble House of Franklin must have a presence in court."

"What about you?" Hobart said, "*You're* a representative of our house. Isn't that enough?"

"*I,*" Lord Franklin said, "am a senile old fool who will be in my grave within a decade. And when that happens, you need to have a reputation in court to precede you. What is at stake is nothing less than the continuity of House Franklin."

Hobart took a step back, and almost tripped over a table. He barely remembered taking all those steps backwards! His lord father had always been shorter than him, but he could be terribly intimidating when he chose to be.

"Now listen to me, boy," Lord Franklin said, in a tone that would admit absolutely no dissent, "I don't care if it's just more of Lord Newton's quackery, or if Lord Mayfax ends up spending three hours whinging about the shortcomings of the Kalmar sewer system! You *will* attend the Queen when she holds an audience! Do I make myself clear?"

Hobart nodded slowly, "Yes father."

"Good," Lord Franklin backed off slightly. Only slightly. "Now then, there is to be another audience later this evening in the Great Hall. I have reason to suspect that Lords Petras and Waldemar will be presenting a boundary dispute, with special emphasis on mineral rights. I trust I shall find you in attendance?"

"Yes, father." Hobart nodded again. Lord Franklin seemed satisfied and turned to pour himself a glass of brandy from the liquor cabinet. Hobart picked up his book and slipped back into the armchair by the window.

It was at times like this that Hobart found himself wishing that his lord father really *was* a senile, doddering old fool. In truth, Lord Barnabas Obadiah Franklin's mind was as keen and perceptive as it had always been, even at seven-and-seventy years of age. He had inherited the senile act from his father, Lord Tarquin Hieronymus Franklin, and he from his father before him, and so on. Lord Franklin credited the act as having preserved the standing of House Franklin for generations.

The scheme was simple enough, at least in concept. Once the heir to the current Lord Franklin reached a certain age, the lord in question would begin to put on an air of absent-mindedness. Subtle at first, simple short-term memory lapses and the like, but slowly increasing, until the lord in question seemed completely out of touch with the world around him. In that way, the lord's heir could slowly ease himself into the responsibilities of lordship, and cultivate the public recognition that came with it. Ideally, by the time the lord died, his successor would have already built up a sufficient reputation and network of connections to make the transition from one lord to another as seamless as possible.

Hobart had to admit, it was a sound plan. However, he hoped it would be a good long while before he had to actually assume lordship. He would not be ready to take on those responsibilities for a long time.

"And another thing," Lord Franklin added, "you will keep away from young Stolos."

Hobart slammed the book closed, "I don't see how it's any of your business whom I choose to associate with."

"You're a member of my House. *That* makes it my business!" Lord Franklin snapped, "Your association with Stolos endangers the House of Franklin, and you will not have any more contact with him. Am I clear?"

"His lordship has a number of interesting ideas," Hobart began, "especially concerning—"

"Concerning the induction of Analeria as a full-fledged province of Aurora," Lord Franklin interrupted, "I don't know what sort of mad scheme he's cooking up in that head of his, but I don't want you having anymore contact with him. Had I known just how radical his private opinions were, I'd never have let you near him to begin with!"

"With respect, father," Hobart said, "You don't know what he's told me about—"

"I know every word," Lord Franklin snapped, "Do you have any idea how long it took me to have this bloody palace bugged? Stolos is either pontificating for the broadsheets, or else laying the groundwork to some long-game conspiracy. Either way, he's dangerous."

"And what if Stolos is genuinely concerned about—"

"Don't be an idiot, boy!" Lord Franklin laughed, "*Genuine concern?* A preposterous notion. There's obviously some hidden purpose behind his posturing."

"Honestly, father," Hobart slumped back into his chair and opened his book again, "I do wish you'd stop being so paranoid."

"What you deem 'paranoia,' the rest of the nobility calls common sense," Lord Franklin said, "This country is rotten to the core with plots and counterplots; everyone's in on it, from the servants in the kitchen right on up to the Queen herself! Do you honestly think Her Majesty really is the slack-brained little simpleton she presents to the world? Mark my words, boy, she's playing the selfsame game as the rest of us." Lord Franklin ceased his bloviating for a moment to take a swig of brandy, "And she is good! She is *very good!*"

Hobart got up and started for the glass door to the balcony. His father's senility may have been just an act, but Lord Franklin surely loved listening to the sound of his own voice! Out of the corner of his eye, Hobart noticed Lucille going about her dusting. As her task took her past Lord Franklin, the man gave the girl a flat-palmed slap on the bottom. Lucille dropped the feather duster and let out a startled shriek.

"No, no, no," Lord Franklin said, "Completely wrong. Absolutely wrong. Nobody's going to believe that."

"Will they not, my lord?" the girl said. All traces of distress vanished from her voice in an instant.

"You're still overselling it, girl," Lord Franklin explained, "You need to keep it subtle. None of this squawking like a parrot. Keep your reaction in the face, eyes, and shoulders. Now try it again." There was the sound of fingers snapping, then a momentary pause. "That's better," Lord Franklin said, "Work on it, girl. You'll get the hang of it in time."

"I shall practice in a mirror every night, my lord!" Lucille declared enthusiastically.

"No, not in a mirror," Lord Franklin said, "That's a terrible habit to be in. You see, when you practice in front of a mirror, it trains the mind to..."

Hobart closed the door to the balcony behind him, and the conversation dropped away to inaudibility. Hobart sighed and made his way to the edge of the balcony. He needed to be away from his father's paranoid machinations for a little while.

Hobart drew in a deep breath and released it, letting his tensions loosen. The sun had long since vanished behind the Mountains of Dawn to the west, but it would not truly be evening for a few hours yet. The most relaxing time of day. Hobart cast his vision across the scene below. The city lay before him, spread out across the mountain slope, like a well-ordered tapestry of wrought iron and brick.

Unlike other cities throughout Aurora, which had grown organically through generations-long cycles of growth and decline, the Capitol had been constructed expressly for its function as an administrative centre. Its design was evident everywhere one looked, from the orderly grid-like streets, to the long promenade before the Dawn Palace, to the administrative buildings conveniently circling the palace itself. Planning for the Capitol had begun shortly after the Founding, and even now, nearly six hundred years after its completion, there was still no city in the world to equal it.

Hobart squinted. There was something off to the northeast.

Something floating against the afternoon sky, drawing ever closer. An airship. No doubt some lord or other is thinking to make a grand entrance. Hobart shrugged and returned his gaze to the cityscape below him.

"Which building, *Bazi?*" the helmsman asked.

Dagan's dark brown eyes scanned the cityscape below him. So this was the chief city of the brotherless? What a miserable little hovel. Dagan had seen cities twice as large as this pitiful shanty along the Illyrian coast! "There," Dagan pointed to a large sprawling building with six towers, each one flying the green-and-gold banner of the Brotherless Army, "That must be the one right there. Bring us right above it."

"I shall do so, *Bazi,*" the helmsman responded.

As the ship changed course, Dagan left the bridge and approached the chamber where the *Môlsôde* sat in quiet reflection. Dagan could feel his heart racing with excitement as he reached out a trembling hand to knock on the steel door. He had only tapped twice when the door opened suddenly.

Dagan shrank back in shock and awe at the man who appeared in the doorway. He was neither so tall as to be burdened by heavy bones nor so small as to be unimposing. His compact muscles, honed and refined by years of training into a work of art, were visible beneath his uniform. But what stood out the most, were the man's eyes: deep brown, almost black, with the calm air of wisdom that could only be achieved by years and years of introspection and contemplation. This was the *Þôzi uimôlsôde,* the leader of the Death Squad.

"The time of battle draws near," Dagan said, trying to remain calm and dignified in the face of such perfection, "Ready yourselves and come to the loading area."

The Þôzi uimôlsôde nodded, "We come, *Balû.*"

Dagan hastily made his way down to the cargo hold, where the rest of the crew was preparing. Their orders had been opened as soon as they crossed over the *Sazolgari* at Longview, and the entire crew knew their task now. Some were lowering the cargo ramp. Others manhandled the two heavy field guns into position. Still others checked the two long, thick ropes hanging from a heavy beam above the ramp. Dagan checked all of it personally—everything needed to be perfect.

After a minute, the *Môlsôde* arrived, filing down the ladder one after the other with a precise rhythm. They all wore the same uniform as the rest of the soldiers, red tunics and brown trousers, the colors of Hadvar, but each one also wore a black band about his forehead. The mark of the Death Squad. Their weapons also spoke of their rank; they carried powerful steel-bowed arbalests, quieter than rifles, and with deadly steel bolts that could be retrieved after firing. Many of their number also carried small explosive charges on great belts slung over their shoulders. They were the finest soldiers in all the world.

"*Bari,*" Dagan addressed the *Môlsôde.* It was a strange sensation; Dagan was significantly inferior to them, but in the present circumstances, exceptions were made, "Yours shall be the honor of striking the first blow in the final conquest of the *Sazodvar.*" Dagan tried not to sneer at the name. *The Far Eastern Realms?* Bah! If he had his way this entire wretched land would be plunged into the ocean, never to rise again.

"In a few moments," Dagan continued, "our guns shall breach the walls of the building you see before you," The orders had named it a palace, but Dagan had seen mud huts built with more majesty, "Then you shall enter and slay as much of the leadership of the *Sazodvar* as can be found. In this way, confusion shall be sown among the upper echelons of the enemy, and when the full force of our invasion arrives, not even their wicked airships will be able to hold back our great crusade!"

Dagan pounded his chest with his right hand, and thrust it into the air, "Earth and blood!" The *Môlsôde* matched his salute, "*Earth and blood!*"

The *Môlsôde* stepped aside, and the two field guns moved into place. At Dagan's signal, the operators fired simultaneously. The roof of the palace burst open in two places. The sound of the explosion echoed back from the distant mountains. Barely a moment later, the deck pitched violently as the airship swooped over the first breach.

As soon as the ship was low enough, Dagan tossed one of the ropes into the breach. The heavy weight at the bottom of the rope landed on the floor of some upper corridor, pulling the rope tight. With that all set, Dagan stepped aside, and the *Môlsôde* came forward. One after the other, they slipped down the rope and into the headquarters of the brotherless to begin their glorious mission!

As soon as the last one was clear, one of Dagan's men untied the rope from its beam above the cargo ramp, and it dropped away. Dagan could not stop to gape in awe; there was yet another part to their mission. The ship pitched again, and Dagan found himself overlooking the other breach. As the ship came into position above the hole, Dagan noticed someone staring out of it—a local woman, dressed in a long black skirt with a white apron and with a small white cap holding her hair back. Some high lady no doubt—these brotherless clearly didn't know the making of silk, and thus could not properly clothe their women. It really was almost pitiable. Almost.

The woman stared dumbstruck for a moment, then let out a terrific shriek. Dagan drew his sidearm and placed a single bullet in the woman's head, cutting off her cries instantly. Dagan shrugged and slipped his pistol back into its holster. It wasn't as if she were anyone important. Just another wretched brotherless sow with the same pale cooked-chicken skin as that assassin.

As if he had summoned her by his thoughts, the assassin appeared at Dagan's side. She was part of the mission as well; the orders had mentioned her, though the particulars of her mission still remained hidden.

Dagan tossed the remaining rope down into the breach, "You know what you have to do, assassin."

The assassin gave Dagan one of her empty smiles. Her pond-scum eyes remained glazed with disinterest. She casually wrapped one leg around the rope and slipped down into the breach. Then she was gone. And good riddance to her!

As the rope dropped away and the cargo ramp closed, Dagan made for the ladder to return to the bridge. He was happy to finally see that blasted assassin off his ship. She had been disrespectful right from the very start, addressing everyone in the Superior Voice, and making light of their mission at every turn. No doubt her poisonous words had been responsible for young Paku's dangerous doubts.

As for young Paku, he was currently making his way back to Hadvar, with the message for the Elders explaining Dagan's actions. No doubt once that letter arrived, they would all be lauded as heroes, perhaps even offered a prime command during the coming invasion. There was much glory to be had!

As Dagan reached the bridge, a thought suddenly occurred to him: Paku was traveling on foot with the message, whereas the airship had just covered the equivalent of two moons of marching in under five hours. If Dagan and his crew returned to Hadvar now, they would arrive at least two months before Paku could deliver the explanation. That would not do at all.

By now, Paku would have melted away into the many ethnic Hadvari enclaves of Analeria; trying to find him with the airship would be dangerously impractical. There was nothing else for it, but to lie low somewhere for two months to give Paku enough time to deliver his message, and for the message to find its way to the right eyes...

"Where shall we go now, *Bazi?*" the helmsman asked.

Dagan considered for a moment. "The Samedvar," he said. He had always wanted to see what it was like down there, "By way of the Southern Gap. And not too fast. We need to conserve our fuel."

"I shall do so, *Bazi.*" the helmsman said. The airship pitched and turned south.

High Admiral the Lord Cecil Robert Hanscom stalked through the Dawn Palace with murder in his eyes. This week had been absolutely dreadful!

It was that no-good son of his! William Travis Hanscom, scion to the lordship of the North Vale, had been carousing with the most awful sort of low-born scum. His nights were spent in alehouses, bordellos, and gambling dens, and that wasn't counting those many times he had been thrown out on his arse to sleep off his stupor in some rubbish-choked alley.

But the worst part was that he had found himself in trouble with the local magistrates. In the past week since being dismissed from the *Dawn Spear,* William had been involved in no fewer than six different incidents. It was never anything especially serious of course—some prostitute brutalised here, a few thugs murdered there—nothing that could get the family in real trouble, like treason or espionage; but still, it was a stain on the Hanscom family name that had to be securely buried beneath thick layers of bribes, concessions, and flattery.

Lord Hanscom's entire week had been consumed with just that sort of political damage control. He had to smooth over the feathers of everyone with a grievance against William. The boy himself would be quietly slipping onto a train back to Norvell at first light where he would remain locked away in the family estate until such time as he mended his ways. *Perhaps I should have sent him to the* Dreadnought? *Like Wingate did with his boy?* Lord Hanscom considered... *No, he likely would have felt well at home there.*

Lord Hanscom's thoughts came back to the exercises. *My exercises!* He checked his chronometer. 17:04... They should be about two-thirds of the way through the day's exercises right now. The last exercise was scheduled to conclude at 22:00. *I should be there right now!* Lord Hanscom fumed, *Not playing custodian to my son's wretched antics!* He only hoped that idiot Bundwick was up to the task of managing the entire ordeal.

As Lord Hanscom turned a corner, he noted a hanging tapestry woven as a map of Aurora and Analeria. He stopped for a moment to consider the map; there were a number of glaring inaccuracies in it, but it served well enough as an artistic representation. With his mind's eye, Lord Hanscom drew up armies and launched them against each other, deftly striking and manoeuvring just so, until Hadvar was defeated once and for all.

That had been his grand plan for final victory. Lord Hanscom had spent the better part of a decade crafting it. He would open with a massive attack in the Eastern Basin, to draw the focus of the ginks. The Auroran ground troops would then withdraw to a preconstructed line of defence-in-depth fortifications on the border hills beyond Jingyu and Fasat, scorching the earth behind them as they withdrew. While Hadvar threw itself against the defensive line as they always did, the ARAF would deliver a massive army directly behind the ginks—an unprecedented use of air power!

With an army to the rear cutting off their supply lines, the ginks would be forced to fall back to meet this new threat, at which point, Auroran reserves augmented by the Analerian Irregulars would spring into action, encircling and destroying the entire gink army. It would have secured victory against Hadvar, proved that airships were more than just mobile artillery platforms, and made Lord Hanscom into a national hero overnight! It was practically a work of art—a masterpiece!

And then the politicians came along and buggered it all up. Hanscom snorted. This confounded peace of theirs had poured cold water over all of his grand designs. *It was the Queen,* he thought, *that previous Queen, suddenly growing a conscience and bending over backwards to make peace with the ginks!* She had given away all their hard-won territory beyond the Green River Armistice Line, and hadn't even made an attempt to secure the Analerian Disputed Zone in return. Any more concessions, and it would have been a surrender! Lord Hanscom didn't know whose idea it had been to assassinate the meddling little bitch, but if he ever found out, he would give the man a bloody medal!

They even made me cancel the test! Lord Hanscom thought. He had been looking forward to that field test of those new ship-killer shells he had commissioned. They were a backup plan of course, but if the ginks ever managed to put together a fleet of their own, it would not do to be caught unprepared. But with the end of major combat operations, the test became impolitic, so all the preparations had to be cancelled and all the equipment returned to Newton and Sons. Those new shells would probably spend the next fifty years or so gathering dust in a warehouse in Marburg, until some bean-counter decided to melt them down for scrap. What a waste.

There was a loud noise from above, and Lord Hanscom jumped; he had been behind a desk for the past two decades but knew the sound of artillery when he heard it. Lord Hanscom drew his sidearm and rushed to find the stairs. Something was afoot!

Lord Hanscom was only two flights up when he heard a woman scream. A moment later, the sound of a gunshot echoed through the palace. He picked up his pace, barely pausing to shove some clumsy servant girl out of his way.

When Lord Hanscom reached the top floor of the palace, he saw a gaping hole blown in the roof. The floor of the hallway was now strewn with rubble, and there was a dark smear on the marble tiles that was almost certainly blood. No doubt, this was the work of the artillery explosion that he had heard from below!

He heard something else as well: the sound of an airship. Hanscom hadn't noted it before; airships were always coming and going in the Capitol; they were practically beneath notice. He stepped over the rubble to peer out of the hole in the wall and ceiling. Sure enough, an airship was slowly receding into the distance. It looked like an older civilian model. Was this a coup?

Lord Hanscom dashed back into the stairwell. Whatever was going on, there would need to be an organised response to it! *And who better to lead it than me?*

Lord Hanscom only got one floor down when he stopped. A trio of steel crossbow bolts just barely missed his chest! He ducked against the wall beside the opening of the stairwell and flicked off the safety lock on his sidearm. *So, it is a coup after all!*

Hanscom fished out his pocket watch and ripped out the portrait of his second wife to reveal a small circular mirror. Hanscom used the mirror in concert with another mirror in the hallway beyond to get a good look at what he was facing. Five men with crossbows were coming up the hallway. And that idiot serving girl from before! What the bloody hell was she doing just wandering about in the open? Why wasn't she hiding? *Bloody civilians!*

With a frustrated sigh, Hanscom leaped out of cover, firing wildly at the men with crossbows, who immediately took cover behind pillars and tables. *Professional soldiers, no doubt.* The servant shrieked, as Lord Hanscom careened into her and dragged the girl into cover behind another pillar.

Lord Hanscom switched the magazine in his sidearm. He had gotten a good enough look at those troops to recognise their uniforms—the red and brown of Hadvar. And *Môlsôde,* judging by their crossbows and black headbands. Hadvar had used an airship to deliver one of their Death Squads.

This is perfect!

Lord Hanscom could barely keep the grin off his face. This attack would certainly spell the end of that wretched peace treaty. Not only that, but the ginks had used airships to deliver troops directly into combat, exactly as Lord Hanscom planned to do in his grand strategy; this entire attack could be presented as a proof of concept. Additionally, now that the ginks had gotten their hands on some airships of their own, that would allow him to restart the ship-killer shell tests. Everything was falling into place!

Lord Hanscom made ready to return fire. Several crossbow bolts whizzed past, implanting in the marble columns behind him. Lord Hanscom counted the bolts: a cadence of three. Only three of them firing to keep him in cover, while the other two held their fire until there was a clear killshot—standard *Môlsôde* small-engagement doctrine. There was a counter for this sort of tactic; how did it go again? Lord Hanscom turned to return fire.

Something struck him from behind!

Lord Hanscom tried to shout, but the wind was knocked out of him, and all that came out was a grunt. Pain blossomed forth from of his back; first small, like an itch, and then burning, as though his back were being torn apart by a wild beast! He tried to reach back over his shoulder to feel what had struck him, and his fingers found blood.

Lord Hanscom's legs buckled, and he collapsed against the column. He saw the serving girl standing over him. She was holding a bloody stiletto knife in a fluid grip that no ordinary servant could imitate. She smirked down at him, thin lips in a smile that never touched her cold blue-green eyes.

The assassin leaned down and gently wiped the blade against Lord Hanscom's uniform. A few strands of loose red hair slipped out of her white linen cap to dangle in his face. He tried to strangle the bitch, but he couldn't lift his arms. He coughed, and a small droplet of blood dribbled out of his lips. His fingertips were growing cold.

The assassin slipped the stiletto back up her sleeve and strolled carelessly out into the hallway. The crossbow bolts had stopped flying.

Chapter XIX

Crisis and Opportunity

T HE Great Hall of the Dawn Palace was likely the only interior location where it was safe to talk. It was much too vast, and its acoustics were too poor to be effectively bugged, and given that it was a public location anyway, there was little point in trying.

Two figures, a man and a woman, wandered about the otherwise deserted hall. Their low words mingled with the sounds of footsteps and the swishing of the woman's silk skirts on the marble tiles and echoed through the columns to shroud their conversation.

"Alright," Harold Barnes said, consulting a small notebook, "again from the beginning."

"The border was originally established along the River Palne," Queen Cassandra recited, "but now that the Upper Palne has changed course to the north, Lord Petras has extended his claim to include this new area. Lord Waldemar, on the other hand, insists that the area remains his by right. It is a question of which border is to be respected: the original course of the river, or the new."

"Correct," Harold nodded, "Lord Waldemar's argument?"

"Lord Waldemar's claim rests on a small farming village that has been under his administration since before the Founding. However, with the changing of the river's course, the village has fallen to famine, and many of the peasants have departed."

"And Lord Petras's argument?"

"Lord Petras's claim rests on the wording of the Treaty of the Palne between the two provinces which predates the Founding by nearly a century. The treaty establishes the River Palne as the border between the realms of Lord Petras and Lord Waldemar. If the new course is chosen as the border, Petras stands to capture a number of recently discovered mineral deposits in the area, which he likely intends to licence to the Southern Mining Cartel."

"All correct," Harold said and closed the notebook, "How do you intend to proceed?"

"I don't know," Cassandra shrugged, "I suppose it shall, as always, come down to which party can most eloquently present their case."

"By which you mean manipulate you." Harold said with a hint of disapproval.

"All the lords do it," Cassandra said, "Even Wingate, that stolid old stick-in-the-mud. Do you remember the night I raised Captain Bowman? Wingate quite obviously wanted to make sure that the man went to the *Dreadnought* as opposed to any other ship in the fleet." Cassandra giggled lightly, "It was adorable to watch!"

"What about my Lord Stolos?" Harold posed, "He's not tried to manipulate you thus far. Not for his own interests at least."

"Stolos is a *boy*," Cassandra rolled her eyes. It felt odd saying such things about a man who was nearly a decade her senior, but it was the truth, "He'll grow up soon enough, and when he does, he'll play the game just like the rest of us. To tell the truth, the one I'm really concerned about is Franklin's boy."

"Hobart Aloysius?"

"Indeed," Cassandra said, "He's the heir to his father's network of spies. Old Barnabas Obadiah is playing up the senility act as expected, but his son has not been making his presence felt at court. There's obviously some—"

A loud noise echoed through the palace.

"What was that?" Cassandra looked about.

"It sounded like it came from one of the upper levels," Harold said.

"Was it a crash?" Cassandra suggested, "I thought I heard an airship a moment ago."

"I don't think so," Harold said, "Majesty, I think it would be prudent if we moved you to the safe room."

"I concur," Cassandra nodded, and the two of them calmly started towards the back of The Great Hall. It was probably nothing serious, but it was always the sensible thing to take precautions.

Just before they reached the doorway to the stairwell at the back of the hall, a stream of red-and-brown-clad figures came barreling down the stairs. Before Cassandra could react, Harold whipped out his pistol and fired three quick shots into the stairwell, then threw his arm around her waist and dragged her behind a marble column. Cassandra put up no resistance; she knew better than to protest when someone was busy saving her life.

"Blast," Harold said calmly, "Stairwells are blocked. The safe room's no good."

"Who are those people?" Cassandra demanded, trying not to sound panicked.

"Hadvari," Harold said, "I don't know how they got here, but there's no mistaking those uniforms." He leaned out from behind the pillar and fired five more shots at the soldiers taking cover in the stairwell. "Majesty," Harold said as he changed magazines, "I recommend we move at once."

"Agreed," Cassandra said, gathering her skirts into her fist, and kicking off her fine satin slippers. The marble tiles were cold on her bare feet, but at least now she could run.

At a nod from Harold, the two of them dashed out from behind the pillar. Harold fired back at the stairwell, keeping the Hadvari soldiers pinned in cover for as long as possible while the two of them put as much distance between themselves and the soldiers as possible. Finally, Harold's magazine ran dry, just as they slipped into a side corridor.

Near the end of the side corridor, Harold stopped, "There's an escape passage in the Southern Audience Chamber," he said as he ran his fingers across the wood-paneled wall, "I'm going to buy you some time."

"What are you doing?" Cassandra asked.

"There's a dead-end passage behind this panel," Harold said as he pulled one of the wall panels back to reveal a great black maw of darkness, "It should draw a few of them away from you."

"Harold, you'll be trapped!" Cassandra said, "They'll kill you!"

"The first eight of them won't," Harold said grimly as he slipped his final magazine into his pistol, "Get moving, Majesty."

Cassandra nodded, "Good luck, Harold." She ducked around the corner, just moments before hearing Barnes fire a single shot. A few seconds later, she heard another shot. Then another faintly. And another...

Cassandra dearly hoped he would find a way to survive. Howard Barnes had been her close confidant ever since her fifteenth year. He was one of those rare creatures, both keenly intelligent, and unimpeachably loyal. He also managed a vast network of informants and spies, nearly as large as the legendary Franklin spy network. If he died, he would be all but impossible to replace.

He'll make it, Cassandra told herself firmly, *The real question is, will I?*

Cassandra carried no weapons on her person. There had never been a need, the royal bodyguards were considered protection enough. *Except when I dismiss them in order to confer with Harold in secret,* Cassandra thought furiously. Well, it was no good castigating herself over what-ifs and maybes right now. Once she made it to the Southern Audience Chamber, everything would be alright.

Cassandra rounded the last corner and collided with a serving maid.

Hobart Aloysius Franklin dove out of the way just in time to avoid being crushed under a chunk of stone. He saw the airship moving in closer, and adjusted his spectacles to see more clearly. A stream of men clad in the red-and-brown of Hadvar slipped out of the ship and into the upper levels of the Dawn Palace. Hobart burst through the balcony door and shouted, "Father!"

"What's that racket outside?" Lord Franklin demanded.

"An attack!" Hobart said, as clearly as he could with adrenaline surging through his veins, "Hadvar is attacking the palace!"

"Don't be sensational, boy!" Lord Franklin snapped and started toward the balcony door, "There are no ginks this side of the Mountains of Dawn. It's likely just an accident."

"Father, listen to me," Hobart protested, "We need to get to the lower levels at once!"

"Not before I get a look at this 'attack' of yours," Lord Franklin said, "Girl, put the kettle on, and brew me up a nice Dalton Gold."

"Yes, my lord," Lucille curtsied and scurried into a side chamber.

"Now then, let's see what's gotten you so worked up," Lord Franklin shoved Hobart aside and stepped out onto the balcony.

Hobart followed his lord father out onto the balcony. "Right up there," he said, pointing to where the airship was still floating above the palace, "That's it! Now do you believe me?"

"I believe there's been an *accident,*" Lord Franklin said, "Some clumsy first-time pilot come too close to the Palace and grazing the stonework perhaps."

"I'm telling you, there were soldiers!" Hobart insisted, "Hadvari soldiers! They took a rope from the ship and—"

"I've had just about enough of your nonsense, boy!" Lord Franklin started back inside, "I'll hear no more of this. Now, you will present yourself at Her Majesty's audience this evening, and you will at least make an effort to—"

Before Lord Franklin could finish, a single crossbow bolt whistled through the door, took him in the eye, and exited out the back of his skull to impact with an iron thud in the doorframe behind him.

Hobart ducked out of sight of the door. He had been right; the Hadvari were really here to kill everyone in the Dawn Palace! What was he going to do?

Hobart's racing thoughts were shattered by a horrible shriek from inside the chamber. *Lucille!* Hobart peeked around the corner; the poor girl was staring in stark horror at Lord Franklin's body crumpled in a heap on the floor!

"Shhh!" Hobart hushed the girl frantically, "Don't make a sound, or they'll come back and finish us off!"

"B-but," The girl stammered, "But my Lord Franklin! He's... They..."

"Calm down!" Hobart stepped gingerly over his father's corpse, "Calm down!"

"What are we going to do?" Lucille had finally brought her voice down to a whisper.

"I'll figure something out," Hobart said quickly, "Something..."

Hobart knelt down over his father. He remembered hearing his father mention that he always kept a pistol on his person, just in case. But where exactly did he keep it? As he rifled through his father's garments, Hobart's fingers brushed against his skin. His body was still warm. *Oh god!*

A finger twitched, and Hobart almost jumped out of his skin! *Is he still aware? How long does it usually take for someone to... to...* Hobart glanced up. His father's right eye socket was a ruined mass of blood and bone, with a line of red dribbling out of it across an empty expression. Hobart felt bile rising in his throat and quickly looked away to keep from vomiting.

Finally, Hobart felt the pistol in one of his father's back pockets. Quickly, he fished the weapon out and turned it over in his hand. It was a very fine instrument; graceful engravings decorated the barrel, and the handle looked to be plated with silver. Hobart stood up, terribly relieved to be away from his father's body.

"Right then," Hobart turned back to Lucille, "Hide yourself," He gestured to a broom closet with the pistol, "I'll fetch you out again once it's safe." Lucille nodded and scurried into the closet. Hobart stepped confidently out into the hallway. *I'm Lord Franklin now.*

Two more bodies lay in the corridor directly outside the door—a pair of unlucky servants—and Hobart's confidence evaporated. *Dammit, What the bloody hell am I even doing?!* He raised the pistol to eye-level and pointed it down the hallway, then in the other direction. Which way had the killers gone? He hadn't actually seen anything. The two bodies were both facing towards the left... but had they been shot in the back or in the front? Maybe their killers were still about? Lurking behind pillars perhaps? Or beneath the tapestries?

Hobart started running. He didn't know where he was going. He didn't know where he *should* go! He had heard his father mention hidden passages that honeycombed the palace, but he had lever learned where any of them were located. His lord father had kept most of his secrets locked away inside his head. *And now they're all gone!*

After about a minute at a full sprint, Hobart's lungs began to burn as exhaustion caught up with him. He trotted to a stop, doubled over, hands planted on his knees, and heaved for breath. Blast it all! He wasn't built for all this exertion, dashing hither and thither like a madman without the faintest idea of where to go or what to do once he got there.

Suddenly, Hobart heard a sound echoing through the corridor. Footsteps! Multiple sets! Heavy ones too; boots most likely! And they were beating a quick pace! The Hadvari troops were doubling back, coming for him! Hobart quickly turned and started running the other way, but stopped in his tracks when he heard the selfsame sound coming from the other direction!

I'm trapped!

Hobart looked about in a panic. There were no doorways nearby, nor any sufficiently large windows from which to make a desperate leap. There was a tapestry, but it hung much too close to the wall for Hobart to conceal himself behind it. A few more bodies lay strewn about the corridor, a group of low-level bureaucrats who had clearly been transporting a set of ledgers when they had been set upon. Each one bore large jagged wounds through the neck, which were leaking out into red puddles on the floor.

Surely one more body won't be noticed.

Swallowing his pride and revulsion, Hobart dropped onto his hands and knees and lowered his head onto the slick floor. It was still warm. *Oh god, don't think about it!* He went limp just moments before a squad of red-and-brown uniformed troops barreled around the corner with crossbows at the ready. Hobart started taking slow shallow breaths, so as not to be betrayed by a rising chest or stomach. *Please don't let them notice me!*

The footfalls slowed and finally stopped. Hobart dared not look up, but he could hear the Hadvari troops. They exchanged several sentences of their nonsense words, and then both parties left by the same way they had come. None had noticed him. Hobart's ruse had worked. He was still alive. *For the moment...*

Hobart waited for almost a minute after the last soldier slipped behind the corner before finally getting to his feet. He tried to dab the blood out of his face with his sleeve, but stopped when he noticed that his sleeve was just as soaked.

Now what?

The Southern Audience Chamber! Of course, that was where one of the hidden passages was! He could remember his lord father talking about a secret stairwell leading from the Southern Audience Chamber down to the rear stables. It was the perfect emergency escape route!

Hobart looked about to get his bearings. The Dawn Palace was large, but he knew it well enough to puzzle out the way to the Southern Audience Chamber. He started off at a brisk pace, careful not to make too much noise, lest the Hadvari troops come back to finish their work.

Finally, Hobart cautiously rounded the last corner. The great double doors to the Southern Audience Chamber were right at the end of the hallway. The doors were ajar. Hobart glanced down at the floor and saw a trail of blood leading to the doors. Someone was wounded in there. But were they friend or foe? Hobart raised his pistol and stalked silently towards the door.

Hobart popped his head in to steal a quick glance. There was only one person in the room. A woman lay face-down on the floor. Unmoving. Hobart ducked through the door, closed it behind him as softly as he could manage, and crossed to get a closer look at the body in the middle of the chamber.

The dead woman wore a dress of stunning violet silk, now marred by a single puncture wound in the back that leaked blood. No doubt that had been the source of the blood trail in the corridor outside. One of her shoes had come off and was lying between her and the doorway. The woman's long brown hair splayed all about her like a mop. But the thing that caught Hobart's attention was the green-and-gold sash that the woman wore.

The Queen!

If Hobart needed any more confirmation, he noticed a small circlet of wrought gold studded with emeralds lying on the floor a few feet away from the body. A desperate hand reached out towards the crown, falling just a few inches short. There could be no doubt. The Queen was dead!

Overcome with horror, Hobart collapsed to his knees. It would be the end of Aurora for certain. Civilisation was over; the future was red and brown. *All I can do now is save my own skin.*

Hobart quickly looked about the chamber. There had to be an escape hatch somewhere. His father had said so, and the fact that the Queen had tried to make her escape this way proved it. But where was it? Behind one of the tapestries perhaps? Or hidden under the throne? Perhaps one of the columns had been hollowed out and fitted with a ladder? Hobart ducked behind the tapestries and began knocking on the walls, listening carefully for the telltale resonance of a hollow space.

Hobart heard a noise from the corridor. Someone was running. *More Hadvari coming to finish the job.* Just one set of footsteps though? Perhaps he could take this one himself! Hobart drew his pistol and peeked through a gap in the tapestries. *Vengeance for Her Majesty!*

The doors opened ever so slightly, and in slipped the last person Hobart had expected to see.

"Percy!" Hobart emerged from behind the tapestry.

"Bart!" Lord Stolos exclaimed, and quickly holstered his own pistol, "What happened to you? Your face!"

"It's alright," Hobart said, snatching up a loose corner of the tapestry and giving his face a few quick swipes to clean off the blood, "I'm alright. What about you?"

"About as well as can be expected, given the circumstances," Lord Stolos said, "It's good to see that you're still safe."

"Percy, do you have any idea what the bloody hell is going on here?"

"Only bits and pieces, I'm afraid," Stolos said, "There was some sort of commotion on one of the upper floors, and then some Hadvari troops came in and started shooting everyone they came across. I just barely evaded them. And then I—" Stolos looked down and noticed the Queen's body on the floor. "Well now, that *is* a tragedy," he remarked in an oddly unperturbed voice.

"They got my father as well," Hobart said.

"I'm terribly sorry, Bart," Stolos said softly, "I suppose that makes *you* Lord Franklin now."

"I suppose it does," Hobart nodded grimly, "Do you know if they got anyone else?"

"I can't be certain," Stolos said, "There were a good number of lords in court today. Lords Dalton, Siebruck, Petras, and Waldemar I know are dead. Downing, Mayfax, and Corwyn managed to make it to the safe room below the palace, so they should be secure for the moment. Last I saw of Lord Harlocke, he was barricading himself in the armoury with Lord Kalstrom and a number of servants. That only leaves Lords Mantussian, Blackpool, Alaban, Norbury, Yarwick, and Hanscom still unaccounted for."

That's five lords already dead, Hobart considered, *Five at least, as well as Her Majesty.*

"Right then, we'd better get moving." Hobart nodded, bringing himself back into the moment, "There's a hidden escape hatch in this room leading down to the stables. We can escape that way, but first we must find the entrance."

"Are you crazy?" Stolos caught Hobart's wrist in a firm grip, "We can't leave now!"

"Percy, there is a Hadvari Death Squad in the palace," Hobart said, "We have to get to safety."

"Bart, this is perfect!" Stolos whispered excitedly, "This is exactly the situation we can use."

Perfect? Hobart could barely believe his ears! *Five lords are already dead, and this is perfect?* What sort of madness was Stolos cooking up this time? "Are you suggesting that we stay here?" Hobart ventured warily.

"Exactly," Stolos said, "Stay, fight, lead."

"But the palace is in chaos," Hobart protested.

"That's what makes this the perfect time," Stolos said excitedly, "You know, the Illyrians only have one word for *crisis* and *opportunity.*"

"They also only have one word for *enemy* and *foreigner,* " Hobart snapped, "And it's *enemy!*"

"Bart! *Bart!*" Stolos grasped Hobart's shoulders firmly with both hands, "Look at me. *Look at me!*"

Hobart locked eyes with Lord Perseus Hiram Stolos. His friend was mad! Completely mad! And yet, there was something about that look in his eyes, Burning with ambition and zeal, but also with a keen intelligence and insight. Maybe... Just maybe...

"I have a plan," Stolos said, "We're both armed, we both know this palace inside and out, and the enemy has lost the element of surprise. We can do this. I know we can. But I need you to do exactly as I say."

Hobart considered for a moment. This must be the very sort of *mad scheme* that his father had been warning him about. If his father were here, he would doubtless tell him to make his escape and never look back. *Well, too bloody bad for him,* Hobart thought, *He's dead, and I'm not!* "Alright Percy," Hobart nodded, "I'm game."

"Good," Stolos grinned, "Now listen carefully..."

"Captain," Hamilton announced, "we're coming up on the Capitol now."

Paul merely grunted in acknowledgment. His eyes were fixed on the terrain below. The *Dreadnought* had been flying at top speed for nearly five hours now, and Paul had not once had to ask for directions from Hamilton. However that would not last for much longer. Dusk was less than an hour away, and tonight was the new moon. Paul knew the lay of the land well enough, but without any moonlight, he would need to rely almost completely on the navi.

So Vaughn had been right after all.

Paul glanced at Vaughn from across the bridge. The woman was standing at the back of the bridge, inspecting the newly installed bulkhead. Barlowe had not done a very enthusiastic job; those rivets would need to be redone in about six weeks or so, likely sooner. Barlowe himself had vanished once his work was done, and Paul was more than happy to be rid of the slacker.

Paul's gaze swept over to the gunboard. Wolfram was back at the controls, but there was something off about him. He seemed... angrier. More determined. *He did just lose his best friend,* Paul reminded himself. Out of all the crew, Wolfram had probably taken Hakefeldt's death the hardest. *He's out for blood.* That could be a good thing. Or not. Anger was a great source of motivation, but it could also make you sloppy.

As the *Dreadnought* climbed up behind the last spur of the mountains, Paul returned his attention to the city emerging from behind the last jagged peaks. The entire bridge crew had been anticipating this moment for the past five hours, dreading what they might find. The rogue airship had turned south as soon as it cleared the Gates of Dawn; it hadn't taken too much thought to figure out where it was headed.

The ship crested the final ridge, and the Capitol came into view. Paul instantly set about scanning the cityscape for the rogue airship. *Alright, you bastard, where are you hiding?* He looked and looked... nothing.

Had he been wrong? Maybe the rogue airship had been headed somewhere else. Newport or Marburg maybe? Had she seen the *Dreadnought* following her and doubled back to evade them? *Dammit, where the hell are you?*

"Captain," Wolfram called out from his position at the gun controls, "I see something!"

"Where?" Paul looked about, "I don't see anything."

"There," Wolfram pointed, "The Dawn Palace. There's been a breach in the top floor."

Paul turned his gaze upon the sprawling palace complex at the center of the city. Sure enough, a gaping hole had been blown in the top level. *Two* holes in fact, Paul saw as the *Dreadnought* circled around the palace.

"Perhaps it's a coup d'etat?" Vaughn said. Paul almost jumped; he hadn't noticed the woman making her way to the front of the bridge.

So our rogue airship was here after all, Paul concluded, *But where did they go?*

"Captain," Wagner called out from the radio console, "I'm getting a transmission from the Capitol Aerodrome Control. They are advising us that, due to a state of emergency, all air traffic within fifty klicks of the Capitol has been suspended until further notice. They are ordering us to come to ground at once."

Paul was about to dictate a long list of curses for Wagner to send back to those idiots in the control-tower, when he realized, *Of course, they can tell us what happened.* "Tell 'em we're with the Fleet," Paul ordered, "and see if they can tell us what happened here."

"Aye, sir," Wagner nodded.

While the boy busied himself relaying the message, Paul circled the *Dreadnought* around the palace one more time to get a better look at the situation. The two holes looked like the only significant physical damage. There wasn't any smoke or signs of internal collapse. When they came in view of the front of the Palace, he saw a crowd of small figures clustered around the great doors—local police by the look of it. They appeared to be shooting into the palace.

"Fighting on the ground," Vaughn said, "Definitely a coup of some sort."

"Captain," Wagner called, "Getting a response."

"Good," Paul called back, "Let's hear it."

"Control reports," Wagner began, "that an unidentified civilian airship opened fire upon the palace and... and apparently delivered some soldiers into the palace."

"Hadvar!" Wolfram burst out.

"Calm down, guns," Paul snapped.

"That's who's in the Palace!" Wolfram continued, "You said it yourself—the airship was carrying field guns. Well, only Hadvari guns are small enough to fit inside a civilian freighter. They must have opened the breaches in the palace with their guns and dropped one of their *Môlsôde* Death Squads inside. This is no coup. It's a decapitation strike!"

"A prelude to an invasion," Vaughn said darkly.

Paul stopped to think. If they were right and this truly was the opening shot of a new war, then what should they do? Should they continue with their mission? Stay and help in whatever way they can? Return to the Gates of Dawn and brace for the inevitable invasion? What was the proper course of action in a situation like this?

"Sparks," Paul said after a short pause, "Did Control say what direction the enemy airship went after it attacked?"

"I'll ask them, Captain," Wagner said and began tapping his message into the radio. A minute or so later, he came back with the response, "South-by-west Captain, bearing one-nine-five. About an hour ago."

"They're making for the Southern Gap," Paul said, "We can still catch them."

"Wait, we're not stopping to help?" Wagner

"We don't have a choice," Paul snapped, "Every second we waste, that airship gets farther and farther away."

"But there's still fighting going on right here," Wagner insisted, "We have to do something to help! What if the Queen is in trouble?"

Paul hesitated for a moment. *The Queen!* He hadn't thought of that. *Dammit, I'm probably the least experienced person on the whole ship! I shouldn't be the one making these important decisions!*

He glanced over at Wolfram; leaning over the gunboard with his fingers at the ready. The kid was clearly itching to kill something, preferably something Hadvari. Paul's eyes darted over to Hamilton who was standing over the map table, and judging by the tension in his shoulders, trying desperately not to look anywhere else. Neither of those kids would have anything useful to add. Paul wondered what kind of advice Lieutenant Hakefeldt might have given in this situation. His mind was beginning to race, *What if I screw this one up too?*

"No. The Captain is correct."

Paul looked up. It was Vaughn who had spoken. She was standing in front of the window, looking down at the scene below with her hands clasped firmly behind her. Her expression was unreadable. *She agrees with me?* Paul wondered, *Why?*

Vaughn continued, "We are not equipped to render assistance. We have no shipboard infantry, nor any supplies to spare, and this area is too densely populated for us to provide fire support without risking collateral damage. We can do nothing to help here. In light of these circumstances, our original assignment must stand."

It was a pretty cold assessment, but Paul had to admit, it was accurate. *She's good at making the hard choices,* Paul recognized, *She'd make a better captain than me.* It was a sobering thought.

Paul was still mulling over the thought as he turned the ship south.

Lord Wingate paused only for a moment as the airship passed overhead. He didn't need to recognise the obsolete broadside-battery configuration of the guns; there was only one ship in the entire Fleet that wasn't at the exercises: the *Dreadnought*. She was headed south-by-west at what was probably all speed for her rickety old first-generation reactor.

Bowman! That upjumped conscript was supposed to be safely tucked away on customs duty at the Gates of Dawn. What in blazes was his ship doing this far south? Lord Wingate growled and spurred his mount back to a gallop; there had better be some answers when he reached the Capitol.

It wasn't his horse. Lord Wingate would have preferred a mount with a little more fire in it than this taciturn mare, but there had only been one horse in the baggage car of the express train. Lord Wingate had appropriated her when the train had been ordered to stop, leaving the baggage attendant with two five-crown pieces to compensate the beast's rightful owner. Ten crowns was probably ten times the true worth of the scraggly old nag, but it was always good to be in the habit of generosity.

Finally, the beast crested the last rise, and the Capitol came into view. Lord Wingate spurred his mount even faster. *Almost there old girl,* He gave his mount a reassuring pat on the neck, *Just a little farther and then you can rest.*

As he reached the gates of the city, a pair of men with rifles jogged to intercept him. Lord Wingate trotted the mare to a stop. In the dying light, these men looked more like municipal guardsmen than soldiers.

"The city is closed," on of the men announced, "No one is to enter or leave."

Closed? "On whose authority?" Lord Wingate demanded.

"Milord Stolos," the other man said, "There's been some trouble at the palace. His lordship is leading the defense of the city."

Defence of the city? "Defence against what?"

"Hadvar," the man said, "The ginks went and dropped themselves into the Dawn Palace. Can't let none of them escape now, can we?"

Lord Wingate looked up at the Dawn Palace. Sure enough, there were two gaping holes in the upper levels; those had certainly not been there the last time he was in the Capitol! And Hadvar? Here, on the other side of the Mountains of Dawn? It was unthinkable! *Everything is unthinkable until it happens.*

"What about the Queen?" Lord Wingate said, "Is there any word about Her Majesty?"

"We ain't been told nothing," the first man said, "Information's bein' kept tight."

I need to get in there! "I'm coming in." Lord Wingate said firmly.

"Nobody goes in or out," the soldiers raised their rifles in unison, "Now you just turn that nag around and go back the way you—"

"I am Admiral the Lord Orpheus Chester Wingate!" Lord Wingate bellowed, "Either you grant me entrance at once, or you shall have to explain yourselves to Lord Stolos himself."

The two men paled and lowered their rifles. "...Why didn't you just say as much M'lord!" One of the soldiers stepped aside, and his partner followed his example, "Go right on through."

Lord Wingate spurred his mount to a gallop once more. He wove through the narrow back streets towards the palace as fast as he dared; this sluggish beast wasn't nearly as dextrous as he was accustomed to, and this was no time to risk a fall.

Hadvari in the palace! Lord Wingate considered the news. This would almost certainly mean an end to the peace between Aurora and Hadvar. Barely four months, and already broken! More immediately, of course, there was the question of the Hadvari soldiers in the Dawn Palace. How many were they? Whom had they killed so far? What forces were in place to oppose them?

So much for Hanscom! Lord Wingate thought, recalling his original purpose for this mission. Lord Hanscom selling military hardware on the Analerian black market now seemed utterly trivial. *He'll get the justice that's due him,* Lord Wingate vowed, *but he'll have to wait for the moment.*

Finally, Lord Wingate reached the promenade leading to the Dawn Palace. He summoned one last burst of speed from his mount to cover this final stretch, and soon he was in Queen Helen's Square, trotting his mount to a well-deserved rest. He left the animal to water itself in the fountain at the centre of the unsettlingly empty square and proceeded to the entrance of the Dawn Palace where a small crowd of men with rifles were clustered about.

"Soldiers," Lord Wingate announced, "full report."

The men only stared. They were municipal guards, like the two men Lord Wingate had encountered outside the city, not soldiers. It was painfully evident by the way the carried their rifles that they were untrained with such weapons.

"Wingate!" said a strong voice from the other side of the crowd. Lord Wingate looked up to see Lord Stolos waving him over to his position, "What a stroke of luck. It's about time we got a professional on site."

"What's going on here, Stolos?" Lord Wingate asked, "Quickly now."

"It's Hadvar," Stolos said, "They blasted a hole in the roof, and dropped a squadron of troops into the palace." He glanced at his chronometer, "They've been killing everyone they come across for nearly five-and-thirty minutes now. You've caught us at the perfect moment. We're about to make our push inside."

"About time," Lord Wingate nodded, "And you're certain they're Hadvari? It's not a false-flag operation with stolen uniforms?"

"It's them alright," Lord Stolos assured, "I caught sight of them a few times, all brown skin and nonsense words. But they're deadly enough with those crossbows."

"Did you say *crossbows?*" Lord Wingate asked urgently. Lord Stolos nodded awkwardly, clearly not understanding the significance of that last bit of information. Crossbows. Only the *Môlsôde* used crossbows. *We're up against one of their Death Squads!*

"What about The Queen?" Lord Wingate asked, "Where is Her Majesty?"

Lord Stolos looked down, "I'm afraid I don't know. There were several audiences scheduled for today, so I know she was present at the time of the attack, as well as a number of other lords. But I cannot say any clearer at the moment."

Other lords? Lord Wingate raised an eyebrow, "*Which* other lords exactly?"

"Well," Lord Stolos said, "let me see... There was Dalton, Corwyn, Harlocke, Mantussian, Blackpool, Hanscom..."

Hanscom!

Not wasting another moment, Lord Wingate charged into the Palace with his pistol drawn! He was only faintly aware of the confused sounds of the men behind him, and of Lord Stolos clumsily exhorting them to follow after Lord Wingate. He didn't know if it was great courage or great foolishness that was driving him, and he frankly didn't care one way or the other. He had to find Hanscom, fast!

Through the Great Hall and up the stairs he ran, letting his sidearm lead the way, just like those lessons in the academy so many years ago. He stopped at every floor and glanced into the corridor beyond. More often than not, the hallways were littered with bodies of servants and bureaucrats, all caught in the throat by crossbow bolts. *Definitely the work of the Môlsôde.*

Finally, Lord Wingate rounded one last corner, and saw a man in a brilliant green-and-gold ARAF uniform slumped against a column. *Hanscom!* Lord Wingate quickly scanned the rest of the corridor, and finding no enemies in sight, he rushed to kneel beside the man. He lifted up Hascom's head. His face was blank, his eyes were sightless and half closed, his mouth was leaking spittle and blood, and when Lord Wingate removed his hand, Hanscom's head slumped forwards again.

If circumstances had been any different, Lord Wingate would have been celebrating the death of his bitter rival. But not like this. He had needed to find Hanscom alive; he needed to learn his contacts, and find out just how much more matériel had vanished onto the black market, and if possible, track it down and recover it. But now all those contacts were lost! All that work! Finding the shells, tracing their production numbers, and then catching the express back to the Capitol when the truth came out! All gone to waste! Damn it all!

Lord Wingate was about to stand up and leave, when he heard footfalls in the corridor. *The Hadvari.* He raised his pistol. *You bastards cost me my lead!* Lord Wingate peeked out from behind the pillar and fired three quick shots.

Two of the shots struck flesh, and two red-and-brown soldiers fell to the ground. The other three dove for cover behind the pillars farther back in the corridor.

Lord Wingate was about to settle into the tedious panic of a firefight, when he heard voices in the stairwell from whence he had come. Auroran voices. Stolos was on the way with backup. The Môlsôde were fearsome fighters on their own, but they were easily swamped by overwhelming numbers. Still, some of those men in the stairwell would die.

"*Kusôtaide,*" Lord Wingate called out to the Môlsôde. There was a whole speech prepared for this sort of situation. They had been forced to commit it to memory at the Academy. How did it go again?

"*Sûśau źîngî žo. Foilkuzide. Źau ŵo iuhašoga akuzide. Kuzide gi šo. Sûxoiřøiĝa.*"

Honorable Soldiers, this battle has been lost. You are isolated. Our numbers are greater than yours. Surrender yourselves. You need not continue to fight.

A few moments of silence, and then a reply came back.

"*Øsûŵô.*"

Lord Wingate shrugged and reloaded, *I didn't think so.*

"We'll be coming up on the Southern Gap in a minute, Captain."

Paul grunted in acknowledgment. Barlowe had relieved Hamilton at the navi position about half an hour ago. He might be a half-decent navigator, but he was still sulking about being forced to do his job earlier.

By now it was almost completely dark. The only remaining light was a thin halo of dark blue filtering through the ragged peaks of the Mountains of Dawn. A few more minutes, and they would be flying blind. Given their proximity to the mountains, that could be dangerous.

Finally, the mountains moved aside to reveal an absolutely spectacular sunset. The sun was just on the verge of disappearing below the horizon, and the sky above it was burning a brilliant gold, which faded to soft blue, then to a deep indigo, and finally gave way to the star-studded inky-black cloak of night.

And off in the distance, just barely visible against the sunset, was the large black silhouette of an airship.

"Guns," Paul said, not wasting a second, "get me eyes on that ship."

"Aye, sir," Wolfram snatched the spyglass off its peg and began adjusting the dials and knobs to bring it into focus. "Civilian airship," Wolfram announced, "Looks to be about five-and-a-half klicks distant. Heading southwest. Not moving very fast, likely trying to conserve fuel."

Paul grinned, "It's them."

"How can you be certain?" Vaughn said, "We're too far away to make out any identifying features. It could easily be a different civilian ship that simply wandered into our path."

"I don't think so," Paul said, "If this were a freighter making for Illyria, they would be heading west-by-north. And if they're headed for Isafar, they would be heading due south. This ship looks like she's making for the *Samedvar* by way of the Illyrian Sea. No question. This is our guy." He turned to Wolfram, "Guns, how long 'till we're in range?"

Hold off, Guns," Vaughn called. Paul groaned. *What the hell is it now?*

"Captain," Vaughn said, "we cannot close range with that ship before nightfall. We'll be firing in the dark."

"Then we'll shoot her down in the dark," Paul said.

"We'll miss," Vaughn retorted bluntly, "and then she'll flee into the darkness. And we'll have lost our target."

"You got a better idea, lady?" Paul snarled.

"Yes I do," Vaughn said without missing a beat.

Paul blinked. He honestly hadn't been expecting an answer to that question. "Alright then," he snapped, "let's hear it."

"Stalk them," Vaughn said, "Match their speed, and creep up on them in the darkness. That way we can conceal our approach and engage them with the dawn at point-blank range."

Paul turned the idea over in his head. There had to be some flaw in her reasoning. But the more he considered it, the more it started to make sense. It was the new moon tonight; that would make it hard to spot their approach. The pale blue light from their impact columns would be difficult to conceal, but if they kept their power low and their speed steady... Maybe lowered their altitude just a bit... "That... actually sounds like a better idea," Paul said awkwardly, "We'll do that."

"One more thing, Captain," Vaughn added, "We'll need to fly dark."

Fly dark? "What does that mean?"

"Light will give away our position. If this ruse is to work, we must dispense with all nonessential illumination." Vaughn crossed the bridge to the loudspeaker console, "Shall I give the order?"

Paul nodded, "Do it."

Vaughn flipped the master switch, "Attention all hands: This is Leftenant Commander Vaughn speaking. Combat condition two is now in effect. At this time, all non-essential light sources are to be extinguished, and all portholes are to be covered up. WAVE complement, make rounds through the unoccupied areas of the ship to ensure that these instructions are executed thoroughly. Good luck, everyone."

Vaughn switched off the loudspeaker and walked to the box that held the bridge circuit breakers. "Bridge auxiliary power disengaging," she announced, "in three... two... one."

The lights went out on the bridge. Luckily there were still a few remnants of twilight left to help ease everyone's eyes into the darkness. Barlowe mumbled a complaint that he could no longer read his charts, but everyone else managed alright.

Paul glanced down at the controls. The numbers on his instrument displays were still visible, glowing pale green. *Of course the fleet would be willing to pay extra for luminous paint on their dials.* Paul brought the *Dreadnought's* speed down to half and adjusted course to point them directly at the enemy airship. "And now we wait?"

"Correct," Vaughn nodded.

Alright then, Paul leaned back and flipped a small switch to lock the main stick into position. It was going to be a long flight; no sense in keeping his hand on the main stick for the whole time. Paul kept his hand on the altitude stick of course. You *never* locked your altitude control. Not unless you wanted to crash.

And then... nothing.

Waiting.

The horizon slowly swallowed up the remaining twilight. The only way to track the enemy airship now was by its silhouette against the stars, and the distant soft blue glow of her impact columns. She did not change course.

The waiting continued.

The terrain below changed; the vast white salt flats beyond the Gates of Dawn, softly pale in the night, gave way to featureless grass-land, pitch dark, visible only by the lack of stars.

And still, the waiting continued.

How long had it been so far? An hour? Three hours? Half an hour? Paul glanced around the bridge. Barlowe appeared to be sitting on the edge of the map table, squinting at his pocket watch every few moments. Vaughn was an indistinct shadow, looming behind the captain's chair. Wolfram sat at the tactical display. The determined look on his face was faintly illuminated by the soft luminescence from the controls; no doubt the gunboard had been done up with luminous paint as well. Wagner was just sitting beside the radio console. *Poor kid is probably bored out of his skull.*

"Sparks," Paul called over to the kid, "you can turn in for the night if you want." The ship probably wasn't going to need the radio for a while anyway.

"Oh!" Wagner jumped at the sudden noise, "Thank you, Captain," he got to his feet and cautiously felt his way back to the stair-well.

The night went on. The grassland below was replaced by the dark, frothing waters of the Illyrian Sea. The enemy airship held its course.

The hours continued. Wolfram switched out at the gunboard, and Zeigler took over. Vaughn retired and passed off the logbook to

Barlowe, who eventually passed it off to Hamilton when he came to relieve him.

Paul remained at the helm.

After a while, maybe an hour or two, his hand began to cramp up. *I'm gripping the damn altitude stick too hard,* Paul thought, *It's all this damn anticipation getting to me.*

Paul carefully took his hand off the altitude stick and rubbed the ache out of his hand. You were never supposed to do that of course; taking your hand off the altitude controls was one of the cardinal sins of flying. But just for a moment... Paul shrugged his shoulders, rubbing the seal-fur collar of his jacket against his neck. He had forgotten how comfortable it was. How warm... How safe... His eyelids were growing heavy.

"I'm back," Vaughn said as she stepped back onto the bridge, "Who has the logbook?"

"Hamilton," Paul croaked through his tired throat. It was an effort to speak.

"Thank you Capt—" Vaughn began, "Captain? What are you still doing at the helm?"

"Flying," Paul quickly grabbed the altitude stick again. Vaughn couldn't have possibly noticed that in this darkness.

"It's almost three of the second watch," Vaughn said, making her way to the helm, "You've been at the helm for nearly sixteen hours!"

"S'nothing," Paul mumbled, "Pulled a thirty-two-hour shift once."

"You should have switched out hours ago!"

"I'm alright." Paul groaned, "A little engine grease, and I'll be good for another few hours." He pushed himself up in the seat. The whole ship suddenly lurched down and forward! Paul had used the footpedals and the altitude stick to push himself up. He scrambled to correct the controls... "Fuck."

Vaughn's hand shot out and yanked the altitude stick firmly back into place. Her other arm dove under Paul's shoulder and began lifting him up from the seat, "Hamilton," she shouted, "take over at the helm."

"A-aye, ma'am!" Hamilton acknowledged.

"Get your hands off me..." Paul mumbled, "Goddammit, I'm fine."

"Look at yourself, Captain!" Vaughn said, "You're half-asleep already!"

"But... The enemy... The airship..." Paul struggled weakly as Vaughn hoisted him up and out of the seat like a sack of potatoes. He barely noticed Hamilton slipping into place beneath him. *I'd forgotten how nice this jacket feels.*

"Captain, please," Vaughn whispered into his ear. Maybe he really *was* getting sleepy, but she almost sounded soothing. Paul didn't know Vaughn could be soothing. "I understand how you're feeling, but you need your rest."

Paul finally stopped struggling. Maybe he was starting to believe Vaughn. Or maybe he was just so dead tired. Maybe both. Thinking was too much of an effort. "Alright," he groaned, "maybe a few hours."

"We'll send someone to fetch you before everything starts, I promise," Vaughn said, "Zeigler, take Captain Bowman back to his quarters."

Paul was faintly aware of being handed off to someone else, then carried somewhere... After that, reality began to dissolve into an uncertain haze of dreams.

Chapter XX

The Mordred Protocol

"**A**TTENTION all hands: This is Leftenant Commander Vaughn speaking. Combat condition one is now in effect. From this point onwards, there will be no further warnings or drills. All hands are summoned to battle stations and are to remain at high alert until ordered otherwise. WAVE complement, stand by to evacuate wounded to sick bay. Good luck, everyone."

Paul was fully awake before the first sentence of the announcement was over. Glancing about, he realized he was back in his cabin. Outside, the rosy-gray sky looked to be about half an hour before dawn, maybe less. He'd slept for less than three hours. It would have to be enough.

This is it, he told himself, *It all ends right here. One way or another.*

Paul checked himself over. He had fallen asleep in his uniform and his coat. At least he wouldn't have to get dressed. He glanced over at the liquor cabinet, but quickly decided against it; he would need all his wits as sharp as could be for what was about to happen. Besides, the cabinet had been empty for the past few days.

With a groan, Paul got to his feet and started for the door. Just as he reached it, there was a soft knock, and Ensign Wagner poked his head through. "Captain?" he said, "They want you on—"

"I heard," Paul said, "I'm on my way."

Wagner trooped down the stairwell after Paul and jumped back on the radio console as soon as they reached the bridge. The sky was slowly turning red. The airship was less than a quarter of a mile away now; close enough to make out details on her hull. They would be spotted before much longer—assuming they hadn't been already.

"Alright, people," Paul said as he planted himself in the captain's chair, "what's our situation?"

"We're about make our final approach," Vaughn said.

"Have they seen us yet?" Paul asked.

"I don't believe so, Captain." Wolfram said.

"Well then, we've still got the element of surprise," Paul said, "Guns, how do you want to play this?"

"Well, we have two broadside batteries on either side," Wolfram began, "It's rather ironic—this configuration has been obsolete for decades, and yet it's ideally suited for ship-to-ship combat. We frankly couldn't be in a more perfect ship for this."

"Get to the point," Paul said.

"Right, sorry!" Wolfram shook his head, "Well, we know they have at least one field gun in their hold, and those Hadvari gun teams are deadly accurate. We'll want to stay behind her at all costs. I recommend we close the distance and cross the T, throw broadsides at her from inside her blind spot. Clean and methodical."

Paul had no idea what Wolfram meant by "crossing the tea" but the kid seemed to know his stuff. "Alright then," Paul said, "Helm, half ahead. Close distance on the enemy."

"A-aye, sir," Hamilton stammered, and he increased the ship's speed.

Paul raised an eyebrow. The kid sounded nervous, "You alright there, Helm?"

"Yes!" Hamilton responded much too quickly, "Of course, Captain. It's just... y'know, long night."

"I know the feeling," Paul said, shooting a quick glance toward Vaughn. The woman stood by the loudspeaker console, checking her pocket watch and making a note in the logbook.

It took about a minute to close the distance between the two airships. "Captain," Wolfram announced, "all gun crews report ready to fire."

"Good," Paul leaned forward in the captain's chair, "What happens next?"

"Now we need to cross the T," Wolfram said. *There it is again! What the hell does he mean?* Wolfram continued, "Turn to one side, so we can bring all our guns to bear on–"

"Captain," Vaughn shouted, "She's coming about!"

Sure enough, the enemy airship was porting around to face them. Her fully open cargo ramp was coming into view. *Well, they've definitely spotted us now!*

"Helm, hard to starboard!" Paul shouted.

The *Dreadnought* pitched violently to port. Dammit, Hamilton was going to take them right in front of their line of fire! "The captain said *starboard!*" Vaughn shouted. Hamilton responded by immediately throwing the ship into full reverse. Now the *Dreadnought* was pulled up right in front of the cargo ramp—a sitting duck!

"Drop!" Paul leaped out of the captain's chair and dove toward the helm, "Goddammit, drop us!" He reached the helm and wrenched the altitude stick into the off position, dropping the ship hard. He felt the familiar lurching in his stomach, as gravity momentarily switched itself off. Barely a second later, two guns fired in the distance. *Too close!*

"Oh, god," Hamilton moaned softly, "Oh god, it's happening again. It's happening again."

"Pull yourself together, Ensign," Vaughn snapped at the boy, "Keep steady on the helm!"

"It's all my fault," Hamilton kept whimpering, "We're all going to die, and it's all my fault."

"Calm down, kid," Paul said gently, as he slipped into the seat, nudging Hamilton aside, "It's alright. I can take it from here."

"Ensign Hamilton," Vaughn shouted, "Get back on the helm this very—"

"Goddammit lady, the kid's having a panic attack!" Paul shouted back, "Lay off him!"

Vaughn seemed to get the message and backed off. Hamilton was now curled up into a sobbing heap beside the helm. "Sparks," Paul called out, "get the kid back to his quarters. Stay with him until he cools down."

Wagner got up and crossed the bridge to pick up Hamilton, "What about the radio, Captain?"

"Trust me, kid," Paul said, "we're not gonna need you."

Paul finally brought the *Dreadnought* to a stable position. They had lost a good deal of altitude; from about half a mile down to about a thousand feet above sea level. That should keep them safe from the gun on the enemy airship, at least for the moment, but their own guns were also probably out of range. First things first, though: they had to find the airship.

Paul pulled the main stick to one side, causing the *Dreadnought* to turn hard. Paul scanned the sky above, searching for the airship.

"I see her," Wolfram called out, "Ten o'clock, heading due south!"

Paul looked, and sure enough, there was the enemy airship, heading south under what looked like all speed. "I'm on her!" Paul responded, and forced the *Dreadnought* into a climb.

"Don't take us too high, Captain," Wolfram said, "Their guns can't fire down angle, but ours can fire up. If we stay below them, we should be safe from counter-fire."

"Good call, Guns!" Paul reduced the vertical thrust just a hair. He pressed down hard on the accelerator, urging the ship forward as fast as she could go. Slowly, the distance between the ships began to close.

"Captain," Barlowe called out from the navi chart, "Land ahead!" Paul squinted. Sure enough, the northern coast of Isafar was beginning to rise out of the sea in the distance.

"Captain," Vaughn said urgently, "we need to engage them now."

"Just another minute," Paul said, "We're closing on them."

"Captain," Vaughn reiterated, "that ship is heading for land. If we shoot them down over Isafari territory, it will precipitate a serious diplomatic crisis, possibly even drive Isafar into war against us. We cannot let that happen. We need to destroy that ship before she makes it to shore."

"She's right, Captain," Wolfram said, backing her up, "We'll have to engage them at range."

Paul shrugged, half a mile was probably close enough for the gunners to eyeball it anyway, "Alright, standby, Guns." Paul wrenched the main stick over, causing the ship to heel over hard to starboard. The guns would now be pointed directly at the underbelly of the enemy airship. "Do it."

Wolfram's fingers flew across the gunboard, "Portside battery!

Firing!"

The *Dreadnought* rocked violently. Outside the ship, seven heavy cannons sounded off in rapid succession. Paul struggled with the controls, straining to keep the ship, already at a steep angle, from tipping over completely. Finally the *Dreadnought* was stable again. "Did we get 'em?"

"Portside gunpit reports no hits," Vaughn announced from the loudspeaker console, "All shots wide. No luck this time."

"We'll try again with the starboard battery," Wolfram said through gritted teeth, "Ordering portside guns to reload just in case."

"Do it," Paul said, "I'm bringing us around for a closer pass."

Paul worked the controls, and the *Dreadnought* swerved hard to port to bring her starboard guns to bear against the enemy airship. The eastern sky was now a deep blood red; true dawn was only minutes away. Off in the distance, the Isafari coastline was coming closer and closer. They would have to end this soon.

"Give 'er another," Paul shouted as soon as the *Dreadnought* was in position. Again the ship shook with the force of the starboard guns, and again, Paul fought to keep the ship upright.

"Hit!" Vaughn called out, "Starboard gunpit reports a hit!"

At last! "I'm bringing us around," Paul said, "Barlowe, take the spyglass and see how she's doing."

"Aye sir," Barlowe dashed across the bridge, (likely as much to get away from the hated navi chart as much as to obey Paul's orders). Through the spyglass, he zeroed in on the enemy airship as it came into view. "I see two holes in their upper deck, one amidships, one astern. Looks like we took off some of their outer hull. It also looks like she's slowing down."

"Slowing down you say?" Paul asked, "And a hit to the stern?"

"That's how it looks, Captain," Barlowe confirmed.

"The reactor!" Paul blurted out, "We pegged that bitch right in the reactor!"

"Yes!" Wolfram punched the air.

"And not a moment too soon!" Vaughn said, unable to conceal her own enthusiasm, "Another pass, and she would have made landfall."

"Alright, people," Paul said, "I'm bringing us in close. Guns, get ready to finish her off."

"Aye sir," Wolfram responded, "Portside guns report ready to fire."

The *Dreadnought* swooped in closer. A third of a mile... A fifth of a mile... Each moment bringing the end a little closer... "In position," Paul finally called out, "Let 'em have it!"

"Portside battery! Firing!" Again the whole ship trembled under the might of her guns.

"Portside battery reports..." Vaughn began, and then petered out. "Captain, they say they've lost contact."

Lost contact? "Maybe the ship dropped before we could—"

The *Dreadnought* shuddered again! "Dammit, Guns," Paul shouted, "call it out before you fire!"

"It wasn't me, Captain," Wolfram said.

"Behind!" Barlowe shouted. Paul hadn't even noticed him being thrown against the forward window by the shaking, "They hit us from behind! They must have pulled a hard reverse and—"

Another shudder, even more powerful than before! Not only that, but the deck began to tilt, backwards and to starboard. "Shit!" Paul jerked the stick to port and forward, throwing the *Dreadnought* into a diving curve!

"What the hell is happening?" Barlowe screamed.

"We just lost one of our rear impact columns!" Paul said, "I'm compensating!"

"I'm getting out of here!" Barlowe shrieked and started climbing up toward the back of the bridge on all fours, "You're going to get us all— "

Barlowe was interrupted by a loud metallic popping sound, and something struck him in the hand. As he slid back down to the forward window to nurse his wound, more popping noises and a deep metallic groan filled the bridge. Then, a large metallic clank, as the bulkhead that Barlowe had half installed less than a day earlier burst its rivets, clattered onto the deck, and bounced forward, shattering the glass of the main window and sending both itself and Barlowe plunging fifteen hundred feet into the churning sea below.

"Goddammit," Paul spat as he finally got the ship stable again, "Vaughn, damage report!"

"Engine room and starboard gunpit report severe damage and casualties," Vaughn said, "And coil number four is gone. It looks like the enemy caught us in the rear somehow."

Coil number four? That would be the aft starboard impact column. Exactly as Paul had felt. *No worries there,* Paul told himself. He'd been on ships that had lost columns and recovered before. *Just so long as we don't lose another one.* "How's the damage in the engine room looking?"

"Not good," Vaughn said, "Multiple breakages on the main coolant line. Backup systems appear to be defective."

Of course the backups are defective, Paul fumed, *Another petty slight from Miranda Babcock and the Consortium.* "Can they stabilize it?"

"Not for very much longer, Captain," Vaughn reported, "Mister Thatcher gives the reactor ten minutes at most before they'll need to shut down and make repairs."

Ten minutes? Paul considered. He glanced over at the coastline, now almost directly below them. The terrain beyond looked to be dense jungle, not a clearing to be seen for miles about. No way they could come to ground and make repairs in that mess. The beach wasn't an option either; he knew from experience that loose sand would not support the weight of an airship.

Then we won't make repairs.

"Where's the enemy now?" Paul demanded grimly.

Wolfram pointed, "Up there, Captain. Two o'clock, and heading west-northwest at half speed. They're not even bothering to finish us off."

Paul was silent for a moment, *I can't believe I'm really about to do this.* "Vaughn," he said at last, "get everyone off the ship."

"Captain," Vaughn asked warily, "What are you planning?"

"I'm going to ram 'em," Paul pointed the *Dreadnought* squarely at the enemy ship, and began to increase altitude, slower now that they were down a column.

"You're crazy!" Wolfram shouted, "You're absolutely insane!"

"The ship is lost, Guns," Paul shouted back, "We can't make repairs in the air, and there's no place to set down on the shore. So I'm going to make damn sure that we complete our mission and take that bastard down one way or another!"

"You're describing the Mordred Protocol," Vaughn said.

"The Mordred Protocol is a myth!" Wolfram said, "It's a conspiracy theory cooked up by—"

"I've seen it done before," Paul said, "At the Southern Gap."

"The captain knows what he is about," Vaughn said, "Shall I make the announcement to the crew?"

Paul hesitated. *If I do this, I'm not coming out alive.* There was still time to back out. He'd done his duty as best he could; surely nobody could fault him if they just ditched the ship and got to shore... *No!* Paul's anger began to surge up inside him. Those bastards had killed Hakefeldt, they'd killed Barlowe, and now they'd killed his ship. And he was *not* going to let them get away!

I am the wind.

"Make the call."

"Attention all hands," came the voice over the loudspeaker, barely audible over the roar of the reactor, and the howling wind blowing through the gaping hole in the back of the engine room, "This is Leftenant Commander Vaughn speaking. Whatever you're doing, drop it or finish it in the next thirty seconds. Engine crew, disengage all safety measures and stand by to come to full power. Armoury crew, lock all blast doors in the open position. All other hands, proceed to your designated breach points, and make ready to abandon ship. The Mordred Protocol is now in effect. You have five minutes. Good luck, everyone. God be with you all."

Thatcher had to admit, those new squawkboxes were damn handy.

Thatcher took a look around the engine room. Two of his people were dead already—Caldwell and Dickson, caught out of nowhere when the back wall exploded. Arnott was still clinging to life for the moment, but he wouldn't last much longer; a sucking chest wound was not the sort of thing you recovered from. Over on the right, Philpot was doubled over, clutching at the bloody stump that had been his pointer finger a minute ago. Still, he was in much better shape than Behringer, who was limping from the shrapnel wound just below his knee; if he still had his leg in a week, it would be a fuckin' miracle.

"Y'all heard the lady," Thatcher shouted, "Everybody out! Move!"

The people began to stagger out of the engine room, toward the breach point half a deck below. Jackson was struggling to hoist Caldwell's body onto his shoulder. "Leave 'im!" Thatcher hollered at the man, "Ya can't do nothin' for the guy! Get yerself outta here!" Jackson nodded and dropped Caldwell. He was one of the few people who hadn't been seriously injured; like Thatcher, he had escaped with only a few superficial lacerations, nothing that couldn't be patched up with a few strips of cloth.

Slowly, the engine room emptied. Soon, only Thatcher and Lieutenant Newton were left. "Well," Newton shouted over the relentless howling, "it looks like we're in rather a state, old man."

"Yeah," Thatcher shouted back. The lieutenant looked as though the shrapnel had passed him over completely. *Trust a fuckin' bungo like you to get all the luck!*

"Right, then," The kid was still so fuckin' cheerful! "Let's get to work. We'd better get to disabling those safety systems."

Safety systems? What fuckin' safety systems? *I keep tellin' people this is a first-generation reactor! Nobody fuckin' listens to me!*

"First things first," Thatcher shouted, "Open that chest over in the corner. There should be a couple'a 'chutes in there."

"Ah, right! Of course. Safety first and all that," Newton dashed over to the box and threw it open. "I've got the harnesses."

"Alright," Thatcher said as he joined the boy, "Let's get yours first." A few seconds of harness and buckle fiddling later, Newton was all set.

"Right," the boy said as he tested the straps to make certain they would hold, "Now let's get yours done up next."

"I can handle it myself," Thatcher shouted, "You just get clear of the ship."

"Are you sure?" Newton shouted back the question, "You might require my assistance."

"I'll be alright," Thatcher said, "Get yourself clear of the goddamn ship!"

Newton thought about it for a moment and nodded, "Right, I'll see you on the ground then." He carefully climbed through the jagged hole, and vanished from sight.

Thatcher turned back to the reactor. *My reactor.* He had personally kept that rickety old first-generation beast running since he was fifteen years old. That had been nearly four decades ago now. He had outlasted four captains and more crewmen than he could remember. He had outlasted them all. *Me and my reactor.*

She was on her last legs now. The main coolant loop was draining fast, and the peripheral systems weren't responding. Soon the reactor would be running completely dry, and then it would only be a matter of minutes before the entire system overheated and her core melted. *At least she doesn't have any body fractures,* Thatcher thought gratefully, *One of those would see us dead in minutes.*

Thatcher made his way to the throttle controls. Soon the order would come to bring the reactor up to full power. Thatcher looked down and noticed he was still holding the parachute harness. He tossed it carelessly aside.

He remembered telling Captain Bowman that he would still be with the *Dreadnought* when she was finally decommissioned and broken down for scrap. But it seemed that was not what fate had in store for the old girl. Maybe it was better like this? Thatcher had never even considered how he would have spent his days after the *Dreadnought* was decommissioned. Sit around in pubs all day, slowly drinking away his pension and bitching about those kids and their newer reactors? No, that sort of a life wasn't really living; it was just waiting to die.

Thatcher was going to go out on his own terms. At his post. Like a soldier.

"I'm staying with you, girl," Thatcher said, inaudible over the noise, "Just a little while longer."

In the far corner, the bell sounded, and the signal light flashed red. *Maximum Output*. Thatcher turned the main feedback dial as high as it would go.

"Clear! Next!" Vaughn shouted over the shrieking wind.

The next jumper moved into position—one of the WAVE girls, Malden or Willingham probably, Vaughn honestly didn't remember. Leftenant Wingate was giving the girl's harness one last quick check.

"All good," He called out, "Move up." The girl edged cautiously towards the opening.

"Hand on the ripcord," Vaughn shouted. The girl gingerly placed her hand on the ripcord, "Count to five before you pull. Ready?"

The girl nodded hastily. Her face was a mask of pure white terror.

"Right, out you go," Vaughn gave the girl a push. She plummeted out of the red sky, nearly vanishing from sight before her parachute finally opened. "Clear!" Vaughn called out, "Next!"

"I think that's everyone," Leftenant Wingate shouted, "We're the last ones left."

Vaughn glanced out of the door. Sure enough, she counted a line of eighteen parachutes in the sky below, with four other lines of parachutes drifting lazily down from the other breach points. Luckily the *Dreadnought* was fairly close to shore; hopefully the sea breeze wouldn't blow them too far away.

"Commander," Leftenant Wingate called out, "I think we have a problem."

Vaughn ducked back in, "What is it, Leftenant?"

Leftenant Wingate was standing beside the emergency locker holding two parachutes, one in each hand, "There's only two harnesses left."

"So?" Vaughn snatched one of the parachutes and began to strap herself into it, "There's only the two of us here, isn't there?"

"This breach point serves the bridge as well," Leftenant Wingate said, "What about Captain Bowman?"

Vaughn hesitated. Three people left, and only two parachutes between them. One of them was not going survive. The simplest course of action would be to simply take the parachutes and go. Captain Bowman probably didn't plan on surviving anyhow. *Besides, that bastard would do the same to me, were he in this position!* Vaughn thought sullenly, *Wouldn't he?*

"There's... an emergency locker on the bridge," Vaughn bluffed, "The captain'll be along in just a minute. In the meanwhile, let's make sure you're all done up properly." Vaughn quickly busied herself checking over Leftenant Wingate's harness. *Don't think about the captain,* she told herself, *there's nothing you can do about him.*

Once Wolfram's harness was secure, the leftenant made his way to the breach point, while Vaughn secured the straps and buckles on her own parachute. Just before he jumped, he turned back to face her, "Hey! Fiora!" he shouted over the rushing air.

Fiora looked up, shocked! It had been ages since someone had addressed her by her given name.

"I just want you to know," he shouted, "I... I haven't always been good at showing it, but..." He hesitated, "But I've always respected you! As a fellow officer!"

Fiora was honestly shocked to hear it! She'd never really thought of Wolfram Wingate as anything more than a substandard officer squandering his already limited potential on vices and bad habits. Sure enough, thinking back on his behaviour towards her, he had ever been scrupulously courteous. And now that she had seen him in action, she had to admit, he was terribly competent. And yet, Wolfram Wingate was only one officer; there were plenty of other people on the ship who would not even look her in the eye.

I can't lead this crew back home again, Fiora realized, *They need Captain Bowman.*

Through her boots, Fiora could feel the reactor coming up to full power. Moments later, the *Dreadnought* began to climb higher.

Time was running out.

"Wolfram," Fiora said, "I need you to do me a favour."

"Of course," Wolfram said, "What do you need?"

"If I don't make it," Fiora said, "look after the crew for me. Keep them safe."

"Wait, what do you mean 'if you don't make it?'" Wolfram spluttered, and he likely would have protested further if Vaughn hadn't shoved him out of the doorway and into the red sky. She watched only long enough to see his parachute deploy, then dashed back up to the bridge, unfastening her own parachute as she ran.

Back on the bridge, Captain Bowman was sitting at the helm controls. Through the shattered glass of the forward window, the enemy airship was visible floating along at half speed. "Captain!" Vaughn called out as soon as she made it back to the bridge, "I have your parachute."

He didn't respond.

"Did you hear me, Captain?" Vaughn crossed the bridge, "I said I have your—"

"I heard you the first time," Captain Bowman's eyes never left the enemy airship.

Vaughn blinked, "Right... well then, you need to... secure it so that you—"

"Put it on and jump," Captain Bowman snapped.

Do it, a voice in the back of Vaughn's head urged, *It's an order. You have an excuse. No one would blame you.*

"No."

"Goddammit, lady! What is wrong with you?" Captain Bowman shouted, "Just take the damn parachute and jump!"

"This parachute belongs to you," Vaughn insisted.

"I don't need a *fuckin' parachute!*" Captain Bowman roared, "Now take that thing and get off this ship! That's an order!"

"Captain, you promised to get all of us back home again," Vaughn said, "How do you expect to do that if you foolishly sacrifice yourself like this?"

"I..." Captain Bowman hesitated for a moment, then said grimly, "You'll have to get 'em home for me."

"I can't lead them," Vaughn admitted bitterly, "They don't respect me. They won't follow me. But they will follow you, Captain."

For a moment, Captain Bowman worked the controls in silence. His face was furrowed with deep frustration. Through the forward window, the distant shape of the enemy airship came into almost perfect alignment with the *Dreadnought*.

"Well?" Vaughn demanded, "What say you, Captain?"

"I say hold onto something!" Captain Bowman shouted, and jammed down hard on one of the footpedals. The ship shot forwards suddenly, requiring Vaughn to take a deep step back to steady herself against the deck. A second later, Vaughn also felt the dreadfully familiar sensation of the deck dropping out from underneath her feet.

"Captain!" Vaughn shouted, "What about—"

Before she could finish her question, Captain Bowman leaped up from the helm controls, and tackled Vaughn into the air. Barely a moment later, both of them were thrown through the forward window as the *Dreadnought* slammed into the top aft deck of the enemy airship with a metallic crunch.

The wind howled and shrieked around the two of them as they careened over the top of the enemy airship and sailed over the bow. The two of them barely noticed as the two mighty airships buckled under the strain of their own weight and finally ripped themselves apart to plunge a thousand metres out of the sky to vanish beneath the churning waters of the Illyrian Sea.

Vaughn and Captain Bowman turned over and over as they fell. Luckily, Vaughn was still holding the parachute. She hastily slipped the thing onto Captain Bowman and fastened all the straps and buckles as tightly as they would go.

"What are you doing?" Captain Bowman shouted over the howling wind.

"They need you more than me, Captain!" Vaughn shouted back as she finished the last strap. Without waiting, she reached for the ripcord and pulled it as hard as she could... *It's better this way.*

The brilliant white silk parachute sprouted out of Captain Bowman's back, and began to fill up with air. Sure enough, Captain Bowman's descent began to slow. *I did it,* Vaughn thought as she closed her eyes, *It's over.*

Vaughn felt something clamp down tightly around her wrist. Around her, the wind slowly died to a whisper, and she began to feel the pull of gravity again. Her eyes shot open; Captain Bowman was holding her by the wrist.

"Let go," she shouted, "The parachute can't hold both of us."

"No!" Captain Bowman shouted back. Vaughn met his gaze; the look of furious, desperate determination in his eye was absolutely unyielding, "I'm not losing anyone else today! Not one more!"

Vaughn was absolutely dumbfounded! Bloody hell, she could still see the bruise she had given him not two days earlier. Even after all the bile and bitterness that had passed between them this past month... Still, he was willing to risk his own safety just to save one more person? To save *her?*

"Pull up," Captain Bowman said, "I can't hold on like this for much longer."

For a moment, Vaughn only stared. Then, slowly, she pulled herself up. Her daily exercises made the task relatively trivial. Soon she was perched with her stomach laying across Captain Bowman's shoulder; hardly a comfortable position, but it was stable. At least, for the moment.

"This parachute isn't going to hold us up forever," Vaughn said as soon as she was secure.

"It doesn't need to," Captain Bowman said, "Once we hit the water, we're in the clear."

Vaughn had to admit; Captain Bowman's assessment was technically correct. The water was growing nearer with every second.

"By the way," Captain Bowman inquired after a few more seconds, "can you swim?"

"Yes, of course," Vaughn said.

"Good," Captain Bowman said, and then sheepishly added, "because I can't."

Dawn was slowly breaking over the Capitol, but the powerful calcium lamps still illuminated the palace garden from the high walls. Lord Wingate watched as the palace guards arranged the last of the bodies in the centre of the garden. Each one wore the red-and-brown uniform of Hadvar as well as a black headband. A neat pile of crossbows stood beside the bodies, with piles of bolts and unexploded hand bombs arrayed out in further piles. A bureaucrat with a ledger walked amongst the piles, enumerating everything for the record.

"Five-and-twenty," Lord Harlocke stood beside Lord Wingate, sporting a bandaged arm, "Aye, that's a full squad. Those *Môlsôde* bastards gave my lads no end of trouble during the war."

"They're about to give us even more trouble," Lord Wingate said darkly. How long would hostilities last this time? How many more good men would lose their lives before the end? *Would* it end?

"That they shall," Lord Harlocke nodded, "Tricksome little sneaks, hard to catch and harder still to hold onto once you've caught them."

The bureaucrat in the corner finished his enumeration and closed the ledger, "All finished, my lords."

"I'll take it." Lord Wingate said, accepting the ledger from the bureaucrat and walking out of the garden. He flipped through the pages as he made his way through the palace. Soon, all of the Hadvari weapons would be repurposed; what couldn't be repurposed would probably be sold off to a local foundry for scrap. The bodies themselves would be disposed of in the palace furnace, and their ashes dumped unceremoniously into a hole in some secret, easily forgotten place.

Lord Wingate made his way to the Great Hall, where more bodies were being gathered. These ones belonged to servants, palace clerks, members of the guard—the Aurorans who had died during the attack. These bodies would be treated much differently: state funerals and burial with top honours, pensions for their widows and orphans, probably a monument somewhere in the city. Their memory would live on as martyrs for as long as the Kingdom of Aurora endured. *That may not be for much longer now.*

Six other bodies were conspicuously absent, the bodies of the lords who had died in the attack: Franklin, Waldemar, Dalton, Siebruck, Petras, and Hanscom. *Six lords at once,* On any other day, it would have been unprecedented, but in the past twelve hours, that word had rather begun to lose it's impact.

Lord Wingate crossed the hall to where Lord Stolos stood talking with some servants. "Here's the accounting of the Hadvari and their equipment."

"Thank you, Orpheus," Lord Stolos took the ledger and began to look it over, "What do they look like to you?"

"They're called *Mólsôdé,*" Lord Wingate explained, "It means roughly *Dead Soldiers.* They specialise in clandestine operations behind front lines—espionage, sabotage, assassination. An operation like this one is exactly the sort of thing at which they excel. The only proven way to deal with them is to back them into a corner and crush them with overwhelming numbers."

"Good to know," Lord Stolos nodded, "Do you think we're likely to see more... incidents like this in the future?"

"I couldn't say," Lord Wingate admitted, "An operation like this one would have to have been in planning for months, probably a hold-over from the war. Perhaps those poor devils were simply never told about the peace. A dead-hand gambit gone horribly wrong."

"Is that what you expect us to tell the press?" Lord Stolos said in an offended whisper, "That 127 people, including six lords paramount, were murdered by a Hadvari Death Squad because of a bloody *administrative fuck-up?!*"

"Of course not," Lord Wingate said calmly, "I'm certain we can come up with something acceptable, given time."

Lord Stolos gave a disgusted snort and snapped the ledger shut, "This was an assault," he said, "A perfidious, premeditated assault on the very core of our nation and our way of life. And it shall be answered with blood and steel."

"That's for *us* to decide," Lord Wingate said firmly, "You might be handling the clean-up around here for the moment, but military action is *our* department, and we shan't be taking any action before first consulting with Her Majesty."

"That reminds me," Lord Stolos's voice suddenly became grave and serious, "It was about an hour ago in the Southern Audience Chamber. The servants have identified another body."

Lord Wingate could already feel his heart lurching into his throat, "The Queen?"

Lord Stolos nodded, "Caught in the back with a stiletto. Palace guards were nowhere to be found. It's a disgrace."

"You know she had no successor," Lord Wingate said in a low voice, "We'll need to assemble the Council of Lords to figure out what to do."

"I've already taken care of that," Lord Stolos said, waving across the Great Hall at a stout man trotting towards them at a steady jog. Lord Wingate didn't recognise him.

"Percy," the man wheezed, "I just got back from the wire office. The messages have all been sent. Exactly as you said."

"Good, good," Lord Stolos nodded, "Orpheus, this is my good friend Hobart Aloysius Franklin, son of the late Lord Barnabas Obadiah Franklin."

Lord Wingate had no idea that old Barnabas even had a son. The man must not be particularly active in court life. *A smart man.* "How do you do," Lord Wingate said as he shook the man's hand.

"And of course you are familiar with Lord Wingate," Lord Stolos said.

"Only by reputation, I'm afraid," Hobart said. His handshake was terribly weak. *Well, it has been a long night for all of us.*

"Hobart has been dispatching word to the other lords throughout the realm," Lord Stolos explained, "as well as the next-of-kin of the ones we lost today."

Lord Wingate nodded grimly. At this very moment, emergency service telegrams would be zipping across the realm, shattering the morning peace for lords and scions and summoning them to the Capitol with all reasonable haste.

Amelia doesn't know yet!

"I need to send a telegram," Lord Wingate said urgently.

"Oh, let me handle it for you, my lord," Hobart said, "They're still operating on emergency service for the next hour or so."

"I appreciate it, but no," Lord Wingate declined, "I need to send it myself." *And probably through regular channels,* Lord Wingate decided as he excused himself from the Great Hall and headed for the stables, *An emergency telegram will cause Amelia more worry, and there's already more than plenty to be worried about!*

As Lord Wingate reached the stables, he noticed three men with rifles holding defensive positions. More palace guardsmen, probably a rearguard to make certain that nobody escaped. Lord Wingate informed the men that the Dawn Palace was now secure and dismissed them, awarding each with a five-crown piece for their service.

Now alone in the stables, Lord Wingate picked out a horse, a fine chestnut stallion, and began to saddle the beast. His mind was busy composing his message to his wife. Which details should he include? Which details *could* he include? Care would need to be taken so as not to leak any critical information to the telegraph operators.

He was pulled from his thoughts by a sudden noise.

Lord Wingate looked about. What was it? A clumsy bumping sound? It was probably one of the horses. No, there it was again! It was coming from... inside the wall?

Did we miss one of them? Lord Wingate drew his sidearm, and started walking slowly toward the wooden wall. There, the panel in the far corner! Lord Wingate drew his pistol and quickly pushed the panel aside.

A young servant woman fell out!

Lord Wingate quickly holstered his sidearm and rushed to help the servant to her feet. "Blast it all, girl!" he said, "What were you doing clambering about inside the walls like that? I almost took you for a hobgoblin! However did you even get inside the—" Lord Wingate stopped short as the woman drew herself up to her full height, and he recognised her. It wasn't possible!

"My Lord Wingate," the Queen said, lively as a bird, "I am informed that the Palace has been secured."

"M-Majesty?" Lord Wingate stammered, "You're alive?"

"I suppose that depends," the Queen said, brushing a mess of cobwebs off her skirt, "Was there a body?"

Lord Wingate blinked, "Y-yes. About an hour ago. The servants discovered your... well, *a* body in the Southern Audience Chamber."

The Queen nodded curtly, "Aye, that'll be Alexandra; my double. Poor girl." The Queen shrugged, "And you said it was the *servants* who identified the body?"

"I believe so," Lord Wingate nodded.

"That's good," the Queen said, "At present, nobody else knows."

"Majesty, we have to..." Lord Wingate trailed off; he had been about to suggest that they make their way back to the Great Hall to proclaim the Queen's survival to the realm, when something occurred to him: In the Great Hall, Lord Stolos had mentioned that the double had been killed with a stiletto knife.

That minor detail, probably an insignificant inclusion by Lord Stolos, didn't add up; the *Môlsôde* did not use stilettos. They would have used a crossbow or one of their blood knives. But a stiletto? That was a fundamentally Auroran weapon. The decoy queen had been murdered by a fellow Auroran.

"My Lord?" the Queen raised an eyebrow, "Is something amiss?"

"Majesty," Lord Wingate said gravely, "I think this whole attack was cover for an assassination attempt."

"What?"

It made sense. The best place to hide a tree was in a forest; the best place to hide a stone was in a quarry. By that logic, the best place to hide a single murder was in a massacre where its grim details would be eclipsed by the larger tragedy. "I am all but certain of it, Majesty," Lord Wingate said.

The Queen shut her eyes. She held a deep breath for a second or two and then breathed out a heavy sigh. "I need to leave the Capitol immediately," she declared.

Lord Wingate blinked. Something had changed about her. Gone was the frivolous little chit he remembered; in her place stood someone much more intelligent, perceptive, even majestic. For the first time, Lord Wingate actually felt as though he was standing before a queen.

"Are you certain, Majesty?" Lord Wingate said.

The Queen nodded, "This is an eventuality for which I've not made any arrangements. I need to marshall my agents and draw up a new strategy."

"If you believe it is for the best, Majesty." Lord Wingate acquiesced and saddled another horse.

"I suppose we'll find out soon enough," the Queen said as she took the reins of her horse and led the beast out into the stable yard. She vaulted up into the saddle, and Lord Wingate followed her out of the stableyard and into an uncertain future.

The Queen is dead. Long live the Queen.

"Alright, I can touch the bottom. You can stop now."

Vaughn finally stopped swimming. She didn't know how much longer she could have managed. It had to have been four kilometres at least, perhaps farther, and dragging Captain Bowman behind her all the way. Her lungs were on fire, and every muscle in her body screamed with exhaustion.

Bloody stamina, Vaughn thought, *No bloody way to train for it on a bloody airship.* Her head slipped below the water; she probably could have drowned right there and not cared.

Something pulled at Vaughn's arm, and she was hoisted back up out of the water. Captain Bowman lifted her up onto his shoulder and slipped his other arm under her waist. "I got you," he said, "Don't worry, I got you."

Vaughn relaxed and let Captain Bowman carry her through the shoulder-high water. *He's strong.* It was hidden under a padding of fat, but the strength was there. Reassuring.

Vaughn tried to raise her head to look at the coastline before her, but her long dark brown hair had come loose and was now hanging in front of her face in great wet sheets. She wanted to lift the curtain of hair, but her arm would not respond. *So tired...*

"You alright?" Captain Bowman asked. The water was only chest-high now.

"My lungs are trying to strangle me," Vaughn croaked.

"Yeah," Captain Bowman groaned, "you're alright."

Slowly, the water became waist-high, then only knee-high, and finally it receded entirely, and Captain Bowman let her drop onto the sand. Vaughn rolled over onto her back and moved her hair aside. Dawn was at least an hour behind them now.

"Here," Vaughn looked up to see Captain Bowman holding her spectacles. She mumbled a thank you and clumsily took them. The world came into focus again; well, if one didn't count the large drops of water dribbling across her vision. Vaughn raised her sleeve to wipe off the lenses, but stopped when she realised that wiping them on her sopping-wet uniform would only exacerbate the problem.

My uniform is completely ruined, Vaughn thought absently, noting how her undergarments were beginning to cling to her skin in a number of terribly inconvenient places, *though I suppose that's the least of my worries now...*

"The rest of the crew is somewhere back to the east," Captain Bowman said, "A few miles probably. Let me know when you're ready to move."

"We move now," Vaughn said, rolling onto her stomach so she could struggle to her feet, but Captain Bowman knelt down and put a hand on her shoulder.

"Rest," he said.

Vaughn tried to bat away Captain Bowman's hand, "I don't need —"her leg gave out before she could finish the sentence. Captain Bowman managed to catch her just before her face hit the sand.

"Trust me," Captain Bowman said, "I was an infantryman. We'll move quicker after a short rest."

Vaughn nodded and sat back down, "Aye, five minutes then."

"Ten," Captain Bowman said firmly.

All of a sudden, they heard a rustling sound from the thick underbrush beyond the beach. A stream of dark-skinned men with rifles poured out of the jungle and circled tightly around the two of them. *So much for that rest!*

Captain Bowman stood up slowly, and raised his hands. Vaughn slowly go to her feet as well and steadied herself against Captain Bowman. She remembered a few useful phrases in Isafari from the academy, but she was nowhere near fluent.

There was a voice from beyond the line of rifles—a woman's voice, loud, clear, and with a musical accent. It sounded nothing at all like Isafari. Vaughn thought she heard the sound of a clicking tongue, as well as the phrase "polboman."

The riflemen moved aside to reveal an ebony-skinned woman in long patterned robes. Her head was shaven completely bare, and two golden hoops hung from her ears. She strode calmly between the riflemen, paying them no heed, as if they were merely servants in a palace.

The woman stopped in front of the two Aurorans. "Yu sorenda."

For a moment, the only sound was the gentle whooshing of the sea.

And then Captain Bowman began to laugh. Just a chuckle at first, then a deep guffaw. The woman smiled warmly, and then seemed to be laughing a bit herself! *Bloody hell, what am I missing here?*

Finally, Paul stopped laughing, "We surrender, Lady Batu."

The End of the *Gates of Dawn*